*L*imned in moonlight, his mane of dark hair wild about his shoulders in untamed waves, he was easily the most breathtaking vision Zahirah had ever seen.

And he stared at her, too, she realized dazedly.

"What mysteries do you hide beneath that veil, Zahirah?"

The question shocked her, but no more than the unexpected feel of his touch. He reached out slowly, bringing his hand up to her face. Though he scarcely touched her, only the merest skate of his fingertips against her cheek, Zahirah felt enflamed. She closed her eyes.

Seduction.

She knew not the first thing about it, but all that was woman in her warned that this man surely did. His touch advanced no further than her face. The callused pad of his thumb swept over her lips, rasping against the silk that covered them and drawing breath from her lungs in a warm, ragged sigh.

His heavy-lidded gaze trained on her mouth, he started to sweep aside her veil. . . .

Other Books by Tina St. John
Published by Ivy Books

LORD OF VENGEANCE
LADY OF VALOR
WHITE LION'S LADY

BLACK LION'S BRIDE

Tina St. John

IVY BOOKS • NEW YORK

An Ivy Book
Published by The Ballantine Publishing Group
Copyright © 2002 by Tina Haack

www.ballantinebooks.com

ISBN 0-8041-1963-5

Manufactured in the United States of America

First Edition: May 2002

OPM   10   9   8   7   6   5   4   3   2   1

For Leslie

There's not a heroine in print
who can match your courage,
your strength of spirit, or your
incredible grace under fire.
You're an inspiration,
and I'm so glad to call you my friend.

Acknowledgments

Thank you to Staci, Marina, Nicole, Debbie,
and my husband, John—the usual suspects,
for the usual reasons.
I love you!

Thanks, too, to my editor, Shauna Summers, for giving me
the green light on this story two years ago, and for
waiting so patiently as I stumbled my way to the end.

Prologue

Quiet and moonless, the night stretched out over the desert like thick black velvet, a cloak of complicity for the slim figure that moved with catlike grace along the maze of narrow alleyways crisscrossing the heart of Ascalon's slumbering city. Garbed in a form-fitting tunic and hose of ebony silk, head and face masked likewise save for the eyes, it seemed as though night itself had sprouted legs to steal through the war-ravaged, abandoned marketplace.

The figure's pace was brisk but cautious as it rounded the corner of an ancient mosque, then continued past a row of merchants' buildings and down another twisting avenue, each step lighting soundlessly on the cobbles and hard-packed sand of the street, the lithe limbs showing no sign of fatigue or uncertainty. The athletic form and flawless stealth indicated none of the strain that yet lingered from the week-long journey made on foot from the mountain fortress of Masyaf—a journey that had led here, to the desert port of Ascalon.

To what would be a final glory or an ignoble end.

For it was here that the leader of the Frankish infidels, Richard Coeur de Lion, had made his camp, and it was here that the savage king would breathe his last. He had offended many powerful leaders since coming to the Holy Land; there was no telling which of them might have paid to see him eliminated. And to the agent sent out to see the deed was done, the *fida'i* who now crept into position along the city's steep wall to observe the royal pavilion, it mattered not who had bought this death. Like Conrad of Montferrat a fortnight past, Richard of England would soon feel the lethal bite of an assassin's dagger.

Although the hour was easily closer to dawn than dusk, the king did not sleep. Camped on the plain among the other soldiers, Coeur de Lion's large tent glowed from within, the flicker of a single candle throwing shadows against the striped silk walls, betraying the fact that its occupant was alone, his bulky shoulders hunched over his desk in thoughtful concentration. As if to mock the very notion of danger, no guards stood sentry outside, nor in the immediate area. Richard's fearless arrogance was widely accepted; tonight it would spell his doom.

With no time to waste, the *fida'i* sent a prayer to Allah, then reached down to withdraw a virgin dagger crafted especially for this occasion. The curved blade slipped out of its sheath as silently as the footsteps that now carried the assassin to within a few paces of the king's pavilion. Suddenly, from somewhere in the distance, a dog began to bark. Then the deep rumble of men's voices carried through the night, their Frankish words serious-sounding, but too low to be understood. Two knights had entered the camp from the opposite end, their broad-shouldered outlines barely visible in the dark, their heavy boots crunching in the rubble that littered the ground as they made their way toward Coeur de Lion's tent.

Concealed in the gloomy darkness, the assassin watched, measuring the distance between victory and defeat, as King Richard lifted his head, then started to rise from his chair. There was time enough to strike before the knights reached him. Self-preservation was of no concern; martyrdom was the assassin's reward. But even more compelling than the promise of awaiting Paradise was the hope that this feat might at last win the approval of Rashid al-Din Sinan.

Feared by most as the mysterious Old Man of the Mountain, King of the Assassins, to the *fida'i* sent to Ascalon on this mission, Sinan was better known simply as

"Father." It was his name, not Allah's, that the assassin whispered before advancing toward the tent that enveloped Coeur de Lion's unarmed silhouette.

"I dinna suppose the king bothered to explain the urgency of this midnight summons, did he?"

Sebastian, Earl of Montborne, and, more recently, officer to King Richard of England in the war against the Muslim infidels, gave a shrug to the soldier walking at his side. "The king is awake and he wishes to have reports of his troops. What more explanation is needed?"

"Ach," grunted his companion, a large Scotsman from the highlands of that wild northern region. "I might have known better than to complain to you, my friend. You and Lionheart seem to forget that we mere mortals require such things as food and rest to gird us for the next day's battle."

Sebastian chuckled. "And here all these months you've been trying to convince me that the Scots' blood ran thicker than English blood. I wonder what your bonny bride would say to hear you now, bemoaning the loss of a few hours' sleep?"

"Aye, my sweet Mary." The Scot sighed. "She would doubtless give me a pretty scowl and say, 'James Malcolm Logan, I told you you were mad to leave me to chase glory in that accursed place. Now get your fool's arse back home where you belong before I—'"

A movement in the distant darkness caught Sebastian's eye. He stopped walking, silencing his friend with a slight lift of his hand. "Over there," he said, when Logan, too, paused. He kept his voice to no more than a whisper. "Something moved behind that row of tents."

Without the moon to offer light to the camp, it was difficult to see anything beyond the pale shapes of the soldiers' tents and the dark, rising swell of Ascalon's crumbling city wall in the immediate background.

Beside him, Logan was peering into the dark and shaking his head. "I see nothing."

"No," Sebastian insisted, certain he was right by the sudden prickle of rising hairs at the back of his neck. "Something—someone—is out there."

And then there was another shift of the darkness up ahead as a slender figure seemed to materialize from out of the gloom. Clad in black from head to toe, the intruder hunched low, creeping toward the center of camp with unmistakable purpose. Sebastian did not have to see the dagger that curved out of one fist like a deadly steel talon to understand what this intruder was . . .

Assassin.

"Blood of Christ!" Sebastian drew his sword and lunged forward. "The king, Logan! Go to the king!"

While the Scotsman raced for the candlelit glow of Richard's pavilion, Sebastian's boots chewed up the space of earth between him and the Syrian agent of death. In the camp, some of the other soldiers had begun to rouse. They tumbled out of their tents and grabbed up weapons, alerted to the situation by Sebastian's shout of alarm.

The ruckus must have taken the assassin aback, for he paused suddenly as if to assess the pending threat of capture. The hesitation proved costly. Sebastian headed him off and was fast on his heels as the would-be assailant turned and ran for the open city gate. If he let him escape to the labyrinth of Ascalon's streets and alleyways, Sebastian knew he would never find him.

The assassin was slight of form, but quick. Sebastian was close enough that he could have cut him down with his sword at least twice, but the agile little bastard dodged away each time, scrambling out of his path like a hare fleeing a hound. The assassin had nearly reached the freedom of Ascalon's arched gate when he suddenly lost his footing, slipping on a patch of loose gravel. One leg skidded from beneath him and he started to fall. Sebastian hurled himself forward, reaching out with his free hand to grab the assassin's flailing arm.

"Uh—no!" he shrieked, the thready voice pitched higher than Sebastian might have expected.

A stripling youth, then, sent down from the mountains to kill a king? It seemed a ridiculous notion, but Sebastian had no time to consider it further.

Without warning the assassin spun on him, and, in pure speed of motion, he hit Sebastian in the side. The blow was not the hardest he had ever taken, but it was swift enough to knock all the wind from his lungs. He lost his grasp on the assassin's arm and the lad broke away in a run. Sebastian followed, but quickly found he could not keep pace. His feet began to drag beneath him; his sword became a weight he could scarcely hold. He took a couple more steps, his boots scuffing in the sand as the assassin slipped around the corner of the city gate and disappeared.

At his back, Sebastian heard the clank of weapons and the heavy beat of footsteps as a company of soldiers jogged up behind him. He had not realized he'd stopped moving until he felt a hand come to rest on his shoulder.

"Are you all right, sir?" one of the crusaders asked.

Sebastian nodded and pivoted toward his men, trying not to let the effort that small movement took show in his face. "Lost my . . . breath." Impatiently, he waved off the assisting hand one of the knights offered him, frustrated that he had let the assassin get away. "The bastard hit me, and I lost my breath. Leave me alone. I'll be fine."

A dozen guards stared at him in mute stupefaction, wide-eyed and astonished beyond words.

"Jesus," a young soldier managed to gasp.

Sebastian looked down to where their gazes were rooted, and acknowledged the source of their concern with a grim laugh. At his waist, a large pool of blood soaked through the fabric of his tunic and down onto his hose, seeping out of him from a wound at his side. The little whoreson had stabbed him—quite efficiently, from the looks of it.

It was no wonder the men gaped at him as if he were a ghost. In a few more hours, he likely would be.

Chapter One

Three weeks later

"You know, my friend, you might have saved the king and everyone else a great deal of effort and worry had you simply said you were determined to kill yourself one way or another." Outfitted in chain mail armor from a morning spent in training, James Logan strode up to where Sebastian stood at the top of a wooden ladder, his bare back baking in the midday desert sun as he set a large brick into place on the partially reconstructed city wall. "A thousand able men employed to rebuild Ascalon's defenses, yet here you are, the king's right arm, half-dead but a fortnight past and out here working as hard as any man. You must have been drained of all good sense along with the blood you lost in camp last month."

With an exhaled curse that brought a twinge of pain from the healing wound at his side, Sebastian pivoted his head to look down at Logan. "I didn't come to Palestine to die," he said as he spread some mortar onto the wall with his trowel and reached for another brick. "No more than I came here to sit idle in a sultan's confiscated palace, supervising repairs to a city that will likely be razed by Saladin before we lay the last brick."

Logan chuckled as he positioned himself near the base of the ladder, leaning his shoulder against the stone wall and grinning up at Sebastian from under arched chestnut-colored brows. "The king had to know the Black Lion of England would bristle at the notion of being caged—even behind gilded bars. Like it or nay, my friend, those were his orders when he left to march on Darum."

"I don't like it," Sebastian confirmed in a growl. "I came here to fight. As it seems I am unable to do that at present, I will at least make myself useful. Why don't you do likewise and pass me another bucket of mortar while you're down there?" He scooped out the last of the thick clay muck, then dropped the empty vessel into the Scot's waiting hands. "In any event, I mean to return to campaign as soon as the king is back from Darum. After nearly a month of inactivity here in Ascalon, I expect I can tolerate another couple of days."

"Then you haven't heard?" At Sebastian's answering frown, Logan blew out a sigh. "Richard has decided to delay his return. He goes to the Valley of the Wells, to seize a castle held by one of Saladin's emirs. I learned of it myself just this morning. Seems one of the men got the news from a supply ship that met the king down the coast a few days ago."

Sebastian cursed roundly. "Has he gone mad?" Ignoring the stares of several workers who turned their heads in his direction, he threw his muddy trowel to the ground, then came down off his ladder to confer with his lieutenant. "We should be saving our energies for Jerusalem, not squandering our few remaining troops on more petty raids and caravan robberies."

Logan shrugged. "You'll get no argument out of me. But with so much wealth to be gained from plunder, mayhap Richard has forgotten that his reason for coming to Palestine was to liberate Jerusalem from the infidels."

"He also forgets that his arrogance is winning him no esteem," Sebastian said, retrieving his tunic from the ladder rung he had draped it over earlier that morning. He shrugged into the airy white linen shirt, too fast, for in his haste, a jolt of renewed pain sliced through him. If he ever caught the devil who sliced him open that night, he would take great pleasure in returning the favor. Slowly. "The king is making powerful enemies on both sides of this war," he continued, slanting Logan a confidential glance. "At least one of those enemies means to see him dead."

"'Twas Richard's opinion the attack that night was an isolated incident—a crazed Muslim acting on his own volition, was his guess. He doesn'a believe he's in any specific danger."

Sebastian scoffed. "Neither did Conrad of Montferrat until the night two assassins, dressed as monks, accosted him on the street and stuck their daggers in his heart." He picked up his sword and baldric and began to buckle the wide leather belt around his waist.

Frustrated from a combination of heat, thirst, and now this news of the king's latest military whim, Sebastian abandoned his work and started for the well at the center of the city square. Logan fell in behind him. "'Tis rumored that Conrad's murder was bought with Richard's coin. Leastwise, that was the tale the assassins told upon their capture."

"A tale, all right," Sebastian replied. "Conrad and Richard were hardly enamored of each other, but they had finally come to terms. I was there when the king decided that Conrad was to be his replacement in Palestine should affairs in England call him home before Jerusalem was secured. He's gained nothing with Conrad's death, save the added knowledge that the crusade's success or failure now rests solely on him."

"Aye, but I wager the infidels found much cause to celebrate, having one less Christian leader to contend with," Logan suggested wryly. He pitched his voice low as he and Sebastian neared the crowded square. "You don't suspect Saladin's had a hand in any of this, do you? Could he have conspired with the Old Man of the Mountain to see both Conrad and Richard eliminated?"

Sebastian considered the idea for a moment, his attention focused on the throng of English soldiers and turbaned Syrian laborers taking rest and refreshment at the well. "Assassination seems too cowardly a tactic for a man of Saladin's honor," he answered, then shook his head.

"However, the sultan has been pushed into a corner many times, and if we are to start counting King Richard's enemies, I warrant no one can be above suspicion."

At the officers' approach, a young boy hopped down from the ledge of the well where he had been seated, serving water to the other men. He filled two cups from the spring-fed reservoir, then rushed forth to offer them to Sebastian and Logan, his smile eager, dark eyes shining. Halfway across the small distance, he suddenly froze.

A woman's scream rent the air.

It sounded from within the main avenue, a wide street that led to what was once an opulent Syrian palace, and now the nearly deserted headquarters of Richard's high-ranking officers. The woman screamed again, shrieking a single word that curdled the blood of both Frank and Saracen alike . . .

"Assassin!"

Sebastian and Logan set off at once, skirting the crowd of dazed workers to reach the mouth of the avenue. "Shut the gates," Sebastian shouted over his shoulder to a knot of soldiers who rushed to join him. "No one leaves the city!"

Boots pounding on the cobble-paved street, he and the Scot raced toward the trouble. They did not have to get within a few yards of the palace to see what had happened. A frantic servant woman stood outside, jabbering hysterically and flailing her hands. At her feet in a pool of blood lay a Christian knight, one of the guards who had been posted at the palace gates when Sebastian left that morning to relieve his boredom by working on the city wall. The man's throat had been slashed—a savage attack delivered upon him not moments before, for his blood was slick and crimson, and still seeping out of his wound.

"Did you see who did this?" he demanded of the woman, seizing her by the shoulders. She feebly shook her head, then dissolved into another fit of wailing. Sebastian released her, turning his head toward the crowd filling the mouth of the avenue. Several prayers were murmured to Allah, but the majority of onlookers seemed capable only of gaping at the scene in mute shock. "Did anyone see who did this?"

A few heads uselessly shook in denial. Sebastian ground out a curse. He was about to turn away when something—or, rather, someone—in the crowd caught his eye. Enveloped in the knot of stunned spectators was a man of slight, wiry build. He might not have been noticeable amongst the others at all, for he was garbed as any other Syrian laborer: the same long, white tunic, the same turban covered his head. But what separated this man in Sebastian's mind was the fact that his gaze was not on the fallen knight . . . but on Sebastian instead.

He stared at him with piercing black eyes, cold eyes, lit with what seemed to be a morbid sort of amusement. Sebastian frowned and started toward him. Was this the same man who attacked him that night in camp—the same assassin who might have killed the king? He could not be sure. But this man had killed the palace guard; Sebastian could see the truth of it in the chilling, almost mocking, gaze peering back at him.

"You, there," he hailed in Arabic. "Come away from the others. I would speak to you."

The man smiled, but did not move to oblige. Several people around him began to back away, as if suddenly sensing there was evil in their midst.

"What is it?" Logan asked, when Sebastian's hand went to the hilt of his sword.

"There, in the crowd. That man. Do you see him?" Sebastian started forward, and the grinning Arab took a step back, slipping farther into the throng. "The bastard's going to run."

The words were scarcely out of Sebastian's mouth before the man did precisely that. He gave a taunting chuckle and then he was gone, ducking out of sight, his white-turbaned head blending in with the rest of the shoulder-to-shoulder crowd.

Sebastian lunged into a run, pushing his way through the tangle of stupefied laborers and servants. Logan was at his heels in no time, shouting orders to the handful of English soldiers to block off all exits from the city. A sea of turbans and white tunics spread out in all directions, a blurring expanse of colorless shapes, almost blinding in the intense light of the desert sun. Sebastian waded into the crowd, scanning the area like a meadowland hawk searching for the slightest movement in the reeds. He found what he was looking for near the periphery of the throng. The assassin had paused to catch his breath just beyond the city square. Hands splayed against the sidewall of a merchant's home, he threw a glance over his shoulder, then took off once more down a narrow alley.

"This way!" Sebastian called to Logan. "He's heading for the souk."

Ascalon's marketplace would be busy at this time of day, far more populated than the city square with its assemblage of workers. The souk was a veritable hive, churning with activity, as vendors having come to the city to trade food and wares set up shop along the narrow streets. They mingled and argued with villagers and folk from surrounding areas, filling the streets with the din of lively bartering, and the press and stink of hundreds of sweating bodies. Sebastian's elusive quarry might be able to hide among this larger crowd for a short while, but once chased into the enclosed area of the souk, with its maze of winding corridors and dead-end alleys, he was as good as a rat in a trap.

With a furtive look back as if to confirm he was still being followed, the assassin plunged deeper into the marketplace, wending his way past rug makers and silk traders, tipping vendors' carts and shoving women and children aside in his haste to get past.

"The spicers' row. Go. Now!" Sebastian shouted to Logan, his abbreviated command sending the big Scot off to meet him at the intersecting avenue while Sebastian stayed fast on the assassin's heels.

Battle rage pounded in his temples as he leaped over a spilled supply of silk fabrics that had been knocked over in front of him. Sebastian sidestepped a cursing vendor and drew his sword, ignoring the gasps of the commoners as he ran up onto a row of tables to pass the confusion in the street. The assassin was but a few yards ahead of him now, his flight slowed by the mass of people browsing the market. He pushed his way through them, then skidded to an abrupt halt, for rising before him was a wall of stone that climbed some ten feet from the ground.

A dead end.

The assassin seemed to take the obstacle in stride, showing little concern that he was now all but caught. He chuckled as Sebastian drew near, then he tossed a quick glance to his left and spied a way out of his predicament. A curtain of colorful rugs hung suspended on a rope in the space between two buildings, marking a narrow alleyway that was the only means of escape from the blocked market street.

Sebastian grinned as his quarry lunged and made a mad dash down the cramped corridor, for the path he was on now was another dead end. One that would first wind past the spicers' row, where Logan should be at any moment.

No sooner had the Arab fled past, did the Scotsman emerge to join Sebastian in the chase. Together they covered the space of the slim alley, both swords drawn and at the ready, both men fueled by determination and the thrill of pursuit. They pushed the assassin farther down the corridor, allowing him no room to so much as think of attempting to slip past, forcing him to the eventual end of his run. He reached the wall that sealed off the street, then whirled around to face his pursuers.

"It's over. You've nowhere left to go." Sebastian growled the Arabic words, watching as the assassin looked to the left and right of him, his gaze flicking from the high wall of a building that hemmed him in at the left of the alley, to the baker's shop crowding from the right. Before him, Sebastian and Logan began to advance—small, cautious steps that brought them nearly within striking distance.

The assassin reached down to pull his dagger.

"Don't be a fool," Sebastian warned. "I'll cleave you in two before you free it from the sheath."

The man hesitated, his dark eyes narrowing as though he saw the truth in Sebastian's threat. His lip curled at the corner and then he started to chuckle, a deep, guttural sound. "Frankish pig," he spat in halting, thickly accented English. "Allah curse you all!"

His laughter took on a maniacal tone and Sebastian considered the prospect that the man might be insane—or delirious perhaps, from the powerful drug the assassin sect was rumored to administer to its agents before dispatching them to their deadly tasks. Either way, he was dangerous, and Sebastian was losing his patience with the game. "You're coming with us," he said, and started to close the distance between himself and the wild-eyed Arab.

He had only lifted his foot from the ground—moving not even a half pace forward—when suddenly the door to the baker's shop creaked open and a young Muslim woman walked out. She was paying no attention to where she was going, a bundle of flat breads and cakes in her arms, her face veiled to just below the eyes. With her gaze downcast as she stepped into the street, she walked unawares directly between Sebastian and the assassin.

"Go back," Sebastian shouted, but it was too late.

The woman screamed as the assassin seized her around the neck and shoulders, hauling her to him. Her baked goods tumbled to the cobbled pavement. She screamed again. Her wide, terror-stricken eyes—extraordinary eyes, the color of silver moonglow—stared at Sebastian from over the edge of her gossamer veil. When she tried to squirm free, the assassin wrenched her tighter against him. The blade of his dagger pressed into the silk that covered her throat.

"*Saadni,*" she cried, her gaze rooted on Sebastian, pleading, desperate. "Help me, please!"

"God damn it," Sebastian grated savagely. "Let her go."

Leering now, the assassin began to creep backward,

inching away from Sebastian and Logan, toward freedom. The outlet to the spicers' row was only a few yards away, an easy escape. He held the woman before him as he went, all but daring Sebastian to make an untoward move.

Logan hissed an oath. "We canna get to him so long as the bastard's using her as a shield."

"Think carefully, coward," Sebastian snarled in Arabic, challenging the assassin's intent as he hedged nearer. He did not wish to bring further harm to an innocent bystander, but he was not about to back down now. "You're a dead man no matter what you do. Release the woman, and my blade will be swift. Hurt her, and I promise you will suffer a prolonged, painful demise. The choice is yours."

"I leave it to Allah to decide," the assassin replied, his voice deep and rasping as he took the last few steps that separated him from the arched corridor of the alleyway.

"Please," the young woman said in Sebastian's own tongue. That one word compelled him to meet her gaze, even when he knew it would be a mistake to risk taking his eyes off his quarry. "Don't let him hurt me. Please, help me—"

She sucked in her breath when the dagger moved lower, sliding down the length of her throat to press ruthlessly beneath her breasts. Dragging her backward with him, the assassin moved farther into the shade of the covered alley. Try as he might, Sebastian could not tear his gaze away from the woman's. She was exquisite, an olive-complected beauty with a mass of glossy raven hair, hidden beneath the modest veil that covered the heads of all respectable Syrian women. He could not see her nose or mouth through the silk that draped her cheeks, but their outlines were delicate, utterly feminine.

And those eyes . . . Sebastian had never seen their like before. Quicksilver. Dazzling. They entranced him, and for a moment, he lost sight of everything else around him.

The assassin took the opportunity suddenly presented. He released his hold on the woman and shoved her, hard. She cried out as she pitched forward in a violent fall.

Sebastian's reflexes sent him into a lunge, catching her before she could hit the cobbles. When he looked up less than a heartbeat later, the assassin was halfway down the alley.

"Look after her," Sebastian ordered Logan as he stepped around the shaking young woman and resumed a determined pursuit of his quarry.

This time, the cagey assassin was not so swift. Anger and impatience had given Sebastian a demon's speed that brought him onto the man's heels as they rounded the end of the alley. Easily within arm's length, he thrust out his hand and caught the assassin by the tunic, harshly swinging him down onto the dusty street. He did not hesitate for an instant to make good on his earlier threat; with a swift descent of his sword, he delivered a fatal thrust. Wide-eyed with surprise, the Arab clutched at the blade that protruded from his chest, convulsed, then went utterly still.

Logan was still trying to assist the young woman to her feet when Sebastian cleaned and sheathed his sword, then returned to the other end of the alley. "You got him," the Scot stated more than asked, likely reading the cold fact in Sebastian's gaze. "Was he the one from a few weeks ago, the bastard who would have killed the king?"

Sebastian gave a contemplative shake of his head, recalling the events of that night. The *fida'i* who had crept into the English camp to kill the king had been slighter of form, youthful. A mere lad, if the shriek he gave when Sebastian caught him was any indication. The man lying dead in the spicers' row was older, wiry built but too substantial, his voice fully mature. They could not be one and the same; Sebastian was certain of it. "What about her?" he asked, glancing toward the young Saracen woman. "Is she hurt?"

"Her ankle was twisted in the fall," Logan answered, supporting her with the strength of his arm. "I doona think she can walk on it." As if to demonstrate the fact, she tried to take a step and nearly collapsed, sharply sucking in her breath and wincing in pain.

"Go take care of the rubbish I left in the spicers' row.

Maybe someone can tell us if they've seen the man before,"
Sebastian ordered his friend. "I'll look after her."

With Logan's heavy gait pounding down the alleyway,
Sebastian crouched before the woman to assess her damage.
Lifting the hem of her *shalwar,* the loose-legged trousers
worn by Arab women beneath their long tunics, he began to
inspect the fine bones of her ankle. She flinched at his touch,
drawing back sharply; no doubt an innocent maiden, un-
used to a man handling her in such a fashion. He glanced up
and was struck once more with the sheer beauty staring
back at him.

"What is your name?"

"Zahirah," she answered quietly. An exotic name for an
exotic woman.

"I'm not going to hurt you, Zahirah. There is no reason
to be afraid." She nodded faintly, and Sebastian returned his
attention to her injured leg. Her skin was light bronze and
buttery smooth, warm against his fingers as he carefully
probed for signs of breaks or swelling. He could feel neither,
only the velvety softness of her bare skin and the delicate
formation of her limb. He moved her foot, holding her
small, sandaled sole in his palm and pivoting the joint. He
applied only the slightest pressure, but still she cried out.

"It's not broken," he said, "but if it pains you so, it
should be soaked and wrapped." He released her ankle, then
came to stand. "Do you live nearby, Zahirah?"

She gave a faint shake of her head, blinking up at him
from beneath heavy black lashes. "I am . . . only visiting for
the day."

"Is there someone here in Ascalon who can look after
you? A friend, perhaps? A relative?"

Another timid denial. "There is no one, my lord."

Sebastian let out a sigh as he considered his options.
There was no one to take her to, no place that he could
bring her where she might find help among her own people.
And he could not very well leave her standing there in the
street, not when he was partly to blame for her misfortune.
But the last thing he needed was to be charged with the wel-

fare of an injured young innocent, no matter how comely she was.

As if she sensed his reluctance to assist her further, the young woman lowered her gaze. "My humble thanks for your kindness, my lord. Peace and blessings be upon you." She took a small step away, moving gingerly and biting her lower lip as her slight weight shifted onto her left foot. Her stifled cry was more than Sebastian's chivalry could bear.

"God's bones," he growled, reaching out and scooping her into his arms. "You're coming back to the palace with me."

Chapter Two

Zahirah clung to the dark crusader as he swept her up off her feet and began the winding trek back through the streets of the busy souk, toward the opulent palace in the heart of the city. She was trembling, hardly able to catch her breath for the way her heart was racing when she thought about everything that had just happened. The attack on the palace guard. The ensuing chase into the market and the crusaders' cornering of the apparent madman in the alley outside the baker's shop. Zahirah's capture and subsequent rescue. Now this: her deliverance to the headquarters of the Frankish invaders—escorted through the heavily guarded gates by one of their own.

It had all gone precisely according to plan.

Perhaps not everything, she amended with a momentary twinge of regret. Jafar's death had not been part of the design, but her *fida'i* accomplice had been too arrogant, acting careless beyond his experience. Zahirah herself had been careless not a month before, when she had the opportunity to kill the famed English king in his tent and failed. The mistake had cost her, but not again. Like a serpent hiding in the oleander, she would lie in wait for her chance to strike. And this time, Richard the Lionhearted would not see her coming until he felt her deadly bite.

Zahirah turned her veiled face into the crusader's thick-hewn shoulder, hiding her eyes from the handful of Saracen servants who stared as she was carried into the mosaic-tiled entryway of the palace.

"Fetch me a basin of cool water and some strips of dry

cloth," the Frankish captain ordered one of the gawking slaves, speaking in their own Arabic tongue, his deep voice reverberating against Zahirah's ear where it rested at his chest. "And tell Abdul I need him to prepare one of his teas—something to alleviate pain."

"As you wish, my lord."

With the servant's feet padding off in the opposite direction, the crusader delivered Zahirah down a long corridor that opened into a spacious apartment chamber. Sumptuous cushioned divans were built into alcoves that burrowed into the high-ceilinged, frescoed walls. From the entrance, the wide floor stepped down gradually to where a large rug spread out, the resplendent crimson-and-gold weave running the full length and width of the rectangular room. At the far end of the hall, carved marble pillars supported a musician's balcony that sheltered beneath it a raised platform and pillowed seating area that would have been reserved for the sultan, were he still in residence. Sandalwood and myrrh scented the air, traces of harem perfumes that clung to the tapestries and bolsters even though the chamber apartments were some long months abandoned.

Forbidden to outsiders for untold generations, now the palace harem stood empty, vacated when Saladin's forces razed Ascalon. The move to bar the Franks from claiming yet another coastal stronghold had failed, for King Richard set up camp regardless of the wreckage, rebuilding smashed walls and seizing the city for his army's headquarters. The knight carrying Zahirah seemed every bit as bold as his conquering king, striding across the once-forbidden chamber of the harem as if he owned the place.

He set her down on the sultan's plush divan, but his hands remained at her waist, making no immediate move to release her. Alarmed to feel his touch linger, Zahirah tensed, her gaze flying to his piercing gray-green eyes in question. He offered no explanation; with one large hand holding her in place, the other efficiently skimmed the flat of her belly and sides. Before she could muster even so much as a gasp of indignation, he moved on to search the length of her legs, each in turn, his strong fingers skating from the uppermost portion of her thighs to the cuffed edges of her ankle-length trousers.

"A necessary precaution," he offered belatedly, not quite an apology for his rude handling of her person. He let go of her and, with a slight wince for the effort, straightened to his full height. He seemed to weather some degree of pain as he stared down at her from under the slash of his heavy dark brows. "Ascalon is rife with hidden dangers, my lady. I trust you understand my concerns."

"Of course," Zahirah murmured. She could hardly hold his level gaze, chagrined to feel a genuine blush creeping into her cheeks beneath her concealing veil. She further masked her unsettling reaction to the barbarian's touch with a suitable, if feigned, look of meek docility. "You cannot be too careful in times of war. I understand your concerns perfectly, my lord."

Indeed, she more than understood. She had been expecting this much from the mannerless Franks, and so, by her own design, she had carried no weapon that day. Instead she had previously made arrangements with another of the *fi-da'i* to deliver her a blade at the palace under the cloak of night. Her arrival at the appointed meeting place that evening would also serve as a signal that her mission was under way, her position secured within the infidels' headquarters. In the hours remaining before dark, Zahirah's foremost objective was simply to gather what information she could and calculate the best plan of attack for the king's anticipated arrival that next morning.

Her gaze slid from the crusader to the arched entryway of the chamber, where a servant had since come to pause. Balanced on his upturned palms was a tray that contained all of the requested supplies: a bowl of water, rolls of linen bandages, and a cup of steaming tea. "Come in, Abdul," the Frankish captain called in flawless Arabic. "See to this woman's ankle. It appears she's sprained it."

"Yes, master."

"And I suppose you'd better have a look at me when you're finished with her," the knight added, moving aside as Abdul crossed the chamber with his tray of preparations. "I had to deal with some trouble in the market this morning. No doubt I've ruined your stitches yet again."

He pulled the hem of his tunic out from under his sword belt as he said it, then lifted the loose-fitting shirt up over his head, baring his torso without a shred of modesty. Zahirah could not help but stare. She could count on one hand the number of times she had been privy to the sight of a man's unclothed chest, but the narrow, athletic builds of the Arabs she had seen in training at Masyaf could not compare to the solid strength of this Englishman.

Thick-shouldered and massive, he was like a wall of muscle and heavy bone. Ridges and planes of sinew, tanned brown from exposure to the harsh Syrian sun, bulged and flexed with his slightest move. Covering his bronzed skin was a mat of crisp dark hair that tapered down his chest and disappeared beneath the bandage that bound his trim waist. It was indecent, the blatant sexuality of his powerful physique, and Zahirah's eyes felt burned by the very sight of him.

She might have gaped for an eternity, had the crusader not turned away when one of his soldiers entered the room and addressed him. It was the man who had accompanied him in the souk, the big knight whose odd manner of speaking made the coarse dialect of the *lingua franca* even more difficult for Zahirah to decipher.

"Our assassin vermin of this morning lies heaped atop a rubbish cart outside, may he rot in hell."

The quip brought a slight lift to the crusader's mouth, but Zahirah could see that his mind was churning on a host of weighty concerns. "Any luck identifying him?"

The soldier shook his head. "I asked several people in the market if they'd seen him before, but no one had."

"I can't say I'm surprised."

"What do you reckon his purpose was in killing the guard? Do you think it was a bid to gain access to the palace?"

"He had no chance of that, employing so bold a move in broad daylight," the crusader coolly surmised. "And he made no such attempt to infiltrate. Indeed, the way he waited in the crowd it seemed that he was more intent on gaining our attention. Taunting us."

"Aye," agreed the soldier, "as if he wanted to be caught."

His captain gave a thoughtful grunt. "Or as if he meant to lead us into some sort of trap."

Across the room, Zahirah's breath caught in her throat. How close the dark crusader was to the truth! She peered at him over her veil, surreptitiously studying his face and trying to ascertain whether his statement was made in true suspicion or mere conjecture. His hard features told her nothing.

"If his aim was a trap," queried the other knight, "what end did it serve, now that the bastard is dead?"

The captain blew out a sigh and shook his dark head. "I don't know, but I mean to find out."

He glanced toward Zahirah then, as if he sensed her interest in their conversation. Abruptly, she looked away, pretending mild distress as Abdul removed her sandal and placed her foot in the bowl of cool water. She spoke to the servant in Arabic, asking him to exercise a bit more care and hoping that her sudden focus on her injury would convince the crusaders that she did not understand enough of their foreign tongue to cause overmuch concern. The ploy seemed to work.

His gaze serious, the other soldier addressed his captain in a confidential timbre. "If the king doubted the threat of an assassin's attack before, there can be no denying it now."

The crusader gave a slight nod. "It would seem that Richard's delayed return to Ascalon could not have come at a better time."

Against her will, Zahirah's head snapped up.

The king was delayed—how could that be? All of her reconnaissance had indicated that the Frankish leader was due to return from Darum on the morrow. How could she have missed this crucial information?

The two men continued to speak about how they would

use the king's absence over the next couple of weeks to scour the city for any more of the Old Man's disciples, but Zahirah heard none of what they said. Her mind sped forward to assess her present strategy, a knot of dread coiling in her stomach. The king's delay would mean certain failure now, for her plan to infiltrate the crusaders' headquarters hinged on his imminent arrival. She had expected her feigned injury would buy her a day or two inside the enemy camp, but to hope for a possible fortnight was dubious at best. The threat of being caught before she saw her mission through was far too great a risk.

There was only one thing she could do now: abandon this plan and move to strike through other means.

So distracted was she by the news of this sudden terrible complication, Zahirah scarcely noticed that Abdul had finished soaking and wrapping her ankle. He now reached up, offering her the cup of aromatic tea.

"Drink this for your pain," he gently instructed her.

She accepted it without a word, vaguely aware of the musky tang of opium wafting off the steam of the herbal brew. She gave the servant an automatic, agreeable smile as she lifted the edge of her veil and brought the cup to her mouth, though she would not permit a drop of the mild opiate to pass her lips. Her ankle pained her not in the least, and even if it had been snapped in two, she would rather suffer it out than willingly drug her senses. She needed a clear mind, especially in light of this new wrinkle in what had been so simple a plan.

She had to get out of there, and soon. Before the crusader's notions of an assassin trap turned to her, as she was certain it would given time. While Abdul left her to look after the Englishman's injury, Zahirah forced her mind toward further stratagems, refusing to consider her more compelling thoughts of immediate flight. She could not leave now without rousing suspicion, no matter how strong the urge. She would simply have to wait, until morning perhaps, when the soldiers returned to their training and work on the city's walls, affording her the chance to slip out unnoticed.

Yes, she assured herself, patience was her only weapon at this moment.

Her confidence returning, Zahirah watched over the edge of her cup as Abdul began to unwrap the bandages at the captain's waist. The strips of white linen grew wet and blood-stained the farther he progressed, hinting at the gravity of the man's wound, until at last the final length of cloth fell to the floor and the long ugly gash in his side was bared.

She must have gasped, for when she finally jerked her gaze up, the crusader was staring at her. "It is not as bad as it looks," he told her with a brief, flashing grin. "Well, in truth, it might have been worse, but Abdul has proven a master with needle and thread."

The servant gave a small snort in reply as he cleaned and inspected the wound. "Praise Allah the assassin who attacked you all those weeks ago did not aim his dagger any higher, master. Then there would have been nothing for anyone to do but watch as death carried you away."

But it was not the ghastly sight of the torn and bleeding wound that stole Zahirah's breath. It was the fact that she had suddenly realized who the dark crusader was—the man who had foiled her attempt to slay the king and nearly captured her that night in the enemy camp. The man she had fully expected she had killed was now standing before her like a warrior of seemingly immortal stock, wearing his wound like a badge, his body insulted but invincible, and much too real for her peace of mind.

Allah, have mercy.

It was *him*.

"Well, Sebastian, my friend," said the other soldier with a deep laugh. "Skilled or nay, I've no wish to watch Abdul truss you up like a Christmas goose yet another time. I'll go tell the men to take the carcass of our slain assassin and burn it with the rest of the rubbish—"

"No," interjected the captain, his deep voice edged with lethal calm even as Abdul's needle pierced his ravaged skin and drew it closed. "I want the bastard sent back to where he came from. Bind his body to a donkey, then set the beast

loose in the mountain foothills below the Old Man's lair."
His lips were tight and bloodless as he said it, his large
hands fisted for the pain he must have been weathering without so much as a sip of numbing wine. "I want my message
to the leader of the assassins made very clear: for every *fida'i* he sends down, I will deliver back a corpse. By my vow,
I will slay every last one."

Zahirah did not doubt for one instant the truth in that
cool promise. She swallowed hard, setting aside her cup of
cold tea before it slipped out of her trembling fingers. Her
wish to abort her present mission had suddenly gone from
prudent decision to desperate prayer.

Chapter Three

Moonlight spilled in through the latticework grilles that covered a row of windows set high in the harem chamber's wall, the pale silver rays breaking over the rooftops of the palace's many towers and splintering against the wall and floor in a thousand diamond-cut pieces. The wait until midnight had been a maddening test of Zahirah's will, but at last the appointed hour had arrived.

With the Frankish knights having sometime before sought their beds, Zahirah slipped out of her private apartment and padded soundlessly down the palace hallway, headed for the garden courtyard. The *fida'i* who was to meet her there with her weapon should be in position now.

By Allah's grace, he would be.

Zahirah had first thought it best to remain in the palace until morning to make her escape, but as she crept along the maze of shadowy corridors, she knew a deep desire to be gone from the place at once. She told herself that her trepidation had nothing at all to do with the barbarian soldier who had brought her there, the man she might have killed—indeed, should have killed—some weeks before. If she fled now, she did so merely because she was concerned for the success of her mission, not because of any threat issued by an arrogant Englishman.

But to her dismay, it was not his threat that lingered in her mind, so much as it was the man himself: that striking, unforgiving face, those hard gray-green eyes. The sight of his warrior's body was seared onto her memory like a brand, and even now, some hours removed from his presence, she still weathered the strangest feeling in her stomach, a queer fluttering that roused with the very thought of him.

Revulsion, no doubt, she reasoned harshly as she turned a corner and stole along the length of a columned open-air arcade. It had to be a bone-deep disgust that assailed her when she thought on him, for to feel anything more than that for any of the hated Franks—the barbarian race she had been raised to despise—would be the worst sort of shame. Indeed, she would rather die first.

Her thoughts occupied with that morbid prospect, Zahirah hastened toward the end of the colonnade. She did not see the dim flicker of candlelight coming from one of the palace bedchambers until she was nearly upon it. Someone was yet awake. Jolted by her near misstep, Zahirah froze. She had to pass that room to get to the garden.

From within the chamber came the soft scrape of a chair on tile, followed by the muffled thud of booted feet pacing slowly, the space between footfalls belying the great height and solidity of the apartment's occupant. Zahirah crept toward the partially open door without breathing, her back pressed to the wall as she stretched her neck to peer inside. She did not have to see the dark-haired crusader to know it was him . . . Sebastian, his friend had called him. Every fiber of her being tensed with awareness, a keen and inexplicable recognition that was confirmed when she spied the massive span of his shoulders, his tunic-clad back turned blessedly toward the door.

He appeared to be in thoughtful reflection, his elbow and forearm braced against the wall, his dark head bent down to study a document he held in his right hand. At the desk where he had been sitting was a pot of ink and a half-written letter, evidence that the rough soldier was also a man of some learning. The notion surprised her, for she had believed the Franks to be a simpleminded lot, crude barbarians bred for war, and as base in morals and thinking as the lowliest beasts in the field.

Was that not what her father, Rashid al-Din Sinan, had always proclaimed? Was that not what she had been taught from the time she first could speak—a lesson too often learned at the punishing end of an olive switch?

Zahirah shut out the pit of black memories before they could take root. Her lessons were many years behind her; she need not dwell on them. She had to trust her teaching now, trust her training.

She fixed her focus solely on the obstacle that stood between herself and freedom, watching as the Englishman drew breath and released it, waiting for the opportune moment to dash by unnoticed. Perhaps he sensed her steady regard behind him, for he raised his head suddenly and turned to look over his shoulder.

Zahirah did not hesitate for even so much as a heartbeat. Before he had the chance to see her there, she slipped past the slim opening of the door in one smooth motion, then fled noiselessly down the remaining space of hallway to the arched entrance of the gardens.

Once outside, she headed directly for the southern wall where a briar of roses grew, the heavy bloodred blooms peaking their highest at this point over the top of the tall perimeter enclosure. Zahirah hastened to the appointed spot and dropped to her knees in the soft grass.

"Halim," she whispered, "are you there?"

Only silence greeted her from the other side of the wall.

She waited for a moment, praying for reply, then blew out a shaky sigh. Had he already come and gone? she wondered desperately. Her mind racing, she crouched and reached into the thick rosebush near its root, negotiating the thorns as best she could without sacrificing speed. Her fingers scrabbled for purchase, her veil snagging in the branches the deeper she reached. At last, she found what she sought: at the base of the wall was a loosened stone, chipped free of its mortar not a week before. Easily accessible from the outside, the small portal lay well hidden from within by the tangle of the briar.

Using both hands to pry the stone out, Zahirah clutched at the ancient brick and wiggled it out of the wall. A rush of cool night air whisked in through the gap, followed by Halim's rasping whisper.

"You are late."

"A few moments," she admitted. "Not all were abed. I had to be careful."

Halim grunted on the other side of the wall. "Jafar is dead, you know. I saw the Frankish pig slay him like a dog in the middle of the souk."

"I know," Zahirah whispered, hearing an uncustomary note of pain in Halim's voice.

He and Jafar were brothers—two of Sinan's best, most proven agents, though on occasion she had bested the both of them in practice at Masyaf. That she was chosen for this mission over either of them had not endeared her to any of the all-male brotherhood of the *fida'i,* but no one would dare question Sinan's whims. Still, she could sense the scorn in Halim's silence, and she knew that what she was about to tell him now would give him great satisfaction.

"Halim, there has been a complication in my plan. The English king is delayed; he will not be returning to Ascalon on the morrow as I had expected, but may be gone another fortnight at least. I think it may be wise to abort this mission—"

"Abort?" Halim bit off a sharp oath. "A true *fida'i* would consider no such thing."

Zahirah chose to ignore the muttered barb. "I need to get out of here at once, Halim. The captain has already voiced his suspicions that the chase through the souk may have been some sort of trap. It won't be long before he starts to wonder how I might fit into the puzzle."

"Then you must take steps to ensure that his suspicions do not focus on you," Halim answered pointedly. "He is a man of some youth and virility from what I have seen; I doubt he'd refuse you. It should not require much to keep him distracted from your true purpose, even for a girl of your limited skills."

Zahirah felt her face flame at Halim's outrageous suggestion. How dare he advise seduction when he—indeed, all of Masyaf—knew she was yet a virgin, unschooled in the harem arts at her father's strict insistence? And to imply that she might willingly whore for the Frankish captain besides!

"This mission ends tonight," she insisted. "I'm leaving this place here and now, if I must climb this wall to do it. And you will help me, Halim."

The *fida'i*'s answering chuckle did not bode well for her cause. "Jafar's life was spent for nothing, and now you expect me to risk my own to assist you in fleeing your mission like a jittery hare, all because you made a stupid mistake in judgment?"

Zahirah hardened herself to the accusation, despite its sting. "Jafar is dead because of his own carelessness. I have made mistakes, admittedly, but I will not wait here to make another."

"The risk would be greater if you were to abandon the plan now," the *fida'i* countered. "After all, you have been seen by these men, and even if you do not know it, Zahirah, you are not a woman soon forgotten. You have lost the advantage of anonymity. Now that you are inside the Franks' camp, it is better that you stay."

"Halim!" she said in disbelief. "I have made my decision in this. I do not seek your permission—"

Behind her, a booted footstep echoed in the colonnade leading toward the gardens, the interruption cutting short Zahirah's argument. Someone approached from within the palace. She cast a nervous glance over her shoulder, but saw no one. No sign of activity, not even the dim glow of the captain's reading candle, the flame evidently snuffed out since she had been there. Curse Halim for making her quarrel with him when she could have been using the time to gain her freedom!

"I have lingered too long," she whispered urgently. "Someone is coming. I must go!"

"Quick. Take the dagger."

Halim pushed a silk-wrapped object through the hole in

the garden wall. Zahirah retrieved it with grasping, frantic fingers, slipping the slim, sheathed blade beneath the waistband of her pantalets. She did not bother with further words for Halim; he was gone in that next moment anyway, no doubt slinking away from the palace wall with the silent stealth of a cat.

Without a moment to spare, Zahirah shoved the stone back into place in the wall, then vaulted to her feet. She had just brushed the dried leaves and dirt from her hands and clothing when a deep voice made her jump with startlement.

"It is rather late for a stroll in the garden."

"Oh. Yes," she answered, turning to meet the large, moonlit figure of the Frankish captain. *Sebastian,* her mind supplied, the foreign name rolling far too readily to the tip of her tongue. "My apologies if I disturbed your rest, my lord. I found it difficult to sleep in a strange place . . . and, of course, after all that has happened today."

"Of course," he replied lightly, but his dark brows were furrowed, his gaze narrowed and trained more on the rose briar than it was on her. "I thought I heard voices out here. Were you talking to someone?"

"None but myself," she said, her nervous little laugh borne of genuine anxiety as the knight came toward her. "I sometimes do so when I have troubling things on my mind."

"Do you?"

He came to stand before her, and Zahirah frowned, unsettled by his sudden nearness. "My lord?"

He gave her a vague smile. "Do you have troubling things on your mind?"

"Y-yes," she whispered. "That is—no."

Her reply was hasty. Too hasty, perhaps, for he looked down at her then, studying her eyes over the top of her veil. Allah preserve her, but there was something dangerously compelling in that level gaze, something that grabbed ahold of her like a physical bond, drawing her in. He stood so close, it was impossible for her not to stare, her eyes taking in the harsh symmetry of his face: the wide brow and sharply planed cheekbones, his stern chin and jaw, the blunt line of his nose . . . the incongruously sensual curve of his mouth.

Limned in moonlight, with his mane of dark hair wild about his shoulders in untamed waves, this Anglo man of war was easily the most breathtaking vision Zahirah had ever seen.

And he stared at her, too, she realized dazedly. She saw the interest in his eyes, saw the spark of male curiosity that flared in their pale depths as his gaze traveled her covered face, then lifted to meet her eyes. There was potency in that gaze, a compelling confidence that should have unsettled her more than it did. He might have known his effect on her, for then he smiled, a slow curve of his lips. His voice was a growl in the dark.

"What mysteries do you hide beneath that veil, Zahirah?"

The question shocked her, but no more than the unexpected feel of his touch. He reached out slowly, bringing his hand up to her face. Though he scarcely touched her, only the merest skate of his fingertips against her cheek, Zahirah felt inflamed. She closed her eyes, and for one mad instant, she considered Halim's advice.

Seduction.

She knew not the first thing about it, but all that was woman in her warned that this man surely did. His touch advanced no farther than her face, yet Zahirah felt his caress in every nerve and pore of her body. The callused pad of his thumb swept over her lips, rasping against the silk that covered them and drawing the breath from her lungs in a warm, ragged sigh.

His heavy-lidded gaze trained on her mouth, he started to sweep aside her veil . . .

"No," Zahirah gasped, finally seizing some thread of sanity amid the tumult of her present state.

What had come over her? She was daughter of Rashid al-Din Sinan! Had she no honor at all that she would allow this overbold heathen to paw her like a common whore? Her skin should crawl from the very notion. What madness did she suffer that she should instead feel so alive?

Terrified by what she was feeling—by what she might yet be tempted to permit this man if she remained another moment—Zahirah shrank back from his touch as if burned. She took a step away from him, then another.

By Allah's merciful grace, he made no move to stop her. Nor did he say a word as she brought her trembling hand to her mouth and dashed past him, her mind reeling as she fled for the safety of her chamber in the palace.

Sebastian stared after her, watching in wry amusement as she made a hasty exit from the garden. Her flight seemed unhindered in the slightest by her injured ankle, running from him as she might from the devil himself. As well she should, he decided, his deep sigh betraying the knot of tension coiled in his loins.

God's bones, but when she stared up at him in the moonlight, her wide, expressive eyes drinking him in with a shattering lack of guile, he had been powerless to keep from touching her. Had she not broken away so abruptly, he no doubt would have endeavored to do far more than that.

He wondered at his interest in her. An interest that had kept him awake that night, made him restless even beyond his usual inability to sleep a night through. His mind had been churning on her from the moment he first laid eyes on her in the souk, a beauty like no other he had known.

Zahirah harbored mysteries that went far deeper than her beauty, that much he was sure of. But as tempting as it was to sate his curiosity and lay each of her secrets bare, he knew he could ill afford the distraction when the king's life hung in the balance. If he had not been sure of it before, this encounter in the garden was proof enough: His pretty desert rose would have to go back to where she came from.

Indeed, the sooner he was delivered of the chit, the better.

Chapter Four

Fatigued from a nearly sleepless night, Zahirah was wide-awake before the dawn. She listened from the sanctity of her chamber as the knights in the palace stirred, the metallic jangle of armor and the tick of spurs on tiled hallways telling her that the company of soldiers was departing for the day's activities. She could only pray their brutish captain was gone with them, for if she never faced him again, it would suit her quite well.

Assuring herself of her rightful scorn, Zahirah crossed the room to see about the commencement of her escape. She reached for the latch on the tall chamber door—at the very moment a soft knock sounded from the other side. She leaped back, her right hand instinctively searching out her dagger, which rested snug against her belly, held in place by the drawstring waistband of her trousers, and concealed by the shapeless length of her tunic.

"Who is there?" she called, ready to draw her weapon and use it if the coarse crusader thought for one moment she would be fool enough to let him near her again.

"It is Abdul, mistress. I have come to offer you a light repast."

Zahirah exhaled a sigh of frustration. Next to the heathen known as Sebastian, the last thing she needed was his well-meaning servant delaying her with his doting. She would take what he brought her and quickly dismiss him, she decided. Gripping the latch, she opened the door and met his smile with a small nod of greeting. "Thank you, Abdul," she said, then frowned when she noticed that he carried nothing in his hands.

"My master has requested that you join him in breaking his morning's fast, mistress. Come with me, I will show you the way."

She would do no such thing! To share a meal with a non-believer was to pollute her Muslim purity; she would rather starve first, especially after her encounter with him last night. Ignoring the servant's outstretched arm, Zahirah remained where she stood, bristling from the top of her veiled head to the open toes of her sandals. "My humble thanks for bringing me his invitation, Abdul, but you may tell your master that I have respectfully declined. His offer is—" She bit her tongue, harnessing the urge to call it grossly presumptuous. "His offer is most hospitable, however, I haven't the appetite to dine with him. Tell him I wish to spend the morning in prayer."

Abdul blinked at her, then dipped his head and awkwardly cleared his throat. "He instructed me to wait until you were ready, mistress."

"Did he." Zahirah could hardly comprehend the audacity of the man. And with the loyal servant standing there, fully intent on observing his Christian master's orders to wait her out, her hopes of a neat escape from the palace that morning scattered like dust in a desert sandstorm.

"Very well," she relented crisply, "then I suppose you should take me to him."

She stepped out into the corridor, and, with Abdul shuffling to get ahead of her, Zahirah marched up the same hallway she had navigated in the dark a few hours before, then followed the servant down a wide colonnade that cut a mosaic-tiled path to an interior courtyard.

Doubtless one of many such pleasure gardens secreted in the palace grounds, the rectangular enclosure was a feast for the senses. More than a dozen tall palm trees shaded the area, the light breeze sifting through their fronds carrying with it the fragrance of countless flowers that bloomed in large clay pots and in carefully tended beds. A bulbul chirped from somewhere above Zahirah's head, its bright morning song echoed by the soft trickle of a fountain located at the center of the courtyard.

"Good morrow, Lady Zahirah. I am pleased you decided to join me."

Decided, indeed, Zahirah scoffed inwardly. She turned away from the pleasing beauty of the garden with some reluctance, glancing to where the crusader lounged, his big frame garbed in a dark tunic and hose, and dwarfing the carved stone bench on which he sat. Spread upon the table before him was an assortment of fruits and flat breads, the sight of all that delicious-looking food setting Zahirah's stomach to growling.

He rose, indicating the empty bench opposite him at the table. "Come. Sit."

"All due respect, my lord, but I would rather not."

At his post near the entryway to the courtyard, Abdul pointedly cleared his throat. Zahirah ignored the less-than-subtle signal to submit to the Frank, her cool gaze trained on the arrogant captain in reproach.

"You are upset about what happened last night," he guessed, resuming his seat when her rigid stance made it clear she would not be joining him. "I expected you might be. I had hoped I might make it up to you in some way."

"That won't be necessary," she replied, steeling herself to his obvious attempts at politeness. She did not want to think what Abdul might make of their conversation. Despite his endeavor to appear disinterested, his gaze now fixed on a point high above his turbaned head, she suspected there was little the servant did not know about the goings-on in the palace.

His foreign master seemed equally attuned.

"How fares your ankle today?" he asked, stabbing a chunk of melon on the end of a narrow knife and eating from the blade like a savage. "It must be markedly improved; I couldn't help noticing when you came in that you have taken off your bandages."

"Yes," Zahirah answered, having all but forgotten about the wrappings she had cut away a short while before Abdul's arrival at her door. After all, she'd had no true need of them, and she had wanted no hindrances when she made her escape from the palace. On second thought, perhaps there would be no call for risky escape tactics, now that it was plain to him that she was well on the mend. "My ankle is much better today, my lord. In fact, that is what I came to tell you. I thank you for your . . . hospitality, but I've no wish to trouble you further. I should like very much to be on my way as soon as possible."

"Understood," he granted her with a slight tilt of his head. "We can leave as soon as we are finished here."

Zahirah's heart slammed against her rib cage. "We, my lord?"

"You and I," he replied. "Abdul has already seen to the horses and supplies." A casual look toward the servant garnered a obeisant nod of confirmation.

"I don't understand," Zahirah blurted. She took a step forward, hands fisted at her sides, her head ringing with the ramifications of what he proposed. "Certainly, you cannot mean to accompany me when I leave here?"

"Indeed, I do. Despite what I may have led you to believe last night, I am a man of some honor, my lady. It would be a smirch to my vows of chivalry did I not see you safely delivered to your home."

She stared at him in mute frustration, unsure of what to think, let alone what to say.

"You do have a home somewhere, do you not, Zahirah?"

"Yes, but, I—" She struggled for excuses, anything to dissuade the man from his course. "My lord, I assure you it is not necessary for you to bother. I am perfectly able to go on my own." At his questioning frown, she rushed to explain. "My village is in the mountains, you see. It is a great distance from here, and it is remote. What few roads there are can be very difficult to travel—"

"All the more reason for you not to go alone."

"But, my lord—"

His smile was unwavering. "I insist."

Zahirah was about to sputter another moot refusal when the sound of raised voices carried down the length of the long corridor. They were too far away to discern the cause of the argument, but there was no mistaking that at least one of the men was Arabic—and hotly combative. Amid the disturbance, a palace servant rushed frantically into the courtyard. The small man executed a quick bow to the Frankish captain, who had since risen to his feet, watching as the servant then turned and whispered something in Abdul's ear.

"What is it?" questioned the dark lord.

"There is a man at the gates, master. He is quite agitated, I fear. He is demanding that he see his sister at once."

"His sister?" The captain pivoted, fixing a pointed look on Zahirah.

"He says he will not leave until he sees her, master."

"Then by all means," he answered, still staring at her, a faint scowl pinching his brow, "have the guards show him in."

Abdul's clipped order sent the other servant dashing back up the corridor. Zahirah could only stand there, praying that her heretofore unknown brother was in fact Halim, come to aid her after all. She breathed a sigh of relief to hear the *fida'i*'s voice booming in the hallway, and had to marshal a rather satisfied grin as he appeared before her a moment later, escorted by the beefy knight who called the captain his friend.

"This is your brother?" asked the captain.

Zahirah nodded, then raced forward to embrace Halim as if to demonstrate her affection. She could not have been more stunned when he raised his hand and struck her hard across the face.

"Whore," he spat acidly as she stumbled to her knees. "You are a disgrace!"

Cradling her burning cheek, Zahirah stared up at him in utter shock. She could not believe what he had just done, nor could she fathom how this degradingly violent display would help get her out of the palace. But all it took was one glimpse at the genuinely heated look in Halim's eyes, and she knew that his purpose in coming that morning was not to help her.

Rather, he had come to ensure she stayed.

"What, by God, is the meaning of this?"

The captain charged forward to assist her, but Zahirah held him back with a shake of her head. "Please, don't. I'm all right," she gasped brokenly, coming to her feet of her own accord.

The captain's voice rolled like thunder, deep and angry. "No man strikes a woman, be he a brother or nay."

"Sebastian," warned the other knight from behind Halim. "Have a care, my friend. This isna our affair."

"Like hell it's not," the captain growled in reply. He leveled a chilling glare on Halim and switched from his own language to Arabic. "This woman was nearly killed in the souk yesterday. What sort of family does she hail from that would send her brother here, willing to beat her senseless without affording her the benefit of explanation?"

"What explanation can she give?" Halim shot back. "There is nothing she can say. Any decent woman would have preferred death to what I see before me here. A woman soiled by your kind is worth nothing in my eyes. Less than nothing!"

Zahirah stood between the two men, staring at the blanket of thick grass at her feet. She was well aware of the trap Halim was baiting for Sebastian. That he had come to her defense so readily was all the information the *fida'i* needed to know precisely where, and how, to strike. Halim would use her in whatever way he deemed fitting—subjecting her to whatever insult or injury that was required to make sure the crusader kept her firmly under his protective wing.

Once a queen in this game of intrigue, Zahirah found that she had suddenly become a powerless pawn.

"If anyone bears cause for shame today, it is you," charged the captain, playing into Halim's practiced hands. "Your sister is every bit as chaste and innocent now as she was when I found her in the souk."

Halim gave an unconvinced grunt. "I am to believe that you brought a woman of her considerable beauty into a den of heathens and no one touched her? You must think me a fool."

"I think you are a man who is bent on jumping to groundless conclusions. I give you my word, no one touched this woman. She has dishonored herself not in the least."

Halim scoffed. "As if I would accept the vow of a Frank." Wrenching Zahirah's arm, he hauled her toward him. "If her virtue be intact, I would see it for myself—here and now."

"Halim!" she shrieked in bald horror. She pulled against his iron hold on her arm, but it did not give.

Behind her, the Frankish captain's sword flew out of its scabbard with a hiss of grating steel. "You will do no such thing, sirrah. I'll not have this woman further humiliated by your filthy slurs, or your presence. Release her. Now."

"And leave her to service you and your men without bringing me any return for the bother she's been to me? I think not." Halim tightened his grip on her arm. "Her looks should fetch me a pretty price at the slave market—"

"I don't think you hear what I am telling you, sirrah. The lady goes nowhere with you. Not today, or any other day. As you are a man who clearly values money more than the word of your own blood kin, then here—" He reached into his tunic and yanked a pendant free from his neck. The gold medallion glittered in the sunlight as it sailed across the courtyard to Halim. "That should more than pay for your troubles. Now begone from my sight, unless you mean to give me the pleasure of removing you myself."

Halim did not argue. He curled his hand around the long chain of gold, slanting a look of cool triumph at Zahirah as he released her and turned to go.

"Halim," she whispered, catching him by the arm and chagrined to hear a note of true fear rising in her throat. "Please. Don't leave me here."

He paused to look at her, and although Zahirah doubted that he cared if any of the other men heard him, he pitched his voice low for her ears only. "If you fail in this, I will kill you. Do you understand? You have gotten only what you deserve, Zahirah. I'm certain you will make the most of it."

She knew he spoke true, knew that he did this to her now

for many reasons, not the least of which being the fact that he held her responsible for his brother's death. She scarcely flinched when he reached out and tore off her veil—one final humiliation, the baring of her face to the other men in the room.

"Congratulations, Captain," Halim called in a caustic, thickly accented attempt at the *lingua franca*. "She's all yours."

Chapter Five

Sebastian knew a swift, violent urge to follow Zahirah's brother out of the palace and see if the bastard was as eager to raise his fist to another man as he was to a defenseless woman. Logan's mind was likely on a similar track; as Halim swaggered past him, the big Scot gave him a deliberate butt of his shoulder, inviting insult and all but daring the Saracen to give him further cause to fall in behind and take him to task outside. Disappointingly, Halim did not rise to the bait. He merely stepped away from Logan to throw one last glance at Sebastian, before he strode into the corridor and took his leave.

Glad to be rid of him, Sebastian turned his attention to Zahirah. "Are you all right?" he asked her.

Without looking at him, she gave a faint nod. He had expected to find her in tears a few paces beside him, as helpless as a lost kitten in need of protection. He would have understood, and he would have pitied her. But while Zahirah was quiet, her face downcast, hands clenched rigidly at her sides, there was no trace of defeat or fear in her stance. Hardly a mewling kitten in need of rescue, in that moment, she more resembled a tigress, taking silent measure of her sudden vulnerabilities and anticipating the next attack.

Or, perhaps, came the odd thought, calculating whether or not to spring first in offense.

Sebastian dismissed his queer misgivings and took a step toward her. In the grass at her feet lay her tattered veil. When she made no move to retrieve it, he bent down and did it for her.

"Thank you," she said, as she slid the scrap of torn silk from between his fingers.

She glanced up then, affording him a first glimpse at her uncovered face. If he had thought her exquisite in partial view, seeing the full measure of her beauty nearly rendered him speechless. Like a goddess kissed by an adoring sun, Zahirah's skin glowed warm honey bronze, as flawless and smooth as the silk that had so prudently concealed it from hungry male gazes until a few moments ago. High cheekbones, flushed pink beneath their Saracen color, flared above her delicate jaw and blunt, rounded chin; her nose was straight and slender, as aristocratic as any queen's, and perfectly balanced with the pouty, sensual curve of her mouth. Zahirah's fine arched brows and wide quicksilver eyes had been entrancing over the edge of her veil, but now, complemented by the striking beauty of her other features, their power to bewitch was staggering.

Her brother was wrong to think he could get a decent sum for her in the slave market; he could have gotten a bloody fortune.

Sebastian had not realized how rudely he stared until he met Zahirah's gaze straight on. Had she sensed his less-than-subtle appraisal? Perhaps she worried that she might yet find herself sold into human bondage, or worse. Those mercurial eyes did not so much as flinch, but deep within them, Sebastian spied a glimmer of uncertainty. It was gone in the next heartbeat, shuttered by a sweep of long dark lashes. Whether witting or not, she took a cautious step backward.

"Abdul," Sebastian commanded, "show Zahirah back to her chamber. She's been through much these past many hours. No doubt she would appreciate a bit of privacy to collect her thoughts."

The servant came forward and bowed his head to the lady, politely bidding she follow. Zahirah went along without so much as a word or a second glance at Sebastian, keeping her gaze down as the servant guided her out of the courtyard and back along the palace corridor.

Once they were gone, Logan pushed away from the frame of the doorway and entered the garden. He said nothing as he approached the breakfast-laden table and plucked a handful of purple grapes from a bowl of fruit. His prolonged silence as he raided the morning's viands was maddening.

"I know what you're thinking," Sebastian said dryly. "It was a mistake to bring the chit here in the first place. I should have summoned a villager to look after her injuries in the market. What sort of fool brings a Muslim woman into a Christian army camp unescorted?"

"Actually," said the Scots lieutenant, grinning as he chewed and swallowed another plump grape, "I was thinking that it might serve you well to be saddled with a ward. Mayhap she'll help keep you out of trouble. God knows I canna do it alone."

Sebastian sharply let out his breath, eyeing Logan askance. "A ward with her appeal will bring her own trouble, mark my words. I haven't the time or the interest to play guardian to the girl—or do you forget we've an assassin to ferret out before the king's return?"

The Scot grunted in acknowledgment. "Sinan's disciples would have to work magic to get past the city gates now, let alone breach the palace. By your command, there are extra guards on watch within and without Ascalon. I've set them to searching everyone who comes or goes."

"And what if our *fida'i* is already in place somewhere in the city, perhaps hiding under our very noses?" Sebastian remarked, almost to himself. The Old Man's agents were known for their ability to blend in with their surroundings, trained to adapt to any role, to assume any mask—from holy man to lowly peasant. Ascalon teemed with a thousand miscellaneous folk; any one of them could be Richard's attacker. How they would root him out before he struck again, Sebastian had no idea.

"You'll find him," Logan said, as if divining the direction of his thoughts from his dark expression alone. "Has the Black Lion ever failed at aught he's set his mind to do?"

Sebastian lifted a brow in wry humor. "Aye, once. That night in camp, when I let the little bastard escape the business end of my blade."

"A mere postponement of the inevitable," Logan quipped, shrugging his broad shoulders.

"Postponement, indeed," Sebastian replied. "My hand yet itches for revenge on his treachery."

"And I daresay none would deny you the pleasure of having it, my friend. If the assassin is within so much as a league of Ascalon, rest assured, we will find him."

Sebastian nodded, his concerns somewhat assuaged by his lieutenant's shared determination. He spoke true when he said his hand itched for vengeance on the *fida'i*. His body, too long in recuperation of his injury, craved the feel of battle, the pound and strain of weaponry and armor, the satisfaction of victory . . . anything to drown out another craving that plagued him. The craving that would set his feet on a path down the palace corridor to where she was, that tigress cub with the quicksilver eyes and the exotic mouth he had longed to taste even before he had been cursed by the sight of it.

She brought her own brand of trouble, indeed, and he had no intention of permitting her to stay any longer than it took to arrange safe harbor for her elsewhere. Abdul would know what to do; he would set the servant to the task before the sun set.

Forcing his thoughts back on course, Sebastian met his lieutenant's expectant gaze. "Have the men begun their morning's practice yet?"

Logan gave a nod. "They had just started to train when trouble arrived at the gates. No doubt they grow restless with waiting."

"Good. Then I should have no difficulty finding someone to spar with me for a while."

"Spar with you?" When Sebastian started for the corridor, Logan grabbed one last handful of grapes, then fell in behind. "You can't be serious."

"My skills have grown rusty," Sebastian replied casually. "I need the practice."

Logan scoffed. "Rusty, my arse. Even if you were, who would be fool enough to oblige you, in training or in truth, when you're but a few weeks this side of death?"

Sebastian answered him with a meaningful sidelong glance as he turned down a corridor that led to the courtyard.

"Oh, nay, my friend." Logan chuckled, keeping pace with him just the same. "You'll not goad me into sharing your madness. I want no part of it."

Sebastian gave a bark of laughter. "Whose skill do you doubt—mine, or yours?"

The big Scot growled an oath as they stepped out into the wide courtyard where the soldiers trained, already sweating under the relentless desert sun. Several groups of knights paused as their captain and his Scots right arm strode into their midst, chuckling and trading good-natured gibes; activity ceased altogether when it became apparent that the two warriors, so equal in size and skill, were intent to spar.

Sebastian paid no mind to the gathering crowd of soldiers. With humor in his eyes and the thrill of combat enlivening his limbs, he drew his weapon and waited for his friend to do likewise.

Logan met the challenge, grinning, every bit as eager for the contest, despite his protests. "You're a lunatic. You do realize that?"

With a shrug of agreement, Sebastian advanced. Someone shouted a bet of ten deniers on the Black Lion, a wager that was quickly met by another soldier, who evidently favored the unhindered strength of his Scot kinsman. The two mock combatants took up their stance, and within moments, the dusty, sun-baked courtyard rang with the cacophony of clashing steel and shouting, cheering men.

The intensity of the blazing noontide sun drove the exhausted knights into shadier quarters some three hours—and several lively wagers—later. Sebastian quit the training yard with Logan and the others, sweating and out of breath, his heart thudding heavily in his chest. The stitched gash in his side throbbed from the prolonged exertion of the morning's combat, but beyond the pain, he could feel his blood pumping through every vein, energizing every muscle and fiber of his body. His strength was coming back, and he could not recall when he had ever felt so incredibly alive.

"God's bones, English," remarked Logan as the two men took their ease near the palace well. He poured a ladle of water into a cup and handed it to Sebastian. "How can you look so satisfied when I know damned well you must feel every bit as abused as I do?"

Sebastian's lip curled in amusement as he accepted the drink from his friend. He consumed half of the cool water in one greedy swallow; the rest he poured over his heated head and face. Instantly refreshed, he slicked his hand over his jaw and met the Scot's gaze from under his dripping forelock. "I had no idea you were so soft, my friend. I'll bear it in mind and endeavor to go a bit easier on you when we spar again tomorrow."

"Go easier? Bloody hell!" Logan sputtered. He chortled over the jest, tossing aside his cup and making a great show of reaching for his sword. "I'll give you something to bear in mind!"

Sebastian laughed. "Save it for the morn," he said, clapping the Scot on the shoulder. "Tell your sergeants on watch at the gates that I want detailed reports before sup each night. And if there is any sign of trouble, I am to be called immediately."

At Logan's nod, Sebastian left the gathering at the well, heading back toward the palace, where he knew he would find a bath and a tankard of good Ascalon wine. Battle usually made him hungry for other pleasures as well, and as he passed a pretty doe-eyed servingwoman near the gardens, for a moment, he entertained the thought of inviting her along to assist him. She had been eager enough company on other occasions, but for reasons he had no inclination to explore, when she looked up and smiled at him, Sebastian merely returned the gesture and walked past.

His strides were long and confident as he traversed the length of a pillared, open-air arcade, his spurs ticking briskly on the tiled floor of the corridor that led to his private quarters. The day's exercise had soaked his tunic, making it itch where it clung to his skin. Impatient to be rid of the offending garment, he stripped it off and tossed it onto a divan the instant he stepped inside his chamber.

Abdul must have been in the room to open the windows sometime that morning, for a soft fragrant breeze whispered across Sebastian's bare chest and shoulders as he unbuckled his sword belt and walked through the main apartment toward his bedchamber. His weapon removed, he was about to set it down against the wall when something made him pause.

A movement behind him.

Subtle, soundless.

Stealthy.

An image of a black-clad youth and a slashing dagger flashed through his mind like a bolt of lightning. *Assassin*, warned the hairs that rose on the back of his neck, an explanation that seemed impossible to believe, but a threat too real to ignore.

He did not intend to wait for confirmation. His hand instinctively curled around the hilt of his sword, Sebastian ripped the blade free of its scabbard and rounded on the intruder.

"Christ Jesus!" he hissed as the sharp edge of steel came to a precarious halt at the base of a slender, silk-veiled throat.

Zahirah's eyes were wide with surprise over the edge of her veil, but she did not scream or faint away. Indeed, she scarcely moved, not even to draw breath, instead standing there unblinking, as if she fully expected him to run her through. There was an audible sigh of relief, however faint, when, with a muttered curse, he lowered his weapon.

"What, by God, are you doing in here?" he demanded, his tone overly harsh for the realization of what he might have done to her. His gaze strayed over her shoulder to a space of carpeted floor in the main area of his living quarters. There, a collection of pillows was arranged to form a cushioned pallet, and beside them was a prayer mat, spread out as if recently in use, its woven design facing toward Mecca, the direction in which all good Muslims sent their praise to Allah.

Sebastian looked back to Zahirah in confusion. "What is this about?"

She had been staring at his bare chest. Evidently, Zahirah realized the fact at the same time he did; she blinked and lifted her chin to meet his gaze straight on. "My lord?"

"Who gave you leave to enter my private chambers?"

"Your manservant, my lord," she answered simply enough. "He brought me here several hours ago with instructions that I was to serve you in whatever way you deemed fitting." She glanced down, suddenly shy. "I assumed those were your wishes as well."

Before he could acknowledge to himself that he could think of nothing more enticing in this world, Sebastian stalked to the open doorway and bellowed for Abdul. The turbaned Saracen appeared within scant moments, somewhat breathless for rushing to the summons from wherever he had been.

"Yes, master?"

"Am I to understand that you delivered Lady Zahirah to my private quarters without my leave?"

Abdul's dark gaze flicked to her, then up at his scowling Frankish lord. He swallowed hard. "I . . . yes, master."

Sebastian had to struggle to keep his voice level. "Explain yourself."

"Well, I . . . after what occurred this morning, master, I suppose I thought her presence would please you—"

"Please me?" he growled. Seizing Abdul by the arm, Sebastian forcibly guided the servant into the corridor. "By the Cross, Abdul. She came up behind me and I nearly took her head off."

The servant gasped. "It is my fault, master. I should not have presumed to know your wishes. Forgive me. I just thought that since she now belongs to you—"

"Belongs to me?" Sebastian echoed darkly. He shook his head, certain he misunderstood. "Zahirah is not chattel, Abdul. She is a free citizen, same as you. She belongs to no one, and I'll not have her kept here against her will—in my chamber or anywhere else."

The manservant's face grew serious, far too serious for Sebastian's peace of mind. "Master," he said softly, "she is yours. Did you not hear her brother say as much in the garden but a few hours ago? In Arab eyes, this woman belongs to you now. You paid for her with the chain of gold you gave her brother."

Sebastian suddenly recalled the angry impulse that compelled him to throw his heraldic pendant at Halim. He had meant it as an insult, a means of getting rid of the man before he was moved to slay Zahirah's brother before her very eyes. He had regretted the decision the instant he had torn the pendant loose and let it fly. Now a deeper dread began to dawn.

Wary for what he was about to hear, Sebastian narrowed his gaze on Abdul. "You're saying I paid for her, as one would pay for a slave?"

"No, not a slave," answered Abdul soberly. "A bride."

Chapter Six

Sebastian's expression must have been dire, for the Arab servant paled a bit as he stared up at him. "Is this your notion of a jest, Abdul? I warn you, I see no humor in it."

"Master, I do not jest. By her brother's word, Mistress Zahirah has been disowned. She is here at your mercy now, as your bri—"

Sebastian halted Abdul's tongue with a glower. "That's ridiculous." He refused to accept that in defending Zahirah that morning, he might have unwittingly tied himself to her. "She must have other kin somewhere who will take her in," he told Abdul in a clipped tone. "Find out who they are, then see that she is delivered to them without delay."

"As you wish, master." The manservant started to say something more, then shook his head. "I shall have her removed from the palace at once."

"What is it?" Sebastian asked, seeing the note of doubt in Abdul's eyes. "You think I am wrong to do this?"

"No, master. I would never question your judgment. It is not my place."

"However . . ." Sebastian prompted.

Abdul hesitated for a moment, as if still uncertain he should voice his opinion. "It is just that I fear for what might become of her should she be forced to leave, master. Arab women are very proud, you see. They value honor above all—even their own lives. Many would rather suffer death than the shame of repudiation."

"Repudiation?" Sebastian blew out his breath in frustration. "This is an army camp, Abdul. It's no place for gentle maidens, particularly maidens of Muslim faith. I'm certain Lady Zahirah will fare better, and doubtless be far happier, once she is back with her own kin."

Abdul bowed. "Of course, master."

Everything that was logical urged Sebastian simply to walk away and have done with the matter. He knew he could count on Abdul to carry out his instructions despite any personal reservations. As for Zahirah, in the short time he had been around her, Sebastian had seen hints of her inner strength. She did not strike him as the sort of woman to cave to antiquated notions of pride and dishonor. And if she was, how was that any of his concern?

Against his own will, he pivoted his head to look back into the room where she yet remained. She stood across the distance of the large chamber, paused before the tall, open windows. Her back was turned to the doorway, spine held rigidly erect. Prideful as she awaited news of her fate.

"Damnation," Sebastian swore softly.

"Master?"

He turned his head back and met Abdul's expectant gaze. "Just remove the lady from my chamber for the time being. I reckon it can do no harm to give her peace for the rest of the day. I'll explain the situation to her myself later this evening, to be sure she understands."

Abdul inclined his head. "Very well, master."

The conversation taking place in the corridor was kept in confidential tones, but with a measure of concentration, Zahirah was able to discern some of what was said. By Allah's shining grace, the palace servant, Abdul, had taken it upon himself to act as her defender with his boorish master, explaining how he had bound himself to her by paying Halim for her hand. The Frankish captain seemed as repulsed by the idea as she was, but her mission depended on his acceptance of the fact, and she could not have hoped for a better ally than the unwitting Abdul. If his appeal did not sway the Frank to let her remain at the palace, she suspected nothing would.

She tried to dismiss the knot of trepidation she felt at the thought of spending any amount of time in the captain's presence. She could still see the surprise, then the thunderous displeasure, in his gray-green eyes when he found she had been installed in his private chambers. She had been shocked to find herself so quickly at the killing end of his broadsword, even if he had borne down on her out of a warrior's sharp-honed reflex.

There had been no mercy in that thrust, only hard determination, and unerring control that stopped the blade a mere hairsbreadth from meeting its deadly mark. Her throat still felt the chill of his blade, and she knew the day would come that she would feel that cold bite again.

Allah willing, she would first know victory over the hated Franks and their king.

It was that thought alone that moved her to smile as she turned to face Abdul, who entered the chamber without his Frankish master. Outside in the hallway, the heavy boot falls of a clipped, long-legged stride echoed on the tiles of the floor, fading away with the captain's cool departure.

"Will you come with me, mistress?" asked Abdul, looking a bit awkward despite his kind expression. "My master believes you will be more comfortable elsewhere."

Zahirah lifted a brow. "Has he told you to turn me out, Abdul?"

"It was his wish that I give you peace for the rest of this day," the servant answered, making an obvious attempt to set her at ease.

She was not sure she should fully trust his kindness, but when he gathered up the prayer mat and pillows he had provided her with, then ushered her to the door, she followed willingly. He led her to another chamber, located on the same stretch of hallway, not a dozen paces from the captain's expansive quarters. It was smaller than those princely chambers, but every bit as bright and clean, furnished simply with a silk-covered bed, and a long divan that sprawled elegantly beneath a large window, shuttered from the heat of the sun with a grate of intricate iron lattice-work.

Abdul turned and caught her smiling as she took in the room. "It pleases you. I am glad, mistress."

She did not like the way he called her that. *Mistress*. It made her feel as if she belonged here, as if she were some-how a part of this place, the way he seemed to be.

How could this Arab man, who appeared to lack no measure of intelligence or good sense, deign to serve a Frankish lord? He did not wear the garb or tattooed mark-ings of a slave, nor, by the absence of a striped *zunnar* sash at his waist, had he converted to the heathen faith of the Western armies.

"You are a free Muslim," she said as he unrolled the prayer mat and turned its head toward the East.

"I am, mistress."

"Does it not bother you to serve those who deny Allah's Law?"

Her question was bold, perhaps overbold, coming from a woman. Abdul straightened, turned to face her. She searched his eyes for anger but found none there, nor in the gentle smile he offered her. "It bothered me more when our defending armies swept through Ascalon not a year ago," he said, pain still raw in his voice. "The city, you see, was razed to keep out the Franks."

"I remember," she said. "Ascalon burned for seven days and nights."

Abdul nodded vaguely. "I had a wife and young son then. My boy was sick, so his mother tended him while I was out assisting the wounded near the docks. Our house, along with the others on our street, was set afire by Saladin's forces. The wind was high that day, and the blaze swept quickly; my family had no chance to escape the flames. They perished within moments."

"Peace be upon them," Zahirah whispered, a blessing that fell simultaneously from Abdul's lips.

"I could have left Ascalon, like many others did after the fires, but this city is my home. I was born here. By Allah's grace, it is here I will die."

"But to live here, in a Frankish army camp," Zahirah said, still unable to reconcile the notion in her mind. "Surely there are other places . . . other means."

"Oh, it is not as bad as that, mistress. These Franks are no different than any other men of war, be they Muslim, Christian, or another faith. There is good and bad in the hearts of all men. Here I have found mostly good. You will see." He laid a gentle hand on her arm, startling her with the unexpected contact. "My master, Lord Sebastian, is among the finest, most noble men I've ever known. I fear his bark might have you believing differently."

Zahirah was tempted to say that she did not know enough about him yet to believe anything, nor did she have any particular inclination to know him. But she would play along with this game for now, if it might win her some valuable insight into the habits of his king. "Your esteem must be shared by the English king, for him to have placed your lord Sebastian in charge here."

Abdul nodded. "From what I have seen of him, Richard of England holds few men in high regard. His trust is hard-won and easily lost."

"I have heard the same said of his promises."

"And his mercy, mistress," the servant cautioned with a sober glance. "If I may give you a word of advice: endeavor to keep yourself out of the king's eye. He likes pretty things, and he takes what he likes."

Zahirah accepted the warning with a grateful nod of thanks. "Does he stay here when he is in Ascalon?" she asked, taking care not to sound too deliberate.

"The king is often on the march, but he keeps chambers here in the palace."

"Where in the palace does he stay?" Zahirah pressed. "So I may know what areas to avoid."

Abdul smiled reassuringly. "Stay close to my master and you will be safe wherever you are, mistress."

It was not the answer she wanted, but to probe further would likely rouse the servant's suspicions. She watched as he finished settling her into the chamber, readily agreeing when he suggested she probably needed to rest a while in private. She was not tired, but she pretended to doze on the bed when Abdul at last took his leave.

With the servant gone to other tasks and his overlord nowhere to be seen, Zahirah slipped out of her chamber and padded off down the corridor. She would no doubt have precious few opportunities to learn the layout of the palace; she had best make the most of every one.

Her exploration led her first down a long hall that passed above one of the many enclosed courtyards. She moved with care and haste along the open-air gallery, taking note of the knights training at their war games below.

He was there among them, too—Sebastian. He surveyed the activity from the shade of the arcade, his heavy-muscled arms folded over his bare chest, his dark brows knit into a scowl. Amid a courtyard ringing with weaponry and arms, thick with a swarm of fighting men, it was he who commanded her gaze. Just standing idle as he was, he radiated raw male power, and not a little fury. Indeed, his presence filled the wide space the same as it filled her senses.

A young servingwoman seemed to feel likewise. Dark-haired and lovely, she sauntered across the courtyard to bring him a cup of wine. She wore no veil to mask her desirous look, nor did she feign the slightest degree of modesty when the captain reached out to brush her bare cheek with his hand. It was a casual touch, but the woman's giggle was full of meaning.

Had he a lover in her, then? Zahirah wondered.

She felt a dart of scorn for the idea, but quickly shook it off. Let him have a dozen lovers—whatever diversions kept him occupied and out of her way would suit her very well.

Refusing to see how long it took the woman to entice him away, Zahirah ducked low and moved hastily to the end of the gallery walkway.

She found the empty harem after navigating a series of winding corridors. The many apartments and common rooms were eerily vacant, some rooms stripped of their rugs and tapestries while others had been left untouched. She passed the bathhouse and eunuchs' quarters, the kitchens and gazebos, noting which rooms opened into hallways— her mind automatically cataloging possible hiding places and escape routes. There was nothing in this section of the palace that indicated the king might stay there, but Zahirah did find something of interest when she peeked inside a chamber that had likely belonged to one of the sultan's wives.

At the center of the far wall was a pair of latticework doors. They opened onto a covered balcony that over-looked the city, and, not much farther beyond, the endless blue of the ocean. A cooling breeze blew off the harbor to skate across the graduated rooftops of the palace, which must have been a favorite spot for the women of the harem.

One of those flat roof terraces was accessible from the balcony. Zahirah walked out and swung her legs over the edge to scoot out onto the roof, where the sun was bright and warm. She sat down on the smooth tiled surface and breathed in the cleansing air of her homeland, her eyes nearly hurting for the beauty of the day Allah had cre-ated.

Here, under the cloudless Syrian sky, there was no dark-ness. No terror or death.

Here, alone with her God, she did not have to hide who she was—or what she was. Her mask could fall away and Allah would still be there, accepting her, smiling down upon her with the warmth of his infinite benevolence. Sometimes, it was enough.

Sometimes, she could only weep.

As was her private ritual from the time she was a little girl, Zahirah removed her veil and tipped her face into the sun. Next she rolled up the sleeves and hem of her tunic, then did the same to the legs of her silk trousers.

She lay back on the roof terrace, her skin exposed as much as she dared, then whispered to the heavens, "Heal me. Allah, please . . . heal me."

Chapter Seven

The Frankish captain was lounging like a bored young emir when Zahirah appeared at his door later that evening. No, not bored, she amended as her eyes took in his powerful physique, which dwarfed the small divan beneath him. His expression when it lit upon her was thoughtful and self-possessed, his dark brow furrowed as if in mild irritation to glance up and find her standing there.

"You sent for me, my lord."

It bothered her that she should blush under his stare, that she should feel the need to explain herself to this man. What bothered her more was the fierce urge she had to scan his lamplit chamber for traces of the woman he had met in the courtyard earlier that day.

Had she been there, Zahirah would never know, for this infidel warlord was discreet and meticulous, a fact evidenced by the way he kept his person—always clean-smelling and well groomed—his thick jet hair longish about his shoulders, but not shaggy like most of his breed; his dark beard was naught but shadow on his broad, shapely jaw, painstakingly shaved close to his skin as was the custom of the heathen Western knights.

Vanity, she accused silently, though she had to admit his masculine pride was not at all misplaced. Hawkish and striking, she supposed he would be handsome to Frankish eyes, and, perhaps even a little to her own, did she not despise his kind to her very marrow.

"Your manservant said you wished to speak to me," she said, an edge of rancor to her voice.

"Yes. Come in, Zahirah." He rose to his feet, albeit be-latedly, and beckoned her forth with a smile. It was a brief baring of straight white teeth, too arrogantly dazzling to bring her any measure of comfort.

When Abdul had informed her of his master's wish for private audience in his chamber, Zahirah had worried that perhaps the Frank had decided to take his use of her. She had seen the way he looked at her when Halim had stripped her of her veil earlier that day—more than that, she had felt it, like the heat of the sun's caress—and while she had no personal knowledge of carnal relations, she had seen enough in her father's harem at Masyaf to recognize the glint of lust in a man's eye.

It had been there when Sebastian gazed upon her naked face that morn. It had been there in the garden the night before as well, when he stared at her in the moonlight, so bold in manner that he would reach out and trace the line of her mouth through her veil.

It was there now, too, although she could see that he en-deavored to mask it with cool indifference as he gestured for her to be seated across from him on a small wooden chair. He had an agenda in mind by summoning her to him, but ravishment did not seem at the heart of it. Somewhat re-laxed to realize that, she stepped inside.

"We must needs talk," he said when she quietly obliged him. "What happened this morning between me and your brother . . . the apparent exchange that transpired . . ."

At his hesitation, Zahirah cocked her head slightly and frowned. Although he wrestled with how to say it, she un-derstood precisely where he was headed, and she would af-ford him no easy route to her dismissal from the palace. She let the silence stretch out between them.

The captain cleared his throat. "My days at court are too long behind me. I fear my skills at politic conversation now leave something to be desired. May I speak plainly, my lady?"

"As you wish, my lord," she replied. "I find I much pre-fer the efficiency of candor to pointlessly talking around a matter."

She was startled to hear him laugh at that. The deep bark of humor filled the room, resonating in her breast long after it left her ears. She did not know what she had said to amuse him, but his gray-green eyes were still dancing with mirth as he reached for a cup of wine that sat on the table before him.

"Would you care for some?" he asked when he looked up and found Zahirah studying him.

"It is a sin for a Muslim to take wine," she said, and while she spoke softly, her words seemed to hurl at him in accusation.

He gave no indication of insult, although he set the cup back down on the table without drinking from it. "There are many differences in our two cultures, as I am learning each day. Abdul has explained to me a few things about your customs. That is, in fact, the reason I asked you here this evening."

"To discuss our differences, my lord? I thought you might have asked me here to tell me there was no place for me in this house."

A smile quirked at the corner of the captain's mouth. He leaned back against the cushioned divan in a negligent sprawl, his legs casually braced apart, one arm flung along the back of the divan. "I see you do prefer candid conversation, my lady. Very well. You should know that it was never my intention to bargain with your brother for a bride."

"Nor was it mine to be that bride," she replied, a truth that rolled easily off the tip of her tongue.

"And yet, alas, my lady, here we are."

She blinked slowly. "So it would seem, my lord."

He studied her for a moment. When he spoke again, his voice, and his demeanor, had gentled. "I apologize for the way I reacted this afternoon, when I found you in here. I had not expected—well, you can see how unaccustomed I am to having a woman so close underfoot. This may look like a palace, Zahirah, but it is a house of war. It's no place for someone like you."

"Like me, my lord?"

"An innocent. One whose eyes are far too lovely to be tainted with the ugliness of war."

Was that how he viewed her? Part of her warmed to the notion, but a less forgiving part of her reminded her of the icy cold dagger she wore at her waist, of the years of hard training and ruthless discipline that had made her what she was: Sinan's own virgin blade, a weapon that had been honed in secret, kept pure from sin and stain and feeling for a single mission. There had never been a female *fida'i* in the history of her clan; by her father's design, she was ordained from birth to be the first—and last—of her kind.

But an innocent? No, she was hardly that. And she was not about to let this Frank and his misguided sympathy sway her from her course.

"I am here because you brought me here," she said pointedly. "I have nowhere to go. If you turn me out, do not say it is out of concern for me when it is plain you would do so because my presence in this place suddenly inconveniences you."

It was unfair of her, certainly, the way she fought him with those words. The captain's expression grew harder the longer he stared at her, considering. He had likely never been spoken to in such a way, leastwise by a woman. Would he strike her, or bring her under his wing? Zahirah steeled herself for either reaction. He could do whatever he wanted; she would accept it, so long as she did not have to return to Masyaf in shame.

"I will do anything," she heard herself say, the tremor in her voice rising up from a well of true emotion. "Anything, my lord. I swear it."

He let out his breath in a long sigh, resignation etched deep into his brow. "This would be a temporary arrangement, you understand. Only for as long as I am here in Ascalon. I'll make no demands of you, nor will I make you any promises beyond these walls."

Zahirah nodded, feeling a wave of relief wash over her. "I will ask nothing of you, my lord."

"Very well," he said, although he did not look entirely

convinced that he agreed. "You may stay in the chamber Abdul has given you. The palace is secured by guards at every gate. You are free to move about the grounds, but you will not venture outside without an escort. And no one may accompany you in without my express permission. Understood?"

Although this was far more advantageous than being turned out, Zahirah felt the pinch of his limiting restrictions. "Have I gone from bride to prisoner, now, my lord?"

He stared at her, one dark brow arching slightly. "You are neither, my lady. But so long as you are here under my protection, you will obey me." He rose then, indicating their meeting was at an end. "I'll instruct Abdul to purchase some clothing and personal items for you from the bazaar in the morning. If there is anything else you require, you need only ask."

She murmured her thanks, but the captain's attention was since turned toward the corridor where the jangle of armor and a heavy-heeled gait announced an approaching soldier. A moment later, the big brown-haired knight with the strange manner of speaking had swaggered over the threshold.

"The reports are in from the gates, my friend." His glance lit on Zahirah and he paused, drawing up short. "Beg pardon. I dinna mean to intrude."

"It's all right, Logan. I believe Lady Zahirah and I have said all there is to say. For now."

At Sebastian's indication, Zahirah got to her feet and followed him to the open door. She wanted to feel triumph as she passed him to step into the corridor, telling herself that she had won this first skirmish with minimal sacrifice, but the nervous flutter in her stomach told her different. It warned that while she had succeeded in securing her place in the palace, she had just put herself directly in the captain's control.

Neither bride nor prisoner, he had said, but she was shackled to him nonetheless. She felt the weight of her new bonds in every step she took down the corridor toward her chamber, her spine burning for the heat of his regard at her back. He would be watching her closely now, and if she were careless enough to slip at any juncture in her mission, she knew that his mercy would be spare; his wrath, swift.

"A beguiling lass, is she not?"

"Persuasive," Sebastian drawled, leaning his shoulder against the doorjamb.

"I take it you decided to let her stay."

He grunted. "We have settled on a mutually acceptable arrangement."

"Ah, of course," Logan chuckled. "An arrangement."

Sebastian pivoted his head and slid a narrow-eyed glance in the Scot's direction. "What the devil are you so smug about?"

Like his captain's had been until that moment, Logan's appreciative gaze followed Zahirah's swift retreat down the corridor. "Me, smug? I haena said a word, my friend."

"And I'll thank you to keep it that way," Sebastian growled. "If you've finished gaping at the lady, perhaps we can go see about those reports now."

Chapter Eight

True to his word, Sebastian sent Abdul to Zahirah's chamber that next morning with four new tunics and *shalwar*. The pretty silks were lovelier by far than any she had at Masyaf, their bright hues and intricate green-and-magenta embroideries glowing like jewels in the sun rays pouring in through the window grate. She luxuriated in the sight and feel of them all, finally settling on a ruby-colored outfit as the first she would wear. Abdul had scarcely departed the room and shut the door before she tore off her old tunic and pantalets to slip into the new.

Indulgences such as this were not permitted at her father's house. There, she was a soldier first, treated thusly in both form and address, for the great Sinan would have it no other way. She was loath to think what he would do to see her garbed as richly as she was now.

Nor would she think about that.

Not now. Not when the crisp silk felt so good against her skin, the fine fabric pleasingly scented with the warm, heady spices of the market. And if the ankle-length embroidered tunic was lovely indoors, she imagined the fiery color would be stunning under the full glory of this new day's sun. But why imagine, she decided, when it would take but a moment to see for herself?

Zahirah fastened her veil across her cheeks, then quit her chamber. Her step was light as she navigated the corridor and maze of inner arcades. None of the servants or palace guards did more than glance up as she passed them on her way to the large courtyard, the folk evidently advised that she was free to walk about by the captain's leave.

Near the pool at the center of the dusty yard, a knot of women worked at washing clothes. They were Frankish, laundresses of varying age and appearance, brought along from their homeland to service the infidel army. From their bawdy talk and ease among the soldiers, Zahirah suspected their duties extended beyond the tub and board, yet they glared at her when she passed as if *she* were the whore.

His whore.

No doubt the story of how the formidable captain had unwillingly shackled himself to a Muslim village girl had already traveled the camp. And here she was the very next day, out among his folk, dressed as fine as a rich man's favorite concubine. Suddenly, her idea to stroll the courtyard seemed worse than foolish.

Zahirah had been raised with great discipline not to call attention to herself, to blend in with her surroundings, one of the most vital weapons of the *fida'i*. Standing there now, she had never felt more conspicuous, nor more exposed. Her gaze strayed to the gaggle of hard-faced washerwomen. She would have needed no amount of studied training in the coarse *lingua franca* to understand what one of them called her through a gap-toothed sneer. Another slur quickly followed, then a third.

Feeling cornered in the middle of the huge yard, Zahirah pivoted her head and found a group of infidel knights watching the scene from several dozen paces at her back. A couple of them were chuckling, clearly enjoying the sport.

If they thought her defenseless, it only made her yearn to prove them wrong. Her skills were thorough enough that she could have fought off the washerwomen's taunts, showing by swift, lethal example what happens to a Frank who is fool enough to tangle with a *fida'i*. But the dagger she wore hidden beneath her tunic was meant for one Frank alone; she would not sully it with the blood of these squawking, petty hens.

She spared the lot of them no more than a glance, turning

on her heel and striding out of the courtyard as haughty as
a queen. Her brisk steps carried her down a hall and through
a wide colonnade, a path she quickly recognized for its pat-
tern of intricate mosaic tilework. Her feet began to slow of
their own accord. This was the same corridor she had traveled the morning before with Abdul, at the start of her troubles, when she had been summoned to join Sebastian as he
broke his fast.

To her dismay, she found that he was there now as well.

She had sensed him even before she saw him, seated at
the same table, his forehead braced on his fist as he studied
something that sat on the table before him. After her embarrassment in the courtyard, the last thing she wanted was
a confrontation with the captain. Hoping to slip by unnoticed, Zahirah picked up her pace, careful that her sandals
made no noise on the tiles as she walked past the arched entryway.

"That color suits you well, my lady."

Faith, but did the man miss nothing?

Zahirah froze at the sound of his deep voice coming from
within the garden alcove. Hands fisted at her sides, she
reluctantly turned and walked the two steps back to face
him.

"Abdul has a merchant's eye for quality," he said, when
she stood at the threshold, mutely meeting his gaze from
across the distance that separated them. "I trust you were
pleased with his selections."

She inclined her head in acknowledgment. "Yes, my lord.
Thank you."

"Won't you join me?" he asked, and although it was not
quite a command, his invitation was compelling enough
that she obeyed.

As she drew near to where he sat, she saw what had so
captivated his interest before she arrived. There before him
on the table was a checkered game board, peopled with rows
of white and black pieces, some half dozen moves advanced
in play. The captain played the white side; he was about to
lose a pawn to the black.

"You know *shatranj*," she said as he studied the board, somewhat surprised to see this Westerner playing at the ancient Arabic game of kingly war.

"I am still learning," he replied, lifting his shoulder in a shrug. "Abdul took it upon himself to teach me a few weeks ago, when I was good for naught but lying about in bed as an invalid."

"After you were . . . injured?" Zahirah asked carefully as she came to stand beside him.

"Attacked," he corrected, glancing up at her. "I stood in defense of my king when an assassin crept into our camp one night last month. The whelp nearly gutted me with his blade."

Chagrined, Zahirah had to force herself to hold that steady gray-green gaze. "Not many would dare to stand against the assassins, my lord. They are said to move as phantoms among the villages and mountains of Syria. Some say they are enchanted by a black brand of magic— that they are devils possessed."

The captain scoffed. "Before he stabbed me, I held this particular devil tight in mine own hands. He was flesh and bone, same as you or I. When next I meet him, he will bleed the same, too."

Zahirah swallowed hard at the bald determination in that statement. Sebastian had since turned his attention back to his game, grabbing up his jeopardized pawn and moving it out of danger. It was a decision that would cost him the match in four more turns, if his opponent had half the skill of Zahirah herself in this game she had played since childhood.

She saw where he had been heading, impatiently clearing a path for the white queen to challenge the black. It was a bold move, she would grant him that, but if he had thought it out more cautiously, he would have seen his mistake. Zahirah looked at the white *ruhk* suddenly made vulnerable, her fingers itching to sit in where Abdul had left off.

"How eager you Franks are for blood," she remarked in

an easy, if somewhat provocative, tone. "You play at war the same way you play at *shatranj*."

Sebastian chuckled. "You sound like Abdul. He says this game will teach me the virtue of biding one's time." He arched a dark brow. "Do you play, my lady?"

Beneath her veil, Zahirah smiled. "A bit."

"Please," he said, indicating the bench opposite him.

Zahirah took her position as the black player and moved without the slightest pretense of hesitation. She advanced her *faras* two squares forward and three to the right, the horse-shaped piece neatly capturing the captain's unprotected *ruhk*.

He grunted, meeting her unapologetic gaze with a look of wry understanding. "I see I can expect no quarter from you, my lady."

She shook her head. "None, my lord."

He smiled a smile that had likely melted a thousand maidens' hearts from England to Palestine. "Then I shall consider myself under no obligation to grant quarter, either, gentle lady."

"Do you presume I would need ask it, sir Frank?"

He laughed aloud, and so began their dance.

At once, Zahirah ruled the board, blocking his every stratagem and driving him back with a steady offense worthy of Saladin himself. Sebastian seemed to enjoy the contest, even though he was losing the battle to a woman—or perhaps, she thought, because of that fact. More than once she caught him eyeing her with a look that she was wont to describe as warmth or interest, maybe even a small measure of admiration. Oh, he glared and sputtered over each forfeited piece, and cursed a bit, too, but his laughter was never far behind, and soon, Zahirah found herself sharing his mirth.

Worse than that, she found herself genuinely enjoying his company. So much so that when the game came down to the last handful of pieces, she almost regretted the haste with which she had played. A quick glance at the board showed

that, depending on what he did next, Zahirah could claim
Sebastian's king in one more move. She sat back, rather
hoping he would see the potential breach in his defenses and
move elsewise to prolong the match.

To her dismay, his hand hovered over the white queen,
the piece blocking her swift victory. He thought for a moment, then started to pick it up.

"M-my lord," she murmured, shocked, and not a little
bemused, to hear the warning slip past her lips. "Are you
sure?"

He paused, staring at her for a moment, as if weighing
her advice. She could see the surprise in his gaze, the question he very likely thought but did not voice: Did she protect him now, or lead him into defeat? He glanced back
down at the game, his finger tapping on the piece he might
have moved, and realization suddenly dawned.

"Perhaps there is a bit of mercy in your heart after all,
Zahirah." He chose another tactic, a better move by far,
then tilted his head to regard her across the table with a wry
grin. "I confess, after this ruthless game, I was beginning to
wonder if the heart of an assassin beat within your breast."

She laughed at his jest, but to her ears, it was a forced
sound. That heart he wondered at was suddenly tumbling
against her ribs. Did he possibly suspect? She dismissed the
thought at once, certain that this warrior lord would not be
sitting there, laughing with her and making jokes, if he
thought for one moment that she was not what she pretended to be.

What was it she pretended at now, she wondered, when
she looked into the face of this Frank—her forsworn
enemy—and felt nary a kindling of proper scorn? What
game did she purport to play when she laughed with him,
sparred with him, but a few moments ago?

And what flimsy ruse could she claim when her fluttering
heart beat as wildly simply to be near him as it did at the
thought of being discovered for the betrayer she would inevitably prove to be?

"It is your move, my lady."

Flustered by the droll reminder, Zahirah reached out hastily to take her turn. As she did so, the wide edge of her tunic sleeve caught on one of the game pieces and knocked it over, sending it rolling to the edge of the table. She made a grab for it at the same time Sebastian did. His hand closed over hers, large and warm and strong.

For a moment, she was unable to draw her breath. She stared at that warrior's hand, the hard sun-browned fingers engulfing her nearly to the wrist in a firm, yet undemanding, grasp. It was light enough that she could have pulled away—should have, certainly—but to her utter bewilderment, she lingered in his hold.

Allah, forgive her, but she reveled in it.

He stroked the tender skin at the juncture of her thumb and forefinger. "Have you ever permitted a man the privilege of enjoying your company with your face unveiled, Zahirah?"

It was a scandalous question, a proposition that should shame her just to hear it. She felt a blush flood her cheeks, but could not fool herself into blaming the heat on humility. "What you suggest is a right granted only to a Muslim woman's husband, my lord."

"A regrettable fact," he drawled, "in light of the terms of our arrangement."

Was that another jest, or something more serious? He was smiling vaguely, but his gaze was too intense to be misconstrued as mockery. Taken aback by his implication, at last, Zahirah found the will to withdraw her hand from his grasp.

It was a struggle to gather her wits so long as he was studying her. She could scarcely see the game board for the effort it took to steady her hand as she reached for the black left *ruhk* and slid it forward two squares.

"Do I make you nervous, Zahirah?"

"N-no. Of course not," she denied quickly. Too quickly, perhaps, for when her anxious gaze darted up to meet his, he was leaning back in his seat, grinning.

"I am glad to hear it," he said, his voice low and rumbling

like the purr of a big desert cat. "It is not my intention to make you nervous. And I hate to leave you thinking that I would take unfair advantage."

She watched in mild confusion as he came forward to have his turn at the board. The gleam in his eye as he made his move was pure deviltry. "*Shah mat,* my lady."

Zahirah sucked in her breath in disbelief. She gaped at him, then to the game board, to where the black king stood, abandoned by the *ruhk* she had moved in her befuddlement, and now, left no escape from Sebastian's advancing queen.

Shah mat. Her king was forfeit; the game was ended.

"That—that's impossible," she gasped, having not lost at *shatranj* since she was an impulsive, careless child just learning to play.

But the truth was irrefutable. This unskilled Frank, an opponent she should have easily trounced, had instead managed to turn the tables and beat her at her own game.

"Perhaps my lady wishes a rematch?" he asked, very full of himself in that moment.

Zahirah arched a brow, her own pride seething for revenge. "I more than wish it, my lord. I demand it."

Chapter Nine

Zahirah promptly won the next round, and would have doubtless claimed a third had the game not been interrupted by one of Sebastian's soldiers bringing news of a shipment that required his attention at the docks. Reluctantly, Zahirah took her leave as well, departing the private courtyard with a promise from the captain that they would pick up again as time permitted.

Her mood was almost gleeful as she wended her way back through the heart of the palace. She could not bear the thought of wasting a beautiful day indoors, so instead of returning to her chamber, she headed toward the long corridor of the harems, seeking out the solitude of the roof terrace, that sunny sanctuary she had discovered on her exploration of the palace the morning before.

As she had done that prior morn, Zahirah climbed out from the sultana's balcony and took her place beneath the glorious noontime rays. She lay on her back with her eyes closed, her skin soaking in the sun's warmth, her senses soaking in the simple pleasure of her surroundings. But where she usually found meditation and clarity of thought in the ritual, today her mind was awhirl.

Although she fought it, Zahirah had but to think on him and there he was: that lazy, devilish grin; those eyes that were such a stormy mix of seafoam and steel; the strong but gentle hand that she could still feel warming her own.

Sebastian.

Quietly, she whispered the foreign name, tasting it on her

tongue the way a child would savor a strange new sweet.
Sebastian. How easy it was to let it roll from her lips.

It should have choked her, this feeling she suddenly
had—this queer and unwanted fondness for a man she
should despise. She told herself it was merely the thrill of
finding a kindred spirit, despite their opposing sides.
Someone who seemed every bit as competitive, and determined to win, as she was. But there was something more to
this feeling. Something that spoke to her in hushed darker
tones, stirring up a confusion of feelings and wants and de-
sires from deep within her.

Zahirah had never known a man's touch; Rashid al-Din
Sinan would have slain any who dared so much as glance
with interest on the daughter he had taken great pains to
raise in his own ruthless image. She had been kept pure in
body and in thought, schooled never to fail in anything her
father demanded of her, a lesson that was easy to abide once
she knew what she would suffer for the most trivial slip.

Darkness.

Even now, under the blaze of the midday sun, she could
feel the coldness of that black place clawing at her. It
was there that her nightmares first began to breed, in the ter-
rifying, endless void of isolation. It nearly drove her mad,
those lightless, empty hours she had been forced to spend in
discipline, left with nothing but the sounds of her own
breathing . . . and, if she dared sleep, the screams.

Allah, the screams.

Bloodcurdling, frightened, sorrowful screams. She did
not know the strangers' voices, nor could she make sense of
what they said, but the terror was so real to Zahirah, it
could have been torn from her own throat. She felt the pain
as her own; she knew the grief, the shocking, sudden sense
of loss. Now, as then, she heard a name carrying from out
of the darkness of her memory, drifting toward her as a tattered ribbon snagging on a savage wind . . .

No.

Zahirah banished the disturbing thought from her mind

before it could take root. She sat up and rubbed off a bone-deep chill, looking up at the heavens and filling her eyes with the burning comfort of bright warm sunshine. Safe, glorious daylight. There was nothing to fear here.

And yet, she trembled.

She did not know how long she had been out there on the roof terrace, but the solitude she found was no longer as pleasing as it had been, and she suddenly needed to feel some of the bustle and hubbub of the palace interior. She fastened her veil and readjusted the hems of her tunic and *shalwar,* then returned inside the sultana's chamber to make the passage back to her own.

To her relief, once out of the vacant harem wing, activity abounded. Servants went about their day's tasks; soldiers trained in the yard. Even the cackle of the washerwomen, goading the men with outrageous jests and innuendo, was a welcome diversion from the ghosts of memory that followed Zahirah in from the roof.

She found herself surreptitiously searching for Sebastian among the other folk, listening for his deep laugh, hoping to see him come striding down one of the many corridors as she made her way back to her chamber. But the captain was nowhere in sight, evidently still detained with his men somewhere outside the palace.

Zahirah tried to deny the little pang of disappointment she felt at his absence, tried to ignore the glimmer of hope she held that she would find him in his chamber as she passed on the way to hers. She slowed as she neared his apartments, but he was not there either. His chamber door was closed tight; naught but quiet sounded on the other side.

Zahirah's own chamber door, however, stood ajar. She approached with caution—curious, and not a small measure suspicious, of what she would find within. Someone had been there since she had left that morning. Abdul, no doubt, she decided, immediately relaxing as she made a quick glance around.

The latticework grate that covered her window had been opened to let in the balmy garden breeze. On the squat table nearby was a pot of fresh flowers, their gay colors and sweet perfumes begging to be enjoyed. But it was the small package on the bed that wrung a smile from Zahirah's lips, drawing her into the room as on winged feet.

What more had Sebastian given her? she wondered, excited as she untied the bindings and tore away the linen wrapper to see what it contained. Every joyful feeling she had fled the instant the package fell open, for the gift was no gift at all.

It was a flat yellow cake that no one would dare put to their lips, for it could have come from one place alone: Masyaf. A token generally reserved for victims of the *fida'i,* this one had come to her as a message—or a warning. Sobered by the very sight of it, Zahirah quietly closed her chamber door, then spread the linen wrapper out on the bed and crushed the crumbly cake in her hands. A small square of papyrus had been baked inside, folded over to conceal a note written in Arabic. It was from Halim.

I have information. Meet me tomorrow at the city mosque. Sabbath prayer. Do not be late.

Zahirah gathered up the crumb-covered swatch of linen and carried it to the window to shake it out. The garden birds and pigeons would dispose of the tiny bits of cake in a matter of moments; Halim's missive would need to be destroyed through more deliberate means. She brought it to where an oil lamp burned in an alcove in the wall and held the note over the thin flame. It smoked and caught fire, but it was still burning when a heavy knock sounded on her door.

"Zahirah, are you in there?"

Sebastian. She swung her head toward the deep growl of his voice in a panic. Allah, what should she do? She dropped the smoldering remnants of Halim's note onto the floor and stomped them out with her sandal as quietly as she could. She considered feigning her absence from the chamber, but could not trust that the captain would not open the door to verify the fact for himself.

"A moment, please," she called from the other side of the room, willing her voice to a calm timbre as she lifted the edge of the thick Persian rug and swept the ashes of Halim's note under it.

Even with the window open to the breeze, the room smelled of smoke and burnt paper. If she allowed Sebastian in, he would surely scent what she had been up to and wonder if she had something to hide. He might even insist on a search of her chambers—or her person. It was a risk she was unwilling to take.

"Yes, my lord?" she asked from the other side of the panel that separated them. "I thought you were yet at the docks."

"I was," he answered, "but my business there is concluded." A pause followed, then: "Will you open the door, my lady, or must we speak through it?"

There was a wry edge to his voice, but Zahirah still bit her lip in worry, fearful that his light request could easily become demand. "I cannot open the door, my lord. I . . . I am not dressed to receive company."

Another pause from him, this time longer. Did he doubt her excuse? Worse, would modesty matter to a barbarian Frank if he was determined to have his way?

"I had hoped to bathe, my lord," she hastened to add, "then spend the evening in prayer."

"Ah," he answered, evidently appeased. "And here I thought I might convince you to let me win back some of the dignity you stole from me this morn at *shatranj.*"

He was waiting for her to answer, perhaps waiting to discern whether or not she smiled on the other side of the door. She was smiling, but she snuffed it with a harsh thought of reprimand, and did not dare trust herself to reply. She remained silent where she stood, scarcely breathing, wishing him away.

"Well," he said after a long moment. "Another time, perhaps."

"Perhaps," she echoed quietly.

Zahirah waited, listening in utter silence, her pent-up breath leaking out of her as he slowly took his leave. She had managed to avoid a potential disaster, but there were sure to be more awaiting her in this dangerous game she played. Sebastian was not a man to be toyed with; the very worst thing she could do was allow herself to warm to him, to let herself feel something for him beyond an adversarial sort of wariness, the respect given to any formidable enemy.

Where that was concerned, Halim's message could not have come at a better time. If her focus had started to slip, the reminder of her duty to her clan had put it firmly back to rights. She had a mission to carry out. She would not lose sight of it again.

The fear of discovery passed, Zahirah turned, then went to retrieve the half-charred remains of Halim's note. With cool deliberation, she brought it back to the flame of the oil lamp and watched with placid calm as the evidence of her perfidy burned to cinder and vanished.

Sebastian walked away from Zahirah's door in a state of mild befuddlement. Not so much over the fact that she had refused him, but rather, over his own reaction to that fact. He was surprised, even a bit angry, scowling as he stalked to the head of the long corridor and into a chamber he had commandeered as an officers' meeting room.

He had to admit, against all better judgment, he had been eager to see Zahirah again. The truth was, he had been unable to put her out of his mind since he had been called away from her some four hours before. He could not remember the last time he had so enjoyed the simple pleasure of a woman's company as he had that morning in the garden with her. That enjoyment had only made him greedy for more. More of Zahirah's time, more of her companionship. More, simply, of her.

Her stammered confession that she was at least partially undressed on the other side of that door had done little to assuage his hunger to see her. It was all too easy to imagine what might greet his eyes if he pushed the panel open. Indeed, had he been a man of lesser breeding, he might have acted on the impulse that urged him to turn the latch and see for himself. Instead, he had stood there in the hallway, cursing his noble upbringing and searching for his voice, which had suddenly left him with the thought of Zahirah unclothed.

He wanted her; there could be no denying that. He had wanted her from the moment he first saw her in the bazaar, and now that she was here, likely to be in his charge for an interminable amount of time, he was finding it difficult to think of much else. Based on the aloof reception he had gotten on the other side of her barred door, he, evidently, was alone in his regard. It should have relieved him. After all, he had been adamant from the start about not wanting the distraction of her constant presence.

He reckoned it was good that he would soon be leaving Ascalon, even if he would be away only for a sennight at most. The harbormaster reported word of a food-and-arms supply heading in from the king's allies in Tyre. The goods were due to arrive in a couple of days, then transfer to caravan to be hauled inland to Richard's depleted forces. Sebastian, Logan, and a company of guards would ride as escort. It was hardly a dangerous mission to require his personal attention, but he expected the time on the road should help clear his head.

God knew, he hoped it would.

And if Richard called him back to action upon his arrival, so much the better, Sebastian thought as he entered his officers' chamber and seated himself at the large oak desk. It had been brought to Outremer by one of the Christian leaders, a nobleman who had no doubt come searching for gold and glory and long since fled back home. The bulky piece of furniture with its equally obtrusive chair was sorely out of place amid the cushioned elegance of the Arabian palace—not unlike the crusaders themselves.

They did not belong in this place of sand and sun and sacrifice. He was reminded of that fact every day, from the blistering heat that greeted each morn, to the sounds of armies marching and women and children screaming in their wake. He was reminded, too, by the healing wound at his side, and the cool gray glances of a certain young woman—a haughty thing who harbored a dislike for the Franks that went a great deal deeper than he suspected she would ever let on.

That he was out of place here did not make him long to return to his old life as it did so many others. He had come to Palestine in search of something: adventure, he had thought upon departing England and the earldom that his brother, Griffin, now held for him in trust. Adventure he had found—enough to last two lifetimes—but it was not yet enough, and he supposed he would wander the world until he discovered what it was that he was missing.

His eye drifted past the maps and papers that lay on the desk, to the letter he had recently received from his castle home of Montborne. He had read it at least a dozen times in the two months since it arrived, so much that he almost knew each line by heart. Nevertheless, he picked it up and let himself revisit the exciting news from home.

He was an uncle again, announced his brother's bold scrawl at the top of the message. There was no preamble, no superfluous greeting, for Griffin was not a man to mince words. Isabel, Griff's lady wife, had given birth to their third child—a son this time, a squalling, robust baby brother for the twin girls born to them in the months after Sebastian had left for crusade.

Griffin's delight was evident in the hasty, often clumsy, strokes of his quill. Born to the sword and raised in a household far from Montborne, Sebastian's only brother had not learned to read and write until recent years, when Isabel had come into his life. She was a gentle lady and a patient teacher—an heiress bride who would have been

Sebastian's, had fate not intervened to deliver her instead to Griffin.

Sebastian did not begrudge the match, for it was made out of love, and forged years before the king had betrothed Isabel to him.

He read the rest of the letter, smiling when he got to the place where Griff evidently had finally given up and turned the quill over to Isabel. Her voice, too, was in her handwriting, light and sweet, asking him about where he had been, the exotic places he had seen. She told him not to fret over things at home, that all was well, and closed by wishing him blessings and Godspeed upon what they all prayed would be his soon return.

Sebastian's reply was long overdue. The letter had come just before the night of the assassin's attack in camp, and he had not been motivated to write in the weeks he had been abed with his injuries. He had not been at all sure he would recover, and he had not wanted them to worry. He supposed, now that the worst of it was past, he should let them know he received their letter in good health.

He retrieved a writing quill and a clean sheaf of parchment, then opened the inkpot and dipped the feather pen into the well. He began his letter with words of congratulations to Isabel for the birth of his new nephew, and a jest to Griffin about the zeal with which he seemed to go about carrying on the family name. He asked after his elderly mother, Lady Joanna, then began to tell about his recent days in Ascalon: the wondrous places he had been, the sights he had seen, like the sandstorm that blew in from the desert valley and turned the sky bloodred a few weeks before.

He wrote about trivial things, avoiding the mention of royal assassins and the many other dangers that lurked in this strange, savage land. He was thinking on the page, letting his mind simply wander where it would, when suddenly he stopped and stared in frank surprise. He glanced down to

where his pen rested, poised at the end of a sentence he had
not at all planned to write:

I have met the most intriguing woman . . .

He stared at those confounding words for a long moment, then he swore an oath and irritably tore the letter in
two.

Chapter Ten

Sebastian endured a restless night abed in his chamber that eve, his mind too preoccupied to give him any better than an hour of peace at a time. His hard-won, dreamless sleep was intruded on more than once by the image of slashing, slender steel, a dagger's blade piercing the thin dark of slumber like lightning ripping across a moonless midnight sky, and letting open a river of blood that rained down all around him. He woke dreaming of death—not his, he felt certain of that—but he opened his eyes with a start, his naked body sprawled across the mattress of his bed and bathed in a cold sweat.

It was nearly dawn in Ascalon. Soon the *muezzin* would climb to the minaret pulpit of the city mosque, and, in his warbling, singsong chant, call the faithful to the morning prayer the way the cock called the sunrise back home in England. It was Friday today, the Muslim Sabbath, a holy day that would see the city swarming with people come to pray at the afternoon *jumah*. The gates would swell with the press of attending villagers; the streets and public bathhouses would jam to overflowing.

Sebastian had never much minded the weekly crush of humanity, but now, when his head was filled with foreboding, he knew a bone-deep dread that on this day, death might follow on the heels of the devout. As a precaution, he would post additional guards at the gates, although he knew he could not expect the soldiers to search every comer on his way to the mosque. Perhaps today he would stand on watch himself.

Resolved to this initiative, he threw off the tangle of
sheets that had snarled around his legs, then pivoted to set
his feet on the floor. His braies were draped on the divan beside the bed. He snatched them up and fastened them about
his hips, the loose linen undergarment just sufficient to
cover his nakedness for the short trek to and from the palace
bathhouse.

There was much to admire about the Saracen people and
their culture, but the thing Sebastian thought he would miss
the most when he eventually left Palestine was the ritual of
the bath. A far cry from the occasional frigid plunge into a
river or the cramped tub of lukewarm water that was generally scorned as a bath in England's drafty castles, here,
bathing was nearly an art form, practiced almost as reli-
giously as the Muslims' five daily prayers. Here, the bath was
meant to be savored, taking place in great tiled rooms with
vaulted ceilings, amid elaborate pools and fountains of clear
water and billowing steam.

The bathhouse of the Ascalon palace was empty this
morning but for Sebastian, for there were few Christian
knights who were liable to indulge in a practice frowned
upon as hedonism by the Church. God knew most of them
could use a good scrubbing, but he was well pleased to have
the space all to himself today.

He took a towel from a supply near the entryway and
brought it with him to the bathing pool. Disrobed, his
braies and towel placed on a bench that crouched elegantly
at poolside, Sebastian waded into the warm, scented water
and submerged himself. He soaped his head and body with
a cake of sandalwood soap, then plunged beneath the water
to rinse.

The pool was too small for swimming, but he could
stretch his limbs easily, and the warmth of the bath felt
good on his tired muscles and the healing injury at his side.
He broke the surface with a measure of regret and hoisted
himself out of the water. Dripping wet and refreshed, he
stood and reached for the towel.

It was then that he sensed a subtle shift in the air behind him.

He wrapped the swatch of cotton around his hips and turned, fully expecting to find Abdul there, for the two men had shared the ritual of the morning bath on occasion, sitting together in a thick fog of steam and trading stories about their families and homelands with an easy camaraderie that was rare between their warring peoples. But it was not Abdul who stood within the arched alcove that separated the bathhouse from the corridor.

It was Zahirah.

She was dressed and veiled in simple morning attire, carrying a folded white towel and a small basket of accoutrements for her bath. Sebastian met her surprised, wordless stare and held it. He stood as still as granite, feeling each bead of water that rolled down his naked limbs and torso to drip onto the tiles of the bathhouse floor. His every muscle was keen with awareness, keen with an instant, coiling hunger. He did not trust himself to move, for the compulsion to cross the room to where she stood would surely carry him there with his first step.

"I—I'm sorry," she stammered, belatedly averting her gaze. "I did not know the bathhouse was occupied."

"You should have asked," he replied, his voice sounding as tight as his present effort at restraint. He watched a blush creep up over the edge of her veil.

"My apologies for the intrusion, my lord. Please excuse me."

She turned to leave. He should have let her go.

Instead, he said, "You're up early, Zahirah. It's scarcely dawn. Did your night of solitude not provide you peace?"

She paused, pivoting to face him. From the faint shadows under her unblinking, exquisite eyes, it did not appear that she had slept much better than he had. Despite that fact, she bowed her head in a slight nod. "It did, my lord. I rose early because today is the Sabbath. There is much to do before I go to attend the *jumah* this afternoon."

At her mention of the special prayer service to be held in the mosque, Sebastian's brow wrinkled. His unsettling dreams were still fresh in his mind, and he did not want to be concerned about Zahirah when he would be else-wise occupied at the city gates. He shook his head in flat refusal. "The *jumah* will have to wait for another time, my lady."

"What do you mean, it will have to wait?"

He could not tell if she was outraged or panic-stricken. Perhaps she was a little of both. "I'll be busy about the city with my men today," he explained. "There will be no time for me to take you to the mosque."

"But, my lord!" She took a step forward, frowning. "I was not asking for your escort—I do not require it."

He leveled an unyielding stare on her. "The requirement is mine, Zahirah."

"Christians are not allowed in a Muslim holy place," she informed him, her customarily even tone slipping toward an edge of defiance. Her towel and basket were abandoned on a nearby pedestal as she came toward him, a fuming tigress on the offense, clearly refusing to let herself be pushed into a corner. "Even should you think to attend, my lord, you would be forbidden from the mosque. I am certain you do not intend to deny me the observance of my faith."

"You're in my charge, under my protection. So long as you are here, you'll do as I say. That was our agreement."

She exhaled sharply, her eyes flashing with ire. "No Frank has the right to lord over me."

"This one does," he answered. "I would ask you to remember that, unless you'd rather find your shelter else-where. You may observe your Sabbath in whatever way you wish, my lady. Just do so from within these grounds."

She scoffed. "You said I was not to be kept a prisoner here. You said you would make no demands of me."

"And I haven't," he replied evenly, no easy feat when she was standing within arm's reach of him, her eyes flashing with anger, her pert breasts straining against the fabric of her tunic with every sharp breath she took into her lungs.

"You Franks," she accused. "All you know is what you want. All you speak are lies."

Finally, she had provoked him enough. He advanced on her now, breaching the last few paces that separated them. Towering over her, he crowded her with his shadow. "If I was not a man of my word, do you think I would have let you bar me from your room last night?"

She drew in a feathery gasp of air, holding herself very still. He could see that she was uncertain of him now, unsure what he intended and likely surprised to find herself all but pressed against his nearly naked body. He saw her trepidation, her sudden awareness, and he leaned closer, so close, he could see the rapid pulse of her heartbeat thudding above the neckline of her tunic. He wanted to touch her. God help him, he wanted to do much more than that.

"Do you think, my lady, that I would have walked away last night, when I wanted more than anything to have you in my bed—when I have been mad with the thought of having you from the moment I first saw you?"

She stared up at him, stunned, evidently, into silence. Her diaphanous veil fluttered with the tremulous little sigh that escaped her parted lips.

"If I were half the unreasonable boor you seem convinced I am, do you think you should be standing here, cursing me for a liar and a beast, when it would take but a moment for me to have you in my arms?" To prove his point, he caught her by the wrist and hauled her to him. She gasped, tensing in his grip, but scarcely made the effort to pull away. "Tell me, Zahirah. Were I the sort of man you think I am, do you expect you'd be safe behind a mere scrap of silk if I decided I wanted to taste that pretty mouth that seems always so quick to condemn me?"

Had she drawn back in the slightest, he would have released her. Had she flinched at all when his free hand came up between them, he would have denied himself the impulse and let his hand fall away. But she gave only the slightest tremble as he reached up under her veil to let his fingertips brush the bare skin of her cheek. He cupped her jaw in his

palm, sliding his hand around to the back of her neck as he
pulled her closer to him.

She was softer, infinitely softer, than the silk that covered
her. He reveled in the feel of her, the warmth of her, the
smell of her. So feminine, so beautiful. He needed to see
more of her.

High on her cheek was the place where the veil was fastened to the silk *kufiyya* that draped her head. He found the
loop that held it in place and gently unhooked it. The wisp
of silk floated away from her face, crushing against her opposite shoulder. He swept aside her head covering with a
light, if impatient, skate of his hand, baring her ebony hair
to his touch.

It was glossy and luxurious, unbound and tumbling
down her back. Idly, he wondered how long it would reach,
wondered how it would feel to have it whispering against his
skin while Zahirah lay naked in his arms. He wondered what
it would look like, tossing about her shoulders in a tempest
as he brought her to a shattering climax. His sex hardened
at the very thought.

"Like heaven," he murmured as he brought a handful of
the raven locks over her shoulder, then gently caressed her
jawline.

Her thick-lashed eyes muted from quicksilver to dark steel.
A blush, sweetly innocent, crept into her cheeks. "Please," she
whispered, her lips moist against the pad of his thumb.

She shook her head, too faint to be all resistance, but he
did not think he could stop himself even if it was. Tipping
her chin up on the edge of his hand, he bent down to claim
her mouth with his.

At the moment of contact, she went as rigid as a lance.
Then slowly, with the artless surprise of a fawn on her first
legs, she opened to him. The hand he had been holding by
the wrist slipped free of his slack grasp and found his bare
shoulder. Her touch was light, uncertain, like her kiss. A
small whimper curled up from the back of her throat as he
led her deeper into his embrace, catching her plump bottom
lip and sucking it lightly, teasing it with his tongue.

Despite his inexperience with purity, he could tell at once that she was a virgin, had likely never even been kissed before this very moment. The thought should have sobered him. Instead it made him burn. God help him, it made him want to possess her.

Here.

Now.

He circled his arm around her back, dragging her against the length of him, trying to show her what she was doing to him, needing her to know. His arousal was stiff and throbbing beneath his towel, rampant as it surged against the firmness of her pelvis. He groaned at the soft pressure that met his groin, then reached down to grasp her buttocks and lift her harder against him. He tested the seam of her mouth with his tongue, thrusting past her lips, past her teeth, the way he wanted to thrust past the offending barriers of clothing and propriety.

Had he said he would make no demands of her?

Now more than ever he saw his noble claim for the grand jest it was. Never had he been so consumed with demand. His kiss was rife with it, plundering where he meant to be gentle, pressing where he meant to be patient. Demand was wild in his touch as well, his hands searching, clutching, taking. Demand was all his body knew, his senses greedily taking their fill, and still wanting for more.

He left her mouth to taste the soft lobe of her ear. Zahirah's breath escaped her in a ragged gasp as he caught the tender flesh between his teeth. Her body arched taut, resisting even as her fingers dug into his shoulders to cling to him. She moaned in weak protest as he dragged an open-mouth kiss down the silky column of her neck, cried out in wordless pleasure when he delved his tongue into the tender hollow of her shoulder.

He brought his hand between them, cupping one glorious breast through her tunic, kneading it to arousal. She squirmed and caught hold of his wrist, as if she meant to push him away, then found she had not the strength to try. He searched out the laces that held the linen bodice to-

gether, untying them with fingers that were surprisingly un
steady.

"Let me see you," he whispered against her warm skin a
he slid his hand inside and started to push the open necklin
off her shoulder. "Let me see all of you, Zahirah."

As if suddenly called out of a dreamlike trance, her eye
snapped open, wide with panic. "No!" she gasped. Sh
grabbed the slack edge of her tunic and wrenched it from hi
grasp, clutching it together in a trembling, white-knuckled
fist. Shaking her head, she took a wary step away from him
She was damp from his embrace, her tunic spotted witl
water where they had been pressed together just a momen
before. "No," she said. "No. You can't . . . you can't."

He swore an oath. "Zahirah, I am not going to hurt you."

Though intended to ease her, his growled reassurance di
nothing to erase the look of alarm on her face. He hac
moved too fast, too bold for an untried maiden new to pas
sion. He had no skill with virgins, no experience in gentlin;
a maid toward his carnal whims. For him, from his first awk
ward coupling at fifteen to the consummate pleasure h
took in the act now, he knew no other way. He was not on
to dance around desire; there had never before been cause.

But he had honor, and being around Zahirah was puttin;
it to a constant test. Sooner or later, if he could not purg
her from his thoughts, he felt certain he was going to g
mad.

"Zahirah," he said, but she was already backing away
looking at him as if he were some kind of monster.

As if he had just proved himself every bit the barbarian
Frank she knew him to be.

Perhaps she knew him better than he knew himself. He
could hardly defend what he had done—what he would have
done if she had not drawn away. There was nothing he coulc
say to excuse his behavior, not when he stood there, stil
taut with wanting, still hungry to take her, the evidence o
his lust still heavy between his legs and utterly bereft o
apology.

He did not even try to stop her as she turned on her hee

and fled the room, upsetting the pedestal that held her basket of bath items in her haste to escape. The reed container rocked in her wake, then tumbled to the floor, scattering its contents while Zahirah's hurried footsteps retreated down the corridor.

"By the Cross," Sebastian muttered, dropping onto the poolside bench and catching his forehead in his hands. "What have I gotten myself into?"

"Trouble, I'd say," answered a thick Scots brogue. "And a fine lot of it, judging from the look on the lass's face as she passed me in the hall just now. You don't look so well yourself, my friend."

Sebastian grunted, sliding a weary glance over his shoulder as Logan entered the bathhouse.

The big knight's spurs ticked on the wet tiles as he strode forward, an expression of wry amusement quirking the corners of his mouth. He noted the spilled basket on the floor at his feet, and paused to pick up a broken cake of soap. Idly, he brought it under his nose, breathing in its essence for a moment before setting it down on the pedestal.

"You know, English, even the most ill-bred highlander will endeavor to employ a little finesse when he sets out to seduce a lass. You might try it next time, so you don't send your bonny new bride into a fit of terror each time she sees you."

"She's not my bride," Sebastian growled, in no mood to be reminded of the situation that had been providing the happily married Scot with overmuch humor these past couple of days. "And I wasn't trying to seduce her." He raked a hand through his damp hair and blew out a sigh. "I don't know what I'm doing when it comes to her."

To his credit, Logan did not attempt to tell him. "I was just heading out to the yard for the morning drills with the men, if you've a mind to join me. In the interest of friendship, I may even let you win a few rounds."

Still occupied by other thoughts, Sebastian shook his head. "I'm overdue at the gates; no doubt the Sabbath crowds are already starting to prove a challenge to the men

on watch. In fact, send up five of your guards once you're
through with them. And Logan," he said when the Scot
turned to take his leave, "send Abdul to me on your way
out. I have a peace offering I would like him to deliver for
me."

Chapter Eleven

Zahirah could scarcely catch her breath for the way her heart was pounding. For some untold time, she stood in her chamber, trembling behind the closed door, wondering what terrible madness she suffered that she would allow herself to be kissed and pawed so brazenly.

By a Frank, no less!

She tried to be offended by the idea. She tried to blame the fierce thrumming of her pulse on mortification, tried to dismiss the heat she felt in her limbs and elsewhere on moral outrage. But there was no prudent explanation for the way her body sang at the memory of Sebastian's mouth on hers. There was no means of reconciling the fierce craving that made her keen for his touch almost as much as she scorned it.

That he had nearly undressed her right there in the bathhouse still stunned her. That he might have seen the shame she strove to hide from all the world shocked her back to her senses like nothing else could have. Chagrined by the weight of her secret, Zahirah pulled together the laces he had so deftly untied, and fastened them into a tight knot. No one could ever know the hideousness that lay beneath the mask of her clothing. Least of all him.

Indeed, she would rather die than let Sebastian know her for the abomination she was.

That, more than anything—more, even, than the risk of being discovered as one of the *fida'i*—terrified Zahirah. It set her to pacing the confines of her chamber, feeling trapped and threatened. Caged and desperate to escape.

Escape.

Yes. It seemed that was her best defense—her only defense—now.

Halim would be waiting for her at the mosque. Somehow she had to get out of the palace to meet him as planned. She would have to manufacture a reason for her flight, perhaps tell him that the captain had grown tired of her and ejected her, that she could not go back to the palace. She could say that her infiltration had failed, and they would have to devise another plan for eliminating the English king. She would tell him anything, so long as it would deliver her away from Sebastian.

By Allah's grace, Halim would believe her.

Anxious now to be gone, Zahirah threw on one of the tunics and pantalets that Sebastian had given her, then retrieved her dagger from beneath the mattress of her bed and secured the blade at her waistband. Hastily, she fixed her veil and opened the chamber door to peer outside. The corridor was blessedly empty.

On silent feet, she crept out of her room and traversed the quiet artery of the palace hallway, each step full of purpose and steely determination. No one stopped her to question her destination until she reached the guarded palace doors. At her approach, two lances crossed before her like a gate, descending to block the way.

"Where do you think to go?" asked one of the knights in his rough Frankish tongue. He bared a yellowed, crooked smile that was anything but hospitable. "Bloody little infidel whore."

Zahirah easily understood both his challenge and his epithet, but she masked her contempt with a level stare over the edge of her veil. Her answer, a similarly insulting explanation, voiced in swiftly spoken Arabic, garnered twin looks of puzzlement from the apes on watch. She stared at them, then finally issued her reply again, this time in flawless *lingua franca*. "I thought I would go to the mosque, to beg Allah to deliver Islam from the repellant and lingering stench of you Frankish dogs."

The knight who had been silent until then suddenly choked. His boorish companion turned three shades of red before his pride finally registered the barb in her attack. He cursed and took a threatening step toward her, but a glance over her shoulder stopped him in midstride.

"Is there a problem here?"

Sebastian's deep voice always commanded attention, and the effect was not lost now, on Zahirah or his guards. They snapped into a stance of deferential address; Zahirah simply froze where she stood, not daring to look at him after what had transpired in the bathhouse and what was presently under way here at the palace gate.

When neither of the soldiers seemed sure what to say about the insolence of the woman in their captain's protection, Sebastian strode forward. "Let her pass," he ordered calmly. The lances withdrew to upright position at once.

Surprised, Zahirah turned to meet his gaze. "You're letting me go to the Sabbath service after all?"

"Isn't that what you want?"

He had dressed, but despite his soldier's attire, Zahirah could not purge her vision of him as he had been in the bathhouse, clad indecently in just a scrap of white cotton slung low about his hips, his powerful body and sleek black hair wet from his time in the pool. The sight of him, all hard planes and bronzed muscular slabs, was burned into her memory like a brand. To her shame, she could not purge it, nor could she banish the queer stirring in her belly when she looked upon him now.

Knowing that if she left the palace she might never see him again, Zahirah swallowed, then nodded. "Yes. It is what I want."

"Very well." He stared at her for a moment, then he flashed her a devil's smile. "You see?" he said, his voice pitched low before his guards and edged with a meaning only she would understand. "I'm not such a terrible tyrant."

Zahirah forced herself not to warm to him as she wanted to, but to show him only cool indifference. "Then, by your leave, my lord . . ."

She broke his gaze and turned toward the open palace doors where freedom awaited. When she would have taken the first step out, Sebastian cleared his throat.

"You can go the mosque as you wish, my lady, however I cannot permit you to go alone." A mere glance from the captain brought Abdul hastening to her side. "Abdul has agreed to go with you in my stead. I trust him to see that you are kept safe."

"I will guard her with my life, master," vowed the gentle manservant. He bowed to the captain, then turned to Zahirah and granted her equal respect. "It is my great honor to be your escort to the *jumah*, mistress."

Although it was better by some tenfold than being accompanied by Sebastian himself, Zahirah battled a wave of dread as she and Abdul were granted leave from the palace. If she had any hope of escaping now, she would have to find a way to lose Abdul in the heavy Sabbath crowds.

Abdul stuck closer to her than her own shadow for the better part of the day.

Zahirah tried to bore him with a languorous meander through the souk, pausing to browse every merchant's stall as if she had never been to market and could not move on until she had peered at and fingered every item set out for sale. Certain that he must be every bit as uninterested as she was, Zahirah told him that he should not feel obliged to tarry with her, but Abdul merely smiled and bade her take her time as he followed along without a single yawn or overture toward impatience.

When they paused to watch a Turk and his performing monkey, Zahirah tried to disappear into the crush of the gathering crowd, waiting until Abdul was thoroughly engrossed in the chattering antics of the simian jester, then slowly inching her way out of the circle of spectators. But Abdul could not be fooled. He was there at her side again before she could take the first step in flight.

By midday, not an hour or so before the call to *jumah*

would sound, Zahirah had become desperate to lose him. She could not fashion a neat escape, nor could she risk going to the mosque to meet Halim so long as Abdul was fast on her heels. He seemed maddeningly intent to carry out his master's orders to watch over her, Zahirah thought with a grimace as they paused to rest near a city fountain.

She watched idly as a young mother passed before them, dragging her unwilling child in tow so she could scrub his face at the well. Abdul chuckled at the boy's irate squall and shot him a playful wink. Before long, both the child and the man were laughing. Zahirah found herself smiling, too, waving to the little boy as his mother finished with him at the fountain, then picked him up and carried him away.

In that fresh-scrubbed face, Zahirah suddenly saw the solution to her own dilemma.

There was but one place she could go where Abdul would not be permitted to follow: the women's public bathhouse.

"It is nearly time for the *jumah*," she said to him, schooling her voice to a casual airiness. "Where will you be, Abdul, so I will know where to meet you when I return from the *hammam*?"

The manservant frowned slightly. "The *hammam*," he remarked, contemplating the notion. "My master has charged me with your protection today, mistress. Perhaps I should go with you."

"To the baths?" Zahirah gave an indulgent laugh. "What sort of protection might I need from a pool full of unclothed ladies?" She stood before he could think of further protest. "I will be fine, Abdul. Your Frankish lord need not even know I went."

And by the time he found out, she would be well on her way to Masyaf to plot a new course of action for the English king's demise. Zahirah tried not to think of the guilt Abdul would feel for failing his master. Would Sebastian be upset over her flight, or would he be relieved? She did not know, and she assured herself she did not care.

Determined to have her way in this, she set her hand on

Abdul's arm. "I know you are a good Muslim, Abdul. And I know you will not deny me the right to proper ablutions before I take my Sabbath prayer."

Abdul's kindly features were pinched with doubt, but, praise Allah, his sigh was relenting. "My master is correct; you are stubborn. Very well, mistress. Go to your *hammam*. I will wait for you outside the bathhouse."

She had to work to keep her gait light, resisting the compulsion to dash for the bathhouse like a mare kept to the bit overlong and finally given her head. Abdul kept pace with her, dropping back only as they reached the squat building that housed the women's pools and fountains. With a quick glance to make sure he stayed, Zahirah entered the dark shade of the bathhouse.

She did not trifle with the pretense of partaking in the ritual baths. Instead, she dashed past the pillared, wide-open chamber where some twoscore women of varying ages and sizes sat about gossiping and laughing and soaking in the steamy pools of water. Zahirah directly headed toward the back of the public house, ignoring a wrinkled crone who scolded her for her haste, and nearly crashing into a servant who carried a tray of depilatory creams and brushes.

At the rear of the building, beyond the private rooms and privy, was an exit that opened onto an alleyway. Servants used it to dump refuse; Zahirah used it to begin her escape. Pushing the small door ajar, she slipped out of the bathhouse and skirted to the edge of the building where it opened onto the wider, bustling avenue. She peered around the corner to where Abdul dutifully awaited her return, then, with only the slightest degree of regret, she stepped into the current of the crowd and let it carry her, fully concealed by the masses, toward the mosque at the city's heart.

She did not even see Halim until he grabbed her by the arm and hauled her out of the churning throng of the faithful.

He took in her fine new clothing, and gave a snort. "He dresses you well. You must have more talents than I give you credit for, O sainted daughter of Sinan."

When she would have snapped back a retort for his implication, Halim took her in hand and led her across the sprawling courtyard of the mosque, to a quieter spot just inside the shaded overhang of the grand arcade. People swarmed about, but the bulk of the populous flowed past without taking the slightest notice of a private conversation, their collective minds set on reaching the prayer hall for the *jumah*.

"You should not have chanced sending your message to the palace," Zahirah scolded in a tight near whisper. "It might have easily been intercepted before it reached me. As it was, the Frankish captain nearly caught me with it."

Halim shrugged. "It was a risk, but I trusted you would know what to do."

And he did not care a whit that his actions might have put her—and her mission—in jeopardy, Zahirah understood from the glint of indifference in his hard eyes. "You said you had information, Halim. Let us have done with it."

"There is news at the docks of a supply shipment en route to Lionheart. The vessel is due in port any day now, where it will be moved to caravan for delivery to the English king. Rashid al-Din Sinan does not want those supplies to reach their destination."

"An ambush, then?" guessed Zahirah.

Halim nodded. "Twenty Masyaf warriors will be loosed on the van once it passes Gaza. Richard's army is weary. If those supplies do not reach him, he will be forced to retreat back to Ascalon at once. Back to where you will be ready and waiting."

Zahirah frowned, considering her present intent to leave the palace—and Sebastian—behind.

"I should think this news would cheer you," Halim remarked. "Are you not anxious to fulfill your mission?"

"I am. But there have been some . . . complications." She steeled herself to the suspicious look Halim gave her and forged on with her plan. "The Frankish captain, he—he is no fool. He scarcely lets me out of his sight. On the few occasions that he does, his manservant is never far behind. When Sebastian himself is around, he affords me no room to think . . . no room to . . . breathe. I can't go back there, Halim. The risk of discovery is too great."

Halim's dubious glare had gone from questioning to coldly accusing. "You fear him, this Sebastian?" He spat the foreign name like an oath. "You fear him more than you fear failing your clan? More than you fear my promise to you the day I left you with the Franks?"

Allah, forgive her, but she did. She feared Sebastian more than everything else combined. She was afraid of what he did to her, afraid of what he made her feel. Most of all, she was afraid of losing her heart to him, a risk she could ill afford and a shame she could never bear.

"My mind is made up," she told Halim, more forcefully now, mustering every scrap of her resolve. "I'll figure another plan to carry out my mission, but I'm not going back to the palace."

When she started to walk away, Halim reached out and grabbed her by the arm. "You haughty bitch. Do you think it's so easy? Do you think you have anything to say in this?"

"Let go of my arm, Halim."

She wrenched it away, but the *fida'i* took two steps forward and hemmed her in, backing her up against a pillar of the mosque arcade. Above the garlic stench and humid rasp of Halim's breath, the *muezzin* called the fourth prayer. The wailing summons echoed through the courtyard and spread over the rooftops of the city, beckoning the faithful to the *jumah* while Halim stared at Zahirah with murder in his eyes. She felt a sudden press of cold steel at her breast, and knew a moment of true fear.

But she refused to cower. Her hand slipped beneath her tunic to wrap around the hilt of her dagger. She would meet him steel for steel if she had to. "If I die, Halim, I promise, so do you."

"Draw your weapon, then," he taunted, "if you think you can reach me before I gut you open."

"Mistress, is everything all right?"

Zahirah turned her head with a start, shocked to find Abdul standing but a few paces from where she and Halim were engaged in a deadly impasse. The manservant looked from her to the *fida'i*, who held the dagger poised to kill at her heart.

"Foolish girl. I told you to come alone," Halim growled at Zahirah.

Abdul took a step forward as if to help her. "Mistress, do not worry. I will not let him harm you."

"Abdul, go!" Zahirah ordered him, too caught up in the moment to trifle with appearances. "I beg you. Go, now!"

He did not heed her warning. Bravely, Abdul walked toward Halim, unarmed but unwary. "Let this woman go. Your sister belongs to my master now. You do harm to her, you do harm to him, and that I will not allow."

Halim gave a snort of derision. "My sister. Oh, yes. I had nearly forgotten."

Abdul frowned, clearly confused. His gaze darted to Zahirah in question. He smelled the lie. Her heart squeezed for the flicker of doubt that crept into those gentle, sagacious eyes. "Abdul," she said, shaking her head, "please, you do not know what you are doing."

"I vowed to protect you, mistress," he said, though it was clear from his expression that if he did so now it was out of duty to his master more than any lingering affinity for her. He turned a look on Halim and strode forward, reaching for his arm.

It happened in the blink of an eye, but to Zahirah, unable to do more than cry a warning as Halim struck, the sequence of events played out as in a dream: slowly, image by agonizing image.

At Abdul's approach, Halim turned, dagger in hand. Abdul reached for it, batting his arm as if to swipe the weapon away. Though slighter in build, Halim was stronger, infinitely better trained. He met the blow with easy defense, following the arc of Abdul's strike before coming back around to deliver a vicious attack of his own. The dagger in his hand was nothing more than a glint of polished steel, a blur of light that cleaved the air before sheathing itself in Abdul's unprotected chest.

Zahirah shrieked, but it was too late. Halim withdrew his blade, and Abdul instantly crumpled to his knees. The wound seeped a crimson stream, a river of blood spilling through Abdul's fingers as he coughed and clutched at his chest to staunch the flow.

"Allah curse you, Halim!" Zahirah cried, racing to the dying manservant's side. "You had no cause for this!"

"I told you to come alone," he said with a killer's calm. "Next time, perhaps you will be more inclined to abide my orders."

"I swear, I will see you dead for this!" she railed at him, but when she looked up, Halim was gone and she was alone with the terrible consequences of what she had inadvertently brought upon Abdul.

"Mistress," he said, looking up at her in stunned disbelief, his voice thready, so painfully thin. "I am dying, mistress."

"No," she said, choking on the word, knowing it for a lie. "Abdul, forgive me, please. I'm sorry. I'm so, so sorry." She held his head in her lap, watching in horror as he wheezed from deep within his chest. Death was beginning to creep into his kind features. Zahirah tugged on the loose fabric of his tunic, trying to cover his wound, trying to blot away the blood that refused to cease flowing. "Oh, Allah. Have mercy, I beg you."

"I am tired, mistress," Abdul whispered. "I will sleep now."

"No. Abdul, you must stay awake. Please do not sleep. Not yet. Please . . . don't die."

A convulsion shook him, deep and thorough, leaving a wash of perspiration on his dark brow. His eyes rolled back to their whites, and he swallowed, parting his lips as if to speak. "You," he said, hardly audible. "You . . ."

Zahirah looked down into his paling face, desperate to know what he needed. "Abdul, I am here. I won't leave you. What is it? Tell me what I can do for you—anything. Please, say something . . ."

He fisted his hand in the sleeve of her tunic, pulling at

her, trying in futility to lift himself up. His eyes were clouding over, his grip slowly going slack, but he met her gaze and held it for all he was worth. A whisper slid past his colorless lips, little more than a hiss of breath, but she heard it plainly. She understood what he said, the accusation in that one final word as clear as the sun's rays beating down from the heavens, and just as scorching.

Staring at her, the last thing he would see, Abdul looked her in the eye, and gasped, "Assassin."

Chapter Twelve

The congestion at the city gates that morning had begun to ease by noontide. An hour later, only a few stragglers had yet to pass through: latecomers, squawking over their delay by the Frankish guards on watch. Sebastian was weary of the process as well, for the hours of search and supervision had yielded nothing more troubling than a bone-thin village youth attempting to breach the gates and make off with a merchant's purse.

The group waiting for admittance now looked to be no greater threat—a dozen women and old men, their sandals worn and dusty from their trek to the city, their faces ruddy and haggard from the heat, dark eyes fixed in contempt on the Christian heathens who would keep them from practicing their faith at the mosque.

Sebastian gave an impatient wave to the guards on post. "Let them by."

He watched the lot of commoners trundle past, relieved when he heard the *muezzin*'s call to *jumah* in the moments that followed. His head was aching, his eyes burning from hours spent under the glare of the too-bright desert sun. And underneath it all was the niggling feeling of foreboding that had been with him since he awoke that morning.

Death. So real he could still taste its acrid tang in the back of his throat.

His apprehension seemed ungrounded now, but nevertheless, he kept a trained eye on the folk milling about the streets as he left the gates. He followed what remained of the thinning crowd, heading toward the avenue that led to the mosque, where he knew he would find Abdul and Zahirah after the Sabbath service.

She had been on his mind that day; indeed, as much as his thoughts were haunted by images of blood and death, so, too, were they haunted by Zahirah. Somehow, she was turning him from reluctant protector to relentless predator. He did not like the change, did not like the idea that he was losing control of his own will. But like it or nay, he was pursuing her, he acknowledged, as surely as he sought her out here in the bustle of the city.

And what a bustle it was—more frenetic than any other Friday crush he could recall. The remaining folk who had yet to reach the mosque seemed almost mindless in their haste to get there. Slower-moving villagers were pushed aside by the more spry; elders were left to toddle on in the waking dust of the youth.

Sebastian paused to steady an old man who was nearly trampled by the passing swarm, and as he set the graybeard firmly on his feet, he looked about him, taking in what his eyes were seeing: the quickly emptying souk, merchant stalls being abandoned—a few toppled over in haste. The villagers at the fountain well, leaving their cool refreshment to hurry toward the minaret and arcaded entryway that sat at the end of the avenue.

The people of Ascalon were not so much rushing to the mosque as they were racing.

Three boys came up from somewhere behind, their sandals beating the cobbled avenue, white robes flapping as they ran past. Sebastian reached out and caught the slowest of the trio by the arm.

"What is it? What is going on?"

"Murder," the boy exclaimed, wild-eyed and breathless. "There has been a murder at the mosque!"

"Christ," Sebastian hissed. Then fear settled in, cold and sharp. "Oh, God. Zahirah."

He loosed the boy to follow him and his two companions at a dead run through the chaos mounting in the street. There were more than a few gasps and several muttered curses when he, a Christian, forbidden in a Muslim place of worship, fought his way past the mosque's sacred arches. He burst into the sun-filled courtyard and with a quick glance, searched out the trouble. It was easy enough to find.

A crowd huddled tight at the far side of a pillared colonnade that surrounded the wide square and its central minaret. People ran to and from the area, some crying, some whispering prayers; some were mute with horror. With his hand fisted about the hilt of his sheathed sword, Sebastian ignored the distressed Saracen faces that gaped at him as his boots tramped over hallowed Muslim ground. He waded to the fore of the onlookers, cursing when he spied the rivulet of blood spilling between the feet of the spectators. It was dark crimson-black. Lifeblood, and too damned much of it.

God forbid it belonged to—

"Zahirah."

His heart clenched in his chest, thudding to a heavy halt at what lay before him. Zahirah slowly glanced up when he said her name, but if she registered who he was in that moment, her vacant gaze said nothing to confirm it. She was sitting on the ground, legs folded beneath her. Her face was streaked with tears, her damp veil askew and spattered with blood. Abdul's head rested in her lap. His sightless gaze stared up at her, fixed, frozen, his mouth slack in death.

The blood was his. It seeped from a deep wound in his chest, covering the front of his clothing and the ground beneath him. Zahirah wore much of it, too. It covered the bodice of her tunic and stained her hands and sleeves, as if she might have been bending over Abdul, trying to staunch the flow. The wound was too grave; she could not have saved him. Nothing could have.

Nor would anything save the fiend who slew him, Sebastian silently vowed.

"Who did this?" he demanded of the crowd, stumbling over the Arabic words in his grief for the loss of his friend. "Did any of you see who was responsible for this death?

Speak now, or by my vow, you'll suffer far worse than this good man."

No one answered. With a snarl, Sebastian drew his weapon. The crowd gave a collective gasp, drawing back as he leveled the blade on one of the handful of Muslims who dared to stare at him in silent contempt. Was this man at the end of his sword Abdul's killer? He listened to the litany of prayers that began to fall from the man's lips, hardly caring if they bore guilt or not, so great was his rage, so strong was his want to spill blood in retaliation.

"God damn it," he growled in his own tongue, the vicious bark of anger needing no comprehension to send several big men back a healthy pace. "Someone must have seen something. Who did this? Who is responsible?"

"I am."

Zahirah's voice was little more than a threadbare whisper. Sebastian pivoted to regard her over his shoulder, frowning at the pained gaze that met his own. She shook her head and blinked as a fresh wash of tears filled her eyes and ran down her cheeks. "Allah forgive me, but I—I am the one to blame for Abdul's death. I should never have . . . He was trying to protect me . . . I tried to stop him . . ."

She broke down before the words were out of her mouth. Her chin dropped to her chest and her tears began in earnest. Sebastian's fury paled at the sight of Zahirah's distress. He lowered his weapon and eased it back into its sheath, then turned and knelt down beside her.

"No, my lady," he said, gentle, despite the tumult of his own guilt and anguish. He wanted to reach out and enfold her in his embrace, but there were too many people gawking, and with all that had passed between them that morning, he was not at all sure Zahirah would accept his sympathy. Strangely, he realized that he, too, needed comforting in this moment. Abdul's death, and the thought that Zahirah had been so close to danger, shook him deeply. With effort, he was able to school his voice and his expression to some semblance of calm. "Do not blame yourself, my lady. You couldn't have seen this coming. There was nothing you could do."

Although he meant to soothe her, his attempt at consolation only seemed to upset her further. As if she could bear no more of what he said, Zahirah held up her hand. She started to get up, tried to find her feet, and failed. When she wobbled, Sebastian caught her and lifted her into his arms. Her head lolled onto his shoulder but she clung to him, sobbing quietly into the crook of his neck.

Sebastian scanned the knot of villagers and met the eye of the boy he had followed into the mosque. "Go to the city walls where my knights are working," he ordered the lad. "Tell them what has happened. Have them bring the body—" He bit off a curse, then corrected thickly, "Have them bring my friend back to the palace."

Zahirah had no strength left at all. It had poured out of her with Abdul's last breath, with the blood that stained her hands and tunic. A queer, empty numbness was all she knew as Sebastian carried her away from the carnage at the mosque. She could feel nothing of her limbs, but her heart beat dully in her breast, and beneath the deadened pall of shock was something else. Something deep inside that ached and swelled like bitter bile.

It was guilt: dark and smothering. She thought it would devour her—prayed it would—for she did not know how she would carry the burden of Abdul's death. She had never intended for him to meet with harm. Would that she had taken Halim's dagger instead. Abdul was a good man; he did not deserve such a terrible end.

And then there was Sebastian. She wrapped her arms around his neck and shoulders, burying her face in the smell of him, the warmth of him, feeling safe and protected in his strong arms where she had no right. It hurt, how badly she needed his arms around her—how thoroughly he would hate her when he discovered the truth of who, and what, she was.

Zahirah closed her eyes and listened to the sound of his boots on the cobbled streets, felt his heartbeat pound against her cheek. She wished he would just keep walking, that he would carry her somewhere far away from this place, somewhere green and peaceful, somewhere that pain and death did not dwell. She was weak to think it.

By Allah's grace, she was too weak to say it.

She must have fallen into a doze as he carried her to the palace, for when Zahirah next opened her eyes, Sebastian was setting her down on the bed in her chamber. He was gentle with her, as if he feared she might break. As if he did not know that it was his tenderness that would shatter her. She had no strength to protest as he removed her damp veil and brushed an errant wisp of hair from her brow.

"It's all right," he said as she blinked up at him. "You're safe now. I will keep you safe, my lady."

Zahirah gave a feeble shake of her head, sinking her teeth into her trembling lip to keep from blurting out a careless reply. When she might have reached for him, instead she fisted her hands at her sides. They were sticky with Abdul's blood, a realization that brought a fresh well of tears to her eyes.

Sebastian touched her shoulder, lightly resting his palm on her. "Zahirah, I am sorry. I should have been with you today. Abdul's death—" He broke off abruptly and let out a sigh. "Ah, Christ. His death is my fault, not yours."

A small flame burned in the lamp at her bedside, gilding Sebastian's face. His pain was etched into the lines that bracketed his mouth, in the flat press of his lips and the slight flare of his nostrils as he breathed. Abdul's death had wounded him. It should not have surprised her, for what little she knew of him, Sebastian seemed a caring man. But that he would mourn the death of a Saracen, more, that he would grieve for Abdul as he would a true friend—no less than any of his Christian friends—touched her.

How hard it was to reconcile Sebastian with the image her father had painted of the Franks: cold uncaring beasts, faithless villains who would not stop until they had destroyed everything that was Muslim. Sebastian had never shown her such blind enmity. His sorrow now was real. His friendship with Abdul had been true.

His sympathy toward her was more than she could bear, but no more burdensome than the weight of her own dishonor for allowing Sebastian to blame himself for the death of his friend. She could not bear his kindness, but neither could she confess her part in the day's tragedy. Summoning the barest shreds of her will, she turned away from Sebastian, rolling onto her side and giving him her back. "Please," she whispered brokenly. "I want to rest now."

"Of course," he said after a moment. He bent down and stroked her hair, and Zahirah choked back a sob for the kindness in his touch, a kindness she could not allow herself to accept. Not when her heart felt so poisoned and black. "Rest, my lady. I will send a maid to help you wash and change your clothes."

"No. Don't send anyone," she said. "I don't want anyone to help me. I don't want to see anyone at all."

"Very well." The mattress dipped under his weight as he seated himself on the edge of the bed. "Then I'll stay until you are asleep. You have been through quite an ordeal. I don't think you should be alone."

But she was alone, especially while she was in this place, and the longer he remained in the room with her, the more painful that realization was. "Leave, Sebastian," she pleaded, the words raw and heavy in her throat. "I don't want you here, either. Please, just . . . I need you to leave me alone."

She waited for him to consider her demand, part of her praying he would go without delay, and a more foolish part of her hoping he would refuse. His pride would never permit that, however. He rose without another word, then left her side to cross the room. His footsteps paused several paces away.

"You know, Zahirah, I am not the enemy."

That said, he stepped outside the room and closed the door behind him. Zahirah lay there, listening to the ensuing silence of her chamber, then she pushed herself up and sat on the edge of the bed. Her dagger was sheathed beneath her tunic where she had replaced it after the altercation with

Halim. The hilt rested against the bare skin at her waist, cold as ice.

She withdrew the blade and held it before her in her palms. There had been a time, not too long ago, that she would marvel at the artistry of Masyaf steel. She had always appreciated its lethal beauty. Now, in her blood-stained hands, her fingers soiled by the death of an innocent man, that curved length of shining steel had never looked so wicked.

It had never looked so wrong.

Disgusted and confused, Zahirah slid off the bed and knelt beside it. She said a prayer for Abdul's soul, then lifted the edge of the thick mattress and shoved the dagger deep beneath, hoping to banish her doubts along with the blade.

What was wrong with her? She knew how dangerous it was to question what she had been raised to believe. She had seen members of her clan killed in cold blood when they questioned the teachings of her father. Who was she to doubt him now? How weak was her heart that she would doubt the validity, the divine purpose, of her mission?

She was the daughter of Rashid al-Din Sinan, she reminded herself sternly. She was a skilled *fida'i,* not some sniveling girl to fall to pieces over the death of one man. Abdul was an unwitting pawn, no more than that. His death changed nothing. Indeed, it only raised the stakes of her mission, for now the Franks would be watching everyone more closely, including her.

Zahirah tried to nurse this new feeling of budding anger, knowing she would need something solid to cling to when she next saw Sebastian. She could not allow herself to soften—not toward him, certainly not toward her cause. She was stronger than this. She had to be.

She had to put aside what happened today. She had to forget it and move on, and to do that, she supposed she would first have to rid herself of the appalling evidence. Efficiently, telling herself she could put things back on

course, she stripped off her ruined clothing, then donned a
clean cotton shift as she walked to a washbasin that sat atop
a pedestal on the other side of the room. She cupped her
hands and brought the cool water up to her face, but before
she could rinse away the day's troubles, Zahirah made the
mistake of glancing up.

Her reflection stared back at her from a plate of polished
glass that hung above the basin.

She did not know the woman in the mirror. She looked
older than Zahirah might have guessed, tired beyond her
less than twenty years of age. Her eyes were haunted and
red-rimmed, her forehead splattered with blood, her cheeks
soiled likewise but streaked clean in places where her tears
had left their tracks.

Was this who she was? Was this what she had become?

Zahirah wiped her wet hand across her brow, watching as
the rivulets of water ran down her nose and past her eyes,
turning red as they met with Abdul's blood. The moment of
his death flashed before her suddenly: the thrust of Halim's
dagger, the lurching sag of Abdul's body as he crumpled to the
ground, the accusation he hissed at her with his final breath.

Assassin.

Zahirah fought the swell of guilt that rose inside her,
gripping the sides of the washbasin when her legs threatened to buckle. "I am Zahirah bint Sinan, daughter of
Rashid al-Din Sinan," she whispered, forcing her wretched
reflection to speak the words, words of loyalty and subordi-
nation that had been demanded of her from the time she
was a little girl. "I am one of the *fida'i*. My destiny is cast; I
will not question it. I will not fail. I will not . . ."

The woman in the mirror knew her for the mockery she
was. Her eyes were sad, pitying.

"You are a fraud," she said.

And as her tears began to fall anew, Zahirah lifted the bowl
of water and hurled it into the face of that weeping young
woman, shattering vessel, mirror, and reflection as one.

Chapter Thirteen

Ascalon moved in a stupor for the remainder of the day. Merchants gathered up their wares and departed without a thought toward profit; villagers cleared the streets and public places, taking to their homes and barring their doors as if to leave death standing on the other side. By dusk, there was but a handful of souls who dared to walk as darkness fell over the city, Sebastian and Logan among them.

They had spent the better part of the day stalking the city, questioning those few who would speak to them about the crime that took place at the mosque. There had been precious little information to be had, for despite the hundreds who had flocked to the Sabbath service, less than a dozen admitted to having been in the vicinity when Abdul was killed.

Their accounts varied widely about what they had seen, but in the end the reports had each come down to one common, disturbing fact: Moments before the murder, Zahirah had been seen speaking—arguing, more than one observer had contended—with a Muslim man just outside the prayer hall. A man who was not Abdul.

"Who do you suppose he was?" Logan asked, as the last of the witnesses was dismissed and he and Sebastian walked alone in the darkening street. "Did the lady say she had plans to meet someone at the mosque?"

"No. Only that she wanted to attend the Sabbath prayer service. She was quite insistent that I allow her to go." The gaze Logan turned on him was dubious, even in the gathering twilight. "In any event," Sebastian continued, "none of this explains how she came to be alone with whoever this man was. I gave Abdul orders to stay with her at all times; he would not have failed me in that."

"Mayhap she escaped him somehow," Logan suggested. "The lass appears to be clever enough. She might have been able to slip away from Abdul's watch."

"Aye, but for what purpose? She claims to know no one in Ascalon. Who would she meet, particularly in secret?"

Logan shrugged. "The witnesses' descriptions could fit any one of a hundred men in Ascalon, her brother among them. Although after what he did to her a few days ago, I don't expect the lass would be too eager to put herself in his company."

Sebastian took a drink of wine from the flask tied to his belt. He considered the suggestion, loath to think that Zahirah might have been desperate enough to meet with her violent sibling. But perhaps she had gone to him. She might have gone to beg his mercy, or to seek to convince him to take her away from the palace shelter she had likened to a prison. If she wanted to leave, he could not blame her, really. After the way he had pawed at her in the bathhouse, she might have been willing to risk just about anything to distance herself from him.

"Could she tell you nothing at all, my friend?"

Sebastian shook his head. "When I found her at the mosque, just after the murder, she said it was her fault, that she was to blame for Abdul's death. She said he had tried to protect her."

"Protect her? If not from her brother, then whom?" Logan drawled. He was quiet for a moment as they walked. "There is, I reckon, the possibility of a lover."

Sebastian swung his head to glare at the Scot. Zahirah with a lover? It was a surprisingly distasteful prospect, but now that Logan had said it, he wondered. Was that the reason she rebuffed him at every turn? He had taken it for granted that she was an innocent. God's bones, could he be so blind? He wanted to reject the idea outright, but he could ill afford to ignore what seemed like a logical explanation.

"It wouldna be the first time one man killed another purely out of want of a woman."

"There was no passion in this killing," Sebastian countered, recalling the efficiency of the blow that ended Abdul's life. "The cut to his heart was cold and unerring. It had been wielded by an expert hand."

"The assassin?" Logan asked with a sidelong glance. "Do you reckon it was our *fida'i* who killed Abdul?"

Sebastian lifted a brow, his thoughts darkening the more he considered the very likely probability. "Only one person can answer that question," he said, as they neared the guarded, torchlit gates of the palace. "And answer it she will."

Someone was calling her name.

Zahirah tossed in her bed, drifting near the edge of sleep and wakefulness, her mind snagged on a weblike dream that wound itself around her, pulling her deeper into the black chasm of slumber. She knew where that lightless path would lead her. She did not want to follow it, did not want to let it drag her under, but she was too weak to fight the dreaming this night.

She heard her name again, more plaintive now that she had succumbed to its beckon. A hand reached out to her through the mist of the dream, pale as ivory, slender fingers stretching and clutching, straining, catching naught but empty air. The mist swirled higher, burning her eyes and throat. Sand, she realized, tasting the grit of it in her teeth.

Sand and wind.

And screams.

Some human. Some beast. Some so hideous, they seemed to belong to nothing of this world.

Her name had since become a wail, sorrowful and broken, so full of despair. So full of fear.

For her? she wondered through the blur of reality and nightmare. Was she in danger? She felt the stark jolt of ter-

ror as the dream seized her, felt her heart rending asunder in
her breast. She heard herself shriek in fright. Then she was
crying.

Crying for them.

Faceless, nameless people whose anguish she felt as if it
were her own. As if she were a part of them somehow. Linked
to them by invisible tethers. She reached for the hand that
stretched toward her own, but before their fingers could con-
nect, she was viciously wrenched away. She could hardly
breathe for the band of iron wrapped around her waist, could
hardly see for the tears that flooded and filled her vision.

But she could hear. God help her, even as the ground
began to move beneath her, loud as thunder and fast as the
wind itself, she could hear the grief left in her wake. She
could hear the pain and violence.

She could hear the sound of a child's voice, small and
helpless, whimpering into the vast emptiness of a world suddenly gone strange and savage and dark.

"Maman . . ." she heard the child cry. "Mamaaaan!"

Sebastian stalked down the corridor his chamber shared
with Zahirah's, the wake of his brisk strides upsetting the
flames of oil lamps that had burned since dusk to light the
way. If Zahirah had a lover—if she had any information
about Abdul's murder or the assassin he hunted—he would
have the truth of it, and he would have it now.

His head was pounding as he came upon Zahirah's door
and found it closed. No light spilled out from under it. She
was, evidently, asleep, though hardly peaceful, if the fretful
sounds coming from the other side of the carved panel were
any indication. Sebastian's scowl muted into a frown. He
heard her cry out, an unintelligible, tortured sound, and instead of throwing open the door as his lingering anger compelled him to do, he hesitated.

His fist hovered between his chest and the door. He
should knock at least, let her know that he was there. But
she was mindless in her sleep, and when she cried out again,
Sebastian put his hand on the latch and carefully entered.

"My lady?" he called into the darkness, to which there came no reply, only the restless tossing of Zahirah in her bed.

He stepped inside the chamber, letting his eyes adjust to the gloom. Something crunched beneath his boot. Glass, he realized, and earthenware. Shards of both littered the floor. God's bones, what had happened in here? At the far side of the room, the washbasin was missing from its pedestal, and where a mirror of polished glass had once hung above it, there was nothing now, save an empty iron frame, tilted sideways on a scarred patch of wall.

And on the bed, caught in a tangle of clothing and coverlets, was Zahirah.

Sebastian walked toward her, wondering at what nightmare she suffered, for it was clear she did suffer, deeply. She thrashed and moaned, clawing at the bolster, clinging to it as if she feared she would be torn away from it somehow. She murmured something, a single word, too faint for him to make out. A name, perhaps, but he could not be certain.

He stepped closer to the bed, close enough to see that her cheeks were wet with fresh tears. Her dark hair was unbound and wild about her shoulders, wrapped around her arms, plastered to her brow. She looked miserable, and so very small. A child, alone and vulnerable, filled with fear.

Warily, watchfully, Sebastian seated himself on the edge of the mattress. He tried to hold fast to the anger he had carried with him into the room, but felt it begin to slip from his grasp to see Zahirah in such distress. He reached out and smoothed her forehead with a brush of his hand, sweeping aside the damp tendrils of her hair. She was breathing hard, nearly panting, mindless in the throes of whatever haunted her sleep.

"No," she moaned, restlessly fighting the sheets and coverlet. "No . . . please . . . nooo . . . ."

Sebastian placed his hand on her shoulder, not sure he should disturb her, but unable to stand by and watch her suffer. "Zahirah," he said, not quite gently. "Zahirah, wake up now. It's all right."

At the sound of his voice, she turned her head toward
him. She opened her eyes, staring wildly and unfocused,
doubtless seeing nothing but the terror of her dream. "So
scared," she gasped. She reached for him, clutching his tunic
in a tight fist as if it were all that kept her from slipping back
into the darkness of her nightmare. "Awful . . . so awful!"

"A bad dream, that's all."

"I didn't want to go," she hiccoughed, shuddering against
him. "Didn't want to leave them, but there was nothing I
could do!"

He stiffened and tried to loosen her hold on him, but she
only burrowed deeper, wrapping her arms around his waist
and crushing her cheek to his chest like a child in need of
protection. Awkwardly, Sebastian stroked the length of her
arm, hoping to calm her hysterics, but her trembling and
sobbing would not cease. She was too far gone into her fear,
too ensnared in whatever it was that haunted her sleep. He
reached down and unfastened the wine flask from his
baldric, flipping open the stopper with his thumb.

He brought Zahirah's head and shoulders into the crook
of his arm and placed the flask to her quivering lips.
"Drink," he told her. "It will ease you."

She obeyed, opening her mouth and sipping from the de-
canter. She coughed at first, but took more as it was offered.
Sebastian fed her the wine until she calmed, her breathing
returning to a normal, if heavy, rhythm, her tears ceasing to
spill from beneath her closed eyelids. She gave a deep sigh
and relaxed in his arms, finally peaceful.

God help him, but Sebastian did not want to feel sympathy for her. Not now. Not when he was still angry with her
for the secrets she obviously kept from him. Not when she
might be responsible, at least in part, for Abdul's death.

Nevertheless, he found himself caressing her unbound
hair, gently smoothing the back of his knuckles over her
damp brow. "Rest now, Zahirah. It was just a bad dream.
There's nothing to be afraid of."

Despite his deep misgivings, looking at Zahirah now, so

fragile and wounded, Sebastian felt a sudden surge of possessiveness. He wanted to protect her. Despite his lingering
anger, and his many nagging suspicions, he wanted to keep
Zahirah safe. And despite his mistrust for the woman who
had pushed him away just hours before and now lay curled
up sweetly in his lap, Sebastian could not deny that he still
wanted her.

"Hold me," she whispered, drowsily turning in his
embrace. Her slender back was nestled against his abdomen, her words muffled by the bolster beneath her cheek.
"Please . . . I'm scared. I need you to hold me."

Reluctantly, knowing himself for a fool, Sebastian
stretched out behind her on the bed and brought his arms
around her. Zahirah snuggled into him, each curve of her
body finding a perfect cradle in his. She was warm and soft
in his embrace, her breasts resting firm and enticing against
his forearm, her long slender legs seeking out his and twining with them beneath the coverlet.

Each shift in movement, each breath she took, was a
sweet torture that brought her into direct contact with the
unbidden need coming to life in his groin. He tried to shut
out that need, tried to ignore the keen awareness of her
body pressed so innocently against his, but he heard his desire betray itself in the gruff timbre of his voice.

"You're safe, Zahirah. Nothing can hurt you now."

"Do you promise?" she asked softly.

He gathered her close, pressing a kiss to her chemise-clad
shoulder. "Yes," he answered, "I promise."

She made a sound in the back of her throat, a quiet purr
of contentment that Sebastian felt as sure as a physical caress. He could not ignore the way she fit so perfectly to his
body, could hardly think for the sweet, subtle pressure of
her buttocks at his groin. His arousal stirred unbidden,
searching out the source of her pleasing heat.

He groaned, and moved slightly in an effort to put space
between them, but Zahirah followed, edging closer and rub-
bing unwittingly against him as she settled further into his

embrace. His sex swelled and throbbed at the prolonged contact, urging his hips into motion. Zahirah sighed sleepily as he rocked against her, slowly, gently, trying to hold his hunger in check.

He whispered her name, but she did not answer. Did she sleep? he wondered, marveling at how her body responded so naturally to his, moving with him in the dark, her soft sighs and tender moans seeming to come from a place of deepest pleasure and peace. He wanted to give her both tonight. He wanted to chase away the horrors that had left her crying and terrified moments before.

In truth, he wanted more than that. Much more.

His body was taut with need, coiling tighter with every heartbeat that thudded hard and heavy in his chest. Zahirah's heart was beating in time with his own. He could feel its steady pound at his wrist, which he realized now was wedged between the fullness of her breasts. Softly, he caressed the underside of one perfect mound, teasing the nipple to erectness through the fabric of her chemise. Zahirah drew in her breath, languorously shifting so that he now cupped her wholly in his palm.

Sebastian reveled in her sleepy, sweet surrender. He swept aside her unbound hair and placed a kiss below her ear, breathing in the warm essence of her skin. She arched into him and let out a feathery sigh. A shudder rocked him as her bottom pressed against his stiff erection, her breasts thrusting upward, filling his hand. He kneaded both in turn, then let his hand roam down the slimness of her torso, his fingers feeling heavy and awkward as he skimmed the front of her chemise and splayed his palm over the pleasing rise of her hip.

He circled his arm around her waist and held her firmly against him, his sex nestled between the roundness of her buttocks as he rocked with her, kissing the tender column of her neck. She moaned when he reached down between her legs and began to stroke her mound. Her thighs clamped together around his hand and she startled somewhat, stiffening in his arms.

"It's all right," he soothed her, whispering into her ear as he gently guided her legs apart with his fingers.

There was no resistance in her now, only a quiet welcome, a trusting acceptance that nearly proved his undoing. She moved so sweetly against his palm, sighing like an angel as he kissed and caressed her, and Sebastian thought he would go mad with desire. He squeezed his hand over her mons, her sensual heat searing his palm and rendering him as hard as pure Damascus steel.

Faith, how he wanted her. He wanted to feel her writhe and buck beneath him in ecstasy, wanted to sheathe himself in her body and drive into her until the lust he carried for her was sated at last. That part of him that was all beast, hungry and savage, urged him to raise her shift and take her, awake or nay, for it was clear her body was ready for his.

God's blood, but if she had another lover—even had she lain with one of the heinous *fida'i*—he did not care. Tonight he would see that she forgot him. Forgot everything but his hands on her body, flesh against flesh, his mouth on hers.

He wanted to have her without further preamble, so fierce was his desire, but more than that, he wanted her pleasure to be complete. His growl was pure triumph as she began to grind against his hand, meeting the increased tempo of his caress and giving a thick little mewl as her climax edged nearer.

"It feels good?" he asked, nipping her earlobe, his query rasping in the dark.

"Yes," she sighed. "Oh, yes . . . so good."

He smiled against her shoulder. "Do you want more, my lady?"

"Yes."

He reached down and found the hem of her chemise, then rucked it up, sliding his hand underneath to touch the satiny skin of her bare legs. He traced his fingers along the shapely length of her calf, past the curve of her knee, and up her slender thigh to the soft patch of her woman's down.

The silky curls were moist with her essence, her tender fold
slick and distended, pulsing and heated with arousal.

His finger slid between the petals and it was all he coul
do to bite back the groan of pure need that shot through hir
at the feel of her sweet wetness engulfing him. He stroked he
gently, laving her with the dew of her body and teasing th
pearl of her womanhood until it balled, tight and quivering
at his touch. Learning the rhythm of her body, he brough
her just to the very crest of release then back again, height
ening her arousal and mercilessly denying her climax until h
knew she could bear wanting it no longer.

"More?" he asked when she whimpered in frustratior
her body arching and squirming against him. "Shall I giv
you more, Zahirah?"

She seemed too lost to reply, but her moan of pleasur
was answer enough. Sebastian let his fingers slide deepe
into the cleft of her body, spreading her to his touch, open
ing her for his caress. She held him to her with her thigh:
tilting her hips forward with a hunger that seemed to matc
his own. Sebastian squeezed her mound, then slid his fin
gertip inside of her. The sheer tightness of her sheath cam
as a shock. He did not move, dared not push too hard, real
izing somewhat dully the truth of what he was feeling.

Zahirah was untouched—a virgin.

Given the fevered raging of his loins, he should have fe
no end of regret for that fact. Instead, all he could muste
was a certain sense of relief, a keen satisfaction that ther
had been no other man in Zahirah's bed. She was pure, a
innocent after all. The knowledge only made her surrende
to him now all the more sweet, her bliss all the more pre
cious. Filled with a new sense of wonder for the angel in hi
arms, Sebastian ignored the demands of his own body and
guided her gently, expertly, to her release.

She cried out as it seized her, the spasm of pleasure rack
ing her limbs and leaving her trembling, gasping. Sebastia
held her as she came undone in his arms, feeling a bolt o
sheer male possessiveness as she shuddered and quake
against the cradle of his palm in a shattering climax. H

kissed her neck, whispering tender endearments beside her ear as she slowly calmed, her heartbeat thudding to an easier pace, her breath slowing, deepening in satiation.

She let out a languid sigh, stretching catlike as she snuggled deeper into his embrace. He was yet too hard, too wanting, to lie there with her any longer. His want for her was too strong, and he did not trust himself to stay and not entertain thoughts of a further seduction. Though his libido cursed him roundly, Sebastian edged his way out of Zahirah's comfortable nest.

She was drowsy and spent, but she must have felt him move, for she yawned and rolled to face him, her eyelids slowly drooping closed. "Mmm, no . . . stay . . ."

"I cannot."

"Don't want you to leave," she murmured, clearly spent, not quite wakeful, but not yet asleep. "Please . . ."

He caressed her cheek and bent to place a kiss on her damp brow. "I must, my lady. I have already stayed too long."

He started to move away from the bed, but Zahirah's voice, impossibly quiet, halted him in the next moment. "Don't want you to go . . . don't want to hear the screaming again . . . can't bear to hear it anymore."

Sebastian frowned down at the shape of her body, now curled up beneath the covers like a child. "Screaming?" he asked softly, knowing she spoke from within the mindlessness of sleep. "Who was screaming, Zahirah?"

"The strangers," she whispered, turning her face into the bolster as she began to drift into slumber. "Screaming . . . and crying . . . for her."

He leaned forward, confusion knitting his brow. "Crying for who?"

"For Gillianne." Zahirah's voice was little more than a sigh as sleep grabbed hold to claim her fully. "They cry for Gillianne."

Sebastian stared down at her in silent contemplation, watching as she slipped into a heavier, peaceful rest. He, however, knew nothing close to peace. Nor did he expect he would, until Zahirah and her many mysteries were solved.

Chapter Fourteen

Zahirah did not wake until the first prayer call sounded that next morning, well past her usual hour to rise. Her sleep had been hard-won, but once it had come, it was deep, so deep that waking now seemed a rude and jarring event. Her head and tongue were thick, the light in the room almost blinding, pouring in through the window grate.

She rubbed her eyes and glanced to the table beside her bed, frowning at the hardened leather drink flask that lay atop it. Hoping it contained water, she uncorked it and brought it to her lips, only to recoil a moment later when the strong and oddly familiar aroma reached her nose. Wine. Who would have brought their heathen's drink to her room?

She put the flask back and rolled away from the light, burying her face in the bolster. She had been dreaming, she remembered now. Dreaming the bad dream. The memory of it was distant, but still heavy in her mind: the terror and sorrow, the sand and wind. The strangers.

And Sebastian.

Zahirah sat up in her bed with a start, clutching the edge of the coverlet to her chest. Had he been in the room with her last night? She wondered at the idea, feeling a queer stirring in her belly as an image of him lying beside her sprang into her head. She tingled everywhere all at once, as if she were being caressed by some ghostly presence, touched in places that still sang from the contact.

There had been another dream, she realized suddenly. A wicked dream that was too scandalous to imagine in the bald light of day. She considered the moist warmth between her legs, the quivering aliveness of her body, and could not dismiss the feeling that she had experienced something magical in the hours before dawn, something she could not fully understand.

"Sebastian?" she whispered, then quickly covered her mouth with her hand, for merely saying his name was enough to bring a flush of heat to her face.

If he had been present at some point, Allah preserve her, but if he had anything to do with the strange feelings she awoke with, at least there was no trace of him in the chamber now. There was no trace of her fit of destruction, either. Someone had swept the floor clean of the glass and pottery pieces she had shattered the night before. Vaguely, she remembered the soft brush of a caress. Soothing words whispered in the dark. Strong arms wrapped about her, making her feel safe and warm.

Impossible, she thought, casting aside the notion with a shake of her head. There was never comfort to be found where her nightmare struck. No one was ever there to console her or wash away her tears. Perhaps that, too, had been part of last night's dream.

Perhaps all of it had been, she thought suddenly, feeling a surge of hope.

Perhaps the entire past day—her encounter that morning in the bathhouse with Sebastian, her meeting in the mosque with Halim, Abdul's terrible murder—perhaps all of it had been naught but vapor, the product of her imagination.

"Please, let it be so," she whispered, flinging off the coverlet and slipping her feet to the floor.

In the corridor outside her chamber she heard activity: the scuff of someone's brisk gait, the clink of pottery rattling on a tray, the low murmur of softly spoken Arabic. She bit her lip and opened the door to peer around it, praying she would find Abdul on the other side, ferrying something to or from the palace kitchens. Instead, two passing male servants paused in the hallway to stare at her crestfallen expression as her eyes lit on them.

"Allah's blessings be upon you this morning, mistress,"

one of them greeted soberly. He bowed his head in deference. The other hesitated an overlong moment, half-glaring, before dipping his chin to offer like courtesy.

"Please, excuse me," she said. "I thought you might have been Abdul."

The men exchanged an awkward look. Then the first one cleared his throat and addressed her with somewhat forced civility. "I am Maimoun, mistress. If there is anything you require, it will be my honor to serve you."

That proper statement, coupled by the uncomfortable, almost condemning, stares of the two servants, told her all she needed to know. It had not all been a dream; yesterday had actually happened. Abdul was gone, never to return, his kindness certainly never to be replaced by these tight-faced men. She closed the door on their damning silence, miserable as she listened for their departure.

Once they had gone, Zahirah changed out of her shift and into a fresh tunic and *shalwar*. She could not stay in the confining chamber when the weight of her thoughts bore down on her so heavily. She quit the room and headed for the roof terrace of the harem apartments. She needed open space and fresh air, room to think about what had transpired the day before . . . and what her mission would demand of her from this point forward.

Deep in contemplation of that matter, Zahirah navigated her way along the labyrinth of corridors to the sultana's vacant chambers. She had been unaware of her haste until she stepped, nearly breathless, out onto the balcony that overlooked Ascalon's walled city. She had forgotten her veil, but hardly missed it at that moment. Bracing her hands on the stonework railing of the covered perch of the balcony, she tipped her face up into the sun and closed her eyes, breathing in a deep, cleansing draught of the clean ocean breeze that blew in from the harbor beyond. It left her lungs in a long, thought-laden sigh that sounded more than a little shaky, expelled into the stillness of the morning.

Zahirah suddenly realized she was not alone. She sensed

that fact even before she heard Sebastian's voice from the flat space of rooftop to her right.

"I see you've discovered one of my secrets."

She whirled to face him, unsure what startled her more: the fact that he was there in the first place, or his low, casually drawled suggestion that he might have something to hide from her. "Your secret, my lord?"

He was sitting near the ledge of the roof terrace, leaning back on his elbows, reclining with his knees bent, his thick-muscled thighs spread slightly apart. His tunic was unlaced at the neck, indecently baring some of the dark hairs that covered his chest. Even at rest, there was sheer male power in his form, although this was hardly the first time she had noticed.

There was danger in him, too, a truth that had never seemed more evident than it did now, when his gray-green gaze was fixed on her, unwavering. Studying her. Making her think of scandalous whispers and dark, forbidden caresses that made her limbs feel oddly boneless beneath her. Zahirah felt a peculiar flood of heat course through her the longer Sebastian stared at her. She tried not to squirm.

"This roof affords the best view of the city," he said, his deep voice and sudden smile doing little to assuage the queer fluttering of her heart. "I come here when I need clarity to think about things. Or when I want to be alone."

Welcoming any excuse to leave his unsettling presence before he noticed her discomfiture, she started to back away from the balcony. "Pardon me for intruding, my lord. I will leave you to your peace."

Before she could retreat into the shadowed vacancy of the sultana's chamber, Sebastian got to his feet, fluid as a cat. "Stay, Zahirah. We need to talk." He held out his hand to her. "Come."

She glanced to where he was standing, his long legs braced apart, perilously near the edge of the high terrace, waiting. What was he about? Zahirah hesitated, not at all sure she should join him as he requested, yet strangely unable to refuse him. He did not repeat his command, as if he knew there was no need. His expectant, outstretched hand was enough to compel her forward even when her every sensible instinct urged her to turn instead and make a prudent escape back into the palace.

She climbed down from the balcony and onto the roof terrace. A light breeze skated across the flat overlook as her sandals touched ground, tickling her ankles as it ruffled the cuffed pant legs of her *shalwar*. Zahirah shook a little despite the warmth of the morning.

Barely a half dozen paces separated her from the ledge where Sebastian stood, his broad shoulders and dark, wind-tousled head framed by a wall of empty blue sky, waiting. Watching. Zahirah considered the challenging arch of his brow, the subtle flattening of his mouth that said he likely sensed her apprehension.

Perhaps intended it.

The singular thought spurred her into motion. Lifting her chin and taking care not to let any bit of her unease show, Zahirah walked the short distance of the roof terrace. She slowed as she approached the ledge, her wary gaze fixed on Sebastian, who had since turned his attention to the sprawling city and the horizon beyond.

She did not have to hazard a glance over the roof's sharp edge to see what lay directly below. The large palace courtyard, with its brick walkways and gurgling marble fountain spread out some fifty feet beneath them, every square inch of it paved in hard, unforgiving stone. One careless misstep, the slightest slip, and—

Sebastian's voice rumbled from an arm's length beside her, startling her out of her grim musings. "When I was a boy back home in England, I used to climb with my father to the highest tower of our castle at Montborne and look out over the vast hills and meadows that comprised the demesne. He would lift me up onto the ledge and instruct me to lean out as far as I could, letting me breathe the air and marvel at the land that would one day be mine, while he held me about the waist to keep me from toppling off."

"You Franks have strange notions of amusement," Zahirah replied archly, but she found it easy, and somewhat endearing, to picture him as the reckless lad he had likely been, a raven-haired wildling who would race pell-mell to the edge of a castle parapet only to thrust his face into the howling northern wind. The man standing beside her seemed not so far removed from the inclination himself. She frowned, chiding herself for admiring him, then or now.

"It wasn't so much about amusement as it was about trust," he replied, turning his head toward her. "You see, as a child, I had a terrible fear of high places. My father saw that it bothered me, and so he taught me to face my fear and overcome it. He took me to the top of the tower each morning and promised he wouldn't let me fall. I trusted him to keep that promise."

A pigeon took flight from a perch somewhere below, its gray-and-white wings beating furiously as it rose up over the rooftop, then careened toward the sun-dappled city in the distance. Zahirah watched the bird until it was gone from sight, grateful for the excuse to break contact with Sebastian's intense stare.

She considered all the mental games she herself had played while growing up at Masyaf—the taxing exercises she had employed to make herself stronger, the relentless training that had given her the will to accept any challenge sent her way. She had certainly had her share of fears as a child, but there had never been anyone to help her through them, not even her father. Rashid al-Din Sinan saw fear as weakness, and weakness was not to be tolerated.

Zahirah had been forced to cope on her own, and she had, understanding early on that she could rely on no one save herself. It was easier that way, less margin for error. Less opportunity for hurt or disappointment.

She was so caught up in bitter memories, she did not realize Sebastian had reached out to her until she felt the firm warmth of his hand on her arm. "Come here. Stand beside me."

She drew back slightly and gave a small shake of her head. "I think I'd prefer to remain at a safer distance."

"From the ledge, or from me?" he asked, a devilish smirk tugging at the corner of his mouth. "Come, Zahirah. There's nothing to be afraid of."

Abruptly, her gaze flew up to meet his. Had he said that very thing to her before? Recently, perhaps, as though not but a few hours had gone between? She was certain he had, certain she could hear that very assurance murmured softly beside her ear, his breath warm on her skin, soothing, seductive . . .

Zahirah shook herself back to the reality of his present challenge, thrusting her chin up as she regarded him straight on. "I am afraid of nothing, my lord."

His gaze seemed to say he thought otherwise, but nevertheless, he tilted his head in acknowledgment. "Then come, my lady."

She presented no further resistance, allowing him to take her hand and guide her to stand before him, the toes of her sandals mere inches from the sheer drop of the ledge. Her heart immediately began to pound against her rib cage, every muscle going taut and alert to the precariousness and absolute awe of her surroundings.

From this vantage point, Ascalon was a visual wonder, a paradox, seeming both enormous and minute at the same time. Like a large bowl, the city's wide perimeters arced toward the sea, hugging a tight-packed collection of buildings, streets, parks, and holy places. Flat, tiled rooftops of varying heights marched crazily in all directions, like a giant's staircase with no beginning or end. People moved about like ants below, small colonies swarming in the markets and the public squares, their chatter blending to rise over the city in a never-ending hum of activity.

Zahirah took in these new sights and sounds, feeling as if she were suspended above it all, an eagle riding the wind. She did not fear falling, not even for an instant, for

Sebastian's arm was firm around her waist, the solid warmth of his body behind her providing all the security she could ever need.

Although it troubled her to no end to admit it, she could not help but notice how easily he held her against him, how natural it felt to be pressed to his body, held fast in his arms. His breath stirred the fine hairs at her neck, and for an instant, she closed her eyes, imagining that they were both flying, soaring high into the clouds together, and leaving the troubles of the earthbound world behind.

"You see? You can trust me," Sebastian drawled beside her ear, the low rumble of his voice sending a quiver of awareness through her very core. He chuckled as if he well knew his effect on her, but when he spoke his tone was darkly serious. "The question remains, Zahirah, can I trust you?"

She sucked in a startled breath. "M-my lord?"

"Do you want to tell me what happened yesterday in the mosque?"

She tested his hold on her and found it troublingly firm. "What happened yesterday was a hideous tragedy, my lord. I would rather not think on it at all."

"Then think on it this once, and I will not ask it of you again."

Clearly, he was not about to let her go until she gave him sufficient answer. "What is it you want to know? It all happened so quickly, I'm not sure I will be able to remember very much," she hedged, her fingers clawing at the arm that bound her like iron between Sebastian's body and a deadly plummet off the roof. She was too trapped, too close to the edge. Too frightened by the power of the man who held her so helpless. "Please!" she gasped. "I cannot think like this. Release me at once, I beg you."

He gave a dubious-sounding grunt and whirled her off her feet, sweeping her away from the ledge. She was no longer teetering above the courtyard, but if she thought she would feel safer on the inside space of the terrace, she had been sorely mistaken. Sebastian now faced her, his sheer size and scorching gaze forcing her backward against the rising

wall of the palace, hemming her in and permitting her no
easy route of escape from his questions or his person.

"In England, my lady," he told her very calmly, bracing
his arms on either side of her head, "when a vassal seeks
his lord's protection, he offers him his pledge of loyalty, a vow
that he will hold the lord's trust in highest esteem. This vow
is sacred—as sacred as any given in marriage—for in exchange of that trust, the lord pledges to provide for his
vassals, guarding them with his own blood and sweat. Even
his life."

She wanted to scoff in arch defense, but her voice would
not cooperate. It leaked out of her like a plea. "A Muslim's
vow is no less binding than a Frank's, my lord."

He raised his brows. "I am glad to hear it, because I
would have yours here and now, my lady. The truth, all of it.
What happened yesterday afternoon? You met someone in
the mosque—a man. I want you to tell me who he was."

Zahirah blinked nervously, certain he could read the guilt
in her face. Her mind rushed to replay the events of the day
before, assessing her potential exposure. How many people
might have seen her with Halim? Had someone overheard
their argument, or seen the confrontation that led to
Abdul's death? She could not be sure of what precisely
Sebastian knew, but she was determined to deny her in-
volvement. "There were many people at the Sabbath service,
my lord. Am I to remember them all?"

"Just the one," he replied, his unwavering gaze too intense, his voice too civil, to be trusted. "There may have
been a thousand people at the mosque, but it took only one
man to murder Abdul in cold blood. I would have his name,
Zahirah."

She squirmed, finding it impossible to maintain any semblance of innocence when he was staring at her so closely.
"Sebastian, please. You are asking me questions I cannot
answer—"

"Can't," he challenged, "or won't?"

She saw the danger she was stoking with her evasiveness,
acknowledged the angry flaring of his nostrils, the slow

knitting of his brows that bespoke the storm doubtless soon to come. "I—I would tell you if I could," she stammered. "I wish I could tell you what you want to know. Would that I could be of more help."

Sebastian seemed less than convinced. He searched her eyes, his face so close to hers that his breath stirred the fine hairs at her forehead. "Am I to understand, then, that you did not know the man at all? That he was a stranger to you?"

She nodded, and lowered her gaze. "That is what I am saying, yes."

He grunted. "Would it surprise you to know that the descriptions I've gathered seem to match your brother? Is that what you're afraid to tell me—that he is somehow involved in this?"

Zahirah considered the lie that had bought her passage into the crusaders' camp, the falsehood that had made her kin to Halim in Sebastian's eyes. The irony of it now made her exhale a small, wry-sounding laugh. "My brother did not kill Abdul."

"You are certain?"

"Yes," she said, the flimsy denial bitter on her tongue.

"When I came upon you in the mosque, my lady, you said Abdul had been trying to protect you. Protect you from whom—this stranger? A man you do not know and who had no good reason to accost you on your way to the prayer service?"

She was slow to confirm her statement, hesitating as she thought about the tangle of deception into which she was knitting herself. She should not feel remorse for her actions, no more than she should feel sympathy for Sebastian's friend for having been another casualty in her mission for Sinan. She should not feel anything, but she did. Allah, she was miserable with herself for what she had done—for what she had yet to do by her pledge to her clan.

"What do you know about the assassins, Zahirah?"

She looked up, praying her indrawn breath did not sound as startled as she was by his abrupt query. "The assassins, my lord?"

"The *fida'i* of Masyaf," he said, watching her expression too closely for her peace of mind. "I've found their stench all about this city of late. Which leads me to wonder if the man in the mosque was one of Sinan's agents. Mayhap your face is known to them from the morning you were held hostage in the market."

The day Sebastian found her and carried her to the palace in his arms.

She gave a weak shrug, forcing herself to hold his steady gaze as the frayed threads of her many deceptions threatened to unravel around her. "Perhaps you are right, my lord. It could have been an assassin in the mosque. All I know is, Abdul is gone, and as much as I wish I could change that—as much as I wish I could tell you who is responsible, I . . . I cannot."

Sebastian frowned in apparent consideration. "This is your word, my lady? You swear that what you've told me here today is the truth?"

She tilted her head, offering him the slightest nod.

He grabbed her chin and made her face him straight on. "Then say it, Zahirah. Give me your oath that I can trust you in this."

She stared at him and found she could not make that vow. She could not, to her utter bewilderment, look him in the eye and swear to him that the lie she fed him about Abdul's murderer was anything else than what it was. Cursing herself a fool for not being able to swear to the falsehood and be done with it, she thrust her chin out, praying she could mask some of the turmoil and confusion that had suddenly begun to churn inside her. "You demanded an answer, my lord, and I gave you one. I am not one of your English vassals to be made to kneel before you in obeisance—"

He backed off, quirking a brow as if to mock her indignation. "You're not my bride, either, but that didn't seem to matter last night."

Zahirah's face filled with a terrible heat. She gulped down the squeak of disbelief that rose to her lips, shocked to hear him reference the past evening—horrified to hear him put words to the fear she had been nursing since she first awoke.

Sebastian had been in her room after all.

He had been there, and she was loath to think of what might have transpired between them. But oh, she knew. She knew with a certainty that bordered on the sublime. She had but to see the wicked gleam in his eye to know that he had come to her in the dark, not as a dream, but as flesh. A man who gentled her out of a nightmare with soft words and tender hands. A man who coaxed feelings and pleasures from her like none she had ever known before.

It was sinful, the things he did to her. Sinful and wicked, and Zahirah should hate him for it with every fiber of her soul. But she did not, far from it. To her utmost shame, she burned just to think on the astonishing things he did to her body, things he did when she was too weak to resist—too dazed with wine, she suspected now, recalling the flask she had found beside her bed that morning.

Allah, she prayed it was the wine to blame, and not her own traitorous longings. Longings that stirred to life like embers fanned to flame under the intensity of Sebastian's knowing gaze.

"How dare you," she breathed, aghast with embarrassment. "How dare you jest about the fact that you would creep into my private chambers with your heathen drink and proceed to drug me senseless for your own base amusement!"

He chuckled, raking a hand through his thick black hair. "Drugged you? Is that truly what you believe?" When she did not answer, he shook his head. "You were having a nightmare. I heard you from the other side of the door, and I went in to make sure you were all right. You were crying, nearly hysterical, so I gave you a taste of wine. A taste, no more. What happened next had nothing to do with the wine. It wasn't planned, and if I had known—"

"What?" she asked, not at all sure she wanted to know what he was hesitant to say. "If you had known what, my lord?"

"If I had known that you had never . . . that you were untouched, I would not have let things go as far as they did last
night."

She scoffed, feeling oddly wounded by his regret. "Is that
what passes for a Frankish apology, my lord?"

"If that is what you seek, then, yes."

"What I seek is leave from this conversation. Excuse me,
please."

He did not try to stop her as she made to brush past him,
but his voice was enough to make her pause, halfway to the
balcony stairs. "A word of warning, my lady: If you're hiding something from me, I will find it out eventually—you
know that. Secrets can be dangerous things. They destroy
lives. Think on it, and let me know if there is anything else
you wish to tell me."

Zahirah stared back at him, uncertain what to say.
Already she had revealed far too much. And she did not fool
herself for one moment into thinking that she would be able
to continue outmaneuvering him for long. He was a match
for her in wit and skill. But what was more confounding—
some hundred times more disturbing—was the fact that it
ate at her heart to deceive him.

Despite all she had been taught to think about the
Franks, despite her prejudices, she liked this one. She respected him.

There was, she admitted to herself, more to her regard for
Sebastian than simple fondness or respect. Much more. But
too soon, none of it would matter. He would discover the
whole truth about her eventually, just as he said. And Allah
help her when he did. Thinking on that black day soon to
come, Zahirah weathered a bone-deep pang of regret, and
not a little fear.

"If you are quite through with me, my lord?"

He gave a vague nod, then seemed to reconsider. "No, actually. There is one more thing before you go, Zahirah."

She met that cool, level stare, dreading another round of
his questions. She expected him to press her further about

the events leading up to Abdul's murder, perhaps question her alliances or demand some proof that what she said was true. She expected any number of interrogations, but never the query he posed to her then.

"Who is Gillianne?"

He said it so casually, at first she did not think she heard aright. But one look at him and she knew her ears did not deceive her. Zahirah bit the insides of her cheeks to keep from screaming. She knotted her hands in the hem of her tunic to keep from striking him. Steeling herself to the tumult of emotion that rose like bile in her throat, she schooled her voice to deceptive disregard. "Should I know this person, my lord?"

"I think you must. After all, it is her name you cried out in your sleep last eve."

If she had doubted it for so much as an instant before, there could be no denying it now. Sebastian had been in her chamber last night, but worse than his seduction was the fact that he had been there through her nightmare, there to witness the terror that always left her trembling and broken. Allah, preserve her, but this man—this Frank—now knew the accursed name that came to her in dreams like a long-buried ghost.

The name that had haunted her nearly all her life.

Gillianne.

Zahirah tried to shut it out of her mind. She did not want to face that demon here, now. Not in front of him.

"I have no idea what you're talking about," she said, inwardly cursing her voice when it came out hardly more than a whisper. "The name means nothing to me."

"Another secret, is it, Zahirah?" His dubious gaze narrowed on her. "I am to believe that you clung to me, weeping and crying as if to perish of terror, fearful over this name—this person, Gillianne—but none of that means anything to you at all?"

"It means nothing," she answered, firm in her denial. Desperately firm.

She pivoted to leave, refusing to let him get close to her. Refusing to let him past the barriers of secrecy that always kept her safe.

"It's English," he informed her before she could take the first step.

Zahirah froze.

English? No. It could not be. She had always thought the name peculiar—definitely foreign—but to think that it was Frankish? That it was likely Christian . . .

Behind her, she felt Sebastian watching her too closely now. She knew he waited, expecting to spy a fissure in her composure. She would not allow it. He was treading too close to the bone, probing where he had no right. Zahirah turned to face him, calling on every dram of composure at her command as she met and held his studious, thoughtful gaze.

"It's an English name, Zahirah. I find it curious, don't you? That you would hear this name in your nightmares?"

She stared at him for a long moment, tamping down the rise of emotion that hung about the queer name like a stench of carrion. Gillianne. The very thought seemed to sit in her throat like a stone. "I know all I need to know about it," she answered at last. "It is English, as you say. It's English, and it's ugly, and I hate it. The same as I hate all things English."

At her venomous avowal, he drew his head back. "Even me?"

She did not know where she found the will to hold his level gaze. Nor could she fathom the font of resolve that allowed her to open her mouth and utter yet another hideous lie, told in a desperate attempt at self-preservation. "Yes, Sebastian. Especially you."

Chapter Fifteen

Two days later, the shipment of supplies promised to King Richard by his allies arrived in Ascalon's harbor. Sebastian met the galley from Tyre at the docks that morning, where barrels of wine and water and crates of foodstuffs and weapons were being unloaded for transfer onto carts and camels that would make the trek south toward Darum, where the king and his depleted troops waited.

All morning, Sebastian and Logan and a dozen other workers labored to ready the caravan, sweating and straining under a sun that would have been ruthless if not for the smattering of cloud cover, which had begun to crouch in from the north just before midday. The fresh ocean breeze was an added boon, but the men still began to tire as the day dragged on. Sebastian was tired, too, but he trudged on, and he had little patience for the weaker men who started to lag behind.

"Look alive, ladies! At this sluggish pace, the van won't be ready for another sennight. You can rest when your work is done."

"You've been in a sore mood these past few days," Logan said as he passed him on the dock.

"Have I?" Sebastian grabbed a barrel of wine from the gangplank and rolled it to the end of the dock where Logan was still watching him, waiting for an explanation. Sebastian gave him a shrug and jumped down to help him move the barrel to the caravan. "I suppose I have a good deal on my mind."

"I'd say one thing, more than another," suggested the Scot, slanting him a knowing look as he reached for the barrel.

"You mean, Zahirah?" Sebastian forced out a chuckle. "I haven't seen her lately to think on her. No doubt she's still upset with me after I confronted her about Abdul's murder. Among other things." He frowned as he lifted his end of the heavy oak cask and walked it toward the cart that would carry it to Darum. "Not that I've had the time or inclination to worry about what she might think of me now."

"Huh. Is that why you turned Leila away last night? And Jada a few days before her?" At his questioning look, Logan added, "None of the women are happy to know you've taken a new favorite into your bed, my friend."

God's bones. He had already forgotten about the lusty serving girl who had come to his chamber during the night, looking to share his bed as they had done on occasion in the days before Zahirah had arrived at the palace. He had refused her outright and none too politely, angered and frustrated at himself for the disappointment he felt upon opening his door and finding Leila there instead of the woman he really wanted.

To his chagrin, that frustration had not dissipated in the hours since. Indeed, if anything, it had only worsened.

"'Tis a shame I'm so besotted with my Mary. I might be tempted to break my vow of celibacy and help pick up some of the slack you've left around here since you've taken up with your pretty Saracen bride."

Halfway back to the docks, Sebastian blew out an oath, meeting Logan's smug grin with a scowl. "For the hundredth time, she is not my bride. And you have no idea what you're talking about. I haven't taken Zahirah to my bed." He climbed up onto the dock and lifted a heavy sack of wheat from the pile awaiting transfer. Pivoting, he tossed the sack down to Logan.

"Ah," said the Scot with a nod, "I think I am beginning to understand."

Sebastian retrieved another bulky sack and slung it over his shoulder. He jumped down beside his friend and cut him a weary look. "Understand what?"

"By the Rood, English! You've got a burr under your saddle

about this woman, so pluck it out. God knows, I and the rest of this camp will thank you for it. Your lady would likely thank you, too. Why don't you just have her and have done with it?"

Striding past the Scot to carry the wheat to a waiting camel, Sebastian gave a wry chuckle. "Unfortunately, that's not an option."

"Why the hell not?"

"Because she's a virgin." Sebastian hefted the grain sack up onto the beast's back, wincing from the lance of pain that shot through the still healing wound at his side.

"A virgin?" Logan threw his burden up onto the camel as well, then walked around to grab the straps that would secure it for the trek. He tossed them over to Sebastian. "What about the man she met at the mosque—the infidel who killed Abdul?"

"What about him?"

"Well, did she tell you who he was, for one thing?"

"No, she didn't," Sebastian admitted. "But I can assure you that he was not Zahirah's lover."

"Was that her claim when you questioned her?"

"She didn't have to make any such claims," he replied, remembering all too well the night he went to her chamber, intent on interrogating her, only to end up in bed beside her. Touching her. Kissing her. Wanting her as he had never wanted a woman before. His blood still heated when he thought on the way she melted in his arms, her sweet surrender that nearly unmanned him—a surrender that she was loath to acknowledge in the light of day.

He wiped his brow on his forearm and harshly tied off the last strap. "She is a virgin. I discovered it on my own, much to my, and, as it turned out, the lady's, regret."

The Scot let out a chortle of laughter. "Well, I'll be damned. I do believe the Black Lion has just confessed to having been spurned! And I reckon that explains what's had you roaring and snarling at everyone these past days." He came around the other side of the camel and cuffed Sebastian on the shoulder. "Here I was beginning to worry that you had tired of my company."

"At the moment," Sebastian drawled, wiping a sheen of sweat from his brow, "I'd say you're not too far off the mark."

Logan gave a grunt as he followed Sebastian to retrieve another sack for loading onto the caravan. "I know you well, my friend, and in these many months I've fought beside you, I canna say that I've ever known you to let anything trouble you the way this woman seems to."

He was right. As much as Sebastian wanted to deny it, the truth was that Zahirah had done something to him that no other woman had before. She intrigued him. He had not realized just how bored he had become in his relationships until Zahirah walked so unexpectedly into his life. She was no powdered, pampered maiden to bat her eyes at him and hang on his every word. Indeed, she was more inclined to fight with him than fawn.

She was maddening and aloof, a challenge at every turn. She was provocative and stubborn, and easily the most bewitching woman he had ever met. She was so different from the vapid court beauties who had pursued him back in England. Too different, most would say. And despite his fascination with her, his instincts warned him toward caution.

"She's hiding something," he said, voicing his concern as he came to pause with Logan near the dock. "I look into her eyes and I can't help thinking that she's lying to me—lying about more than just what happened that day in the mosque. When I talked to her the next day, I thought I might be getting through to her, but she kept shutting me out. I'm sure I went about it the wrong way, but I won't abide dishonesty, and I can't afford to let her stay here if she won't be truthful." He shook his head, staring at a dust whorl that kicked up around his boots. "I thought that maybe if I gave her space—time to consider things—she might come to me on her own. It's been two days now, and she continues to avoid me."

"Mother of God," Logan breathed. "You're falling in love with this Saracen lass."

"Falling in love with her?" he scoffed. "Come now, you jest."

Zahirah had captured his interest, certainly, but his love? Hell, he didn't know the first thing about falling in love. Love was for the bards and poets, not a man bred to rule an earldom—a man who had seen too many people, too many futures, ruined by the fickleness of the heart. Love was for his brother, Griffin, and his lady wife, Isabel. Or Logan and his Mary, the bonny highland bride he so adored. Not him. And certainly not for him and a woman who professed to despise his very breed. A woman who might well harbor secrets that could put his life—or his king's—in grave jeopardy.

Logan was grinning. "I don't hear you rushing to deny it, my friend."

"I don't love her," he said firmly, but he found it difficult to meet Logan's smug, knowing gaze. "I don't trust her."

"But you want her."

God, yes. "I think I could go mad from wanting her."

Logan chuckled, but his eyes were serious. "Do you want to know what I think?"

"Probably not."

"I think you ought to stay here tonight, instead of riding out with us to deliver the supplies to Darum. There's no good reason for you to go, but there seems to be plenty of reason for you to stay. The men and I can easily manage the escort without you. Stay here with your lady—"

Sebastian shook his head. "Out of the question. I'm the captain of this garrison; this mission is mine to command. I'm bloody well going to take it."

He said it forcefully enough to keep the Scot from pressing him further, but there was more to Sebastian's vehemence than just a captain's desire to ride with his troops. More even, than a warrior's itching to be out of his idle recovery and back on his mount, back in his armor and ready for battle. Sebastian was desperate to go on the escort mission as planned. He would not allow himself to consider the very tempting notion of staying behind to mend things with Zahirah.

He'd had two days to think about what was best for himself and his duty to the king, and he had decided that unless she came to him with the truth—all of it, whatever she was hiding—before he left for Darum, upon his return, he would arrange for Zahirah to be removed from the palace.

"I want to head out before dusk," he said after a long moment. "Tell the men to rest and take their sup, then we'll go."

Logan nodded. "Aye, Captain. As you wish."

It had taken Zahirah all morning and most of the afternoon to work up the nerve to see him. The two days that had passed since their confrontation on the roof terrace had been among the longest of her life, days she had spent alone in her chamber, too mortified—too utterly confused—to venture much past the threshold when it would mean the risk of running into Sebastian again.

But as prudent as it seemed to maintain her distance from the Frankish captain and the danger of his certain suspicions, there was a foolish part of her that mourned his absence. A part of her that wondered if he might be missing her just a little bit, too. It was that part of her that finally could take the avoidance no longer and set her feet on a determined, if reckless, course down the palace corridor.

It was easy enough to find him. A succession of servants and soldiers filed in and out of the courtyard alcove where he seemed to like taking his meals. Slowly, she stepped into the arched entryway of the garden and paused there, respectfully lowering her gaze as one of the crusaders brushed past her. He had delivered something to his captain—a scroll of some sort. The large roll of parchment lay on the table where Sebastian sat, eating a kingly supper of lamb and cheese and flat, aromatic bread.

He was garbed in a tunic of polished steel links and a surcoat of red silk that drew her eye to the broad width of his shoulders. He was dressed for war, she realized, frowning at the idea. He glanced up as his man departed the courtyard and his gaze locked with Zahirah's. She smiled warily beneath her veil but he did not return the gesture. As quickly as it had lit on her, his gaze was gone. He turned his attention back to his half-eaten meal, stabbing a chunk of meat on the end of his knife and washing down the mouthful of food with a long draught of wine.

Though she had not been invited to enter, Zahirah walked forward. He saw her coming toward him, surely, but he neither acknowledged her nor instructed her to go.

No, he ignored her entirely.

Flanking his table some six feet on either side of him were two Arab servants dressed in white robes and turbans. They eyed Zahirah's intrusion with looks of marked discomfiture, waiting, evidently, to see if they were expected to serve her, or pretend, as their Frankish lord was doing, not to see her at all.

Uncomfortable with this prolonged, and, she suspected, fully intentional, silence, Zahirah tipped her head up to observe the late-afternoon sky that soared high above them. A heady breeze ruffled in the twisting tops of the cedars. The tall palm trees were swaying slightly, their wide green fronds shifting and clacking against each other in a lazy, almost hypnotic, rhythm. There was, she noted, a hesitance—a mild, but building, chill—in the air that could not be entirely attributable to the unresponsive man seated before her.

"It feels as though it might storm this evening," she remarked, watching a thin gathering of clouds drift overhead and begin to bunch together like tufts of newly culled cotton. "Perhaps we might even get a bit of rain."

Sebastian set his cup down with a thump. "Why are you here, Zahirah?"

She flinched to hear his clipped tone, wondering at first if he was questioning outright her presence at the palace. She knew a jolt of alarm and was unsure how to reply. But then, seeing the irritation in his eyes, she understood that he spoke now out of impatience rather than a warrior's blunt suspicion.

Nevertheless, she felt her smile wobble a bit under the coolness of his glare. "Why, I—I suppose I thought perhaps we might play a game of *shatranj* this afternoon. You seemed to enjoy it when we played before, and as you said you were interested in bettering your skills, I thought, if it pleased you, I could set up the board inside and we could play a round or two. I mean, if you'd like that . . ."

She was rambling, her sudden nervousness lending speed to her words even as it reduced them to little more than a whisper. Sebastian listened, his gaze narrowing in scrutiny before dismissing her altogether with a downward sweep of his lashes. He looked back to what had been brought to him by the soldier and unrolled what appeared to be a map of the kingdom's southern coastline. "I haven't the time for playing games with you, my lady."

She was sure there was more to his refusal and his queer tone of voice than a merely casual dismissal. No doubt he was still angry with her after their confrontation over Abdul's death and the uninvited intimacy they had shared in her chamber the night of her bad dream. In truth, she was still somewhat angry herself, but she was determined to put it behind her.

She wanted to make peace with Sebastian, to end the stalemate that had kept them apart these past couple of days. She wanted to be back on friendly terms with him— for the benefit of her mission, of course, she assured herself.

"Actually," she said to the top of his dark glossy head, "I thought that perhaps we could talk, my lord."

"Talk?" That impatient gaze flicked up once more, his chin rising to an arrogant, expectant level as he leaned back on the bench. A nod to one of the waiting servants brought both pairs of hands to the table to clear away his ravaged meal and refresh his cup of wine. While they attended him, Sebastian folded his arms over his chest and stared flatly at Zahirah from across the table. "Then talk if you will, my lady, but pray, do it quickly. As you can see, I am rather busy at present."

Zahirah waited for the two servants to depart the courtyard before she ventured to speak again. "I had hoped that we might talk in private, my lord."

Pursing his lips, he seemed to consider for a moment, then gave a curt shake of his head. "If you have something to say, it must needs be said here and now, Zahirah. I've a mission awaiting outside with my men. I'll be leaving Ascalon within the hour, and I cannot indulge anyone with a private conference at the moment."

"Of course. I understand," she said, stung by the inference that she was of no greater import to him than anyone else he might deign to speak to at that moment. But aside from the smart of her pride, she was surprised, and more than passing disappointed to hear that he would be leaving the city. His stoniness chilled her thoroughly, but she swept aside her own discomfort and held his icy gaze to say what needed saying. "I wanted to apologize for what I said to you that day on the roof terrace, my lord. I was upset, as you must know, and I'm afraid I spoke rashly. I didn't mean the things I said to you. I don't hate you."

A long moment passed, a moment filled with an agonizing, endless waiting. She swallowed hard, watching a muscle tick in Sebastian's tightly clenched jaw. Finally, when she thought she might go mad for the weight of his damning silence, he spoke. "Is that all, then?"

"Yes," she replied quickly, praying that her apology would thaw some of the frost still lingering in his eyes. "I wanted you to know that I was—that I am—sorry, Sebastian."

His answering grunt did not bode well for her hopes of winning his cry of peace. "Well, you needn't have troubled yourself, my lady. It wasn't the first time I tasted a woman's scorn. I don't expect it will be the last."

Then, as if he could tolerate the interruption of her presence no longer, he gathered up the map and rose from his seat to take his leave, pausing only to grab his cup of wine and drain it. He set it down somewhat heavily and gave Zahirah an exceedingly polite, if dismissive, nod. "Was there anything else you wished to discuss with me, my lady?"

She shook her head.

"Very well, then. This supply escort should take no more than a few days. Once I am returned from Darum, I think it best if we seek more suitable living arrangements for you elsewhere in the city. Your protection will be assured, but I expect you'll be happier, and rest more securely, away from here. No doubt you'd agree."

She should have been alarmed that he was intending to remove her from the palace, but it was something else he said—his mention of the supply caravan heading for Darum—that sent her pulse into a crazy lurch. Sebastian was providing personal escort to the shipment.

The same shipment that Halim and his band of *fida'i* soldiers were planning to ambush before it reached King Richard in Darum.

"Everything is in readiness," said a familiar voice from somewhere behind Zahirah. It was Sebastian's friend, Logan, she realized dully, catching the wildness of his accent in his rolling baritone voice. "The carts are packed and assembled, and the men are eager to ride. I must tell you, my friend, I don't like the look of the sky. With the way the winds are kicking up, I reckon we've a healthy storm brewing along the northern coast. It could well be upon us within the hour."

"Then let us be off without further delay," the captain answered, looking past Zahirah as if she were no longer there. His sheathed sword scraped the table as he came around it, and Zahirah had a jarring, all too vivid vision of the violence that awaited him on the road to Darum.

There would be carnage and brutality. Bloodshed and death.

And he was walking into it wholly unawares.

"Sebastian, wait! Don't go." Before she could stop herself, Zahirah was reaching out to him, catching him by the arm as though trying to physically prevent him from leaving. "Please . . . I . . . I don't want you to go."

"Why not?" He paused, scowling down to where her white-knuckled hand gripped his tunic sleeve, the hard steel links biting into her fingertips. Slowly, he lifted his gaze to meet hers. "Why should I stay, Zahirah?"

She sank her teeth into her lip, thinking of a hundred reasons why she did not want him to ride escort for the king's supply caravan, but numerous as they were, they all amounted to the same basic fact. If he left on this ill-fated mission, Zahirah was afraid she might never see him again—at least, not like this. Not as they were in this moment: merely man and woman, at odds certainly, but not, as yet, mortal enemies.

The threat of the ambush Halim was hatching was very real. Sebastian could be hurt in the skirmish—or, Allah, forbid, he could be killed. But even if he survived, he would return to the palace wise to the conspiracy. He would know for certain there was a traitor in his ranks, and, before too long at all, he would know that traitor was Zahirah. He might well suspect her, even now.

But if he stayed . . .

Allah, if he stayed, he would be safe from Halim and his assassin troops, but then what of her mission for her father, Rashid al-Din Sinan? Halim had said the caravan must not reach Richard, that without those supplies the king would be forced to return to Ascalon, where Zahirah, and his preordained fate, awaited him.

Her head was swimming with this mess of conflicting concerns, her heart entangled in a sudden, confusing jumble of warring alliances. She could taste them all equally, but not one would make its way to her tongue.

When she could only stare up at him, shaking her head, mute in her torment, Sebastian exhaled an impatient, mirthless laugh. He wrested his arm from her slack grasp and stood there for a moment, considering her at length.

"Good-bye, Zahirah," he said at last.

Then he turned away, and he was gone.

Chapter Sixteen

Zahirah stood on the very edge of the roof terrace, watching in helpless frustration as the caravan departed. The groaning calls of the camels, the creak of cart wheels burdened with their heavy loads, and the jangle of the soldiers' armor, had all since fallen into silence as Sebastian and the supply escort left the city and started off on the ancient trade route that would lead them to Darum. She watched them until they were out of sight completely, until the dust left in their wake had blown away, leaving naught but an empty stretch of road as far as the eye could see.

And, still, she stood there . . . watching, worrying.

She tried to tell herself that for the sake of her mission, she had done the right thing by letting Sebastian go. That she had no choice. She tried to tell herself that he and his soldiers were not in grave danger, that Halim's intent was to stop a shipment of supplies, not needlessly slaughter the men who were carrying it. And even if the ambush were to escalate into something worse, Sebastian would survive. She had seen his skill with the sword, and knew of no one in Sinan's army who could match him steel for steel.

But still, fear niggled at her heart, cold and unrelenting.

She heard a great clap of thunder in the distance and realized it was raining. Her tunic and trousers were already soaked; her veil hung, sodden and limp, at her chin. The air had begun to churn, dark clouds wheeling overhead, gray and roiling, fat with rain. The tiles of the roof terrace had grown slick with water. It ran between her feet and over the ledge in rivulets, smacking hard as it spilled onto the stones of the empty courtyard below.

It was a sign, surely, this freak, violent swell of rain in an otherwise arid season.

Perhaps it was the voice of Allah issuing a warning, a portent of evil soon to come. But if it were, did the message bode ill for the fate of the Frankish caravan or for her own designs? She waited, contemplating the fury of the gathering storm and praying for guidance. God gave her nothing, save the steady pound of the rain and the grim crackle of lightning above her head.

A huge crash of thunder followed, shaking the building beneath her. Zahirah turned and ran for the shelter of the balcony. She sluiced off the chilling wetness that drizzled from her hair and nose, then dashed inside the palace, heading for the warmth of her chamber.

But as she neared the room, her feet would not slow. They carried her past her private apartments, then past Sebastian's quarters, too, and down the corridor, to where the colonnade leading to the palace outbuildings was located. She was running by the time she reached the stables.

"I need a horse!" she shouted to the stablemaster, her accented *lingua franca* echoing in the cavernous building. "Please, I need a mount at once!"

When she started inside, her eyes looking past the sturdy Frankish destriers to find a horse bred for speed, the gray-bearded guard stepped in front of her. "Now, wait just a moment, girl," he sputtered. "These beasts belong to the king—"

Zahirah pushed him aside with a cry of impatience, hastening to the stall of a sleek black Arabian mare. She unlatched the gate and quickly walked the beauty out. A saddle and tack were draped over the far wall of the berth; Zahirah retrieved them and began readying the horse for riding.

"What is this about?" demanded the stablemaster. He grabbed her by the arm and wrenched her away from her task. "Horse-thieving is a serious offense—"

"I'm not stealing it," Zahirah hissed. "Please, you don't understand! They're in danger—I have to warn them!"

She twisted loose and went back to the mare, dropping to her knees to cinch the saddle, then dashing up to fit her with the bridle and bit.

"Warn who, girl?"

"Sebastian," she told him, stepping into the stirrup and slinging her leg over the mare's back. "The caravan is heading into an ambush. I have to warn him!"

"God's blood," swore the old soldier. "Let's get you out of here!"

He whistled to call another knight to mount up and accompany her, then ran ahead to order the guards to lift the palace gates and let them past. Zahirah jabbed her heels into her mount the instant the huge wooden doors opened, charging headlong into the rain and setting off at a breakneck pace for the road to Darum, praying she would reach Sebastian and convince him to turn the caravan around before Halim and his assassin raiders struck.

Some two hours into their trek, the rainstorm that had been threatening all day finally broke. It swept down on the caravan from out of the north, a dark wall of fast-moving clouds, alive and churning with the slash and crackle of lightning and the raucous clap and boom of thunder. The rains, once they started, were swift and furious, a blinding onslaught that made travel difficult for a lone horse and rider, but near to impossible for the lumbering bulk of the supply caravan.

Sebastian had wanted to make the eight-hour journey to Darum by dawn, a plan that had meant pushing the van on past midnight. Now, riding at the head of the sodden escort alongside Logan, he cursed as the water began to gather and run on the road, turning the hard-paved track into a small, but racing, river. His white warhorse, indignant from the start of the laborious march, tossed its head in protest of the inclement weather. Its hooves splashed in the rising water as it sidled away from the camels, which were tethered and bunched in a tight line behind them on the road.

Thunder rolled above, bringing with it a sudden, violent gust of wind that buffeted the group from the back and rattled the tarps that covered the supply carts. A rope on one of the loads came loose with a snap, lashing about wildly in the spitting gale. Sebastian gave the signal to halt and waited as Logan and two of the caravan's attendants sloshed through the deep puddles in the road to secure the strap.

While they worked to batten down the cargo, Sebastian motioned for the chief caravaner. "Is there someplace safe for us to camp along this road?"

The portly Saracen foreman nodded, his white tunic sleeve dripping water as he pointed into the distance ahead. "There is a place in the next village that might shelter us. The owner is Muslim, but he is also a merchant. For a price, he'll give you space to wait out the storm."

"Excellent," Sebastian shouted over the roar of the storm. "You can show us the way."

He was about to give the call to resume the march when something on the road behind them caught his eye. Far off yet, little more than a dark and growing splotch in the midst of the storm, was a rider—two of them, he corrected, watching as the one in front galloped toward the caravan as if to outpace the devil himself.

"Riders coming," Logan advised him, returning to the head of the caravan. "Could be trouble. Should I take a couple of the men down to see what they're about?"

Sebastian shook his head, peering into the distance. "They're not the infidel," he said, watching as the unarmed figure in front came into better view. He saw the petite frame, the long black hair. "It's a woman. Christ Jesus—it's Zahirah!"

Heart lurching to see her caught in the storm, Sebastian gave his mount his spurs and charged past the stopped caravan, racing toward her as quickly as she was racing toward him. The rain was beating down around them at a relentless rate, but even through the deluge, Sebastian could plainly see that Zahirah was upset. Her eyes were wild, her face stricken with fatigue and worry.

"Don't go!" she cried, her voice nearly swallowed up by the driving wind and rain. "Oh, Sebastian, I'm so glad I reached you in time. Please, you can't go!"

He reined in before her and vaulted from his saddle to catch the reins of her prancing mount and bring her to a halt. Zahirah all but fell into his arms, exhausted and breathless from her hard ride. Behind her was one of Sebastian's men from the garrison at Ascalon. The knight's destrier was lathered and huffing, struggling to keep pace with Zahirah's sleek Arabian mare. With a look, Sebastian sent the guard on to meet the others at the caravan.

"God's blood, woman!" He grabbed Zahirah by the arms and gave her a shake for the jolt of worry still fiercely thrumming in his veins. "Are you mad? What are you thinking coming out here like this?"

She clutched at his wet surcoat and buried her face in his chest, her body cold and shuddering as he held her. "I couldn't let you go, Sebastian. I couldn't—it's too dangerous!" She tipped her face up and met his confused gaze. "You must turn the caravan around at once."

"Turn it around?" He smoothed her rankled brow, furious with her for being there, yet pleased beyond all reason to be holding her in his arms. "The caravan will be fine, Zahirah. It's just a bit of bad weather."

"No," she choked. "Sebastian, you don't understand! You have to go back. There's going to be an ambush."

Sebastian grew very still as he stared at her fear-stricken, rain-spattered face. "An ambush," he echoed, feeling dread coil and twist in his gut. "How do you know this?"

"Halim." A pained look crept into her features, a look that seemed part regret, part guilt. "H-he told me about his plans to raid the caravan and keep the supplies from reaching the king in Darum."

"Bloody hell." Sebastian absorbed the bigger truth in her admission and felt his blood run as cold as the bitter downpour. "It was him, then. You met Halim that day in the mosque. You lied to me."

She gave a weak nod. "It was Halim."

"When is it going to happen? The ambush, Zahirah," he growled when she did not answer right away. "I need to know where and when Halim plans to strike."

"I—I don't know! He didn't tell me—I swear it. I know only that the attack is coming somewhere between here and Darum."

He hissed an oath and set her away from him none too gently.

"I'm sorry, Sebastian. For everything. I . . . I should not have kept it from you."

"You're right, madam," he bit off harshly. "You shouldn't have." Hardening himself to her look of remorse, he turned and stalked away from her to remount his waiting destrier. "Get your horse, Zahirah, and let's get out of this rain. The storm is growing worse."

Chapter Seventeen

And Sebastian was right. The storm did worsen, but the
bluster and battering of the unseasonable torrent was nothing compared to the chilly silence Zahirah had endured
upon joining the caravan with Sebastian. He had given her
no eye contact, not a single word of conversation, in the
endless half hour it took to find shelter for the traveling
party along the road. He purchased rooms for the group at
a village caravansary, then left Zahirah to her own devices
while he went off to confer with his men.

She had no idea how long she sat there, alone in her modest chamber in the small, two-story inn. The owner and his
wife brought Zahirah a prayer mat and a light repast to eat
at her leisure, but she left both courtesies untouched. All she
could think about was Sebastian, and the horrible mess she
was making of both their lives.

More than once, she thought about slipping away from
the caravansary and disappearing into the night, before she
let her feelings toward Sebastian get any further out of her
control. She could leave with a clear conscience where he
was concerned. She had warned him of the raid; his safety
was assured. In the morning, he would turn the caravan
back toward Ascalon, and Halim's designs for an ambush
would be foiled.

It should have been the easiest thing to do, getting up
and walking out of that unguarded lodge. It should have
been the most logical thing in the world to seize this chance
to flee the Frankish captain who was but a hairsbreadth
from discovering her for who—and what—she really was.

But to her dismay, Zahirah found that her limbs would not obey logic.

No, she realized, it was her heart that refused to obey.

It leaped into her throat not a moment later, when a hard rap sounded on her door. The panel creaked open, but to her alternating relief and disappointment, it was not Sebastian standing at the threshold. His brawny lieutenant seemed attuned to her uncertain reaction, for he gave her a small but reassuring smile.

"The captain wishes to see you now, lass. Come, I'll take you to him."

She followed the big knight through the heart of the caravansary lodge, past a common room of tables and benches where some of the soldiers and caravaners were having food and drink. The room opened out onto a courtyard, not unlike the ones at the palace in Ascalon, if far less lavishly appointed. Ordinarily, it would be there, under the stars, where pilgrims would converse and take their rest, but not tonight. The rains were quieting at last, Zahirah noted, glancing out into the dark of the courtyard before she was directed up a short flight of stairs. Gone was the furious beat of falling water, replaced now by a steady, soothing patter on the ground outside.

The worst of it had passed, she thought, feeling a measure of relief . . . until she was brought into another chamber and met with Sebastian's stormy gaze.

Divested of his armor, and limned by the wobbling flame of an oil lamp that burned on the table beside him, Sebastian sat on a divan, thoughtfully twisting the stem of a wine goblet between his fingers. He glanced up as she entered the room, then stood and gave a short nod to his friend. The big knight left her to Sebastian's mercy without a word, closing the door behind him as he departed. For the time it took his boot falls to die away, and for an interminable time thereafter, an awkward silence filled the small room. Finally, his brow rankled by a frown, Sebastian turned away.

"There is food here," he said, indicating the meal on

the table beside him as he seated himself once more on the divan. "Eat, if you like, Zahirah. Unless you fear it will taint the purity of your faith to break bread with the enemy."

She drew a shaky breath, stung by the barb in his voice. "Are we enemies, my lord?"

"I had hoped you might tell me," he said tonelessly, regarding her from under the heavy fall of his forelock. "I must admit, you've had me wondering these past couple of days."

She thought about the uneasy standoff that had existed between them since their confrontation on the roof terrace, her angry, defensive reaction to his questioning of her about Halim and the nightmare Sebastian had witnessed the night he had been with her in her chamber. She had said she hated him, but what she felt for him was far from that. "You are not my enemy, Sebastian. I would not have left Ascalon to be here if you were."

His gaze narrowed on her, untrusting. "What made you decide to come? You must have known about the ambush for some time. Why wait, only to tell me now?"

"I did know about the ambush," she admitted. "I knew, but I didn't realize you were planning to provide personal escort for the caravan until today—"

He grunted. "So, I am to believe you came forward out of concern for me?"

"It's the truth."

"The truth," he replied, eyeing her dubiously. "The same as when you told me the man you met in the mosque—the assassin who killed Abdul—was not your brother? That was the truth, too, so you said."

"A partial truth," she said quietly.

His face hardened, the bones in his jaw seeming sharper now, his gaze scathing in the dim light of the lamp. His voice was calm, far more painful to her ears than had he bellowed at her in anger. "A partial truth is no better than a lie, Zahirah. And by your own admission, Halim was there with you at the mosque. Do you now deny that he was the man who killed my friend in cold blood?"

"He did kill Abdul," she agreed, "but when I said I did not meet my brother, that was no lie. Halim and I are not related."

The news surprised him, she could see it in his expression. But his acceptance of her confession now was not furious, as she might have expected. It was cool, a mere shade away from indifferent, as if he had known her for a liar for some time but was only just now assessing the depth of her perfidy. "That day he found you at the palace, when he struck you, he said he was your brother. You said he was."

"We were raised in the same household," Zahirah admitted, "but we are not kin. There is no bond between us."

"And his threat that he would harm you? How much truth was there in that, my lady?"

"His threat is real. Halim will kill me if he gets the chance. Especially when he learns that I warned you of his plans for the caravan."

"You could have told me this before, Zahirah. In all this time, have I given you any reason not to trust me?"

"You are Frank," she answered simply. "In the past, that was reason enough."

"And now?"

"Now," she said, "it has become . . . complicated."

"Indeed, it has, my lady. You are a complication I did not expect." He frowned, then ran a hand through his damp hair. "God's truth, Zahirah, but you are a complication I do not want."

She swallowed hard, hearing the edge of frustration in his carefully schooled voice. She did not know what to make of the storm of warring emotions that swelled and churned inside her. She knew her mission should be paramount, but it meant little when she was standing there before Sebastian, needing to be near him, yet knowing how difficult it would be for him to look past her lies. How impossible it would be for her to stay now, if he despised her.

"I'll leave, if you wish, Sebastian. I will understand if you would prefer that I not return with you to Ascalon . . . if, after all of this, you wish never to see me again."

"What of Halim and his threats to do you harm, lady?"

She dropped her gaze to the floor and shrugged, thinking about the certain reaction of her *fida'i* accomplice, thinking about his promise that he would see her dead if she failed in her mission. She feared Halim, certainly, but no more than she feared her own emotions when she stood anywhere near Sebastian. Already her feelings for him had steered her away from her true course. The ambush was key to the commencement of her plan, and yet, here she stood, a willing saboteur. Allah forgive her, but she was weak, and growing weaker with every beat of her traitorous heart.

"Come here," Sebastian said when she could only stand there, torn between her loyalty to her clan and her growing attachment to the man who now held his hand out to her, beckoning her toward him with a gentle, if commanding, stare.

She went to him, feeling drawn as if by physical force and unable to contain the shiver of awareness that went through her as he grasped her hand in his and drew her close. He reached up to her, tipping her chin down to face him.

"I gave you my promise that I would keep you safe, my lady. My protection is yours, Zahirah, so long as you need it. I won't require you to leave, now or when you return to Ascalon."

"You would do this for me?" she whispered, astonished. "After everything I have told you tonight—"

"I don't deny my displeasure for your having withheld information from me, but nothing you've said tonight changes my promise to you. My word is my honor, Zahirah. I don't give it lightly, and I have never broken it."

By all that was good and true in this world, she believed him. It was there, in his eyes. She looked at this man, this dark, dangerous warrior, and she believed unequivocally that he would protect her—even now. Despite her lies, despite her unworthiness of the gift, she knew that his promise was good. And it shamed her to the very core of her being. She reached out to him, letting her palm rest against the determined line of his jaw. "My lord," she said, "your honor humbles me."

He held her stare for a long moment, then turned away from her touch, distancing himself from her with a scowl. "I warrant we've said all that needs saying tonight, Zahirah. You should go now and seek your pallet. Before it gets too late."

She saw the blaze of interest light in his eyes, heard the warning in his choice of words and his low tone of voice. She knew he wanted to touch her, knew there was an anger in him tonight, and a wildness that seemed on the verge of breaking, but she was not afraid.

Not waiting for her to comply with his order to retire, he glanced down and began to unfasten the bandages that bound the mending wound at his waist. The wound she herself had delivered him all those weeks past, before she knew him. Before she understood the depth and nobility of the man who stood before her now.

Before she could have imagined the true cost of this mission she had come to loathe.

Her eyes rooted to the ugly evidence of her deception— a deception she was continuing to perpetrate with her very presence in the room—Zahirah touched him once more, pressing her fingertips to his forearm and stilling his hand on the bandage.

"Please, my lord," she said, urging him to sit. "Let me help you."

Then she reached down, somewhat hesitantly, to take the tail of the bandage from his hands. Zahirah knelt before him on the floor, in the V of space he made for her between his knees. His powerful thighs radiated heat, a warmth that was eminently stronger than the flame glowing from the lamp beside them. He lifted his arms and watched in guarded silence as she bent forward and reached around him, carefully unwrapping the thin lengths of cloth. She heard his constricted exhale, felt the warmth of his breath against her brow, as she freed him of the last of the bindings, then set them aside on the floor.

The gash was sealed clean and healing well, but the cut had been deep, and the scar would be with him for the rest of his days. Zahirah gently touched the place where her dagger had bitten him, her fingertips skating over the ravaged skin. She felt a rush of regret flood her to know that she had done this damage.

"Would that I could take it away," she said, her voice catching in her throat.

Sebastian did not answer, but she felt the heat of his gaze, and when she looked up, she saw that his eyes were dark and hooded, his jaw held tight. His elbows rested easily on the back of the divan, but his hands were fisted, his knuckles glowing white in the spare lamplight.

She realized with startling clarity the eroticism of her position: she on her knees before him, her head at a level with the firm plane of his abdomen, her breasts nestled mere inches from the bulging juncture of his thighs. It was a position she had surreptitiously witnessed in the harems at Masyaf, when a slave girl endeavored to pleasure her lover with her mouth. She remembered the look of ecstasy on the man's face as the odalisque kissed and suckled him, and found herself imagining what it would be like to do the same now for Sebastian. Her gaze traveled the length of him, slowly appreciating the strength and contours of his hard warrior's body. She moistened her lips and dared a quick glance at his face.

"Lady, be warned," he growled. "You are stoking a fire tonight that may not bank."

She knew what he was cautioning her against, but she could not find the sense to care. Not when she wanted more than anything to be with him—even if just for this one night. She wanted to show him why she was there, why she could not let him go to Darum. She wanted him, the way a woman wanted a man, and as much as it terrified her to know what that meant, she could not turn away from it.

Zahirah brought her hands up from her lap and lightly braced them on his thighs. The fabric of his hose was coarse, and molded to the shape of his strong legs. She watched her hands slide up the sinewy length of his thighs, felt the muscle clench beneath her palms as she neared the heat of his groin. A flood of sudden shyness made her stop short of reaching it.

She heard Sebastian growl low in his throat as her hands retreated back toward his knees, but when she looked up to gauge his response, she saw that his head was tipped back on his shoulders, his eyes closed tight. The tendons in his neck were drawn taut; the planes and angles of his face seemed somehow harsher, stark and feral. His nostrils flared with the deep breath he sucked in as she leaned forward and pushed her hands up onto the steely smoothness of his abdomen, then let her fingertips wade higher, into the crisp mat of dark hair that covered his chest.

Something coiled deep inside of her as she touched his bare skin, something warm and alive. Something needful. It ignited like the flame he warned her about, slowly burning away her inhibitions and leaving only a keen yearning in its place. Zahirah let it guide her fingers, let it command her beyond her inexperience.

She bent forward and pressed a kiss to his abdomen, then another, lower this time, nuzzling him and letting her mouth linger meaningfully against the satin warmth of his skin. Sebastian's breath rasped out of him as he brought his hands down onto her shoulders, his touch blunt and heavy, his entire body going rigid beneath her. His thighs pressed in at her sides; the bulge at his groin swelled and hardened, lengthening where it nestled between her breasts.

He moaned, and with a vicious curse, came forward to seize her by the arms and set her away from him. "Zahirah," he rasped, "if you care about your virtue, you will leave me now. Go back to your room. Bolt the door." His gaze flashed, searing and hungry, raking her like a caress, so hot it nearly stole her breath. "Don't think I'll be gentleman enough to tell you again. Not when I am wanting you the way I am right now."

Ignoring the tremor of fear racing through her for what she was about to invite, she reached up to touch the muscle that jumped in his stern jaw. "If you want me, then I have no wish to leave. I am where I want to be, my lord."

His smile was brief, a baring of straight white teeth that was at once exultant and tortured. "Foolish girl," he chided softly, but then he plunged his hand into her hair, catching her behind the neck and hauling her closer for his kiss.

He slanted his mouth over hers, sliding his hips forward on the divan so that their bodies were pressed hard against each other, his fingers gripping her tightly at her nape. It was a possessive hold, a possessive kiss. Zahirah nearly wanted to drown in it. She felt Sebastian's other hand slide down the length of her spine, felt the soft friction of her silk pantalets as his palm curved around the arc of her buttock. Then, both strong hands were there together, kneading and parting the mounds of sensitive muscle as he pulled her higher, deeper into his embrace.

His tongue pressed insistently against her lips, and like the wanton he made her, Zahirah let him in. She plunged her fingers into the thick gloss of his hair, her mouth and hands becoming as questing and hungry as his. There was need in their kiss, and in their touch. So much need in their bodies; they both trembled with the force of it.

Allah, here it was, Zahirah realized through the dizzying haze of her senses. Here was the one truth that could exist between them despite who they were, and what they could never be together. This need was real. It knew no power above its own, and tonight it would abide no pretense or denial.

"Make love to me, Sebastian," she demanded as his mouth left hers to explore the tender skin beneath her ear. "Please. I need you to make love to me."

He moaned against her shoulder and reared his head up to look at her. His eyes were dark and stormy, the harsh planes of his cheeks somehow tighter than she recalled. "What you're asking for," he said thickly, "once given, it cannot be taken back."

She gave him a faint nod of understanding, then touched her fingertips to his lips. "Make love to me," she whispered.

Sebastian's curse was low and reverent. He turned his face into her palm, his breath raggedly leaving his lungs. "Come up here," he said.

He took her hand and helped lift her to her feet. She stood before him in trembling anticipation, waiting for him to tear her clothes off and ravish her. Part of her wanted their mating to be fierce and swift—all the better to snuff the fevered raging of her body—but another part of her was just a little bit terrified and uncertain of precisely how to proceed.

Sebastian seemed to be at no such loss. Seated on the divan, his hands were at her hips, his caress both soothing and exciting. He found the hem of her tunic and slid his hands beneath it to stroke the line of her ribs, then he splayed his fingers and held her waist in his hands, as if measuring the petiteness of her form. He looked up at her as he cupped her naked breast in his palm. Zahirah sighed, transfixed by the intensity of his gaze and the sheer witchery of his touch.

She realized somewhat dazedly that he now had one hand at the front of her waist, his fingers nimbly loosening the ties of her trousers. He tugged the drawstring waistband open and pushed the fabric off her hips, leaving it to sag low around her thighs. Then his hand was on her skin, his knuckles brushing the place where she ached for him, and Zahirah sucked in a ragged breath.

"Do you remember my touch?" he whispered, pressing his mouth to the dip just below her navel. "That night I came to your chamber . . . do you remember?"

"Yes," she gasped, mindless as his breath stirred the down between her legs.

"Do you remember the pleasure?"

"Oh, yes."

"I've been burning for you ever since," he said, nudging her thighs apart with the barest stroke of his thumb. "I've been wanting to taste you, to feel you melt around me the way you did that night."

"Sebastian," she sighed, her legs going boneless as his fingers slid between them and into the moist cleft of her womanhood. "Oh, yes . . ."

He stroked her with an artistry that left her quaking and panting, seeming to know just when to alternate from a slow, rhythmic slide of his finger between her petals to a frenzied titillation that had her clutching at him and clenching her teeth in exquisite torment. She thought she would go mad with the raw pleasure of the moment, but it was nothing compared to the bolt of awe that struck her the instant he put his mouth to her flesh. His tongue touched her, warm and wet and hot against the pearl of sensation nestled high in her woman's place. She cried out and tried to push him away, for the intensity of the contact was too much, too raw.

"Shh," he sighed against her skin. "It's all right. Trust me, Zahirah."

He held her hips to keep her steady, and bent his head back down to taste her again. He was gentler with her now, coaxing her back under his spell with tender kisses and tentative brushes of his mouth and tongue. The wonderment she had felt before returned quickly, then swelled into something stronger, something far more demanding. She began moving her hips in time with Sebastian's carnal kiss, finding that she wanted more than he was giving her.

"That's it," he murmured. "Reach for it, Zahirah."

She moaned in frustration, not sure what it was that lay just beyond her grasp, but certain she would perish without it. She buried her fingers in Sebastian's hair and pulled him closer, but still he wasn't close enough. She was still empty, still needing. She clung to him, half-sobbing as the hunger twisted tighter. "Sebastian," she whimpered, "I can't . . . please, I need you now."

She was vaguely aware that he was moving her, pivoting her until she was lying back on the cushioned divan, her legs bent over the front of it, her pantalets bunched around her ankles. He pushed up the hem of her tunic and she gasped, jolted momentarily by his apparent intent to disrobe her completely. The light of the oil lamp was slim, but it would not keep her secret if he wanted her naked beneath him. She stilled his hand and he looked up in question.

"Please," she whispered, shaking her head.

His frown was curious, but slight, and his need was strong. He moved his hands down her bare abdomen, kissing her belly before descending to suckle her throbbing mons while he worked to remove his hose and braies. Zahirah saw him through a mist of sudden tears, saw the shadowy form of his body, thick-muscled and beautiful, his limbs and torso bronzed by the sun and cast into intriguing relief by the thin flicker of the lamp.

She saw the glory of his sex, the stiff member thrusting proudly from the thatch of dark curls at his groin. She saw the sheer power in his organ, the frightening size of him, and she knew that this was what she wanted. He was what she needed to fill the void in her that ached like nothing she had ever known before.

"Are you sure?" he asked her, bracing his hands on either side of her shoulders as he brought himself up between her legs. The hard length of his erection pressed against her belly, hot as fire, and smooth as silk. A droplet of pearly moisture beaded on the thick, blunt head of his penis. It slid between them, warm and slick on her skin as Sebastian moved against her, torturing her with his intimate caress. "Tell me this is what you want, my lady."

"It is. This is what I want, Sebastian. You are what I want."

He whispered her name like a prayer, then lowered himself to kiss her, tilting his hips to let his sex slide into position at the juncture of her thighs. Zahirah parted her legs, and her pelvis rose up to meet his, her loins flooding with anticipation, pulsing for want of completion. She did not realize she was holding her breath until she felt Sebastian push past the barrier of her maidenhead. There was a fiery tearing as he thrust the length of himself into her virgin sheath, a burning that lanced through her and left a wash of perspiration on her brow.

But there was pleasure, too. An infinite pleasure that came from the exquisite fullness of her womb as it stretched to accommodate Sebastian's sensual invasion. He moved within her, slowly, as if he held himself back from taking the full measure of his passion. He was careful, but he was large, and his steely shaft proved unforgiving to the small mouth and tender skin of her body.

Zahirah clung to him, suspended in a dizzying place somewhere between pleasure and pain, as he plunged and withdrew, each deep thrust of his hips seeming to impale her to her very soul. She would take all that he gave her tonight—the pleasure and the pain. The pain she had earned, certainly; the pleasure was hers because in taking this bliss from their union, she also shared it with him.

She felt him hesitate as if he meant to stop, as if he knew he was hurting her and was deciding whether to continue. Zahirah arched into him, lifting her hips to encourage him further, squeezing her eyes closed against the discomfort and holding fast to the sweet ache of passion. She buried her fingers in the crisp hair at his chest, clutching at him as he rocked into her, his hips pumping faster as she panted and whimpered beside his ear.

She was losing hold of the world around her. She felt it slipping, felt the pain of her breached maidenhead dissipate, and a coiling wonderment begin to swell deep inside of her. Her world was tilting wildly, the force and passion of Sebastian's lovemaking pushing her higher and higher, into an oblivion of weightless, breathless ecstasy. She cried out as she brushed the edges of that place, digging her finger-nails into Sebastian's shoulders for fear that she would slip away completely.

"Allah," she gasped, her back coming up off the divan as

Sebastian pumped deeper than ever before, burying himself to the hilt inside of her, each thrust getting faster, and stronger. She soared higher into the void of pleasure, nearly to the point of shattering, holding him to her as he began to thrust with a sudden intensity. She felt the rapture coming, felt the earth fall away beneath her as a dizzying wave of release scooped her up and swept her high into the heavens. Distantly, she heard herself cry out as she climaxed, heard herself sobbing Sebastian's name as she floated slowly back into herself.

"That's it, my lady. Let it go," he growled, nipping at her slack mouth as he continued his sensual assault on her quivering, too-sensitive body. "God, Zahirah, I can't take much more . . ."

With a wordless groan, he impaled her fully, shuddering as he then withdrew nearly all the way. His curse was savage-sounding as he reared up and grabbed her hips, holding her in a bruising grip as he pumped furiously into her, his every muscle tense and strained. She felt him swelling, growing harder, becoming bigger, filling her more than she dreamed was possible. He lifted her pelvis off the divan, angling her higher to meet his fierce thrusts, his face contorting in evident anguish as a spasm began to shake him. With a shout, he jerked out of her, and Zahirah clung to him as he shuddered atop her, his member throbbing between them as a rush of hot moisture spurted onto the flatness of her belly.

The wonderment of what they had just shared, the awe of what their bodies had been together, left Zahirah trembling with emotion. It was all she could do not to cry in that moment, feeling Sebastian warm and heavy atop her, hearing his breathing begin to slow along with hers, their heartbeats thudding strongly, matched in time. She had given him her virginity this night, and he had given her wings. Her heart was still soaring, even if her body remained tethered to earth by the pleasing weight of her lover and the more substantial press of her regrets.

A brush against her cheek made her dazedly open her eyes. Sebastian was there, watching her face as he braced himself on one elbow above her. Her vision was watery; she felt a tear slide down her temple and into her hair. Sebastian swept its track away with his thumb, frowning. "It was too much," he said, his words hoarse in the darkness as he caressed her cheek. "You should have told me to stop."

"No," she whispered. She shook her head and blinked away another swell of hot tears. "No. I didn't ever want you to stop."

He gave her a rueful smile. "I should have been more gentle, but you just . . . God, you felt so good." He leaned down and kissed her, a sweet but heated joining of their mouths that stirred her, even in exhaustion. It stirred him, too. His sex began to rouse, lengthening and growing harder where it rested between her thighs. "You should know that deflowering maidens is not something I do very often," he confessed, his deep voice a heavenly rumble below her ear. "In fact, you are the first."

"I am?" she asked, surprised.

He drew back to look at her and inclined his head, but his expression was oddly distant as he traced his finger along the line of her shoulder. "The women I have known before have all been . . . experienced."

She felt a sudden twinge of embarrassment, suspecting her own awkwardness should he now lie beside her and compare her to the lovers that had come before her. Lovers like the pretty dark-haired serving girl at the palace, and the Frankish washerwomen who likely charmed him into their beds with their witty banter and expert methods of seduction. How she must have paled in his regard. "Was I . . . was I a disappointment to you, then?"

"God, no," he breathed, quelling her doubts with a look of complete sincerity. "Zahirah, my lady, you were exquisite. Too exquisite by far, and I had no right taking all that you have given me tonight. I only pray you won't come to regret this evening and look upon me with loathing come the morn."

"Never," she vowed, a similar prayer edging its way to the

tip of her own tongue. "Sebastian, I will never regret this. I've never known anything as perfect as what you have just given me."

Her smile trembled on her lips, but his was prideful and sensual—dazzlingly male. He bent toward her and captured her mouth with his, teasing the seam of her lips with his tongue as he shifted above her on the divan. Zahirah welcomed him into her mouth the same as she welcomed him back between her thighs, spreading her legs to accommodate him as he slid into position at their juncture. His arousal nudged into the moist cleft of her body, blunt and warm and hard. She moaned as he moved against her, teasing her with his rigid length as his erection cleaved her quivering flesh, then withdrew short of penetration.

Zahirah wrapped her legs around his hips, arching hungrily for that which he denied her. She deepened her kiss, taking his tongue into her mouth and nipping his lip when she could stand the wanting no longer. "Please," she gasped, arching into him.

He did not make her ask again.

A subtle shift of his pelvis put him at the mouth of her womb, and this time, when he gently thrust into her sheath, there was no pain, only a faint tightness that blurred quickly as Sebastian gathered her into his arms and slowly made love to her. She gave a shaky sigh as her body wakened to his once more, her heart and soul unfolding and rising toward the heavens.

"Tell me if you want me to stop," he whispered roughly, slowing his pace when she bit her lip to hold back a cry. "I only want to give you pleasure, my lady."

"You are." She sighed. She cupped his jaw, and, holding his stormy gaze, she arched her hips against him, then back again, moving her body around his when it seemed he might deny her the sweet friction of their joining. "Don't stop, Sebastian."

Sliding her hands down the hard muscle of his back, she grasped his firm buttocks and lifted into him once more. This time, he met her with a deep, shuddering thrust. She smiled as he slowly withdrew, then began his rhythm again, his strokes long and purposeful, achingly sensual. "Please . . . don't stop," she begged him.

And, by Allah's grace, he didn't.

Chapter Eighteen

It was not yet dawn when Sebastian called his men together in the courtyard of the caravansary to discuss the day's new strategy. Despite the warning of ambush by the *fida'i*, they were continuing on to Darum as originally planned. A rider had been sent on ahead of them the night before; unencumbered by the slowness of the caravan, he should have reached the king's camp some hours ago to communicate the news of the pending raid.

Once alerted to the danger, Lionheart would no doubt send reinforcements to meet them on the road. The hope of aid, coupled with the foreknowledge of the attack, would likely save not only the shipment of supplies but also the lives of the men gathered before Sebastian that morning. His own life, too, more than likely, he reflected with a sober sense of acceptance. And he had Zahirah to thank for it.

Zahirah.

He could not so much as voice her name in his mind without reliving the passion they had shared together in his chamber. God's truth, but even though he stood outside amid a dozen soldiers and caravaners, all he could see was Zahirah, glorious and beautiful, arched in rapture beneath him. He breathed in the rain-washed air of the open courtyard, but it was her scent that filled his nostrils like sweet, heady perfume. Her soft moans and sighs still echoed in his ears, and the memory of her touch, her unexpected and willing surrender, made it difficult to focus on anything but the present quickening of his blood and his fierce desire to

return to his chamber where she yet slumbered, spent from
their night of lovemaking.

It had taken every bit of his will to leave her undisturbed
when he had awakened beside her on the divan a mere hour
or so before. Her back had been curved into his chest, their
arms and legs entangled, her buttocks nestled far too pleasingly into the cradle of his groin. Sebastian had come awake
hard and wanting, ready to have her then . . . again . . . still.

"Blood of Christ," he growled, shoving his hand through
his hair in frustration.

At his muttered outburst, Logan and the chief caravaner
looked up from the map they held before him. "You prefer
another route, perhaps?" asked the Scot.

"What?" Sebastian scowled, having no idea how much of
the discussion he had missed because of his present state of
preoccupation.

That preoccupation showed no sign of improvement, for
in the next instant, Zahirah appeared just inside the common room of the caravansary. She walked toward the pillared entry to the courtyard, dressed in her tunic and long
pantalets, her face devoid of its veil. Her hair was unbound
and somewhat tousled, crushing in waves against her shoulders and spilling all around her in a loose tumble as if she
had risen from bed but a moment before. Sebastian's groin
tightened at the thought. She looked at no one save him,
and when she smiled, it was the shy, slow-curling smile of a
well-pleasured woman. Her every glance and gesture glowed
with sensuality, and it was all Sebastian could do to keep
from crossing the space of the yard to show her just how
thoroughly she affected him.

And he did not particularly like the fact that several of
the other men staring at her now seemed to be entertaining
similar thoughts.

"Excuse me," he said to Logan and the caravan foreman,
his gaze, and the whole of his attention trained squarely on
Zahirah.

He walked to where she stood waiting, her eyes shifting
downward, fingers fidgeting with a loose thread on her tunic

hem as he neared. "Good morrow, my lady," he greeted her quietly, reaching out to lift her hand to his lips. He knew the men were watching as he kissed her palm, and he did not care. She was his, and he wanted there to be no mistaking it when he would soon send one of the soldiers back with her to Ascalon while he and the rest of the caravan continued on to Darum. "Did you sleep well?"

She nodded, then, biting her lip, glanced up and met his gaze. "I did, until I felt your absence and realized you had gone."

He grunted. "Regrettable, but necessary."

She looked past him then, her eyes taking in the garrison of soldiers and caravan attendants assembled in the court-yard and awaiting further orders. "Will we be leaving soon?"

"Within the hour," Sebastian replied. "The carts and camels are being loaded as we speak."

"Begging pardon, sir," interrupted the merchant owner of the caravansary. He waved a trio of Saracen men forward as he approached from within the common room. "Here are the weapons you requested, good sir. Eight crossbows and half a dozen spears."

"Set them down over there," Sebastian answered, indicating a nearby table.

When the weapons were laid out before him, Sebastian picked up one of the crossbows and inspected its quality. The piece was solidly made, as the rest of the lot appeared to be. Crafted of good English oak, it had no doubt been scavenged from a fallen crusader, only to be sold back to whomever would have it by vultures of profit, such as this man.

"They will do," Sebastian said at last. He paid the merchant the inflated price he demanded, his pride irritated to know he was being cheated but grateful to have obtained the arms at whatever cost.

Zahirah came up beside him, frowning slightly. "Do you expect trouble between here and Ascalon, my lord?"

"No," he said, taking up one of the spears to check its deadly point.

"Then I don't understand. Why did you feel the need to buy arms if we are returning to the city within the hour?"

Sebastian set down the weapon and faced her. "We are not returning to Ascalon, my lady. The caravan will resume the trek south to Darum, as scheduled. One of the guards will escort you back to the city, where you will be safe until I return."

"Until you return?" she asked, distress edging her voice. "Then you're not coming with me?"

"I have supplies to deliver to the king, then I'll be back as soon as I can."

"But the ambush—" she blurted. "I told you about it so you would not go. It's too dangerous to continue on to Darum knowing that Halim plans to raid the caravan."

Touched by her concern, Sebastian brushed his hand against her cheek. "It's far less dangerous now that you have made me aware of that fact, my lady. We'll be ready for Halim and his *fida'i* dogs, whenever and wherever they choose to attack."

She reached up and curled her fingers around his, her silver gaze wide and determined. "Take me with you."

"Absolutely not."

"I can help you," she argued. "I know these roads, and I know Halim. I know how he thinks. I can help guide you past the areas where he might be inclined to strike."

Sebastian shook his head. "Halim is my concern now. And the caravan foreman is familiar enough with the terrain—"

"Then give me a weapon and I will ride beside you. The more arms you have at the ready, the better your chances of meeting the ambush. I was raised around men; I am no stranger to fighting."

Although she seemed bravely undaunted, Sebastian was loath to give credence to her bold claims. He knew no woman whose stomach was strong enough to withstand the sight of battle, let alone wield a weapon and join the fray. And he was not about to permit this woman—a woman he was coming to care for more than he liked to admit—to put herself in the way of any man's blade.

"Zahirah," he said, "this is not a matter for you to decide. I will not risk your safety or that of my men by allowing myself to be distracted over concern for your welfare. I cannot permit you to come with me to Darum. There is too much at risk."

"But after last night—"

"Especially after last night," he said, catching her chin and bringing her gaze to meet his. "I want you to be safe, Zahirah, that's all. I would ask you to try to understand."

"And I would ask the same of you, my lord. Understand what I have done in coming here to warn you—the risk I am taking merely by standing here. I have made an enemy of Halim, now more than ever. I did it for you," she said, emotion catching in her throat. "I did it for you, Sebastian, because I could not bear the thought of you meeting with harm. If you won't walk away from the danger, then what makes you think I will?"

Sebastian looked into her courageous, beautiful face and knew that it would be futile to argue with her. She was determined, and she was right in that she had risked much already by coming to him with the news of Halim's intended raid. He could insist on sending her back to Ascalon, but he could not be certain at all that she would obediently remain there while he rode for Darum. And there was a selfish, possessive part of him that loathed the idea of parting with her, even for the space of a few days. Against his better judgment, Sebastian found himself agreeing to her request.

"You will stay by my side at all times, and you will not, under any circumstances, disobey my orders. If there is any sign of danger, I will instruct you on where to seek cover and you will go without hesitation or argument. Understood?"

God help him, but he should not have felt so proud to see her nod in acceptance of his decision. Nor should he have been so damnably pleased to look over and see her canter-

ing alongside him once the caravan was assembled and the
escort party set out for whatever peril awaited them on the
road to Darum.

Zahirah had no idea what madness she suffered that
she would insist on accompanying Sebastian into Halim's
trap. She knew only that in those desperate moments when
he had informed her that he was going to Darum despite
her warning, she had to be with him. She rode at his left
on the track of ancient Roman pavement, watching him
observe their surroundings with a keen, steady eye, his command of the caravan no less sure or regal than that of a
king.

As a lover, he had proven equally magnificent. Zahirah
blushed just to think of their evening together, the shattering passion he had shown her in those precious hours before
dawn. He had loved her thoroughly, and yet she had awakened hungry for more. His gaze now, intense as he glanced
over and found her watching him, seemed to say that he understood what she was feeling.

That he, too, knew the hunger.

His mouth curving into a sensual smile, he guided his
mount next to hers and reached for her hand. He was just
about to bring it to his lips when something ahead in the distance caught his eye. His grip tightened on her as he scanned
the horizon and brought his mount to a slow halt on the
road. He released her hand to motion soundlessly for the
caravan to stop.

"What is it?" Zahirah whispered, her ebony mare sidling
away from the stamping and huffing of his large white steed.

"A reflection near that knoll," he told her in a low growl,
indicating the same to his lieutenant when the big knight
cantered to the head of the caravan to join him.

Zahirah followed the line of the men's vision to a small
rise in the terrain some several hundred yards directly
ahead. At first she saw nothing but a shapeless jut of rock
and scrub brush, but then, something moved behind it. And
on the other side of the road, reflecting from the rubble of a

uined stone outbuilding, came a sudden glint of steel, the edge of a weapon breaking the sun's rays and betraying the location of more of Halim's men. The caravan was hemmed in on both sides, she realized, swallowing down a lump of apprehension that rose in her throat.

It was all the warning they were to receive.

With a shrill battle cry, a score of assassin raiders erupted from their hiding places and charged forward on foot. Some brandished scimitars and iron-tipped lances; others were armed with bows and vicious-looking spiked clubs.

"To arms!" Sebastian shouted, moving his charger in front of Zahirah's as a shield while he grabbed for his crossbow. "Go, my lady," he ordered her, jerking his chin toward a copse of cypress trees to his left. "Find a place to hide until this is ended. Go, now!"

Recalling her promise to obey him, Zahirah hauled on her mare's reins and started to wheel the beast around. But when she would have urged the black off the road to seek cover, she was stopped by a sudden hail of flaming arrows that rained down in front of her. The fiery bolts ignited the dry grass of the plain, spreading a wide sea of flames across her path. She pivoted her head over her shoulder and saw a group of archers emerge on the other side of them as well. They nocked their arrows and released them. Within moments, both routes of sideward escape had been cleanly cut off by a wall of flames.

"Bastards," Sebastian growled, noticing the predicament at the same time she did. "Stay behind me, Zahirah. Don't move unless I tell you to."

With that, he swung his crossbow up into position and let the first bolt fly. It ripped through the smoke-filled air and hit true, lodging into the unprotected chest of one of the ambushers and knocking the dead man off his feet. The rest of the caravaners had issued similar insult to the band of *fida'i* attackers, their shouts of war and the reports of their discharged weapons filling her ears with the chaotic din of combat.

Zahirah screamed as an enemy arrow shot past her, narrowly missing both her and Sebastian. One of the camels behind them was not so fortunate. Pierced through the neck, the beast went down in a weighty heap, its packs of grain bursting open and spilling onto the road. The other animals bleated in fright, shifting and bumping into the carts of supplies as the battle waged on around them.

Zahirah had never felt so powerless. She clung to her mare's reins, ducking to stay behind Sebastian as he had ordered, when her every instinct urged her to help the crusaders hold the caravan. The assassins were moving in closer, escalating the skirmish into a vicious hand-to-hand combat.

She gasped as one of the Frankish soldiers near the front took a blow from a *fida'i* sword and toppled from his mount. Another fell to the bite of a lance, horse and rider crashing to earth with a reverberating thud.

Sebastian's quick aim with the crossbow had eliminated several of the advancing ambushers, but his supply of bolts came to an abrupt, inopportune end. As he grappled for a missile that was not there, two of Zahirah's clansmen rushed at him with weapons raised, bearing murder in their eyes.

"Sebastian, watch out!" she cried, but he had already seen the danger.

He threw aside the useless crossbow and reached for his sword, drawing the deadly length of steel from its scabbard with a hellish howl. He swooped down on the whooping assassins, cleaving one in twain with a single swipe of his arm. The second man came at him with a spiked club, readying a blow that would have crushed Sebastian's arm had Logan not come to his aid at the last moment to shoot the man dead with his crossbow.

Zahirah could barely stand to watch as the road began to run with blood. She turned away from the carnage and heard a thready voice carry over the cacophony, coming from the rear of the stalled caravan.

"Mistress . . . mistress, please! Help me!"

She looked down, and, through the billowing smoke and dust, saw the pain-riddled, begrimed face of the chief cara-

aner. The old man was trapped beneath one of the fallen
amels, his legs engulfed under the dead, unyielding weight
f the beast and its sizable burden.

"Help me, mistress, I beg you . . ."

Zahirah threw a glance over her shoulder to where
ebastian and the other men fought. He had told her to stay
ehind him, but surely he would not expect her to stand by
dly and let this man die when she might be able to help free
im. Even if he did expect as much, her conscience would
llow no such thing. Leaping down from her mount, she ran
o the side of the old man.

"Can't get . . . up," he gasped. "Hurts . . . to . . . breathe."

Zahirah peered through the blinding fog of the smolder-
ng grass to assess the situation more closely. It did not look
ood. The camel had crushed the caravan foreman to the
vaist, likely rupturing any number of his vital organs. She
ould not hope to move the huge beast off of him alone, but
hen she doubted it would matter much longer. The old man
vheezed as she inspected his ribs, coughing up a trickle of
lood that oozed from the corner of his mouth.

"My . . . legs," he whispered, "are they . . . broken?"

"No," she lied, her smile of false reassurance wobbling as
he held his searching, terrified gaze. "Don't speak now. Try
o relax. The pain will be over soon."

He nodded weakly and closed his eyes. Then, within a
ew short moments, he exhaled a deep, rattling breath and
vent utterly still.

"Allah protect you," Zahirah whispered. "May peace be
ipon your soul."

She got to her feet and pivoted, intending to regain her
nount, but drew up short when she met with a chilling pair
f Saracen eyes. They stared down at her, black and cold
ind contemptuous, from the length of an arced scimitar
lade that hovered at her breast.

"Halim," she choked, her hand sliding to the waistband
f her trousers, where her dagger might have been. The dag-
;er, which, in her haste, she left behind at the palace when
he rode out to warn Sebastian of the ambush.

"You traitorous slut," he spat at her, the Arabic word
more grating than the heavy sounds of combat carrying
through the smoke of the skirmish. "You told him! You
warned the Frankish pig that we would be here."

Zahirah saw no sense in denying it. All around her
Halim's *fida'i* soldiers battled with Sebastian and his fully
armed crusaders and caravaners. What might have been a
surprise attack and slaughter had instead become an equal
fight—more than equal, for despite the ambushers' greater
number, the Franks on their heavy warhorses were beginning to succeed in driving them back, pushing them toward
retreat.

But Halim showed no such signs of backing down where
he stood, facing Zahirah. He edged forward through the
ash-filled smoke that surrounded them, forcing her back a
pace to avoid his blade. She stumbled over the massive bulk
of the dead camel behind her, but righted herself before she
lost her footing completely. Halim was there as she started
to come up, the razor-sharp tip of his scimitar lifting her
chin and malevolently encouraging her to rise.

"I should have known you could not be trusted," he
sneered. "You are too weak for this mission. You are no
fida'i."

Zahirah swallowed hard, willing her voice not to wobble
under the cold, cruel edge of Halim's blade. "I am more
fida'i than you ever were. I would not slaughter a dozen innocent men and call it Allah's will. Nor could I stand by and
allow you to do so."

"Innocent men," he scoffed. "You think any one of these
Franks is innocent? Oh, would that our vaunted lord and
master were here to see you now, slavering at the heels of
these Christian dogs like a bitch in heat. He would thank me
for killing you." He flexed his hand on the grip of his scimitar, readying to strike. "Indeed, I expect he shall."

Acting on a sudden surge of instinct, Zahirah flung herself backward, rolling to the ground before Halim could
draw another breath. A crossbow, loaded with a single bolt,
lay just out of her reach in the road. She stretched for it, tri-

mphant as her fingers closed around the wooden throat of
1e weapon. That triumph was short-lived. A heavy boot
ame down hard on her wrist, pinioning her hand to the
tone cobbles of the road.

"Think again," Halim snarled from above her.

Zahirah turned her head to face him, scarcely able to see
im through the swirling smoke and dust. But she could see
is sword, and she could see the tight grip of his hand on the
veapon, fury turning his dark knuckles nearly white.

Allah, but she was certain, this—here and now—was to
e her end. She could not move, could do nothing to defend
erself; Halim was going to kill her. The realization sank
1to her brain like a piercing shard of ice. She was going to
ie.

Her eyes burning from the thick black haze that filled the
ir, Zahirah strained to find Sebastian amid the confusion
f the ambush. Just one last glimpse of him would be
nough. She would not fear death if she could be certain he
.ad survived. She peered hard through the ash and soot and
umble of fighting men, but to no avail. She could not find
im, could see nothing beyond the shapeless mass of the
talled caravan and the chaos of combat beyond.

She must have voiced Sebastian's name aloud, for Halim
egan to chuckle. "Such a pitiful end for the great Sinan's
laughter. Was it worth it, Zahirah? Was *he* worth the cost of
etraying your clan?"

"He would have been," Zahirah replied fiercely, prepar-
1g herself for the deadly wrath she was inviting. "But I have
ot betrayed my clan today, Halim. Only you."

His answering chuckle was pure malice. "I see. Then the
leasure of exacting justice now shall be mine alone. It will
e an honor to take your traitor's head back with me to
Aasyaf."

Zahirah forced herself not to flinch as Halim's blade re-
reated slightly, cutting a thin trail through the smoke as he
Irew his arm back to deliver a fatal blow. She kept her eyes
pen, feeling tears spring forth in the endless moment she
vaited for his blade to bite into her neck.

The din of battle died away in that exaggerated space of time, leaving only the heavy thud of her own heartbeat pounding in her ears. She heard Halim draw a sudden sharp breath, saw his arced blade poised high above her head. Praying for a swift end, Zahirah kept her eyes trained on the muted glint of steel, bracing herself for the imminent impact.

To her astonishment, it did not come.

Halim seemed frozen above her, and through the smoke she saw a look of shock coming over his face. Zahirah felt frozen as well, unable to do anything but stare in confusion as Halim's shock turned to horror. Then she saw the reason.

The bloodied tip of a broadsword had sliced through his chest from behind, cleanly impaling his wicked heart. Halim stood there, staring at her, his dark eyes wide and condemning as his scimitar dropped from his slack grasp. His weight was no longer supported by his own legs, which had begun to buckle beneath him, but by the strength of the blade that had just delivered his death. Once removed, Halim crumpled to the earth like a puppet on severed strings.

Behind his lifeless form stood Sebastian. Face soot-streaked and spattered with blood, his black hair wild and windswept about his face, he had never looked more breathtaking or deadly. He reached down to Zahirah, his gaze steady, intense. "Come, my lady. Take my hand," he said when she could not summon the strength to stand of her own volition.

Zahirah could not hold back her tears as he lifted her to her feet and enveloped her in a fierce embrace. Clutching him to her as if to never let go, she wept into his chest, burying her face in the tattered folds of his silk surcoat.

"Hush now," he soothed, his deep voice like a balm to her nerves. "'Tis over, Zahirah. The fighting has ended. You're safe with me now."

Still ensconced within the circle of his arms, Zahirah drew her head up to verify what Sebastian said, that the fighting was indeed over. Although it was difficult to assess the outcome, she could see that he spoke true. The caravan and its escort party, while not without damage, was, for the most part, intact. Only a few of Sebastian's men had fallen in the skirmish; Halim's forces had suffered easily twice as many casualties. Some of the surviving *fida'i* soldiers had retreated, while still others lay wounded in and around the road.

"It's over," Sebastian said again, pulling her closer and kissing the top of her head.

But as if to belie his reassurances, in the not too far distance, came the rumble of horses' hooves—another army come to join the fray, by the sound of it. Fearing that Halim had provided additional men, Zahirah cried out in alarm, but Sebastian seemed unconcerned. He shielded his eyes from the glare of the sun and smoke as he peered at the approaching company of riders. He chuckled, then he and the rest of the crusaders standing around them went down on one knee, bowing over their swords in deep deference as more than a score of Frankish soldiers thundered forth, then drew to a halt before them on the road.

Borne on tall lances were twin pennons of red silk, adorned with three golden lions. The triangular flags snapped and fluttered in the wind like dancing flames, framing the leader of the newly arrived party in rich, regal color. Zahirah gaped at the splendor of the man riding at the fore of the contingent, a broad-shouldered knight who swept off a crownlike helm and mail coif to reveal a head of fair brownish hair and stern, kingly features.

"Your Majesty," Sebastian said, respectfully bowing his head.

And Zahirah suddenly found herself staring into the questioning blue gaze of Lionheart himself.

The man she was sworn to kill.

Chapter Nineteen

"It appears we have arrived too late to assist," said the English king, a note of disappointment in his voice. He glanced to Sebastian, who straightened to his full height beside Zahirah, his spine erect, wide shoulders held back with pride before his king. "You guarded my supplies well, Montborne. I commend you on your service. As ever, you do not disappoint."

Sebastian returned Lionheart's smile. "I am honored to serve, Sire."

"Assassins, were they?"

"Yes, Sire. They were agents of the Old Man."

The king clucked his tongue. "Vermin cowards," he growled. "Which of them do you suspect was the one who attacked me in the camp some weeks past?"

"Their leader is over there," Sebastian answered, gesturing toward Halim's lifeless body. "He also killed Abdul a few days ago."

The king grunted, flattening his mouth. "And this?" he asked, looking once more to Zahirah. "Have we taken a pretty little hostage from our infidel raiders?"

"No, my lord," Sebastian answered, moving closer to bring her within the shelter of his arm. "This is the Lady Zahirah. 'Twas because of her that we were prepared for this raid." He pitched his voice a bit lower as he turned his head down to meet her gaze. "She risked much to bring me the warning. I am grateful and indebted."

Lionheart's tawny brows rose slightly. "Indeed? Well, then, Montborne, I should like to hear more about this.

Perhaps the lady will indulge me in the tale upon our arrival at Darum."

Zahirah inclined her head at the king's comment, uncomfortable with the way his eyes roved so freely over her person as he spoke. In a flash of memory, she recalled Abdul's warning soon after she first arrived at the palace in Ascalon.

The king likes pretty things, and he takes what he likes.

"Perhaps, my lord," Sebastian answered when she knew not what to say. His tone was casual, but the muscles in his arm went a little tighter around her shoulder, subtly letting her know that, should she need him, he was there to protect her.

The king's gaze lingered a moment longer, then flicked past Zahirah to the caravan of supplies. "Did we lose much in the skirmish?"

"Three of my men are dead, as is the caravan foreman," Sebastian replied. He waited as the king dismounted, then left Zahirah to walk with his liege around the carts to inspect the condition of the caravan. "We lost some of the grain to spillage and scorching, but the bulk of the shipment is intact."

"Excellent." Lionheart gestured two of his soldiers forward with a curl of his gauntlet-covered hand. "Wixley, Fallonmour—assist Montborne's men in transferring the spilled supplies to the carts. And remove these dead beasts from the road. I want to be loaded and en route to Darum within the hour."

"My lords!" shouted one of the crusaders. He pointed toward the thicket of brush off to the distant left, where one of Halim's surviving soldiers was attempting to flee.

The king seemed wholly unfazed. He pivoted his head toward a huge knight clad in black chain mail, and gave a curt nod. Like a hound of hell suddenly unleashed, the warrior broke from Lionheart's ranks astride an ebony destrier. He gave the beast his spurs and sped across the plain, easily flushing the straggling *fida'i* out of hiding before cutting him down with a mighty sweep of his sword.

Zahirah looked on in horror as another assassin soldier pulled himself to his feet and tried to run for cover. Limping from his injuries, he did not get far. The king's demon warrior wheeled his mount on its hocks and gave chase with a roar. He bore down upon the *fida'i* within mere moments, cleanly beheading him in midstride.

"Don't watch, lass," whispered the voice of Sebastian's lieutenant from where he now stood beside her. He caught her chin and turned her face away from the carnage. "Blackheart takes no prisoners, and no one possessing a soul should be made to witness him in action."

But there was little need to see in order to understand what was taking place in the field. The moans and prayers of Zahirah's wounded clansmen were silenced one by one as the devil knight and two companions swept the outlying plain and road, efficiently executing every last man.

Less than an hour later, the caravan was reassembled and once again on the road for Darum, led this time by the formidable duo of Sebastian and the English king. Zahirah rode along near the rear of the group with Logan, who gently schooled her gaze back to the fore when she pivoted in her saddle, compelled to take one last glimpse of the smoking plain and bleak, body-strewn field she was leaving behind.

"The future lies this way, lass," he said, indicating the horizon with a sweep of his hand. "There's no sense in looking back."

Zahirah nodded, but her smile felt weak on her trembling lips. Despite her bravado with Halim, she could not deny the truth in his accusation. She had indeed betrayed her clan today. A betrayal that had cost many lives. And when she looked ahead of her, feeling her heart clench to gaze upon the proud carriage and handsome features of Sebastian of Montborne, she feared a future that would soon force her to betray her clan again . . . or commit the greater sin of betraying her own heart.

They reached the English king's army near Darum some five hours later. It was twilight in the dune-set encampment, the sun having dipped behind the score of Christian tents assembled on the plain, making way for night to rise in deepening shades of azure and ruby-gold. Around the camp, soldiers busied themselves with various tasks. Some scoured weapons; some tended cookfires; still others cared for the injured, those men wounded in previous battles or made sick from lack of water and the stinging bites of the desert's vicious black flies.

Every able man rose to his feet and cheered when King Richard arrived, Lionheart proudly heading up the caravan of supplies as if the victory over the ambushers had been his personal triumph, more than it belonged to Sebastian and his few troops. Zahirah glanced at Sebastian to gauge his reaction to the king's assumption of credit, but his face showed no trace of resentment. He was not the sort to crave recognition or praise, she realized, watching as Sebastian coolly accepted the greetings and good-natured jests of some of the other soldiers who came forward to welcome him to the camp. Indeed, in that moment, Sebastian seemed more kingly than the king, the black-haired captain's tall stature and easy, noble demeanor setting him apart from the ranks of the common men who swarmed around the caravan.

Zahirah's pulse gave a little jump of pride as she surreptitiously watched him reunite with soldiers and friends he had likely fought beside in the months before his injury had grounded him at Ascalon. As if he sensed her warm regard, he glanced back and caught her looking at him. His gaze met hers and lingered, intense despite the buzz of activity around him.

There was desire in his eyes, and an unspoken invitation in his smile that sent a tingle of awareness through her. Zahirah bit her lip to keep from beaming back at him, mindful of the curious stares she was now receiving from several of the Frankish knights.

"A feast this evening!" shouted the king, his baritone voice immediately turning all heads toward him as he dismounted from his prancing, huffing steed. He waved some of the men forward to begin unloading the goods from the camels and carts. "We've foodstuffs and wine, and great cause to celebrate. Today's victory was but a taste of the glory soon to be ours when we march on Jerusalem!"

"God wills it!" came the collective reply from the soldiers. Bedraggled and weary, the crusaders roused to their king's call of war, applauding and chanting, "Help, help, for the Holy Sepulcher! Death to the infidels!"

Zahirah felt as uncomfortable as her suddenly skittish mare amid the throng of rallying Franks. She tried to calm the beast, but in the end it was Sebastian who gentled the sleek black horse. He did not join his countrymen in their fervent song and shouts of war. Instead, he swung down off his destrier and walked to Zahirah's side, calming her mare with low, soothing words as he stroked its sweat-sheened neck. Then he turned to Zahirah and offered her a hand in dismounting. "The king has arranged a tent for me here in the camp," he said. "I warrant you'll be more comfortable there, my lady."

She nodded, grateful for the opportunity to remove herself from the boisterous crowd of knights. Sebastian assisted her to the ground, then led her into the heart of the encampment. Along the way, they came upon a red-striped tent, set off on its own near the pen containing the army's horses. From within the tent came the sound of women talking and laughing in Arabic, the chorus of feminine chatter punctuated now and then by the hollow thump of a drum or the soft jingle of bells and tambourine. Dancing girls, she realized as she and Sebastian approached the pavilion and Zahirah ventured a glance inside.

The front of the tent was rolled high to permit fresh air and easy entry, the open portal shaded by an awning that was held up by tall, twin poles and flanked by burning torchlights. Inside, incense and opium burned, the curling tendrils of smoke wreathing the heads of five young Saracen women who lounged like odalisques in a harem. The dancers sprawled on cushions and carpets in various states of undress, their comely faces unveiled, dark hair unbound, modesty clearly unabashed, garbed as they were in filmy silk pantalets and skin-exposing bodices that left little to the imagination.

They giggled over something one of them said, but their prattle ceased the instant their eyes lit on Sebastian. The one holding the tambourine rose up from her reclined position and sauntered forward with a fluid grace, the bangles on her wrists and ankles ringing with tinny music as she moved. She posed herself artfully near the mouth of the tent and gave Sebastian an inviting smile, revealing a bright gold tooth that glimmered in the wavering flames of the torches.

"Well come, my most handsome lord," she said in the crusaders' tongue, her speech heavily accented and halting, but the gleam in her eye requiring no interpretation. She wrapped one hennaed hand around the tent pole and slid her fingers suggestively up and down the length of it. "You like, Fahimah play for you."

Sebastian's head turned, though he all but ignored the comely young woman's offer, his long-legged strides slowing not the least as he passed her and her whispering companions. Taking Zahirah's hand in his, he turned down a boot-worn track that led toward the row of colorless silk tents belonging to the king and his officers. A yellow-haired Frankish youth met them halfway. A mere boy, Zahirah corrected, as the lad jogged forth to greet them, his ruddy pink cheeks seeming scarcely old enough to grow the sparse beard that fuzzed them like the skin of a peach.

"My lord Montborne," he said, bobbing his head before Sebastian. "This way, if you please. I will show you to your quarters."

The lad brought them to the designated tent, then pulled back the flap to permit them entry. The shaded space was empty of its prior occupant and sparsely furnished with bedroll, table, and a single wooden stool. A half dozen overlying carpets covered the earthen floor of the pavilion, their Arabic weaves of russet, gold, and green glowing warmly in the scant light of an oil lamp that burned at the edge of the squat, scarred table.

"Will it serve, my lord?"

"Aye. It will more than serve," Sebastian replied from be-side Zahirah, turning to look back at the boy where he stood behind them, awaiting the captain's approval. "Who has my arrival displaced, lad?"

"This tent was Sir Cabal's, my lord."

Sebastian grunted, quirking a dark brow. "Blackheart's? Well, perhaps the king was less pleased with my service today than he is letting on."

Smiling at the jest, the boy gave a quick shake of his head. "Sir Cabal is on guard watch tonight, my lord. In truth, I rather think he prefers sleeping out of doors than in the confines of a tent."

"Don't assume that one sleeps at all," Sebastian quipped, winking when the lad's eyes widened in alarm. "What is your name, squire?"

The boy drew himself a little taller, puffing out his slen-der chest. "Joscelin d'Alban, my lord."

Sebastian offered him his hand. "We are well met, Joscelin d'Alban. This is Lady Zahirah. Will you see to her needs while I am meeting with the king?"

"Of course, my lord." He bowed his head to Zahirah. "My lady."

Zahirah smiled at the Frankish youth, impressed by his courtesy. She saw no trace of falsehood in his greeting, no sign of hatred for the woman who was as much an outsider in this camp as the Christians were in Outremer. She turned away to look at her surroundings as Sebastian gave Joscelin orders for bathing water and refreshments, half-listening as the lad departed the tent to carry out his tasks. A moment later, Sebastian's hands came to rest gently on her arms.

"Will you be all right by yourself for a while?"

Zahirah nodded, coming around to face him. "Yes. I will be fine."

His mouth curved at the corner, not quite a smile. His dark brows were pinched together over gray-green eyes that reflected an unspoken concern. "I might have lost you out there today."

"And I you," she said, "but we're here." She placed her palm against his beard-grizzled cheek. "By Allah's grace, we are both here."

He turned his mouth into her hand, kissing the tender skin of her palm. Reaching up, he took her fingers between his and held her hand to his chest. Although his touch was gentle, her wrist was yet too raw from where Halim had earlier crushed it into the stones of the road with his boot heel. Zahirah winced, drew in her breath. She tried to slip her hand from Sebastian's grasp but he caught her fingers and looked down to see the abrasions that crisscrossed her skin.

"Halim did this?" he asked, anger flaring in his gaze. At her shrug of admission, he exhaled a low curse. "He'll never hurt you again. So long as I have breath in my body, none of his kind will ever hurt you again."

How fraudulent she felt, hearing those words, seeing the concern reflected in Sebastian's eyes. Zahirah's smile wobbled as he brought her into his embrace and held her there, his heart beating steadily against her cheek, his arms warm and strong around her shoulders. Allah forgive her, but she clung to him, too, letting herself believe for one precious moment that she deserved his affection, that she might always know the peace she found within the shelter of his arms.

"How I wish we could stop time right here, and stay like this," she whispered, startled to hear the reckless words slip from her tongue.

Sebastian stilled where he was stroking her hair. He brought his hand beneath her chin and lifted her gaze to his. Bending toward her, he brushed his mouth against hers in a kiss that was too sweet, and far too fleeting. He drew back just as the young squire returned with the requested water and food.

"Set them over there, lad," he said, his eyes on Zahirah as he directed Joscelin to the table with a gesture of his hand.

Perhaps sensing the ill timing of his intrusion, the boy put down the tray as requested, then made a hasty exit from the tent.

"The king is waiting," Sebastian said, when the lad was gone. "I don't know how long I will be in conference with him, but if you need anything, summon Joscelin. I'll see that he maintains a post nearby until I return."

Zahirah gave a bob of her head, missing him already. "I shall be waiting for you, my lord."

Sebastian gave her cheek a brief caress, then turned and crossed the space of the tent to take his leave. He swept aside the flap, then hesitated, pivoting to look at her. "Join me at the feast tonight, Zahirah."

"Join you?" She shook her head. She knew how unwelcome women were where Arab men gathered; she could only guess at the reception she would receive amid a tent full of drunken warrior Franks and their king. Surely Sebastian knew this, too, but his expression showed no hint of doubt or reservation at all. Perhaps, rather, a calm defiance. "Do you really think that would be wise, my lord? No one there will want to see me at their table. After all, I am a woman, and the enemy."

Sebastian's gaze was steady, intense. "You are my lady," he answered simply. "Join me, and you will make me the envy of every man in the room."

Although she was not quite fool enough to believe that, Zahirah blushed at his flattery, warmed beyond reckoning that he would want her beside him at the feast. "For a man who professes to recall little of courtly manners, you seem well in command of them now, my lord."

His answering smile sent her heart into a crazy flutter. "Is that a yes, my lady?"

"I'm not sure I could refuse you anything when you are looking at me like that."

He grunted, lifting a brow in devilish interest. "A confession that will haunt me every moment I am kept away from you," he growled. "Rest and refresh yourself. I'll send for you when the feast commences."

She nodded, giddy as a lovesick girl, and watched him duck under the tent flap to take his leave. With a gladness that left her smiling some long time after Sebastian had gone, Zahirah made grateful use of the washbasin the young squire had brought her. She rinsed away the morning's grit and grime, the dirt and blood and ash of Halim's ambush clouding the bowl of bathwater.

It struck her, staring into the swirling filth of the basin, that with the cleansing of her skin—with Halim's death that morning—she was, for the moment, freed of the burden of her mission. No one here knew or suspected what she was about, least of all Sebastian. To him, as he had said, she was simply his lady. His lover, not his enemy.

What a dangerous, delicious feeling that was, to be unencumbered by the weight of her destiny, unshackled from her commitment to her father and her clan. How easy it would be to pretend that deadly promise never existed, that the ruse she played to infiltrate Sebastian's camp could in fact be molded into some sort of truth. . . .

Her heart raced so with the notion, Zahirah had to seek the chair to sit and catch her breath. What she was thinking went beyond blasphemy. To turn her back on her mission would condemn her to eternal damnation. Worse, it would doom her homeland to the continued destructive presence of King Richard and his infidel forces. And for what? To fulfill the romantic longings of her silly woman's heart?

"Yes," she whispered aloud, miserable, pressing her hand to her mouth as if to staunch any further corruption before it could spill from her lips.

Allah forgive her, but if she thought Sebastian would have her, she feared that she would indeed be willing to risk it all.

Chapter Twenty

"To victory over the infidels!"

King Richard's voice boomed, lionlike, over the din of celebration and feasting. Seated at a long wooden table that dominated an entire side of his enormous meeting tent, he raised his goblet of wine high in the air, encouraging assenting shouts and thunderous applause from the knights gathered. To the right of the king at the high table, Sebastian lifted his cup as well, murmuring the credo that had become second nature to the crusaders.

"*Deus le volt!* God wills it," he said, his voice disappearing into the chorus of the other men, his gaze fixed not on the magnificence of his liege, but on the entryway of the lanternlit pavilion.

There, a succession of pages and servants scurried in like ants on the march to their hill, their arms laden with trays of food and flagons of spiced Saracen wine. Sebastian looked past their numbers, searching for Zahirah's face and brooding with a scowl when he did not find her. Joscelin had been dispatched to get her and returned twice already, each time bearing a look that said Zahirah would not be coming to the feast after all. Wondering at her seeming change of heart, Sebastian began to calculate an excuse to leave the festivities and go see about her.

"You've been watching that spot for an hour, Montborne," remarked the king, eyeing him sagely over the rim of his jeweled goblet. "I've never known you to be so plainly distracted."

Sebastian tried to shrug off the observation with a

chuckle. "I was just wondering if I should send a squire to fetch my sword that I might actually cut through this meat sometime tonight."

Lionheart laughed, stabbing a chunk of the tough, gamey brown stuff on the end of his poniard. "What, you don't care for roast camel?" He bit off the large mouthful and spoke while he chewed. "Apparently you have had things too good in Ascalon. Don't tell me your time recuperating has spoiled you for life on the march?"

"Not at all, my lord," Sebastian answered, turning now to meet the king's stare. "I am mended well enough and ready to march on your orders. Indeed, I welcome the return to action."

"Good," Richard proclaimed, cuffing him on the shoulder. "I will need you when we join up with our allies in Beit Nuba and head for Jerusalem."

"Do you expect that will be soon, my lord?" Sebastian asked, well aware of the criticism the king had received for his continued delays in marching on the Holy City. The general feeling among the Christian leaders was that if they did not move to seize Jerusalem soon, their cause would be all but lost.

"I came here to free the Sepulcher from infidel hands," Richard answered soberly, as if recalling for himself the censure that had followed him on every minor campaign that seemed to take him farther away from that goal. "I will reclaim Jerusalem for the Cross, or," he said, pausing in thought, "if it be God's will, I shall die trying."

It was not until that moment Sebastian noticed how drawn the king's face was beneath his trim, tawny beard. His cheeks were sallow, his eyes piercing but haunted, their blue hue somehow bleaker than Sebastian recalled. All of the men were thinner than they had been upon leaving Ascalon some weeks ago, but the king wore a sickly shadow under his eyes, and his mouth, which was always ready with a boast or a leonine roar, was bracketed now with deep lines that bespoke a sickness or a pain he might have sought to conceal. He had never appeared more human, nor more frail, and, looking at him, Sebastian knew a jolt of doubt for the likely success of their remaining days in Outremer.

"I am yours to command, Sire," he told the ghost of his king. "My sword is now, as always, at your service."

Richard eyed him for a long moment, then gave a curt nod, as if he expected no less. Then he blinked, and the apparition of his weaker self vanished, replaced with the bold façade better recognized by all who knew him as the great and mighty Lionheart. Rising from his chair, he opened his arms with a flourish of grand royal showmanship.

"Bring on the entertainment!" he shouted, clapping his hands and sending a couple of idle pages scattering out of the tent to oblige.

Sebastian nursed his cup of wine, deep in thought and scarcely paying attention as the troupe of Saracen dancing girls was ushered into the pavilion. They set up quickly, one seating herself cross-legged on a carpet near the center of the tent and propping a goatskin drum between her legs; another joined her on the floor, blowing a musical trill from the long reed instrument she carried. The remaining three women jogged barefooted into position, leaping up onto tables, their scant, nearly transparent attire and flirtatious looks rousing the lusty, drunken knights into a frenzy of whistles and stomping feet before the dance had even begun.

The one who had propositioned Sebastian earlier that day—he had forgotten her name, but he remembered the gold tooth when she smiled at him now—headed directly for the high table, beating her tambourine and shaking her bosom as she sauntered forward with sleek, graceful strides.

"Fahimah smells fresh blood," drawled the king, grinning as he leaned toward Sebastian. "Keep your head around this one. The bitch bites when she's in heat."

Sebastian gave a reflex chuckle, but he was not the least bit interested in Fahimah or her companions. He downed the rest of his wine as the music started, the deep, staccato beat of the drum and the accompanying stomp of the dancers' bell-adorned feet on the tables filling the tent with a heady, primal rhythm. Before he could give the king his excuses to leave, Fahimah swung herself up onto the high table before him, leering suggestively as she pivoted on her rump and spread herself in front of Lionheart and his officers like a pagan altar offering. The king ran his hand over her smooth brown belly, then bent down and kissed her, thrusting his tongue deep into her mouth.

Mildly appalled at the orgiastic display, Sebastian turned his head away and rose from his seat at the table. The other two dancers were indulging in similar lewdness, shrieking and tossing their hair, spinning and gyrating to the music amid a sea of groping hands and vulgar shouts.

And, there, in the far corner of the tent was a different disturbance under way, a disturbance that instinctively rose the hackles on the back of his neck. One of the knights, a craven nobleman whom Sebastian rather despised, was harassing one of the Saracen girls. She was petite, more than a head shorter than the half dozen soldiers who moved in to surround her, knitting her into the wall of the tent like a pack of wolves cornering a hare. Sebastian caught a glimpse of a torn blue tunic sleeve and the raven's wing gloss of a familiar ebony pate, and his blood went into an instant, furious boil.

"Get away from her!" he bellowed, vaulting over the high table and lunging across the space of the crowded tent. The reed player blew a discordant note, ducking out of his way as he shot toward the knight who pawed at Zahirah. "Fallonmour! Get your hands off of her!"

He shoved past the few leering onlookers to seize the nobleman by the shoulder, forcibly throwing him out of the way. Logan was at Sebastian's elbow, the Scot having evidently noticed the trouble at the same time and rushed from his place at table to assist. He caught Fallonmour as he stumbled back on his heels, clamping his meaty hands down on the knight's arms and holding him away from Zahirah.

"Did he touch you?" Sebastian asked, ready to tear the

bastard apart if he so much as bruised her delicate skin. Zahirah shook her head, her gaze stricken, arms crossed protectively one over the other.

"There's no cause for conflict here, Montborne." Fallonmour shook off Logan's hold and sniffed, indignant as he straightened the hem of his mussed tunic. "If you'd but said you wanted some, too, I might have been willing to share the chit once I was through with her."

Sebastian whirled on the arrogant lord. With a vicious snarl, he hauled his arm back and smashed his fist into Fallonmour's face. "Don't come near her again," he warned, "or I'll kill you."

Doubled over from the cracking blow, the knight coughed and wheezed and spat out a mouthful of blood. His voice was shrill. "Ugh! You thun of a bitch—you broke my nothe!"

Ignoring the sudden resounding silence of the tent, and the disapproving, sphinxlike stare of the king from where he stood, fists braced upon the high table, Sebastian reached for Zahirah's hand and led her away from the shocked assembly, his combative gaze daring anyone to say a word or to make an untoward move. No one did; those standing in his path cleared quickly to let him pass, some shaking their heads, others too stunned to do more than stare after him.

Sebastian's temper cooled somewhat once he and Zahirah were outside in the crisp, starlit blackness of night. His pace, however, remained brisk, his pulse hammering, every muscle coiled and ready for attack. He realized belatedly that Zahirah nearly had to trot to keep up with his long strides, so he slowed and gave her hand a squeeze.

"I'm sorry," he said, exhaling a sharp breath. "I'm sorry for what happened back there—all of it."

"No, I should not have come," she answered. "I wasn't going to, but then I heard the music and it sounded so inviting, I could not resist. I didn't belong there."

He rounded on her, cursing aloud when he thought about what his countrymen might have done to her. "You belong wherever you wish to go. And any man who thinks to tell you different will have to answer to me."

"Even if you have to make enemies of every Frank and Saracen alike?" she asked, her eyes shining in the moonlight. She shook her head, calm as the gentling night breeze, but her smile seemed a little sad. "You would risk too much for me, my lord. I'm not worth all that."

Sebastian grunted. "Assaulting Garrett of Fallonmour was no great risk, I assure you. He's a court hound and an ass, and one of these days his arrogance is going to get him killed." He reached out, touching the smooth line of her cheek. "And you *are* worth it, Zahirah."

She glanced down, silent as they resumed the path that led deeper into the camp. All was dark and quiet here; everyone would be at the feast for some hours yet. Distantly, as if in testimony of that fact, Sebastian heard the music start up again in the king's pavilion on the other side of the encampment. They passed the paddock that contained the army's horses, and the striped awning of the vacant dancers' quarters, then turned the corner that brought them before Sebastian's tent in the officers' row.

Sebastian released Zahirah's hand to unfasten the ties on the flap. He swept the panel aside and stood at the open portal, waiting for her to enter. She stepped in front of him, then let out a soft sigh. Hesitating, she turned toward him, shyly it seemed, her eyes downcast. Her hands came up slowly, her fingers spreading as she laid her palms on his chest. At that mere touch, his heart was slamming against his ribs. His body quickened at once, desire thrumming and thickening in his loins. She leaned into him slightly, tipping her head back to look at him.

As if she meant to say something, her lips parted, glistening moist, tempting. It was too much for him to bear. Sebastian bent forward and kissed her. Her mouth was soft and sweet, like the nectar of a rare, exotic fruit. He could have easily gorged himself on her, so hungry was he for her touch, for the satin pleasure of her body.

His need for her was strong, and Zahirah's eager re-

sponse proved his undoing. She met his kiss with equal
ardor, rising up on her toes and twining her fingers in the
hair at his nape, clutching him to her as if to never let go.
Sebastian groaned, feeling his arousal stir between them, the
pressure of her body against his own searing him like a
brand. He pulled her deeper into his embrace and flicked his
tongue along the seam of her lips, coaxing them open, pen-
etrating the silky heat of her mouth.

Had it only been last night that they had made love at the
caravansary? Faith, but it seemed an eternity to him now,
the way his body responded so swiftly, so needfully to hers.
Zahirah seemed to understand. She seemed to share his torment, her breath coming urgent and shallow, her back arching as he reached down to cup her breast in his palm, his
mouth plundering hers in a kiss that was fast becoming savage. She opened for him like the night-blooming blossom of
desert jasmine, her response pliant and giving, all softness
and warmth and willing, wondrous surrender.

Breathless, fevered with want, Sebastian broke their kiss
before he lost all sense of control. With his fingers laced
through hers, he led her into the dark sanctuary of his tent.
The bedroll was a black rumple on the floor, the only cush-
ion to be had in these sparse soldier's quarters. Sebastian
brought her to the pallet, and she sank down before him on
the blankets. He kissed her again, holding her face in his
hands and nipping possessively at her mouth before moving
off to divest himself of his clothing.

There was no need for words, no need for the pretense of
patience. There was only this shared want, this fierce desire
that pulsed in the air around them like a living thing, hot
and wild and consuming. Ruled by an elemental craving,
Sebastian threw his tunic aside, then stripped off his boots,
hose, and braies. Naked, needful, his flesh tingling with anticipation in the chill of the lightless tent, he knelt before
Zahirah on the pallet and reached for the laces of her tunic's
bodice. He tore at them, exhaling a sharp chuckle of surprise to feel his fingers tremble in his haste. Fumbling in the
dark, he managed to snarl the garment's network of slim

ties, and, in that frenzied moment, considered the virtue in simply ripping the damned thing open. He cursed his clumsiness, then felt Zahirah's hands come up to assist him. Her fingers, praise God, were infinitely more agile. She loosened the last of the knots, then lifted her arms so he could draw the long silk shirt up over her head.

Unaided by the extinguished oil lamp, it was too dark to see more than the shape and shadow of Zahirah's body before him, but his hands suffered no such loss. They told him of the glory his sight was denied, his fingers skating over the velvet softness of her shoulders, the firm shapeliness of her arms. He found her breasts and kneaded them with his palms, reveling in their buoyant perfection, in the delicious fit of them in his hands. Her nipples pearled between his fingers; he longed to taste them. Leaning down, he bent his head and captured one tight bud in his mouth, sampling the sugar sweetness of her flesh.

Zahirah let out a throaty, breathless gasp as he laved and suckled her. He felt her fingers weave into his hair, her hands fisting at the back of his head, her body trembling, breath rasping shallowly in the dark. Sebastian rejoiced in her pleasure, smiling against her skin as he moved from one breast to the other, intent on giving equal worship. He kissed his way there, drawing her nipple deep into his mouth and circling the sensitive peak with his tongue.

He meant to give her pleasure, to ready her for their mating, but it was his body that seemed to teeter on the verge of succumbing. His penis strained heavily between his legs, tight and throbbing to the point of pain, leaping with the need for contact, with the humbling need to sheathe itself within her womb. With a groan, he rocked back on his heels and reached for Zahirah's hand, disentangling it from the hair at his nape. Holding her by the wrist, he guided her down the length of his chest and across the bunched muscles of his abdomen, leading her with plain purpose to the root of his manhood. With her hand covered by his, he wrapped her fingers firmly around the width of his shaft and squeezed, encouraging her to stroke him.

"You're so hard," she whispered, sounding curious and awe-stricken as she explored the full length of him. "Like steel under velvet. You're beautiful, Sebastian."

He chuckled at her innocent praise, settling back to give her free rein of his body for however long he could bear it. Dropping his head back on his shoulders, he savored her roving touch, her artless palming of his wet, sensitive glans bringing him to the brink of an exquisite madness. Her fingers slick with his essence, she traced the underside of his member, wringing a shudder from out of his very core. Racked with a wave of pure male lust, every fiber of his body clenched taut as she stroked him.

"Come up on your knees," he growled, tugging at the waistband of her pantalets. She obeyed at once, holding on to his shoulders as he pulled the ties free and slid the loose-fitting trousers off her hips. He caressed the curve of her naked bottom, then came around and buried his fingers in the downy cleft of her thighs. She was beyond ready for him, her body weeping and quivering for what he would give her. He slipped inside that dewy haven, stroking its swollen folds and teasing the bud that nestled high within them.

Zahirah sighed as he made love to her with his fingers, and Sebastian caught her wordless exclamation in a soulful joining of their mouths. He pressed her down onto the bedroll, urgently removing the rest of her clothing as he covered her with his body. Her thighs fell open to him with only the slightest nudge of his knee; he positioned himself at their juncture, then he sheathed himself to the root in one deep stroke.

For a moment, the bliss of their joining was so complete, all he could do was hold himself there, not moving, scarcely breathing. Zahirah clung to him in like silence, her fingernails scoring his shoulders, her breath coming shallow and uneven beside his ear.

"Am I hurting you?" he whispered, his voice ragged, strained with the effort to remain still.

"No," she answered. "Oh, God, Sebastian. It feels so good."

"Yes," he agreed. He drew his pelvis back and thrust forward once more, cleaving her soft flesh with the rigidness of his own, filling her, feeling the crest of her womb rub against the head of his sex.

He rocked on his elbows, propping himself above her so that he could kiss her as he loved her, wishing he could watch the pleasure play on her face. He could see the outline of the table beside the pallet; the oil lamp and striking box should be nearly within his reach. Regretful that he did not think of it sooner, Sebastian paused to withdraw from Zahirah.

"What are you doing?"

"I want to see you." He gave her a kiss, then started to rise off of her. "It's all right. I'm just going to light the lamp."

"No!" She grabbed his arm, her fingers tightening around him in a grip that felt like panic. "I prefer the darkness," she said, calmer now, although he wondered at her strange reaction—a reaction she'd had in his room at the caravansary, too.

"There's no need to be shy with me," he told her gently, stroking the fingers that still clung to him in an urgent grasp. "Our bodies, and how we share them, is nothing to be ashamed of."

She made a sound of distress in the back of her throat. "Please, Sebastian. Come back, I beg you. Don't . . . don't spoil it."

He frowned in the gloom of the tent, part of him more determined than ever to light the lamp and get to the bottom of her apprehension. But he would not force her to it, not now, not when it was clear that she was terrified of the idea. "Very well," he said, returning to the pallet where she waited. "But we should talk about this, Zahirah. No more hiding, no more secrets between us, agreed?"

It seemed the only answer she would give him at that moment was the tender brush of her palm on his cheek. She circled her hand around the back of his neck and brought him down to kiss her, eager, it seemed, to resume their joining. His body was more than willing to oblige.

On his knees between her legs, he entered her again, bringing her hips up onto his thighs to meet the deep thrust of his penetration. He held her there, hooking his arms underneath her so that he set their pace, his muscles accepting the burden of her slight weight as he made love to her, guiding her at a gradually increasing rhythm along the hard length of his sex. She moaned with the first tremor of her release, her sheath convulsing around him.

"Ohh," she gasped, whispering his name, her mewling sigh of ecstasy like a siren's call, beckoning him to join her in the blissful tide.

Sebastian was not far behind her. Mindless with passion and the desire to please her further, to possess her fully, he lifted her higher and plunged deeper, his hips pumping, arms straining to hold her tighter, bring her closer. She was panting as urgently as he was, her body quaking, trembling. Then, with a sharp cry, she arched against him and shattered.

Sebastian gave a growl of prideful male triumph as her release washed over her in waves of breathless pleasure. Bending over her, he hastened his strokes, worshiping every inch of her slack, sweat-dampened body with his mouth, raining hot kisses on her breasts, her ribs, her belly. Her flesh throbbed and contracted around his pulsing shaft, coaxing him toward a swift, wrenching climax. He felt the coil of rapture build and wind tighter, clutching his core as if to twist him inside out.

He told himself to withdraw, feeling the tenuous bonds of his self-control stretch thinner with every greedy, glorious thrust of his hips. But then the liquid heat of release seized him. It rushed, molten and quicksilver, through his loins, and he knew he was lost. He roared with the stunning force of his ejaculation, plunging himself to the hilt and spilling his seed deep into Zahirah's womb.

"God's blood, woman," he swore in awe, once he was finally able to find his voice. He lay atop Zahirah and inside her, shuddering, each breath he dragged into his lungs shaky and uneven. She held him like an angel, caressing his back, her mouth pressed against his shoulder, kissing him sweetly.

He should have been wholly spent, dead and drained from exertion and the exquisite wringing of his body. He should have been beyond sated, but when Zahirah shifted slightly underneath him, her pelvis rocking against his as she moved to better bear his weight, he felt his arousal begin to stir anew. Before the beast could wake completely, he withdrew, rolling off her with a groan.

"What's wrong?" she asked. Following him on the pallet, she turned into his side and rested her hand on his chest. "Was it something I did?"

"Yes. You should have never let me touch you," he muttered, sounding a good deal more repentant than he felt. He gave her a serious look. "You realize, now you're going to have to put up with me chasing you into my bed every moment we're alone together."

She exhaled a soft laugh, her breath warm where it fanned his cooling skin. "What makes you think you will have to chase me, my lord?"

He stroked her bare arm, letting his fingers play in the silky tresses of her unbound hair while she rained a trail of kisses along his ribs. "Have a care, my lady, lest you spoil me. The king already suspects I've been living too well at Ascalon these past weeks. Indeed, at sup tonight he tried to imply I may be growing soft."

Zahirah gave an offended sounding cluck of her tongue. Her hand slid on a languorous, but purposeful, downward path. "Hmm," she purred against him, surprising him when her fingers brushed his turgid shaft. "No, my lord, not soft at all."

"Vixen," he accused, too weak to resist the urge to thrust himself into her palm. Her thumb flicked the sensitive crown of his manhood and he sucked in his breath for the sheer pleasure-pain of her inquisitive touch. "Do you not desist, you could very well tempt me into desertion of my cause. Worse for my pride, you'll have my bones so depleted of strength, I'll not be able to march on Jerusalem, now that the king has called me to it."

She stilled abruptly; for a moment, he could not even hear her breathing. "Jerusalem," she said at length, her voice rasping softly in the dark of the tent. "When will you go?"

"Not now," he said, "but soon."

He felt her withdraw into a thoughtful silence and cursed himself for reminding her of the prolonged conflict raging between their worlds—the very reason they had found each other in the first place. Two souls, born into enmity oceans apart and thrust together by the tides of war. Their differences did not seem so great a chasm to cross when they were lying in each other's arms, but Sebastian could not deny that he was, first and foremost, a soldier.

"I am sworn, Zahirah. I made a vow to God and my king that I would defend this cause. I have pledged my life to it."

"I know," she said. "I understand."

There was a note of weary acceptance in that statement, and for a moment he wondered if she truly did understand. Wondered how she could. He was sworn to his duty; when and where his king commanded him, he would go. Even if it took him leagues away from where his heart longed to be, with Zahirah. Even if it took him to his death.

"Come here," he said, when his thoughts and the growing silence between them became like a physical weight, too heavy to bear. He turned toward Zahirah and gathered her to him on the pallet, covering the intimate tangle of their bodies with the cocooning warmth of the blanket. "Close your eyes, my lady . . . tell me what you feel."

She snuggled into him, sighing deeply and nestling her cheek against his shoulder as he brought her farther within the circle of his embrace. "What do I feel? I feel the warmth of our bodies pressed together, naked and alive," she whispered, her limbs relaxing beneath the coverlet. "I feel your arms wrapped around me, so warm and strong, holding me tight. I feel our hearts beating in time with each other, and our legs entwined as if we were one."

"Yes," he agreed, kissing the top of her head. "In here,

like this, there is only us. There is no room for talk of war or duty where we are together like this. No room for anything but you and me, and the joy we can bring each other."

Her stillness troubled him, but no more than the trace of sadness in her soft-spoken reply. "Can you promise me that, my lord?"

Sebastian caught her chin on the edge of his hand and gently turned her face up to his. Bending to meet her, he brushed his mouth against hers, claiming her lips in a slow, sensual kiss that left them both breathless. "My lady," he said, "I have never given a more solemn oath."

Then he moved over her, and proceeded to demonstrate just how profound the depth of his promise truly was.

Chapter Twenty-one

Night had a way of muting the steel edge of reality, but dawn proved less forgiving than her benevolent sister. She called Sebastian away within moments of her rising, the first pale whispers of light summoning him out of Zahirah's arms and back to his role as officer to the English king. Lying on her side, wrapped in the blankets of the pallet they had shared, Zahirah watched him wash and dress and don his weapon, scorning the new day that had taken her lover and made him a soldier once again.

"I won't be too long," he said, buckling his wide leather sword belt over his knee-length tunic. "My conference with the king and his other officers should take but a few hours, then we can begin assembling for our return to Ascalon."

She offered him a weak smile, missing him already.

His hair was damp and glossy from his recent toilette; he raked the inky waves back from his brow, then strode over to her and knelt down beside the pallet. His touch on her cheek was gentle, his gaze intense, loving. "Stay near the tent until I come back," he instructed her. "If you need anything before then, Joscelin is here. He will assist you." He leaned forward and kissed her. "Last night was amazing. You, my lady, are amazing."

Zahirah blushed at his praise, her belly fluttering from the satin caress of his mouth and the remembrance of the passion they had shared just a few hours ago. Her body was spent, but her hunger for him seemed without end. She twined her fingers through his, bringing his hand to her mouth and brushing his hard, battle-scarred knuckles

against the pads of her lips. "Must you go now?" she asked,
holding his gaze as she dragged her mouth over his skin and
licked her tongue into the crevice between his fingers. "I
wish we could blink and be back at Ascalon this very moment . . . back in your bed."

"Tonight," he growled, his eyes darkening as he watched
her tease him. Finally, with a groan, he curled his fist around
her hand and pulled her to him, savaging her mouth in a kiss
that left her dizzy and trembling with desire. He drew back,
his eyes like ocean pools: stormy, fathomless. "Tonight, my
amazing, wicked lady."

She did not try to hold him longer when he released her
hand and got to his feet. She relinquished him to his king
and his duties, tossing herself onto her back on the pallet
and staring up at the shadowed rise of the tent ceiling as the
scuff of Sebastian's long strides outside faded away into
the coming morn. Her ablutions and prayers awaited; using
the pitcher of water Sebastian had left her, she bathed, then
dressed and knelt toward the direction of Mecca as she re-
cited the first of her five daily praises for God.

Sebastian still had not returned by the time she had knelt
for her third prayer that day. Impatient with the waiting and
inactivity, Zahirah got up and quit the tent. Joscelin was
posted just outside, sitting on a stool and polishing a tunic
of chain mail, his mop of blond hair slung low over his forehead, his boyish face screwed in concentration. He looked
up with a start as she emerged from the tent.

"Apologies, milady. I did not hear you call for me. Is there
aught you need?"

She shook her head. "I did not call you, Joscelin. I am
merely tired of sitting inside doing nothing. I had hoped my
lord Sebastian would have returned by now. Have you seen
him?"

"Aye, milady. When last I passed the king's pavilion, he
and the other officers were yet in conference."

Zahirah grunted in disappointment, loath to contem-
plate any further hours of boredom spent in the lonely
gloom of the tent behind her. Indeed, she could not abide

the thought. Excusing herself to find the privy, she took a leisurely stroll through the back fringes of the encampment.

In the adjacent plain, the lesser officers were taking the army through battle drills and exercises. At one end of the field, two groups of mounted soldiers were forming for a mock charge. Their horses stamped and whinnied, churning up a fog of yellow dust that snagged on the thin morning breeze and sped across the sandy space of land. Zahirah leaned against an outcrop of jutting rock, pausing to watch the start of the skirmish, waiting with breathless anticipation as the companies prepared for the charge.

Sebastian's wild Scottish friend was positioned at the head of the right guard, a position that would put him first in line of attack. On his order, the two groups of opposing soldiers lunged into action. Mounted astride his brown destrier, garbed as the others in full chain armor and steel helm, Logan brandished a long, blunted lance, shouting orders to his men while he held off three enemy knights with the flat of his shield. With his head turned to watch his flagging rear guard, he did not see the man who rode up fast on his blind side.

Zahirah gasped when the Scot took the unexpected blow on his left shoulder. He lurched in his saddle, then righted himself with a roar, wheeling the beast around with the power of his thighs alone before bearing down on the soldier who struck him. In war, the offending knight would have been hacked in two; here, in training, a cuff to his helm marked him as a casualty and took him out of the game.

"It is called the melee," boomed a richly schooled Frankish voice from behind her.

Zahirah jerked her head around, unable to mask her surprise at finding the King of England himself striding toward her, his fair head uncovered and glowing like a burnished crown in the morning sun, his hands clasped elegantly behind his back as if to frame the trio of yellow lions that emblazoned the front of his red silk surcoat. A jewel-studded weapon belt winked at his waist, not to be outdone by his fine leather boots and golden spurs, which gleamed in defi-

nce of the dust that swirled and eddied around them as he
alked.

At his approach, Zahirah scrambled away from her seat
n the rock, worrying her hands in the loose fabric of her
halwar as she stood to face him. She could not force herself
nto a false show of deference for the reviled Frankish king,
ut neither could she hold his piercing blue gaze as he came
p next to her.

"Excellent! Excellent, men!" he shouted to his soldiers on
he plain, his lauds and hearty applause earning him low
ows from all, and murmurs of salute from Logan and his
nen, who had emerged the victors of the mock skirmish.
Zahirah felt the questioning stare of Sebastian's friend light
n her from across the field and, knowing how it must ap-
ear, she tried not to squirm.

"If you will please excuse me, I imagine you would prefer
o observe your men in private," she said to the king, trying
o sound casual and polite as she took the first step toward
er escape.

"On the contrary," he replied, bracing his legs apart and
ubtly blocking her path. "I would never refuse the com-
any of a beautiful woman." He flashed a disingenuous
mile. "Stay. I insist."

Cornered, she slowly backed away and took her seat once
nore on the jut of rock. For a long while, neither she nor the
ing spoke, both of them sitting in awkward silence, waiting
or the army to regroup on the field to commence with an-
ther melee. More than once Zahirah ventured a hopeful
lance over her shoulder, hoping to see Sebastian swagger-
ng over to rescue her. Each time, her hopes met with disap-
ointment.

"If you are worried about where Montborne is," said the
ing, "he's still in conference with my advisors. Evidently, a
ew of them seem to think my health has been compromised
f late. I disagree, of course, but all morning they have been
rying to convince me that I should return to Ascalon and
ake some rest before I continue on in this campaign." He
urned his head to stare at her then, appraising her with an

unblinking, appreciative gaze. Lust glittered in his eyes
"What do you think?"

Stunned by his question and his sudden encroaching
nearness, Zahirah swallowed hard. "W-what do I think?"

He pinned her with his sharp, predatory stare. "Would
you like me to return to Ascalon, lady?" he asked, not
flinching in the slightest for the brashness of his overture
His smile, when she did not immediately answer, was arro
gantly royal as he leaned into her, crowding her with the
broad spread of his shoulders and chest. He reached out
and confidently traced his bejeweled finger along the curve
of her upper arm, the gesture just brief enough to escape
undue notice, yet blatant enough for Zahirah to understand
its intimation. She drew away from his unwanted attention
bristling when he chuckled low under his breath at her re
treat.

"That was quite a display in my feast hall last eve," he re
marked, his gaze turned back to the practice field as the men
charged into another bout of fighting. "You know, I have
seen days where Montborne has slain a score of infidel sol
diers as cool as you please, but never have I seen him so vir
ulently enflamed—leastwise against one of his own."

"What happened last night was my fault," Zahirah
blurted, hoping to curb some of the king's displeasure from
the night before. "My lord thought I was in danger. He only
sought to protect me."

The king's brows rose slightly on his forehead, the only
indication he gave that he was actually hearing her. "When
a woman stirs that kind of passion in a man," he said
thoughtfully, "well, it does something to those who would
look upon it. It makes them curious." He pivoted his tawny-
bearded chin, turning a wolfish look on her. "That kind of
passion makes a man—even a man who is king—want to
know what it is that woman possesses that makes her worth
killing for."

Zahirah's every nerve went taut as Lionheart's words
sunk into her brain. In the awkward moment that followed,
when all she could see was the leering smile and red-and-

old wall that was the enemy king, when all she could hear
as the pounding of her heart and the din of combat rolling
ff the plain, Zahirah felt the years of her own battle train-
ng begin to whisper to her of strategies and opportunity.

Right here, in the bald light of day, before the whole of
is army just scant yards away, the king was inviting her to
is bed. The idea sat in her belly like a stone when she
nought of Sebastian's loyalty to this man, his willingness to
ledge his life in service to a lord who would so easily betray
im. But as appalled as she was, part of her—a colder part
f her, bred to make use of any advantage if it furthered her
nission—saw the providence here. That part of her warned
nis might be her best chance, her only chance, to fulfill her
romise to her clan.

"You needn't fear Montborne finding out," she heard the
ing say distantly. "Arrangements can be made . . . a mission
o one of the coastal forts, perhaps. A few days on march. I
rill leave that to you to decide."

But Zahirah was no longer listening to what he was
elling her. Her mind was speeding ahead, calculating her
ptions, factoring in the pleasant convenience that the king
ras sitting nearly shoulder to shoulder with her in that mo-
nent, unguarded, his dagger easily within her reach on his
weled baldric. Surreptitiously, without moving even to
raw breath, she slid her gaze to the golden handle of his
lade; she could almost feel the press of its elaborately
arved grip in her palm. One quick lunge and she could have
. One heartbeat more and she could drive the knife home.

The soldiers on the practice field were too far away to
top her. She would never escape them all, but in the time it
rould take the guards to realize what she was about, it
rould be much too late to save their king. They would be
hocked dumb at first. They would kill her, certainly.

She would never see Sebastian again. . . .

Zahirah tried to thrust aside that miserable truth, forcing
er thoughts around what she had been sent there to do—
he mission that would liberate her homeland and fulfill her
lestiny as daughter to Rashid al-Din Sinan. How Sebastian

would hate her when he learned the ugly truth. She tried to tell herself that her heart had no right to lament the inevitable loss of his love; it was never hers to claim. She tried to will herself to act, to seize this opportunity and see it through to its fruition—no matter the consequences. Sitting there in utter stillness, every muscle coiled to pounce, she was not a hairsbreadth away from flying at the king and ending his life as she was sworn to do.

But she could not do it.

Allah forgive her, but if she wondered before, she knew it without doubt now. When she thought of losing Sebastian, losing his love through this act of treachery, she realized that the cost of her pledge had become too great. Sebastian's trust, though she did not yet deserve it, was a gift too precious to forsake.

She understood, in this moment of ultimate inaction, that she was now less *fida'i* than she was simply woman.

Her stomach pitched at the enormity of what she was admitting. She braced her hands on the rough surface of the rock beneath her, clinging for balance while her world tilted on its axis. The king was saying something; she could not hear him. She felt his hand clamp onto her wrist and she jumped, wild-eyed, yanking herself out of his grasp. She leaped to her feet, scarcely registering the king's look of confusion and mild amusement as she backed away from him.

"Don't touch me," she heard herself say, her voice coming to her ears as if in a vacuous tunnel while she edged toward flight. "Don't come near me again."

She did not wait for the king's leave. Heart hammering, breath hitching, she ran for the safety of Sebastian's tent. To her relief, he was there, just arrived from his meeting with the other officers. Zahirah had never seen a more welcome sight. She went to him at once, throwing herself into his waiting arms.

"Where were you?" he asked, enveloping her in his steadying embrace. "You're trembling like a leaf. What's wrong?"

"N-nothing," she stammered, trying to sound unruffled and failing somewhat. "I missed you, that's all. I'm glad you're here."

She could tell from his silence that he did not entirely believe her, but he held her tight nonetheless, keeping near her for the rest of that day and for all of the journey back to Ascalon that night. A journey they made, to her great discomfort, in the watchful company of several dozen Frankish knights and their returning king.

Chapter Twenty-two

Zahirah was having a bad dream. Nay, it was worse than that, another savage nightmare, Sebastian realized as he held her restless, trembling body in his bed at the Ascalon palace. She had been exhausted from the eight hours of travel, dozing off and on atop her mount, until finally Sebastian had taken her onto his destrier to ride with him. She had slept fitfully then, too.

Something had been troubling her since Darum, although she seemed determined to keep it from him. Having observed the king's keen sidelong looks at her on the road, Sebastian hardly needed to guess at what caused her distress. Richard had his eye on her. Sebastian bristled at the notion. He had been too long on the battlefield with his king; he knew how relentless—how single-minded— Lionheart could be when he set his sights on something he wanted. But where he did not fully trust his king, he trusted Zahirah. As he knew she trusted him when he promised he would protect her.

He felt the weight of that pledge now, when she lay like a helpless babe in his arms, thrashing and fighting an enemy he could not see. She murmured something in Arabic, muffled, indiscernible words. She moaned, breathing quick and uneven, her lungs laboring as if they might burst. Sebastian tried to calm her, but she was too far gone, too lost to the demons that seemed to hunt her in her sleep.

"Noo," she sobbed brokenly. "No, not her . . . not my Gillianne . . ."

God's blood, but here it was again, that English name

Zahirah had called out before in her sleep. The name she claimed meant nothing to her.

Gillianne.

Although he wondered what more she might reveal if he let her play the nightmare out to its end, Sebastian could stand her suffering no longer. "Zahirah," he said, smoothing a web of hair from her damp brow. "Zahirah, it's all right. It's just a dream." He touched her shoulder, and gave her a small shake. "Wake up now, my love. You're safe."

"Noo," she cried, still engulfed in the shade of terror. She kicked at him beneath the coverlet, violent and bucking, scratching at his arm that still held her around the waist. Her voice climbed to a shrill, strangled gasp. "Oh, God, no. Let me go! Let me go!"

She threw off his hand and vaulted from the bed in a panic, abruptly jolted awake. Wild-eyed, her hand shaking at her mouth, she gave Sebastian a look of pure anguish before her bare feet carried her swiftly to the open doors of the balcony. She gripped the railing and sucked in great gasps of the predawn air, her petite frame quaking, setting the cuffed pant legs of her dark blue trousers trembling with the aftershocks of a deep, terrible fear.

For a long moment, Sebastian could only stare after her, sitting naked on the edge of the bed. His arm burned where her nails had raked his skin; his legs would bear a score of bruises from her punishing heels. She had fought him like a wild animal, crazed and mindless in her fright. Like a tigress trying to claw her way out of a hunter's snare.

And now she stood across the room from him in shuddering silence, haloed like one of heaven's own angels by the pink-gold hues of the newly rising sun. She had never looked so fragile, or innocent, and Sebastian had never known a love stronger than that which he felt for her now.

He got up off the bed and slowly drew up behind her. She gave a ragged sigh as he wrapped his arms around her. She was cold, her clothing made damp from her distress. She did not withdraw from him, but it pained him to feel how very still she held herself within the circle of his arms, waiting, it seemed, perhaps uncertain of what she should expect from him in that moment.

Sebastian scarcely knew himself. He held her without speaking, listening to the fluttering beat of her heart, his own thudding hard at her back. He felt a tear splash onto his wrist and he pressed a kiss to the top of her head.

"I can't let you go on like this," he whispered, not wanting to distress her any more than she was already, yet needing to know what haunted her. "We need to talk about this, Zahirah. All of it, here and now. You have to tell me who Gillianne is. You have to tell me what that name means to you, why the mention of it should terrify you so."

She swallowed thickly, and Sebastian felt her head shake slightly beneath his chin. "I can't."

He turned her around to face him. Her cheeks were ruddy and streaked with tears, her pale silver eyes shimmering and ghostly with unspoken pain. He scowled to see that pain, to know that she would not share it with him and let him help her through it. "Without honesty between us, Zahirah, we have nothing. You must know that."

She tipped her head down, unable, or perhaps unwilling, to look at him. "I would tell you if I knew . . . if I thought it mattered—"

"It matters to me," he cut in, not allowing her to dodge the subject. "It matters to me that you wake up some nights drenched and shaking, that you are plagued by something so awful you cannot bear to speak of it." She let out a sob and he grabbed her chin, forcing her to meet his gaze. "It matters to me, Zahirah. We have an agreement. No secrets, remember?"

Her mouth quivered uncontrollably. "You don't understand. You couldn't possibly understand what it's like—"

"I want to, damn it," he ground out, unable to curb the harshness of his voice. "God's blood, lady, I need you to make me understand."

"Sebastian . . ." She shook her head, twisting her arm against his hold. Desperation swam in her eyes. "Please, Sebastian . . ."

He gripped her tighter, probably bruising her. He wanted answers, needed them, but he could see he was getting nowhere. He swore a gruff oath and released her. "You're shivering cold in those damp clothes. Take them off and let's get you into something warm."

He waited for her to oblige, but she did not so much as budge. Quite the contrary, she wrapped her arms around herself a little tighter, a protective stance that spoke as plainly as a flat refusal. Sebastian scowled, suspicious. "Your tunic and *shalwar*, my lady. Take them off."

She shrank back from him, her face pinched with distress and a dread that lanced him as sure as any blade. She shook her head. She would not look at him, but he could tell that she had begun to cry once more.

"Oh, yes, I forgot," he growled, sounding every bit as savage as she was making him feel. "I am only permitted to see you—to love you—in the dark. Well, that's not enough, Zahirah. I need more than that." He leveled a fierce glower on her. "From now on, if there is to be anything between us, we will share the daylight and the dark, my lady. No more hiding. Now, take off those clothes."

For a maddening space of time, she merely stood there. Silent. Still. Even her tears ceased to flow. Then, slowly, while Sebastian's heart slammed heavily against his ribs, Zahirah brought her hands up to the neckline of her tunic and began to untie the laces that held the garment together.

It was hard to watch her obey him, hard to abide knowing he had pushed her into this wordless, damning compliance, but he forced himself not to flinch, not to sway. Not this time.

It was nearly impossible to hold her defeated, yet calmly defiant gaze, as she gathered up the hem of the tunic and peeled it up over her head, baring herself to him, just as he had commanded. She held her arm out and slowly released the long silk shirt from her fingers, letting it fall next to her on the floor. Her trousers followed a moment later; the waistband slackened, she slid the pantalets over her hips and left the fabric to crush in an indigo pool at her feet.

Sebastian's breath leaked out of him in a harsh sigh as he looked upon his lover's naked body for what was truly the first time. "Jesus Christ," he swore, staring at her in stunned disbelief.

Beneath her clothing, beneath the honey-brown color of her skin—a color that faded away in a gradual band at her breasts and across the downy triangle of her pelvis— Zahirah was as creamy white as the finest pearl.

As white as the fairest Englishwoman in any king's court.

So, now he knew, Zahirah thought, miserable as she stood before him, watching him gape at her like the freak she knew herself to be. Now he saw her disease, the thing that ate at her heart, at her soul. The sickness that set her apart from her countrymen and her clan. The secret, which, until this very moment, only she and Allah shared.

"Zahirah," Sebastian said, "what is the meaning of this?"

She glanced down, ashamed. "I have been asking God that very question all my life."

"This must have something to do with your night-mares. Perhaps it explains your connection to the name Gillianne."

"No," she said, desperate to deny the suggestion. "No, it can't have anything to do with this. My dreams are just that, dreams. They don't explain anything. They're not real."

"The fear they bring you is real enough. I think they would explain much, if you would only listen to them."

She thought about the anguish and violence of her night terrors, the hideous screaming, the feeling of helplessness and loss. If they held an explanation to anything in her life, she did not want it. She did not think she could bear that cold a truth.

"What about your mother?" Sebastian asked, his voice pulling her out of her dark musings.

"I never knew my mother," Zahirah answered. "She died when I was a babe."

"Was she English? Could your mother have been Gillianne?"

Zahirah gave a sharp shake of her head. "No."

"Why not?"

"Because you don't know my father. He is—" She broke off abruptly, wary of treading down a dangerous path from which there would be no return. "My father is a devout man. He would never taint his blood by taking an Englishwoman to his bed."

"Then how do you explain it, my lady?" He paused, intensely watching her expression, as if he searched for gentle words but could not find them. "Zahirah, it is obvious. Your pale eyes, your fair skin. My lady, you are not Arab."

"Yes, I am," she replied, the shrill forcefulness of her avowal betraying her defensiveness, her rising panic, at his challenge.

It was a charge she herself had never dared whisper, not even when she was banished in punishment to the dank cell at Masyaf, a space so deep and dark within the bowels of the fortress that no one could have heard her, even had she screamed it. She had never dared speak the question aloud, not to her father certainly. Not to anyone.

But she had thought it.

She had thought it every time she bared her skin to the sun's rays, begging Allah to heal her. She had thought it in the throes of the nightmare that woke her in this very room just a few moments before. She had always been able to push the question aside, denying it by example of her devotion— her willing sacrifice—to her father and her clan, but hearing Sebastian voice it now stirred a fear in her so profound it nearly robbed her of breath.

"I am Arab," she whispered fiercely, needing to believe it. "I am Arab in every way it matters: my heart, my soul. My convictions." To her dismay, a sob wrenched up from her constricted throat. "Don't you see? This life is all I know. It's all I have."

"No." Sebastian stepped toward her, reaching out to take her hand. "Not all, my lady. Only if you choose it to be so."

Zahirah looked up into his serious, steady gaze as he closed his fingers around hers and slowly brought her into his embrace. His chest was warm and solid against her naked breasts, the crisp mat of hair rasping against her nipples. He traced the line of her jaw, her chin, his eyes caressing her as sweetly as his touch.

He bent his head down and kissed her mouth. "I love you," he whispered, his lips brushing hers. "I don't care if you're brown or white. I don't care if you're English, Arab, half of each, or not of this world at all. I love you, Zahirah."

She squeezed her eyes shut against the flood of relief and sorrow and pure shattering joy that swept her upon hearing those precious words. That he could mean them, that his acceptance of her could be so genuine, so complete, humbled her as greatly as it elated her. She had never heard those words before, never felt this love. Never knew how keenly she had needed it until now.

Tears burned behind her eyelids and in her throat. "Oh, Sebastian . . . I'm so scared."

"Don't be," he told her. "You don't have to be scared, my lady. Not anymore."

He lowered himself before her, taking her breasts into his hands, into his mouth, kissing the variegation of her skin, worshiping the places where she was neither tan nor pale. He knelt at her feet, there, in front of God and the unblinking eye of the rising sun, and he learned every inch of her body, bringing all of her passion, all of her pleasure, into the light.

And then, as she splintered apart in a wave of trembling, perfect rapture, he pulled her down atop him on the carpeted floor, and he loved her further, showing her an ecstasy that would never again abide the smothering pall of the dark.

Chapter Twenty-three

For better than a week, all the time they had been back at Ascalon, Zahirah knew the boundless warmth and light of Sebastian's love. It was a wondrous thing he gave her, a freedom of feeling that seemed to lift her very soul heavenward. It was joy just to look upon him and think that he was hers; bliss to know the wonder of his regard, his touch . . . the sensual skill of his glorious body. And when he was gone, doing work for his king in the city or beyond its sheltering walls, she missed him with a keenness that surpassed anguish.

That morning, he had left the palace to oversee more repair work on the city walls. By noontide Zahirah was mad to see him, the empty space of the chamber they shared closing in on her and making her yearn to be outdoors. She would bring Sebastian a picnic, she decided, eager to surprise him with an excursion to one of Ascalon's garden parks. With a meal and a blanket and a board for playing *shatranj* bobbing along in the basket on her arm, she quit the palace. The knights on watch at the outer gate had come to know her as their captain's lady; they let her pass unmet to head into the bustle of the city.

Beyond those guarded palace gates, the streets and market teemed with a new day's commerce: tightfisted Muslims and Christians haggled over goods with squawking vendors; soldiers and peasants strolled the alleyways and loitered about the common square, each group eyeing the other warily, while a pack of dirty, laughing children and two yapping dogs raced hither and yon, oblivious to all but the merriment of their game.

Zahirah saw a Muslim holy man heading for the mosque, his fine white robes looking crisp and pristine among the filth and dust of the city, and she realized with a jolt of surprise that this was Friday, the Sabbath. How could she have forgotten? A group of veiled women huddled in a knot near a fountain at the end of the main artery through town, whispering amongst themselves while they waited for the prayer call that would summon them to *jumah*. Zahirah passed them with her gaze averted, telling herself she should not feel ashamed that on this holy day she was going instead, bare-faced and eager, to break fast with her Christian lover.

She spied him but a moment later, there, at the far end of the street where the brick in the soaring city wall was still damp with new mortar. He stood on scaffolding at the top of that high perimeter, talking with a mason, his legs braced apart, balancing him as easily as a great cat on a bough. His tunic was tied about his head like a *kufiyya* to shield him from the heat of the sun; the tail of the shirt hung down past his neck and huge bronzed shoulders, the edges of its hem lifting in the thready breeze. He gave an order to someone on the ground, then glanced out and saw her approaching from up the street. Zahirah felt his welcoming gaze reach out to her across the distance, and her heart skipped a beat.

Beaming, she sent him a wave of greeting. He said something to the mason, then clapped him on the arm and turned to descend the ladder. Zahirah did not even try to bite back her giggle of excitement as she watched him jump the last few rungs to the ground, disappearing into the thick crowd of folk that stood between them on the avenue. She took a quick step forward, about to rush on to the end of the street to meet him, when someone suddenly stepped into her path.

"Oh!" she cried, drawing up short to avoid a collision with the hunched, slim form of a beggarly old man. "My apologies, sir. I did not see you—"

The graybeard lifted his hooded head and Zahirah's gaze locked with a pair of chilling black eyes. Those knowing eyes stared hard at her, narrowed in something that went deeper than mere disapproval. She felt all the blood drain from her face. Her picnic basket hung on her arm like a weight of a hundred stones.

"Father," she gasped, scarcely recognizing the reclusive King of the Assassins for the unexpectedness of his presence there in public and his ragged commoner's disguise. "W-what are you doing here?"

"Come to ask you much the same, *daughter*." Sinan leaned heavily on the word, his calm voice sounding infinitely more lethal to her than would the loudest bellow. "I have been hearing nothing but disappointing news, Zahirah. News of unsuccessful attacks and delays, a score of my best men dead . . . these failures concern me greatly. Now it is my understanding that the Frankish king is here, with you, in Ascalon—here for a week or more, from what I have gathered. Yet still Lionheart lives."

In the periphery of the milling crowd, Zahirah saw three of her father's *fida'i* bodyguards. They were dressed to blend in, but she knew their faces, and she knew each of them would be as well armed as Sinan most certainly was beneath his pilgrim's rags. Like hounds, they watched her, hanging at the ready and waiting for their master's command. From the feral looks in their eyes, she had no doubt that any one of them would be happy to tear out her throat. She swallowed down a knot of stark cold fear. "Father, I can explain—"

"I'm not interested in explanations," he cut in sharply, although his tone retained its deceptive calm. "I am interested in action. Swift action, Zahirah. I am tired of waiting."

"Yes, Father. Of course, I understand."

"Do you?"

Zahirah nodded, but her attention was suddenly drawn elsewhere. Amid the hubbub and shuffle of the busy street, she heard Sebastian's voice, heard its deep masculine rumble as he greeted someone in Arabic. He was likely halfway through the crowd, drawing nearer by the moment. She did not dare venture a glance in his direction, fearing her father would scent her worry. Too late, she realized, nothing escaped the notice of the almighty Old Man.

"The Frankish captain seems quite taken with you." Sinan's thin lips flattened. "Oh, yes, daughter. I've been watching. Is he the reason you have not yet fulfilled your mission?"

"No," she denied in a rush. Then, with forced casualness, "No. There have been complications to my plan, that is all. He has nothing to do with it."

Masyaf's Old Man grunted, and slid a look to one of his hovering guards. "Perhaps I would be a better judge of that."

"W-what do you mean?" she asked, but there was a sinking feeling in the pit of her stomach that warned of her father's intentions.

He would have Sebastian killed—right there, in the middle of a crowded street, if he thought the captain a threat to his goal. Sebastian would never see the daggers coming. And at this very moment, Zahirah was leading him directly into the trap.

"Please, Father," she whispered, desperation making her reach out to take ahold of Sinan's vein-riddled leathery hand. She gripped the lean fingers that would not respond to her touch. "Please . . . I beg you. Don't."

"You have a task to carry out, Zahirah."

"And I will," she said, praying he would believe her, recommitting herself to her mission. "I have not forgotten my pledge."

"I am glad to hear it," said Sinan. "You have two days."

"Two days," she gasped. "But that won't possibly be enough time—"

"Two days, Zahirah. And do not fail, or your Frankish lover dies."

"I will do it," she vowed, sick with the blood promise that stood to cost her so much. "I will not fail you, Father. But please, swear to me you won't do anything to him."

Stoic and inflexible, he would give her no answer, and there was no time for further entreaty.

Shrugging into his tunic, Sebastian stepped around a passerby and gave Zahirah a warm smile. Then his eyes flicked to Sinan and he paused, his easiness replaced with a look of mild suspicion. "Is anything amiss here, my lady?"

"N-no," she replied, shaking her head in quick denial. She released her father's hand and went to Sebastian's side. Her smile felt pasted on and tight; her lie seemed cemented to the roof of her mouth. "I'm afraid I was not looking where I was going, and carelessly I bumped into this gentleman. I was just offering him my apologies."

Sebastian's chin went up a notch in acceptance of her explanation. He looked once more to her father, who stood in watchful silence, holding himself as still as a viper waiting to strike. "Well, I'm sure he pardons you of any offense," Sebastian said in their tongue. With a studying glance, he took in Sinan's rumpled clothing and gaunt features. "Are you hungry? We have food. Zahirah, what have you got in your basket for this man to eat, my love?"

She winced inwardly at the endearment, feeling her father's condemning eyes fix on her like a slew of poison-tipped daggers. Nervously, she stuck her hand inside the basket and fumbled around for something—anything—to give him. Her fingers closed around a velvety peach and she jerked it out, bruising the tender skin and almost dropping it in her state of near hysteria. She held the fruit out to Sinan, willing her hand not to tremble as he took it from her and offered her a fractional nod of thanks.

Sebastian added a large round copper to the gift, retrieving the coin from a pouch on his baldric and placing it in Sinan's palm. "Peace be upon you," he said. "Go with God."

Though the Arabic blessing was customarily polite, it contained an undercurrent of dismissal that would not sit well with Masyaf's assassin king. Unable to speak, unable to so much as breathe, Zahirah stared at her father while he absorbed the situation. She could almost hear the wheels grinding and turning in his head as he evaluated Sebastian, his gaze as emotionally vacant as a vat of the blackest pitch.

Slowly, his fingers closed around the coin. Then, with a meaningful glance toward Zahirah, he simply turned away and left them, becoming just another faceless figure on the wide avenue, trundling along in a sea of the same.

"This is a pleasant surprise."

Zahirah startled at the sound of Sebastian's voice beside her ear. He kissed her cheek and took the basket from her arm. Her pulse was racing. Willing it to slow, she returned his smile, praying her fear of the moment before would not be evident in her expression. "I'm glad you're pleased. I thought you might welcome a break from your work."

"Indeed, I would," he said. "Shall we find a place to sit and enjoy this meal you've brought me? Perhaps there will be a spot of shade in one of the parks."

Although it had been her plan when she set out from the palace, suddenly the thought of sitting in a busy city garden held little appeal. Nor did she think she could force down one bite of food so long as her stomach was churning with worry over her father's deadly ultimatum. But as distressed as she was about the prospect of being forced to fulfill her mission with the king, she could not afford to let Sebastian know that anything was wrong.

To chance that he might suspect something now, when her father and his bodyguards lingered around the city like ghosts, would be to place his very life in jeopardy. She had to keep him unawares; now more than ever, the totality of her deception would be paramount.

"Yes," she said. "The park will be lovely."

Linking her arm through his and holding on to him perhaps a little tighter than she should have, Zahirah walked with Sebastian to an unoccupied pocket of lawn in a park that overlooked Ascalon's shore. There, some near dozen ancient Roman pillars stood among tall cypress and palm trees, creating a strange, sparse forest of stone and wood that shaded the edge of the silvery dune and framed the sun-dappled gem green water that tossed and rippled beyond. Children's voices carried up from the beach on the breeze, their laughter and shouts of mock battle joining with the calls of sea terns that wheeled overhead, looking for charity from the folk who had come to rest and refresh at the park. Somewhere not far was a lemon grove; the citrus fragrance twined pleasingly with the perfumes of myriad spices wafting in from a merchant galley docked at the harbor.

God had given them a perfect day, but Zahirah found it difficult to appreciate any of the peace and beauty surrounding her. There was only Sebastian, the enemy she had come to love. There was only this man, a noble man who had given meaning to the words honor and acceptance.

And now, suddenly, there was only this moment and the precious few that remained between here and the time she would be forced to betray him. Two days. So little time.

Sebastian was looking at her as she knelt in the grass and unpacked the basket. She handed him the blanket, returning his smile when their fingers brushed and lingered for a heartbeat. While he unfurled the large square of cotton and spread it on the ground, Zahirah set out their meal. She had brought them a round of flatbread and some cheese and wine. There was fruit in the basket as well—less one peach for the token she had been made to give her father. But she would not let him invade this moment any further.

Pushing aside all thoughts of Sinan and the unpleasant business that awaited her, Zahirah broke the bread and offered a chunk to Sebastian as he took his place beside her on the ground. He must have been hungry, for he made quick work of his meal, eating like a ravenous youth still growing into his bones. It was pleasure to watch him at the simplest things, and she knew this day would be burned into her memory for all eternity. She wanted to wring everything from it, to make the day last, and so, despite that she was in no state to concentrate on strategy or diversion, when Sebastian found the *shatranj* board in the basket and offered her a game, Zahirah agreed.

Happily, she watched him set up the board, admiring the agility of his strong fingers as he placed each piece in position in its proper-colored square. "Ladies first," he said, when the last pawn had been set in its spot. He propped himself on his bent elbow, stretching out to recline on the blanket, his long legs extended, big leather boots crossed at the ankle.

Zahirah glanced at the new game and bypassed her vanguard of pedestrian white pawns with nary a hesitation, instead moving the horse-shaped *faras* into play.

"Feeling a bit ruthless today, are you, my lady?"

She laughed at his jest, though in truth she felt anything but ruthless. His gaze on hers in challenge, he moved a black pawn and the dance of mock war began on the board. It went back and forth for some time, an equal match; they had been playing often, and Sebastian had a natural skill for the game—a skill that had come into its own when they played in the privacy of his chamber as he preferred, where the cost of each lost piece meant the surrender of a kiss, as determined by the victor. Zahirah blushed, thinking on the many games she had lost to him in the past week, some not entirely accidental.

"I am loath to intrude on whatever it is that has you smiling so prettily, but it seems you have left your *ruhk* wide open." He slid one of his pieces onto the square and neatly captured hers. His smile was dazzling. "Sorry, my love."

"Hah! As sorry as a falcon on a mouse," she replied with arch humor, giving him a suitably offended glare. She sized up the board with a shrewd glance, then moved her *faras* deeper into his ranks, getting a minor revenge on an unsuspecting pawn.

Sebastian's eyes were on her as she collected his lost man and set him aside; she felt their heat, felt the potent male interest in his gaze as surely as she felt the sun, warming her skin through the silk of her clothes. He reached out then, taking her hand in his and bringing it to his lips. His kiss sent a tingle of desire through her, but she could not keep from nervously glancing around, could not keep from withdrawing her hand when her gaze lit on the inquisitive and mildly disapproving stares of a group of Muslim matrons.

"Let them stare," he said, as she averted her eyes, embarrassed, and sat back on her heels. "In England, it would not be improper for a gentleman to kiss his lady's hand in a public park."

Zahirah felt a smile tug at the corner of her mouth. "In England, you also eat off the ends of your knives and dance around bonfires like moonstruck wild animals."

Sebastian let out a bark of rich laughter. "We are not entirely lacking sophistication, my lady. We have manners of our own, much like here, and we have parks and pleasure gardens and places of higher learning. I wish I could show you. You'd like England, I think."

How easy it was to forget he had another life, a privileged life far away from the scorching deserts and forbidding mountain crags she called home. That life of castles and court and loving kin awaited him, and she should not feel sorrow at the prospect that he would one day go back to it. "I'm sure it's beautiful," she said, somewhat wistfully. "You must be eager to return."

"Oh, not so eager, my lady." He gave a nonchalant shrug, but there was an intensity to his gaze when he looked over at her. "England has much to recommend it, but it doesn't have *shatranj*."

Zahirah smiled. "A problem easily remedied. In the souk just the other day, I saw a merchant selling a fine board with carved ivory pieces—"

"It doesn't have you."

At first, she did not think she heard aright. She sat frozen, unable to do more than stare at his serious expression, her heart squeezing as though caught in a vise. "Me? My lord, I . . ."

"Come with me," he said when her voice drifted off and abandoned her. "When this war is over, should God will that I survive, I want to take you with me back to England. Back to my home at Montborne."

Stunned, humbled, miserable with all that he was offering her—with what she could not possibly accept—Zahirah felt her head shaking slowly back and forth. She wrapped her arms around her waist where a steel-cold knot had begun to settle. "Sebastian, I . . . I don't know what to say."

"Say you'll come with me." He put his hand out and gently turned her face back to him. "Say you'll spare my pride and think about it, at least."

Zahirah smiled despite the cumbersome weight of her heart. "Oh, Sebastian," she whispered, "you have no idea what it means to me that you would ask. That you would think so much of me—"

"I think the world of you, my lady. I ask because I love you."

"And I love you," she said, her throat thick with emotion. "I love you, Sebastian . . . so much."

"Well, that's a good enough start," he replied, grinning. He leaned in and kissed her.

Zahirah closed her eyes, wishing for things she would never have, things she would never know. For a moment, while she was kissing him, feeling his arms around her, she could almost believe that she might one day know another life with him—a life far away from the pain and brutality that was so much a part of her homeland. She could almost believe that there was a way, somehow, for them to be together.

In the shelter of Sebastian's arms, she could almost believe their love might be stronger than the power of Rashid al-Din Sinan, and that was dangerous thinking, indeed. That sort of thinking could get Sebastian killed, a prospect she would do anything to avoid, even if it meant she would lose his love forever.

"I must go," she said, breaking out of his embrace before she had no strength to leave him at all.

He arched a brow. "You will quit now, when the game is this close? You're hardly one to walk away from a challenge, my lady."

"It is the Sabbath today," she said, pressing her forehead to his. "The third call will come soon, and I really should be in prayer."

It was an excuse, but one he did not rise to challenge. Growling in exaggerated protest, he released her. "We will finish our game—and our conversation—later this evening. Agreed?"

Zahirah gave him a small nod. He pushed himself to his feet and helped her gather together the *shatranj* board and pieces. While she packed it away and threw their food scraps to the gulls, Sebastian shook out and rolled up the blanket, then returned it to the basket. With his hand resting easily on the small of her spine, he walked her out of the tranquillity of the park and back to the sweltering chaos of the street.

"I'll take you back to the palace," he said when she hesitated to bid him farewell.

"No. There's no need," she replied. "It's not so far. I'll be fine."

"You're sure?"

Nodding firmly, she caressed his face, savoring the feel of his strong jaw against her palm. "I will see you tonight, my lord."

She pivoted before he had a chance to say anything more, and stepped into the busy current of the street.

Sebastian waited where she left him, watching as Zahirah weaved back into the throng and headed up the avenue toward the palace. He had surprised her with his offer to bring her home with him to England; in truth, he had surprised himself with it. But he had meant what he said, and now that he had said it, he was determined that he would not leave the Holy Land without her.

Behind him some distance, someone hailed him, drawing his attention away from the place into which Zahirah had since disappeared. It was Logan calling him, he realized, hearing the brogue roll off the soldier's tongue. The Scot had been patrolling the city that morning with a group of other knights, assigned to help keep order on a busy Muslim holy day.

Sebastian turned to greet his friend's approach when something else drew his attention. He jerked his head to the right, where his scalp prickled with warning. The sun's mid-day rays were strong, beating down in a heavy wash of light that bent off a roof tile to blind him. But something was there, buried deep within the crowd. A pair of coal black eyes, watching him, the gaze steady where others darted or hid within the folds and shadows of veils and *kufiyyas*.

Could it be the queer old man Zahirah had bumped into in the street? He had seemed peculiar somehow, his reticent manner oddly belligerent. Sebastian brought his arm up to shade his vision from the glare and get a better look. He peered hard into that knot of shuffling, talking people, but the eyes—and the gaunt, gray-bearded face he felt certain he would find—was gone.

"Damn," he swore, scanning the crowd to no avail. Logan drew up beside him nearly without his notice.

"Anything wrong?"

"I thought I saw something—or, rather, someone." Sebastian ran a hand over his scalp, scowling.

Logan followed the direction of his gaze and gave a shake of his head. "Things have been quiet for more than a week, my friend. No sign of trouble anywhere, and we've been looking. I reckon we got our man when we got Halim and his pack of *fida'i* dogs."

"Did we?" Sebastian asked. "I'm not so sure. Something doesn't feel right to me."

The Scot grunted. "Well, at least we can take some comfort in the fact that Lionheart is out of danger now that he's here under guard in Ascalon."

"He may be under guard," Sebastian said, turning a serious look on his friend, "but I don't think the king is out of danger yet at all."

Chapter Twenty-four

The knights on watch at the palace gates nodded to Zahirah as they parted their crossed lances and opened the heavy iron grate to admit her entry. Her sandals clipped on the tiled walkway of the interior hallway at nearly a run. She was unable to shake the feeling that her father, now that he was there at Ascalon, was watching her every move. Zahirah had felt his eyes on her in the street outside, felt that cold, cunning gaze following her as she had left Sebastian to wend her way through the crowds, fleeing for the palace as if bedeviled by Shaitan himself.

Down the corridor, coming from within a large meeting room but a few paces ahead of her, Zahirah caught the sudden sound of a brash baritone chortle. It was met with an echoing chorus of the same, then a murmur of Frankish male voices. Someone offered fawning praise for the king's political acumen, commending Lionheart on his recent victory at Darum and pledging his support when the king moved the battle on to Jerusalem. There was a general round of agreement, then the shuffle of furniture as chairs were backed away from tables, followed by the jangle and clop of shifting armor and heavy soldiers' boots as the meeting broke and the attendees began to disperse for the hall.

Too late to turn and avoid it, Zahirah found herself standing face-to-face with King Richard and several richly attired officers. One of them wore a long shaggy beard and a belted surcoat of white silk, its front divided in four quarters by a large red cross. His garb marked him as one of the Christians' warrior monks, a Knight of the Jerusalem Temple, a man of some import, judging by the haughtiness of his expression. Piously arrogant, he seared Zahirah with a disdainful look, as if it offended him to be sharing the same space of hallway with her. Lionheart, on the other hand, looked like a cat who had just been handed a dish of cream.

He dismissed the Templar and the other men with a brevity of words, his gaze fixed on Zahirah in unapologetic interest. She clutched her basket in tight fists, holding herself very still, her eyes downcast as the group of Franks said their good-byes to the king and strode on past her up the corridor.

"My, my, this is an unexpected pleasure," he drawled once the officers were out of earshot. "Here I was beginning to think you were avoiding me."

Zahirah gave a weak shake of her head and forced herself to bare her teeth in a smile. His widened exponentially.

"No? Well, then. It would seem my good fortune knows no bounds today." He took her in with a slow meaningful glance, pausing when his eyes lit on her basket. Without a thought toward permission, he leaned forward and flicked open the lid to peer inside. "*Shatranj?* Hardly a maiden's sport, this game of kingly war. Tell me, lady, are you good?"

He closed the basket, but his hand lingered, his cabochon-ringed fingers skating up her forearm. Zahirah recoiled inwardly at his unbidden touch, but she saw the purpose in it, and with her father's threat still ringing in her ears, she knew she had to put that purpose to prudent use, no matter how it disgusted her to play the role of whore.

"I would not presume to guess at my own skill, my lord," she said, carefully measuring her words. "Your opinion, however, would be of great interest to me. I've no doubt there is much I could learn from you."

Richard's answering chuckle was more a purr than reply, low and throaty and very self-satisfied. Zahirah ventured a look up and saw over his shoulder that two armed knights had since come out of the meeting hall to stand in the doorway, guarding the king's back. One of them was the demon warrior she had come to recognize as Blackheart; the other she had seen about before but did not know by name. Stone-faced and silent, the two men hung back, far enough to grant their liege a modicum of privacy, yet near enough that they could see, and hear, all that transpired in the corridor. That these men knew Sebastian, and no doubt knew that she was his intimate, needled her with unbearable shame, but Zahirah tried to put it out of her mind, concentrating instead on the trap she baited for the king.

"I knew you would come around eventually," he said, grinning as he planted his hand beside her head, boxing her in against the stone of the corridor wall. "Perhaps you'd like to start your lesson now."

He bent forward to kiss her and Zahirah jerked away, a reflex reaction that brought a perturbed scowl to the king's brow. She covered the slip quickly. Tilting her head, she feigned a sudden shyness. "Not here, my lord," she said quietly. "I must insist on discretion. No guards."

"My chambers, then. Tonight."

"Too soon," she said with a shake of her head. Her father's threat provided her two days to fulfill her mission; she refused to forfeit this one last night that she would have with Sebastian. She could not go through with her deadly plan until she was certain she had no other choice. And she needed to be assured that Sebastian would not be there to see her betrayal firsthand—nor the aftermath, for there would be no escaping once Richard was dead, and she had decided that she would not attempt to elude his guards when they moved in to kill his assailant. She could face their hacking blades, but she did not think she could face Sebastian once the ugly mask of her deception was stripped away. "When we spoke at Darum, my lord, you mentioned that you could make certain arrangements . . ."

Lionheart inclined his head, his blue eyes glittering. "Consider it done."

The smile she gave him hurt her cheeks, but it paled compared to the stab of misery that pierced her when she thought of what she was about to do—not only to this immoral and arrogant man who would cuckold one of his most loyal subjects, but also to Sebastian. And to herself.

A feeling of sickness began to churn in her belly. Before it could seize her entirely, she hissed out the rest of what needed to be said. "Tomorrow evening, my lord. After sup. I will come to you."

At his nod of agreement, Zahirah sidled away from him and began a hasty retreat down the corridor. Her hands were shaking and damp, her heart beating furiously in her breast. The *shatranj* pieces clacked and rolled in her basket, their bobbling racket bouncing off the high walls of the corridor as she dashed around a bend and headed down the harem colonnade.

She was nearly out of breath, her legs quaking beneath her. Her stomach clenched in revolt, twisting violently. Zahirah flung one hand out to brace herself on a tall column, doubling over and on the verge of retching into the bed of bright flowers that lined the walkway. Behind her some way, a group of knights came in from an adjacent courtyard, talking about their eagerness to march on the Holy City. Zahirah straightened before they could notice her and willed herself to calm. Gathering her wits as best she could, she took off at a dead run toward her chamber. Distantly, from the minaret tower of the city mosque at the center of town, she heard the *muezzin* call the faithful to prayer.

The city had settled down for nightfall by the time Sebastian returned to the palace. Not that he had wanted to be kept away for so long. The building on the wall had taken most of the daylight hours, and, come dusk, he and Logan had decided to make one last sweep of Ascalon's streets and courtyards, looking for any hint of the unusual.

Their search had yielded nothing out of the ordinary,

but the day's long hours had left him tired and hot and hungry. Those petty needs fell away at the welcome sight of Zahirah waiting for him in his chamber when he opened the door. She quenched all his wants . . . all, save one.

She poured him a cup of wine from a carafe on a nearby table while he unbuckled his sword belt and laid it down near the door. He took the drink gladly, tossing back the rich red claret in one long draught, then setting the cup aside to take his beautiful lady in hand instead. He fell back on the room's plush divan and pulled her down onto his lap. "I've been wanting to kiss you like this all day," he said, plunging his hands into her thick black hair and covering her mouth with his.

She was sweet and clean, and he suddenly became aware of how filthy he was from being outside, standing in the hot sun and working with the brick and mortar. "I should bathe," he murmured against her lips. "I'm getting my dust all over you."

"I don't care," she whispered. She wrapped her arms around his neck and kissed him with a needfulness that seemed but a shade away from despair. "I've been waiting for you too long, my love, and I'm not about to let you go now."

"Then come with me," he growled, pushing her up and taking her by the hand.

Their fingers laced together, he brought her out of his chamber and down the snaking corridor to the bathhouse. At this hour, they would have the place to themselves; the rest of the garrison had already gone to supper in the meeting hall of the palace, where food and wine and the presence of the king would keep them occupied for the better part of the night. Sebastian opened the door to the lamplit sauna and ushered Zahirah inside.

A fragrant steam enveloped them beneath the high dome of the ceiling. It hissed out of vents hollowed into the smooth stone walls, whispering softly, and carrying the scent of sandalwood and myrrh. The fine mist swirled over the tiles of the floor and skated in ribbons across the surface of the small bathing pool in the center of the chamber. Water trickled in a small fountain-fed basin, echoing like primeval music in the damp solitude of the room.

Sebastian brought Zahirah around in front of him, kissing her hungrily as he worked to unlace and strip off his tunic.

"Let me," she said, placing her hands over his and pulling the cotton shirt up over his head. She dropped it to the floor, then bent to press a kiss to his bare skin. Her tongue teased his nipple to instant hardness; her breath blew warm and uneven into the mat of hair on his chest. The air around them was humid, but it rushed cool against him when she broke their kiss and backed away, leading him to a small stool beside the water. "Sit, my lord."

He sat, and watched with keen interest as she knelt before him and slid his feet out of his heavy boots. She rubbed his tired soles and heels, her touch like heaven as she moved up to massage the tight muscles of his calves and thighs. His hose came off next. Zahirah came up between his legs to unhitch the points fastened at his waist and tug the leggings down. The brief friction of her body, the slight press of her breasts against his thighs, sent a bolt of lust shooting through his loins.

When she moved to rise, Sebastian brought his knees together, trapping her there before him. He remembered another time that they were in this very stance—the night in the caravansary outside Darum, the night they had first made love. She had been seated before him like this then, too, and well he remembered how badly he had wanted to keep her there, to feel her mouth moving and suckling on his hard flesh. He looked at her upturned face now, holding her questioning gaze and knowing the one he fixed on her was harsh and dark with need.

She understood that need. Her lips curved sensually, her eyes smoldered in the dim lamplight. With graceful fingers, she unrolled the waistband of his braies and freed him

of the loose undergarment. Unrestrained by the confining
linen drawers, his erection thrust up past his navel, stiff and
substantial, leaping under the heat of her appreciative gaze.
She smoothed her hands up his thighs, and when she
wrapped her fingers around the solid width of his shaft,
stroking him from root to tip, he quaked with a sudden jolt
of white-hot pleasure.

She toyed with him for an unbearable while, teasing and
touching him, driving him to the edge of a perfect madness,
but then she rose up and took him into her mouth, and
Sebastian thought he would splinter on the spot. He could
not contain the low oath of anguish that curled up from his
throat when her tongue sucked and swirled around his
swollen member, nor could he stop himself from reaching
down to catch her behind the neck with both hands, burying his fingers in her hair and holding her head in place as
she took him deeper, impossibly deeper, into the hot velvet
sheath of her mouth. He felt his climax building with each
upward pull of her lips, each subtle scrape of her teeth, her
little mewls of arousal vibrating against him to wrench his
loins tighter and tighter.

"Zahirah," he managed to croak thickly. "God . . . curse
it."

Savagely, before she had sapped him of every bit of his
control, he seized her by the arms and hauled her up onto
her feet. "I need to be inside you," he rasped, fumbling with
her pantalets and finally ripping the laces loose. He shoved
the wrecked silk down her hips, while she quickly took off
her tunic and tossed it aside. Naked and beautiful, she stood
before him, lips glistening and moist, breasts rising with
each panting breath she drew into her lungs. She stepped
forward to straddle his legs and Sebastian gripped her pelvis
in his hands, positioning her over the top of his straining
sex. Their gazes locked and hungry, he brought her down
onto his lap and sheathed himself to the hilt in one long
stroke.

The rhythm they found was fierce and passionate, too
powerful to deny. Sebastian felt Zahirah's release come

along with his, heard the quickening of her breath, felt the delicious squeeze of her body around his sex as climax shuddered through her. She cried out, clinging to him as he gave one final thrust and spilled his essence deep within her womb. For a long while, they merely stayed there, holding each other, still intimately joined, loath to disrupt the moment.

"You feel so good, I don't want to move," he murmured beside her ear.

"Let's not, then," she whispered. "Let's not ever move."

He chuckled, nipping her shoulder and savoring the taste of her salty-sweet skin. "We'll have to eat sometime, my love. And sooner or later, someone is sure to come here looking for a bath."

Zahirah drew out of his embrace and met his gaze. She stared at him, looking so serious, so utterly sober, it took him aback. "What is it?" he asked, smoothing her frown with a brush of his fingers over her brow.

She shook her head slowly, her eyes rooted on his. "I just . . . I never want to forget this moment. I want to remember you always like this, the way you're looking at me right now."

"We'll have many moments like this," he said, smoothing her hair away from her face, loving her so keenly it put an ache in his chest. "If I have my way, sweet lady, we will have moments like this for the rest of our lives." She gave him a smile, made all the more endearing for how it wobbled on her lips. She glanced away, but not before he saw the shimmer of tears welling in her eyes. He scowled, wondering at her sadness, at what felt oddly to him like regret. "You still haven't answered me, you know."

"Answered you?"

"Today, in the park. I asked you to come back with me to England."

"Yes," she said softly. "Yes, you did."

"I know it would not be easy for you to leave. This is your home. I would not ask you to give up your faith—"

"Sebastian," she said, turning an earnest look on him, caressing him with her eyes. "My love. I would give up everything for you. Nothing would make me happier than to see your home, to be with you there, or wherever you go."

He saw the deep love in her gaze, felt his heart swell in the warmth of her regard. His mind sped forward to the day he would bring her home to Montborne, the day he would take her as his wife in truth. "I'll speak with the king as soon as possible," he said, stroking the smooth slope of her cheek. "He must be made aware of my intentions."

"Let's not talk about him now," Zahirah whispered. "Let's not talk about anything now. Just hold me. I need you to hold me."

She burrowed into the circle of his arms and Sebastian wrapped himself around her, rocking her gently, caressing the slender arch of her back. He rose from the stool and lifted her with him, and together they slipped into the small bathing pool to wash. They soaped each other in the warm water, silent but for the intimate hush of their breathing, joining in a slow tangle of slick wet hands and twisting, twining limbs. They made love once more, there in the shallow pool, then they gathered up their clothes and Sebastian carried Zahirah back to his chamber and placed her in his bed beside him. With legs and arms entwined, they lay together in the moonlight, engulfed in a reverent brand of silence, kissing and caressing each other for some long hours, until sleep began to beckon. Sebastian pulled Zahirah close and let his eyes drift shut, surrendering to a calm—a soul-deep fullness—he never thought he would know.

Zahirah lay in his arms, listening as Sebastian fell into a sated, heavy sleep. There would be no such peace for her this night. Indeed, not ever again. This would be the last time he held her. The last time she knew the wonder of his love, the last time she knew the bliss of his body joined with her own.

Paradise, if such a prize was truly to be hers upon the success of so heinous a mission as the one she had been called to do, could not possibly compare to what she had with Sebastian. Nor could Shaitan's fiery domain be worse than the guilt and pain she felt now, looking at the man she loved more than life itself and knowing that in a few short hours he would hate the very notion of her.

The understanding of that eventuality was like a vise around her heart, squeezing as if to wring the very breath from her lungs. She could not sleep, nor could she bear the oppressive weight of her thoughts. Carefully, she freed herself from Sebastian's slack embrace and rose from the haven of his bed. Outside, beyond the gentle soughing of the curtains that framed the balcony terrace, the moon hung full and bright in the deep black sky. The milky light spilled into the chamber, bathing everything with a pale, other-worldly glow, washing the vibrant weave of the carpets nearly colorless, and throwing long shadows beneath the pieces of the *shatranj* board that sat where she had returned it that afternoon, ready for play on the small table across the room.

Zahirah walked toward the idle game as in a trance, her gaze straying to the checkered board with its orderly rows of pieces—small enemy soldiers, facing off to do battle unto the death. In *shatranj*, war was neat, so clearly an issue of black-and-white. Life was a far crueler game, indeed. She plucked the white king from his place between his queen and guards and held the piece up in the moonlight, idly examining it. How she envied that cold chunk of carved stone. To feel nothing, to move as directed without grieving one's losses, without wishing for things that could never be—she had known that sense of purpose once. Long ago and far away, it seemed to her now.

She needed that sense of purpose again. Allah help her, she had never needed it more.

Steeling herself to what had to be done, to the shattering idea that tomorrow at this time her world and everything in t that mattered would cease, Zahirah laid the white king down in the center of the board. With remorse pricking her eyes, she glanced back to Sebastian, sleeping soundly in a naked, masculine sprawl on the bed.

"*Shah mat,* my love," she whispered. "Your king is dead."

Chapter Twenty-five

"You're awake," Sebastian said when he opened his eyes a few hours later.

Her head on the bolster next to his, Zahirah nodded, giving him a small smile. She had climbed back into bed with him some time ago, but she had not slept, and now that it was dawn, she mourned the night's swift passing. Sebastian's strong legs were wound around hers; he slowly flexed his knees, pulling her toward him until her hips were flush against his. He was hard beneath the coverlet, and her body responded to that knowledge with a sudden quickening in her veins. But she shied away from wanting him now, forcing herself to deny the longing that would keep her there with him for as long as he would have her.

"My morning prayers," she said feebly, "I cannot neglect them." She pressed her fingers against his bare chest in tender resistance, but instead found herself closing her eyes at the contact, memorizing the feel of his heart thudding against her palm.

The feel of him, so alive and warm beside her, seared her now, scorching the resolve she was fighting so hard to keep. Before it crumbled any further into ash, Zahirah rolled away from him and swung her legs over the side of the bed. With a groan and a shifting of the mattress behind her, Sebastian did likewise. While Zahirah donned a morning gown, he padded barefoot to the door and summoned a servant to bring them breakfast.

Meekly, her limbs and heart lethargic, Zahirah went to the washbasin and performed her daily ablutions, then unrolled her prayer mat on the floor. She knelt on the woven square of cotton canvas and began the ritual of her praises for Allah. It was a farce today, little more than a performance of the motions, for she could not concentrate on the words. She rushed through the last of her prayers, finishing just as a knock sounded on the door.

"Maimoun is quick today," Sebastian said when her head snapped up in startlement. He shrugged into a long tunic and went to admit the servant entry.

But it was not Maimoun come to bring them their meal. It was Logan. He was outfitted in chain mail, his helm tucked under his arm, his sheathed broadsword slung low on his hips. "Where are you off to so early this morning?" Sebastian asked, stepping aside for the other man to enter.

"Not just me, my friend, but you as well. 'Twas the king's order not a moment ago."

Zahirah swallowed hard. God help her, her betrayal had begun already.

She got to her feet as Logan came inside and gave her a polite nod of greeting. "The king has obtained information recently about Saladin's movements," he told Sebastian. "According to Templar spies, the sultan has been poisoning area wells in an effort to impinge our march on Jerusalem. Lionheart has assembled a scouting party to ride out and assess the situation for himself."

"What's this about?" Sebastian asked, a dubious edge to his voice as he tugged on his braies and hose, then fastened the points and ties. "He doesn't trust the information he's received?"

"I couldna say, my friend. 'Tis my understanding that the king is not well today and still abed in his chambers; these orders came from one of his lieutenants." Logan slanted him a wry look. "All I know is what I've been told. The king wants reports, and he wants you and me to head up the scout. We're to leave without delay."

"Were you told how far we are to scout for these reports?"

Logan nodded. "North, toward Jaffa."

"God's blood," Sebastian swore. "That's a day, easily."

Logan grunted, looking no more enthused with the prospect than Sebastian. In the corridor, Maimoun arrived with a tray of dates and oranges and a loaf of bread. Before the servant could usher in the food, the big knight grabbed a handful of dates and popped one in his mouth. "I've had no time to eat yet," he said, talking around the chunk of succulent fruit.

Sebastian retrieved his gambeson from a T-shaped rack beside the bed and shrugged into the padded leather vest. Draped beneath where the gambeson had been on the stand was his shirt of steel armor links; he gathered it up and slung the tunic's jingling bulk over his arm. "Regrettably, duty calls, my lady," he said to Zahirah. He came over to where she stood and cupped her cheek in his palm. "I'll be back as soon as I can."

Too unsettled to speak, Zahirah gave him a shaky nod. It was all happening so fast. Now that he was going, she wanted to reach out and hold him back, to plead with him to stay. She wanted to blurt out the truth of what she was hiding from him, pray that he would forgive her, and hope that somehow, together, they could puzzle a way out of this coil of lies and destruction. But her father's threat echoed roundly in her ears, and, so, instead, she kept her tongue and willed her hands to stay at her sides.

Sebastian leaned forward to place a quick kiss of goodbye on her lips, and she accepted this last gift of affection, feeling as treacherous as a snake as she watched him turn and grab his sword belt, then stride out of the chamber with Logan.

In the large courtyard outside the palace, four squires were already saddling and provisioning the mounts that Sebastian, Logan, and two other men would be taking on their scouting errand for the king. One of the lads saw the officers approach and rushed around to assist Sebastian into his chain mail. As the heavy armor shirt settled onto his shoulders, a movement near the palace caught his eye. It was the king.

Robed in a hooded white caftan, Lionheart stood on the balcony of his second-floor chamber, idly observing the assembly of the riding party. Behind him, the silken curtains that framed the portal ruffled in the soft breath of the morning. The king watched for a moment, still as a hawk. He met Sebastian's gaze across the space of the yard, by accident, it seemed. He stood there, simply staring, then he turned away and headed back inside.

"Let's go," Sebastian ordered, jerking his head back toward the squires as they strapped on the last of the packs and moved aside.

He took his destrier's reins in hand and swung up into the saddle. Logan and the other two knights followed, bringing their mounts around to join him. With a queer feeling of suspicion beginning to gnaw at him, Sebastian gave his steed a kick of his heels and the scouting party headed out for Jaffa.

Zahirah remained behind the closed door of Sebastian's chamber for the rest of the morning, receiving no one. Maimoun had brought more food at midday but she refused it, sending the servant away without admitting him entry. He obeyed and withdrew, unquestioning her request that she not be disturbed unless she called. Which, of course, she would not.

Today she would fast; she had only room for prayer and reflection, for reconnection with her faith and her clan, and her obligations within them. Devoting herself to that goal, she bathed and dressed and braided her hair, then left Sebastian's empty apartments for the solitude of her own.

But it was more than mere solitude that drew her to the room she had occupied upon her arrival at the palace some weeks ago. With cool-headed purpose, she went at once to the mattress of her small bed and reached far beneath it, her fingers sliding and groping for purchase along the flat of the

bed frame. It was there, where she had left it: the dagger that
had been forged and fashioned especially for this night.
Zahirah curled her hand around the knife's leather sheath
and brought it out of hiding.

The weapon was heavier than she recalled. The slender
blade whispered softly as she drew it from the sleeve, its
razor edge glinting deadly silver in her palms. She lifted the
dagger to her lips and bowed her head to kiss it, murmuring
a prayer that she be granted the strength and skill to deliver
it as He willed. She knelt on the floor, praying for clarity and
focus, for the courage to face these next few hours without
emotion, and to accept whatever should come after them.

It sustained her for a while, that steely marshaling of her
directives, her determined adherence to the code of her clan.
But the space around her was alive with memories of her
time with Sebastian—moments they had shared, places
where they had loved—vivid memories that edged their way
into her meditations like a tender sapling slowly cleaving the
granite core of a stone. She would never forget him. May
Allah forgive her, but she would never stop loving him.

Before the room's many memories and thoughts of her
days there with Sebastian could form a wider fissure in her
resolve, Zahirah returned her dagger to its sheath and hid it
beneath her pantalets, then she quit the small chamber and
headed for the roof terrace to put herself closer to Allah,
where she would use the remaining few hours to prepare
and wait until the time to act drew near.

Chapter Twenty-six

"What do you think, my friend?"

"It's poisoned all right," Sebastian answered, tossing the putrid contents of his cup into the sand below the well. "Just like the last two towns we've been through today. Just like the Templars' spies reported in their meetings with the king." He raked a hand through his hair, slanting Logan a look of frustration. "I've no doubt we're going to find the same thing at every well from here to Jaffa."

It was past noon, but they were just a few leagues out of Ascalon, not yet halfway finished with their mission for the king—a mission that was seeming oddly more and more a boondoggle with each village they investigated. Richard could be frivolous where his whims took him, but it was not like him to squander his resources, be they horses and supplies or men, and the idea that the king had chosen him specifically to head up the trip had niggled at Sebastian's mind since they left the palace that morning.

He wondered if the scouting mission was intended as some form of chastisement, a way for the king to show his displeasure with something Sebastian might have done. His thoughts returned to the night of the feast in the Darum camp, when he had bloodied Garrett of Fallonmour's nose. It would certainly be like the whining earl to appeal to Richard for some form of reparation, but Sebastian knew the king's indifference toward the man and he rather doubted he would trifle with coming to Fallonmour's defense. Certainly not with a pointless exercise of this nature.

No, this was something else.

Against his will, he considered the king's interest in Zahirah. He had taken note of it in Darum and again upon their return to Ascalon. It concerned him, Lionheart's lascivious eye, and it concerned him that he was now some distance from the palace, on a superfluous mission where he was unable to watch over Zahirah and keep her safe from Richard's lustful attentions.

But where his confidence wavered in his king, he had to trust his lady. She was savvy; she would not put herself in the king's company if she felt him any sort of threat. He soothed his anxiety further with the fact that the king had been reported ill that morning. Richard was still in his bedclothes when he watched from his balcony as the party rode out. If he was ill, he would likely remain in his chambers all day. If they were quick about their business with the testing of the area wells, Sebastian and his men could be back in Ascalon come the morrow. His concerns were likely unwarranted.

But still his mind churned on, sick himself, with the feeling that he was being played.

"I've seen enough here. Tell those two we're heading out," he said to Logan, pointing with his chin toward the knights who had accompanied them from Ascalon. They were young and lazy, avoiding the heat of the sun by volunteering to tend the horses. They had all four mounts standing in the shade of a cluster of palm trees, watering them from their own supply and brushing them down from the day's ride. A bunch of naked village children crowded around them, trying to touch the huge warhorses and jabbering in Arabic while they begged for food and money. Logan put two fingers in his mouth and whistled, waving the knights over with a sweep of his arm and a shout to bring the horses.

Sebastian took a handful of coins from his purse and gave them to the town's gnarled elder, thanking him for his cooperation and instructing him on where he could get clean water for his village. "Peace be upon you," he said, granting the old man leave as the two soldiers loped toward them with the mounts.

"I trust you lasses are rested enough to move on?" Logan drawled to their youthful companions, smirking as he took his destrier's reins from one of them and swung up into the saddle.

Sebastian grinned at the jest, but his thoughts were still on Ascalon. "The next town is about an hour's ride," he said. "I want to make it in less that, so let's get moving."

The four of them rode out onto the dusty path that was the road and spurred their horses into a brisk canter. When they had gone some way, Sebastian pulled his water canteen from its strap on his saddle and took a long drink. He passed it over to Logan, who rode beside him on the narrow track.

The Scot and the other two men had been talking most of the time since they had headed out from the last town, comparing stories and discussing the trials of warring in so foreign and forbidding a land. One of the young knights had been on the march with Richard in Darum. He launched into a rather detailed account of the various plagues that beset them: intolerable heat and sunburn, stinging flies that ate the men raw, and rotted foodstuffs that left most of the army sick with dysentery for weeks. "Not the king, however," said the knight, his voice edged with awe. "He seemed to take every setback in stride. Some of the men say he's another Roland."

Logan grunted, and threw a sage look at Sebastian. "Well, hero of legend or nay, I reckon those days on the march are catching up to him, lad. Lionheart was sequestered in his chambers when we left; no doubt he will still be abed when we return."

From behind them, the Darum knight chuckled as he uncorked his wineskin with a pop. "In bed mayhap," he sniggered, "but not sick today. And not alone, as I hear it."

The other man shot him a quick, quelling look, his lips flattened, eyes widened in warning. The youth raised his hands, seeming unaware of how he offended, but he snapped his mouth closed at once. It was a brief, surreptitious exchange, but Sebastian had turned in time to see it all. His mouth went instantly dry.

"How's that, Sergeant?"

A beat of uneasy silence answered his question while the two knights traded uncertain glances. The young man who had made the jest glanced down quickly, shaking his head, his previous jocularity gone at once. "Beg pardon, sir. I—I spoke out of turn. I am obviously mistaken."

Something cold and heavy settled in Sebastian's gut at that feeble denial. He felt the blood rushing in his temples, felt his skin begin to prickle with apprehension. He brought his mount to a halt on the road. "Tell me, Sergeant," he growled, looking from the sheepish soldier to the one who had sought to hush his tongue. And when neither man would respond or meet his gaze, he said it again, barking the command with all the fury that was now drumming like a black tempest in his head. "Tell me, goddamn it!"

The two knights jumped, rightly startled. The second youth looked up, eyes darting and frightened, his face the bloodless color of fishmeat. His news, evidently, was bad indeed. "Apologies, my lord, but d-do you know John Bradford, sir?" The name registered vaguely in Sebastian's mind: one of the king's handful of personal guards. He gave the young knight an impatient glower. "Aye, well, my lord . . . we're friends, John and I. He told me how he was there yesterday, when the king met with the Templars and some other noblemen. And, well, sir, you see, John was there afterward, too . . ."

"Afterward," Sebastian prompted, having no patience for a nervous, fumbling explanation. "Spit it out, man."

It was a feat that seemed to take some doing. The knight swallowed, glancing helplessly to his companion before dropping his gaze once more. Finally, he blurted the whole of it out in one gulp. "He was there after the meeting adjourned, when the king made plans of an intimate nature with a lady he encountered in the hallway."

"A lady?" Sebastian's voice was wooden.

"Aye, sir. The Saracen woman." He swallowed hard. "Your lady, my lord."

The knight from the Darum company gasped at this news, evidently unaware of the connection until now. Logan let out a bark of incredulous laughter, no doubt to cover for Sebastian's sudden lengthening silence. "That's impossible. Tell your man Bradford to check his eyesight. He's got it wrong."

But as disbelieving as Sebastian wanted to be, he could not join his friend in challenging the soldier's tale. It hit too close to what he feared, to what he was beginning to suspect in his heart. He drew back as if physically struck, but his instinct warned to absorb the information with prudence and logic. "What else did he tell you?"

"Not much, my lord. Just that the king had dismissed him and the other chamber guards."

"Dismissed them. Why?"

The knight gave a weak shrug, his gaze meek and edged with something that looked sickeningly like pity. "He said he would be taking to bed early this evening . . . that he wished to have privacy. 'Tis my understanding she—your lady—wanted it that way."

"No guards," he said, his gaze sliding to Logan in sinking alarm.

His mind spun, disbelieving, calling back the weeks he and Zahirah had spent together at the palace—everything, from her appearance in the souk and her request for his protection, to the ambush she had saved him from, and nights they had shared in each other's arms. He thought about Zahirah's behavior over the last day, her quiet withdrawal; her strange comment that she wanted to remember him as he was the night before, when they had made love in the bathhouse; her quiet acceptance of his unexpected orders to head up the scouting party that morning, as if it came as no surprise to her. And then there was her association with Halim, a proven assassin. She had claimed he was her brother, only to admit later that she had lied.

She had too many secrets; how many of them were lies? How many had he believed—worse, still hoped to believe, despite what his gut was telling him now?

"I have to stop her," Sebastian said. He jerked his reins and wheeled his mount around, the stamping hooves stirring up a low fog of dust on the road. "We have to go back to Ascalon. Now."

Logan was staring at him, a look of dawning realization darkening his eyes. "Oh, Jesus. You don't suppose . . ."

Numb with the weight of his suspicions, Sebastian shook off the hand that came to rest in sympathy on his shoulder. "Let's get out of here," he ordered, his voice quiet but deadly steady as the Scot brought his destrier around on the road. "Let's go, Logan, and pray to God I'm wrong."

Zahirah let out a deep sigh as the sun dipped below the horizon. She was almost relieved to see the fiery red orb begin to sink into slumber. Her waiting was nigh at an end. Dusk was coming quickly, and, with it, the task she was solidly resolved to carry out.

The king would be taking his supper now. Less than an hour separated her from the deadly ruse that would lead her into his private chambers. Less than an hour between this next breath and what was sure to be her last. She felt oddly detached from the notion now, having at last come to peace with the idea that through the king's death—indeed, inevitably, through her own—Sebastian would live.

She had to believe that. In these final moments of reflection and meditation, it was all she had left, all that mattered to her now.

Clinging to that singular purpose, she knelt on the hard tiles of the roof terrace and bowed deeply in one last prayer.

It was dusk when Sebastian and Logan galloped their exhausted horses through the opening gates of the Ascalon palace. Sebastian threw his reins off and leapt down from his saddle. He crossed the twilit courtyard in a handful of urgent strides, skidding around the column of the adjacent colonnade. His chamber was down the connecting corridor; he ran for it in a haze of dread, hoping beyond hope that he would find Zahirah there waiting for him. That he would feel more the fool for doubting her now than he did to think she might have been betraying him all along.

When he reached his apartments, he found the door slightly ajar. He threw the heel of his hand against it and knocked it open, letting it crash against the hind wall like a clap of thunder. "Zahirah!" he called, lunging over the threshold, his voice echoing in the stillness of the vacant space.

He made a hasty search of the antechambers, knowing in his gut that despite his hope, he was not going to find her there. As he passed back into the main room, one of the curtains that framed the balcony caught on the sleeve of his mail. He tore the wisp of silk from the rod and flung it away, enraged.

The flimsy streamer fluttered down onto the small table beside him, draping the *shatranj* board that sat atop the pedestal. Sebastian's eye was drawn to that board suddenly, snagged by the neat rows of pieces beneath their silken shroud. He pulled the scrap of fabric away and saw the white king lying in the center of the board. It was a symbolic death. The piece had been placed there deliberately, signaling the forfeit of the game to the black player.

"No," he growled. "God, Zahirah. No. Not you."

He felt like a man drugged and beaten, his surroundings shifting out of focus, stretching into a twisted blur of light and sound, as indistinguishable and elusive as vapor. But he had never seen more clearly. Pivoting, his every muscle clenched with urgent dread, he crashed into the hallway. "The king!" he shouted to a loitering knight as he passed him in the corridor. "The king, damn it! Where is he?"

"Taking his sup last I knew," answered the soldier.

"Where?"

"His chamber, sir. What is it? What's going on?"

Sebastian impatiently waved him off; he had no time to answer. His spurs biting into the polished marble floor of the corridor, he bolted for the king's quarters on the other side of the palace.

Dear God, he prayed, *do not let me be too late.*

Chapter Twenty-seven

Zahirah hesitated outside the door of the king's chamber, her heart pounding against her ribs like a caged bird. She had waited until it was fully dark outside before she climbed down from the roof terrace, wanting to be certain the king would be alone. Standing there now, she had no doubt of that fact. There was no guard posted in the hallway. One subtle squeeze and a click of the cold iron latch in her hand told her the door was unbarred from within. Lionheart was waiting, and it seemed he had met her conditions just as he had agreed.

She exhaled deeply, willing her last remaining shreds of doubt to be expelled along with her spent breath. Cleansed and steady, she gripped the latch and pushed open the door.

A single oil lamp burned in a marble alcove in the far right of the room, providing meager light for the large, lavishly appointed chamber. It limned the wide carpet on the floor and cast a fiery glow on the solitary figure clothed in a hooded white gown and standing at the open window of the balcony.

"My lord," Zahirah said quietly, announcing herself as she entered, her gaze sweeping the apartment, searching to make sure no guards were secreted in the corners before she focused once more on the king's broad back. She pulled the door closed behind her and took a step farther into the room. "I hope I have not kept you waiting overlong, my lord."

He grunted, and for a moment she tensed, wondering if she had irritated him with her delay, for there was a dark undercurrent to his tone, an air of restrained anger in the growl that seemed to answer from deep within his chest more than off his tongue. But then he raised his hand out to his side and beckoned her forward, and that particular anxiety ebbed.

She moved on silent feet, the soles of her sandals not so much as whispering on the thick weave of the rugs beneath them. She could steal up behind him in a heartbeat and have done with it, she realized, weathering a giddy sense of relief to think her task would be so easy, so quick. Slowly, she gathered the hem of her tunic and slipped her hand up to her waist, feeling for the handle of her dagger. She took care not to rush, knowing he could turn around at any moment and discover her purpose.

As if just then sensing something amiss behind him, he lifted his head and pivoted his chin over his shoulder. Listening? she wondered. Zahirah froze where she stood, letting her tunic fall back around her legs. "W-would you care for wine, my lord?" she asked, spying a carafe and goblet on a table near the divan.

He slowly dipped his head, a wordless nod of agreement. Cautiously, Zahirah walked over to the table and poured him a cup of the strongly aromatic wine, watching with satisfaction as he returned his gaze to the moonlit courtyard outside. She had no intention of seducing the king this night, and so long as he remained where he was, his back conveniently turned to her as she prepared to steal up behind him, she was mere moments away from completing her odious task.

With one hand wrapped around the carafe as she poured, Zahirah used the other to efficiently retrieve her blade from its sheath, the soft hush of the steel clearing the leather sleeve swallowed up by the gurgle of the flowing wine. She held the dagger close to her belly, the king's drink steady in her left hand, and carefully crossed the space of floor to the balcony where he waited, unsuspecting.

He seemed somehow larger in the moment she neared him, not more than an arm's length between them. This close, he seemed more substantial, his shoulders wider, standing perhaps taller, certainly more dangerous, even without the benefit of his leonine countenance turned on her in ferocious confrontation. He held himself still, but he seemed to crackle with power, leashed and restrained, but, given its head, lethal.

She could do this, she assured herself when doubt rose to seep insidiously into the steel of her resolve. God help her, she had to do this.

As by instinct, her training leapt to life like a fire in her soul, showing her the way. She inched closer to the king's unmoving bulk, her fingers flexing on the grip of her blade.

"Your drink, my lord," she cooed in an easy, soothing voice, all warmth and promise. All deadly falsity. She stood behind him and reached around the thickness of his left shoulder with the goblet. He turned slightly, bringing his right arm across his chest to take it from her. His fingers brushed hers, a momentary, searing contact. She drew away from that unsettling touch with a gasp, and the instant his hand closed around the jeweled stem, Zahirah lashed out like a viper.

She raised her dagger up and brought it down in a savage arc at his back, thrusting the blade into the space between the wide slabs of his shoulders. She struck true and hard, but something was not right. The blade jarred in her hand, buckling. It skidded down with the force of her blow, rending the back of the king's pristine white robe. She grunted in surprise, jolted momentarily in utter astonishment. The king did not fall. He merely leaned forward slightly, shifting but a half pace forward from the contact.

Before he could move, before he could call for his guards, Zahirah shook off her dazedness with sheer force of will. He had to die. She had to finish this! Regrouped now, with a cry of animal fury, she lunged wildly and drove the dagger home once more.

Another strike, another grating skid.

Impossible!

She tried to blink away the madness before her eyes, but

it was there, glinting in the lamplight, indisputable. She had hit metal, not flesh; hard steel links, not bone, not the heart of the English king.

And then, in the instant it took for the realization to set in, she began to understand the true depth of her mistake. For at that moment, between one breath and the next, the king turned to face her. Only it was not the king beneath that hooded white rag she had savaged.

It was Sebastian.

Staring at her, his nostrils flaring with every breath he sucked into his lungs, he took a single step forward. He flung the cup of wine at the wall; it crashed and clattered like a bell.

Zahirah stumbled backward. "No," she whispered, putting her hand to her mouth. "Oh, no. No."

She shook her head, praying he was not real, desperate that the hate-filled face before her was but a trick of her mind. She prayed she would blink and find that this was just a cruel mirage. But God was not hearing her prayers now. Sebastian was real, as real as the enmity flashing in his eyes, as real as his roar of fury as he advanced toward her, making her cower before him, craven and shaking.

With a harsh oath, he gripped the front of the caftan and tore it off. His surcoat went with it, falling to the floor and leaving him standing before her in bare chain mail, a warrior honed of steel and cold hard purpose. "All along you've been planning this," he accused, his voice deadly calm. "All along, Zahirah, from the day I first saw you in the market, you have played me for a fool."

"No," she said, rushing to deny it. She never thought him a fool, never intended to hurt him like this. "Sebastian, no. It wasn't like that. Not at any time—"

"Oh, no?" he fumed. He stepped forward, his boots trampling the tattered silk that lay beneath them. "Even now you prove it. Your very denial is an insult. A further betrayal."

"Sebastian, please. You must believe me. I never wanted to betray you." She choked on a sob. "I love you."

He scoffed, and it scalded her like acid poison. "Don't

say that. I won't be fed any more of your lies. We're well past that now, my lady."

Zahirah backed up, fearing the look in his eye. Belatedly, she felt the dagger, still gripped in her fist. She heard her father's promise repeating in her head, his threat that Sebastian would die if she did not fulfill her mission. "The king," she murmured numbly. "Sebastian, I need you to take me to him. I need you to tell me where he is—your life depends on it!"

He laughed at that. It was a terrible sound, bitter and contemptuous. "The king is safe, somewhere you'll never reach him."

Zahirah shook her head. "I have to find him! Sebastian, you don't understand. I have to do this. He has to die, or else—"

"Or else?" he snarled. "What, will you kill me to get to him? Here. I'll make it easy for you." He yanked at the neckline of his mail tunic, clearing the bare column of his throat. An open, easy target. She stared at him, appalled. "No?" he taunted viciously. "Mayhap you'd rather finish what you started all those weeks ago in camp. It was you, wasn't it? The whelp who nearly gutted me when I intercepted the attack on the king. It was you."

"I had no choice, Sebastian. I was sworn. I *am* sworn. It's no different than you, pledged to fight this war for your king. I have taken the same pledge, made the same vow to my people and my God."

"No," he growled. "We are not the same, Zahirah. When I fight, I do it openly, with honor. I fight face-to-face and hand to hand with my enemies. Your kind would creep in under cover of night to stab yours in the back. Do not deign to compare us; we are not the same. Not in any way." His jaw hardened, the muscles in his face stretching tight across the bone. "You and I were never the same."

"Sebastian, please, hear me out. Let me explain."

"I think your presence here explains everything plainly enough."

"It is not the way it seems—"

"Hah! That is rich, Zahirah. Spare me your further contortions of the truth. I have heard enough of them."

"No," she said. "You must know the whole of it. It was me that night in the king's camp. I stabbed you, and if you had not stopped me, I would have killed your king. I didn't know you, Sebastian. All I knew was I had a mission to complete. I had made a pledge to my clan . . . to my father, the head of that clan."

Sebastian's hard gaze narrowed in dawning comprehension; there was ice in his voice. "Rashid al-Din Sinan is your father? Good God. It was him—the Old Man of the Mountain—whom I found you speaking with in the street yesterday, wasn't it?"

Zahirah nodded, hating to admit that she shared Sinan's blood, shamed that this was one more lie between them. "Everything changed once I met you, Sebastian. I changed. I didn't want to deceive you. I knew that if it meant I would lose you, I could not go through with this task. I wasn't going to do it, but then my father was here in Ascalon. He knew I had weakened, and he knew that I had fallen in love with you. He threatened me, Sebastian. He said that if I did not fulfill my pledge, you would pay for my failure with your life. I could not let that happen." In spite of her fear for the man who stood tense with fury before her now, Zahirah reached forth to touch him. "He will kill you, unless I kill Lionheart first."

Sebastian stared at her, absorbing her revelation in judicious silence. She could see that he was uncertain he should trust her, perhaps he was unwilling to now. She had given him so little truth since she had known him, how could she hope that he would believe her now? And even if he did believe her, would he care?

He looked down to where her fingers rested on his arm. With an oath, he jerked away from her touch. "Get out."

Zahirah recoiled at the venom in his command, feeling his withdrawal from her as though he were slamming a door in her face, forcibly shutting her out. "Sebastian, please don't push me away. What I've told you is the truth. I swear it—"

"I said, get out." His eyes blazed furious in the dim lamplight. He put his hand out, pointing to the open balcony. "Get out, Zahirah. Before I decide to throw you on the mercy of the king as you well deserve."

It slowly registered to her that he was giving her freedom when he had every right to hate her, to hold her accountable and see her pay with her life for the crime she would have perpetrated this night—despite her reasons. Dimly, she recognized that there was feeling there, that the searing intensity of his gaze might hold more pain than contempt. Desperately, she clung to that hope.

"Come with me, then," she said, her voice quaking for the uncertainty of what lay before her. "Come with me, Sebastian. Let's both go now, while we have the chance. We can leave this place. We can go somewhere new, and be together as we had planned."

He stared hard at her, considering, she prayed. She flung aside her dagger—the hateful symbol of everything she was—and reached out to him, palms up, beseeching, nothing to hide. He looked at her hands, but he would not take them. And then he was stalking toward the bed in heavy silence. He threw off the coverlet and with one firm yank of his arm, tugged the sheet free. Twisting it into a rope, he tied one end to the balcony railing and kicked the length of it over the ledge.

"Go," he ordered woodenly. "Take the rear gate. The guards don't yet know who, or what, you are. They'll let you pass."

Zahirah shook her head slowly from side to side, bringing her hands up to the place in her breast that felt as if it were being rent asunder. "Sebastian . . . don't. Don't make me go without you."

He shut his eyes and turned his head away from her. He would not look at her. He would not listen. "Leave now, Zahirah. I never want to see you again."

She hesitated, unable to move.

"Now, goddamn it!" he shouted, startling her into motion.

With tears burning her eyes, sorrow clogging her throat, Zahirah crossed the space of floor to the balcony overhang. She climbed over the railing and took hold of the knotted sheet, then shinnied down to the garden below and raced, headlong and heartbroken, into the bracing chill of the night.

Chapter Twenty-eight

The king looked up with alarm when Sebastian was granted entry to the heavily guarded chamber deep in the heart of the palace encampment. Richard had been seated on a cushioned divan, with a dozen attendants and bodyguards hanging about him like useless gargoyles. Now the king rose at the center of those watchdogs, standing tall with some effort on unusually shaky legs. His prolonged ill health from campaigning had weakened him, but Sebastian supposed it was this recent brush with death that had him pasty-faced and trembling beneath his voluminous purple robes.

He summoned Sebastian forward with a wave of his bejeweled hand. "Tell me," he said. "It was as you suspected? An assassin?"

Sebastian gave a grim nod.

"The woman?" asked the king.

"It was she, my lord."

Lionheart cleared his throat and glanced away from Sebastian's level gaze, chagrined, evidently, to have been caught so neatly in what might have proven a deadly indiscretion. Possibly, he was more humbled to have been warned of the danger by the very man he would have deceived. "Leave us," he said to his guards and minions.

In an obedient shuffle of booted feet and shifting armor, the men filed out of the room and into an adjacent antechamber to provide a less immediate measure of security and await the king's further requirements. When they had gone and closed the door behind them, Richard let out a heavy sigh.

"Perhaps I owe you an apology for my recent dealings with the woman, Montborne—I am aware you had some fondness for her." When Sebastian said nothing, merely inclined his head in acknowledgment, the king continued. "Be that as it may, I cannot help thinking that in some way this little discovery, unpleasant though it was, has in fact turned out to be a boon for us both. I am all the wiser for having escaped harm tonight, and you have been spared making an even graver mistake in letting yourself get any more attached to the treacherous chit."

"Your logic is indisputable, my lord," Sebastian replied, bowing his head and taking care to show none of his emotion where Zahirah was concerned. The king was right, after all. It was good that he learned of her duplicity now, before he made a greater fool of himself by asking for permission to take her back to England. Before he did the idiotic and costly thing of petitioning the king for special license to wed her.

He nearly laughed aloud at that thought. What a distant, ridiculous dream it was now. Nay, worse than a dream; it was a bloody farce, made all the more pitiful for the way he wanted to cling to it still. After everything she had done to him, after all the lies. Even after the events of this night, he wanted her still.

"You know," said the king, "Ascalon was Samson's city, long ago. It was here that he met Delilah, where he slew a thousand men and met his ultimate destruction—all for the love of one treacherous woman who would shear him of his power and use him for her own designs. You were fortunate. All your Delilah took from you was your pride." When Sebastian looked up, Lionheart was smiling. "But I warrant you will win that back soon enough. You'll have your revenge when she swings at the end of a rope for her crimes. Unless you've already taken the pleasure of cutting out her infidel heart."

"No, Sire." Sebastian held the king's questioning gaze. "I did not kill her. I did not arrest her."

"What are you saying?" There was a note of outrage percolating in the king's voice, his previous tremors of distress replaced with a sudden firming of his stance. His jaw rose along with his tawny brows. "Where is the woman now?"

"She is gone, Sire. Once she was discovered, she threw down her weapon and she fled."

Lionheart looked as if he might explode. He coughed instead, a deep hacking rattle. "She fled," he slowly repeated once he had regained himself. Accusation began to darken his eyes. "Well, then. How disappointed you must have been at that. Let us pray she does not elude capture again."

"Yes, my lord," Sebastian replied, knowing that he should be fearing the king's certain reprimand, but instead calculating the time Zahirah would have had to make her escape from the palace grounds.

The king stared for a long moment, then he slammed his fist against the back of the divan. "Guards!" he shouted, his summons inciting a jumble of urgency in the other room. The lot of his armed attendants hustled in to heed his call. "There is a fugitive woman on the loose somewhere in this city—an assassin. Find her. I want her apprehended at once. Go to it. Now!"

The knights jumped into action, rushing past Sebastian and out the chamber door. They clopped like a pack of horses in the corridor as they ran to do their king's bidding. They had little hope of catching Zahirah; Sebastian had waited to bring the king his report of her escape until he had given her ample time to leave the palace grounds. By now, if she was as quick as she was clever, she would be well on her way out of Ascalon—hopefully heading deep into the craggy hills for cover.

Here in the lamplit room of the palace, with the echo of his soldiers' boot falls dying away in the hall, Richard clasped his hands behind his back and began to pace like a caged, agitated cat.

"Tonight marks the second occasion you have saved my life, Montborne. More, if I think back and count the number of times we've been stirrup to stirrup in battle. I am indebted, but I am also your king and commander. Letting that girl go, whatever your reasons, was an act of defiance against me. Against my orders."

At the king's pause somewhere to the left of him, Sebastian said, "Yes, my lord."

"It is not my preference to be beholden to any man, so I will give you a boon now and this debt between us will be done. In light of your past service, until we return home to England, I will refrain from considering further reprisals where your properties are concerned, however, effective immediately, you are relieved of your command here. Your rank shall be reduced to that of foot soldier, under the officer of my choosing."

If he wanted Sebastian to plead for appeal, the king would get no such satisfaction tonight. Sebastian was in no mind to beg or bargain, not even if Montborne itself hung in the balance. He accepted the king's mercy—such as it was—with a respectful bow of his head. "As you wish, my lord. I thank you for your benevolence."

Lionheart grunted. "Very well, then. Remove yourself from these chambers. You have my leave, sir."

Sebastian pivoted on his heel and quit the king's temporary quarters, stalking past a duo of new knights who stood on post in the hall outside the door—common knights he had once commanded, now, suddenly, his equal. He told himself that he did not care. He had thrown away much this night: his office, his pride, perhaps even his land and titles when all was said and done.

He had thrown it all away on a lady who was no lady. A Delilah, just as the king had said. Zahirah was every bit as conniving and dangerous as the villainess of that Bible tale, and he no less a fool than blind and broken Samson, shorn of his strength for trusting her, and mad to feel anything but enmity toward her as the world he once knew came crashing down like rubble around him.

Zahirah pitched and stumbled through the winding streets of Ascalon's lower city as though in a fog, her head swimming, feet sluggish beneath her as she ran. She was in the shabbier part of town now, where cobbled streets gave way to worn and narrow paths, where crumbling stone houses and dilapidated shacks lurched one against the other, their flat-topped roofs hairy with grass that had taken root in the sand and long gone to seed. Here, whores and drunkards loitered about in every dark corner like rats, slurring and jabbering their filthy talk to anyone who chanced to pass by. Zahirah knew little of this part of town, but she knew enough to guess that the *fida'i* might have friends here.

She had just one cogent goal as she fled the palace and Sebastian's rightful rage: she had to find her father. She had to find him, and beg him not to blame Sebastian for her failing to slay the English king. She did not know how she would convince him, but she was determined to bargain anything to spare Sebastian, even her own life, if Sinan's fury demanded it.

At the end of a crevice alleyway was a tucked-away tavern, the only source of light to be found in this shadowy underbelly domain. Zahirah headed toward the glow of the establishment's lanterns, stepping over a pair of outstretched legs that lay in her path. The vagabond at her feet roused to mutter something unintelligible as her sandals scuffed past him in the debris of the alley, then he slumped back into his doze.

Two Arab men stood huddled together in hushed conversation outside the tavern; they ceased talking and looked up as Zahirah approached. She must have been a sight, her hair falling out of its braid, her face unveiled and streaked with tears, the wide cuffs of her *shalwar* soiled and muddied from the filth of the streets. Even bedraggled and in despair, she knew she did not look as though she belonged there. The two men exchanged a glance that seemed to acknowledge that fact, then one of them smiled and Zahirah instantly mourned the loss of her dagger at the palace.

"Hey, pretty, pretty," said the younger of the two men, the one whose leering grin was giving her gooseflesh.

This close, they smelled of opium and danger, but they

were all that stood between Zahirah and the help she might receive on the other side of the tavern door. She could hear the din of loud talking and laughter inside, and she was determined to get past these two one way or another.

"I'm looking for someone," she said. She took a purposeful step forward and reached for the latch. She was stopped, as she fully expected. The smiling man blocked her reach with his body; his friend moved in from the side to knit her in. Zahirah backed away, just a pace, but enough for them to scent her apprehension.

"Where you going, pretty? We've got all you need right here. Come talk with us. We'll make you happy."

"I'm supposed to meet someone," she replied, deliberately hedging. "My father. He said to meet him at this tavern. He's probably already waiting for me inside."

"Down here?" challenged the first man. "At this hour?"

The one on her left chuckled. "If you think he's here, then call him out. Maybe we'll let him play, too."

Zahirah stood there, factoring out her options, while the two thugs chortled and made jests about what they would do with her whole family. The smiling man began to laugh, his stupid, drug-induced guffaws ringing out in the deserted street. He reached out to grab her arm, all confidence and wolfish amusement. Zahirah seized her chance and struck out, just as she had been trained to do in her many drills at Masyaf.

She grasped his arm as he took hers and yanked him forward, putting him off-balance. Her knee came up between his legs, swift and unerring. He howled, but only for a moment. Zahirah gripped his head in the crook of her elbow, and, using her other arm as a lever, wrenched his neck. He dropped in a heap at her feet, dead as dust. When she looked up to deal with his companion, she saw nothing but empty air, the man's fast-retreating feet beating a frantic tattoo down the far end of the alley.

Suddenly, a movement sounded behind her; a hand reached out of the dark. She whirled, ready to meet whatever trouble greeted her next with like malice.

"Mistress, do not be afraid." It was the vagabond she had tepped over to get to the tavern. He came into the lamp-ight and she saw that he was no mere drunkard. He was one f her clan, a *fida'i* agent posted in disguise to watch the treets. That he was here meant her father could not be far.

"Take me to him," she ordered her kinsman. "I must see ny father at once."

She was brought along another jointed alley, ripe with he stench of offal. There was no light here, only the occa-ional slice of moonlight and the shadowy form of her *fida'i* ;uide to lead her through the slippery darkness beneath ler sandals. She covered her nose in her sleeve and used ler other hand to steady herself in the narrow walkway hat seemed too vile for human habitation. Zahirah knew at nce why her father chose this place to headquarter him vhile in Ascalon; no one but the most determined visitor vould venture this far into the bowels of the lower city. Sinan would be as unmolested here as a beetle in a moun-ain of dung.

Ahead of her some half a dozen paces, crouching low and unassuming at the end of the alley, was a hovel. Like a crone hunched over her kettle, the squat little building rose ip from the street in a lump of sandstone and fallen away ile. Zahirah's kinsman paused at the rickety board that erved as its door. "Hurry, mistress," he whispered, rushing ler forward as he held the portal open.

She ducked beneath his arm and went into the pit of larkness beyond him. No lamps, no sound, just black si-ence. She froze where she stood, wondering if she were being led into another trap, but then the *fida'i* was at her ide saying, "This way, mistress. You will see better in a mo-nent."

Warily, not certain she had any better alternative, she fol-owed the rustle of his robes deeper into the abyss. There vas a soft creak of leather hinges from in front of her, then le turned and took her hand. "We are going down now, mis-ress. Stay close, and mind your step."

They descended some countless steps, down and down,

until the air grew chilly and damp. From somewhere distant
came the low howl of the wind. It sounded like a storm was
blowing in. Slowly, Zahirah's eyes began to adjust to the
lack of light. She saw shapes take form: the arc of crudely
hollowed-out stone walls surrounding her, the flat slope of
the stairwell below her feet, the slim outline of her guide's
shoulders, shrouded in his ragged disguise. And up ahead,
what seemed yet a day away, glowed the faintest sliver of
light.

A torch burned somewhere before them, the orange
flame a wagging beacon. They followed that scant light, and
as they drew nearer, above the crashing din outside, Zahirah
began to hear voices. Low, Arabic rumbles carried to her
ears. She heard her father's among them, and weathered a
shiver of dread for the news she brought him now.

The stairwell ended abruptly, leveling off to smooth, flat
ground. Zahirah's sandals sifted with each step she took,
and she realized she was walking in sand. And as she followed her kinsman toward the end of the track, she understood now that the roar of the wind she heard was rather the
roar of waves. They were very near the ocean. The deeper
they walked into the cave, the heavier the smell of brine; it
permeated the air and clung in her nostrils. She sneezed, and
the murmur of conversation up ahead came to a quick end.
The sudden silence was broken by the sound of weapons
hissing out of their scabbards.

"Who goes?" asked a menacing Arabic voice.

"Jalil," answered Zahirah's companion. "I bring the master's daughter."

He walked her around a wide bend in the rock, and there
before them was Sinan, his trio of bodyguards, and several
other men who stood with weapons ready. Fida'i, all of
them, and a nervous-looking Muslim man who was the
Assassin King's likely patron in the city.

Sinan stared at Zahirah, but he spoke to Jalil. "Your orders were to stand guard and make certain no one found us
here. Do you recall these orders?"

Beside her, the *fida'i* shifted nervously on his feet. "Yes, master."

Zahirah felt a chill snake up her spine at the cold look her father turned on his man. At Sinan's back, two of the other assassin guards stepped forward to flank their leader. One of them drew a dagger.

"B-but master," Jalil stammered. He brought his hands up as if to hold off the advance of Sinan's guards. "She's your daughter. She was in danger. I thought—"

"Yes," hissed Sinan with lethal calm. "And that was your mistake." He slid a glance to his men and the two *fida'i* moved on Jalil.

"Father," Zahirah cried. "Father, no!"

Too late, and to no avail. With an efficiency she herself had trained for years to perfect, the assassins leapt on Jalil and slit his throat. His blood spilled into the sand where he fell, staining it black as pitch under the dim glow of the torch.

"Toss him over the ledge," Sinan commanded. "Let the river take this rubbish out to the sea."

The guards hefted Jalil's slack body up and carried him off a short distance. In the dark it seemed they walked toward a sheer wall of stone, but then Zahirah realized there was a gap of space before it. The wall rose up from behind a cliff of jutting rock. Sinan's men paused at this ridge and swung Jalil out. He hit the water that rushed some distance below, the smack of his weight swallowed up in an instant by the roar of the ocean current.

Zahirah blinked back her outrage and stared at the monster who was her father. She was horrified at what she saw, but she was also afraid. He turned a glare on her and she inched away from him, a retreat that brought a knowing glint of amusement to his coal black gaze. "Tell me you are here to bring me good news, Zahirah. Is the Frank dead?"

She could not reply; her tongue seemed cleaved to the roof of her mouth. Sinan's answering chuckle was thin and malevolent. "I should have known you would not have the

heart," he accused in a brittle whisper. "You are weak. Yo
are a woman. You disgust me."

There was a time that Zahirah would have bristled at h
condescension, when she would have risen to her own d
fense, when she would have explained how she had tried t
carry out her mission, and insisted that she was not weak o
deserving of his disdain. But it bothered her more that sh
could share the same blood, that she could be in any wa
like him. It bothered her how she had for so long wante
this cruel man's approval and would have done anything t
earn it.

It bothered her that she could fear him so much that sh
would rather betray the man she loved—risk losing him fo
ever—than muster the courage to face Sinan's wrath. Tha
was weakness. That was disgust.

"Father," she said, the word tasting bitter on her tongu
"I have never asked you for anything, but tonight I hav
come here to beg of you a favor. I have come to ask you fo
my freedom from the clan, and for your vow that you wi
not harm Sebastian."

Sinan's drawn face showed no reaction to her plea. H
eyes stared flatly, his mouth a thin line within the grayin
wires of his beard. "You had both those things in you
grasp, if you'd only done what you were sent to do. Yo
failed, Zahirah. You knew what was at stake; you under
stood the price you would pay. And the price your Frankis
lover would pay."

"I don't care what you do to me," she said, dropping t
her knees before him. "Father, I am begging you. Please, d
not make good your threat against Sebastian."

"I don't make idle threats, Zahirah. You should know
that."

"You will kill him, then?" she choked, sick with despera
tion. "Can I say nothing to persuade you? Is there nothin
I can do to change your mind?"

She could see no mercy in his unblinking stare, no trac
of human emotion in the darkness looking down at her. Hi

oice was as hollow as the abyss surrounding them. "You
ishonor yourself in coming here to beg before me now.
Ioreover, you dishonor me." He turned to walk away from
er.

"No, Father," Zahirah said, forcing herself not to quake.
You are the one lacking honor."

A buzz of tension swelled around her as the other *fida'i*
urmured amongst themselves, shocked, no doubt, to hear
eir vaunted leader challenged so recklessly. Sinan paused,
en pivoted back to face her charge. He bore murder in his
es, but Zahirah stared back with equal ferocity.

"You rule through blood and terror," she accused. "You
ink that because you are feared—because with a snap of
ur fingers you can order another man's death—that you
re respected. Well, you're not. Fear and respect are not the
me." She shook her head, feeling some of her own fear
issipate under the blaze of her rising anger. "The obedi-
ce you demand is nothing close to devotion or honor.
ou're no leader. You're a monster."

The force of Sinan's ensuing blow knocked her down into
e sand. She touched her bruised and ringing jaw, momen-
rily stunned. "You think you know what I am, girl? Let me
ll you what you are." He reached down and grabbed her
in, his brown bony fingers digging into her cheeks as he
anked her face back toward his. "You are nothing—my
wn creation. I made you out of dust and tears and the
eating cries of your own people as I trampled them under
y heel." Zahirah recoiled from the hateful words, her heart
rching as the horror of what he was telling her sank into
er brain. "You beg now the way your mother begged me all
ose years ago. The way your father begged me to spare his
ife and child. You're all weak, all worthless. I should have
illed you along with the rest of them."

"No," Zahirah moaned, squeezing her eyes closed as if to
ot out the nightmare that began to repeat as memory trig-
ered by the brutality of Sinan's confession.

She saw it all now, the English pilgrim caravan lumbering

across the desert toward Jerusalem, a journey she could no
fully understand at just two years old. But she could under
stand the fear that descended on her family when a band o
Saracen raiders spilled down from the crest of a hill to harr
the group of Christian travelers. She understood the dange
the panic that set her mother screaming when her father wa
beaten and dragged away from the van. They had been cry
ing, all of them, the adults pleading for mercy, the childre
shrieking.

One of the raiders seized Zahirah from her mother'
arms, taking her onto the saddle of his sleek black horse
Zahirah had thrust her arms out but they were not lon
enough to reach her mother. Their fingers brushed, the
separated, and the horse beneath Zahirah began to move
She screamed for her mother, turning her head to see he
watching through her tears as a mob of black-clad Saracen
converged on the caravan and demolished it with thei
swords and clubs and burning torches. Zahirah heard th
screams behind her. She heard her father shout in agony
heard her mother call her name over the din.

"Gillianne!" she had cried. *"No! Not my Gillianne!"*

"Oh, God," Zahirah sobbed, every muscle in her bod
sagging, her legs and arms gone boneless. Sinan release
her, thrusting her away from him with a snarling chuckle.

She fell to her hands on the ground, weeping, not carin
what happened to her next for she was already dead. Sina
was wrong; he had killed her all those years ago, when h
killed her parents and the other pilgrims.

Sebastian had given her a chance to live again, to b
something more than the lump of clay Sinan had manipu
lated into his own wicked design, but she had thrown tha
chance away. And she did not dare hope for another. Sh
had nothing now, and she had no one to blame but herself

Sinan was standing over her like a vulture eyeing carrion
She kept waiting for him to tear into her flesh, hoping h
would, just to be done with the pain of all that was lost t
her now, but that would have been an act of mercy, and h
had none. Leastwise, not where she was concerned.

"Take her," he ordered his bodyguards. "I may still have a way to use her."

Zahirah did not fight the binding hands that clamped down around her arms like cuffs of iron. They hauled her up and dragged her after him like so much baggage, her feet slogging through the sand as they brought her to another section of the cave and bound her to await her fate.

Chapter Twenty-nine

"Twelve deniers, graybeard. 'Tis my last offer."

Leaning back under the shade of a vendor's awning in the heart of the busy souk, Sebastian pivoted his head toward the exchange in progress. It was not going well. One of the English knights, a wellborn lad from Yorkshire, had been slacking in his watch duty to haggle instead with a merchant over a particular treasure. The fruitless negotiating had been under way for nearly half an hour, and it was beginning to irritate Sebastian to no end. "God's teeth, boy. Give him what he's asking, and have done with it, will you? The piece is worth twice that and you know it."

"What it's worth, and what I should be made to pay are separate issues," said the lordling in his native Norman tongue, shooting Sebastian a haughty glare for his interference.

That this green youth with his arrogant manner would be with him all day on guard duty grated Sebastian, though no more than the idea that the king had decided it fitting to place him under Garrett of Fallonmour's direction. As his newly appointed commanding officer, Fallonmour had made sure to put him in the most tedious tasks with the least tolerable company.

He watched halfheartedly as the noble-bred pup dug into his purse and dispensed with a fair sum. The merchant took the coin and handed him what he had purchased: a fine wooden *shatranj* board with pieces carved of shining, bone white ivory and glossy jet stone. Sebastian could hardly look at it—not without thinking of Zahirah, too.

Come nightfall, it would be two full days since she had been gone. The king's search parties had been dispatched and all came back empty-handed. She was likely many leagues away by now. For that, Sebastian was glad. But part of him missed her keenly, and he could not help himself from checking every veiled face that passed him for a pair of bewitching silver eyes. He did not think he would ever stop watching for her, hoping.

As furious as he had been two nights ago, as betrayed as he had felt to learn that she had been deceiving him all along, he could not deny that she had meant something to him. He wanted to believe that there had been some truth in her, that her deception had not been so thorough, so calculated, as it seemed to him that night.

He could not put out of his mind her assertion that Sinan—her father, repugnant though it was to accept—had forced her into undertaking the terrible task of killing the king. If he would do that to his own flesh and blood, if he would use her affection for Sebastian against her, what would he do to her if she returned to her clan a failure? Although Zahirah had told Sebastian that his own life was in jeopardy if she did not complete her mission, he did not fear for himself so much as he did for her.

He had sent her away, thinking to spare her the king's wrath, but he had since begun to worry that he might have sent her into a far greater danger. A danger that might await her with her own treacherous people. He swore under his breath, cursing himself for letting her go without him. Maybe it made him the devil's own fool, but he would never forgive himself if something were to happen to her.

"Damnation," he swore, wishing he'd still had his rank so he could assemble his own search party to ride out and find her, instead of hanging about the marketplace awaiting another man's orders.

The young knight on watch with him trotted over with his prize, grinning now, and pulling Sebastian from his thoughts. "I've a brother back home who just turned four. He loves toys like this," he said, as if he had no appreciation for the work of art he held in his hands. "Will you cover for me while I go put it away in the palace garrison?"

Sebastian gave him a disinterested shrug, although he expected he would well enjoy the solitude. "Go on. And don't hurry back on my account."

As the youth sought his nearby mount from where it was tethered with Sebastian's, and then cantered off, Logan rode up from the opposite direction of the street. "Have you heard, my friend? They found a body on the beach this morning."

Sebastian's heart clenched. "Jesus, not—"

"Nay," Logan said, with a quick shake of his head. "'Tis a man. A Saracen peasant with his throat slit from ear to ear."

"Sounds like the work of the *fida'i.*"

"Aye. I thought so, too. Fallonmour and Blackheart, along with some of the others, are heading down now to have a look. I reckoned you'd want to know."

"Thanks, my friend," Sebastian said. "Go on ahead of me. They don't need to know you told me about this."

Logan gave him a nod, then wheeled his roan about and went off down the street. Sebastian walked over to his white destrier and freed the reins from the post. He put his boot into the stirrup, ready to mount and follow his friend down to the beach, when someone drew up from behind him.

"Buy something pretty for your lady, master?"

Sebastian pivoted his head to regard the skinny Saracen vendor with an impatient stare. "Not interested," he growled back in Arabic. "You'll have better luck elsewhere."

"Are you the captain, master?"

Sebastian paused, stepping back down into the street. "Who's asking?" He narrowed his gaze on the little man, every muscle going taut in warning. "Who are you?"

"I've got something for the captain," said the man, and he withdrew a sparkly gold chain from a pocket in his trousers. He held it up for Sebastian to see the pendant dangling from the end of the loop—his black lion medallion,

the very one he had lost to Halim the day Zahirah first came
to the palace.

"What the—where did you get that?"

Sebastian reached out and snatched it from him, but
when he would have seized the Saracen, too, the wily little
man was that much quicker. Slippery as a fish, he spun on
his heel and darted off down an alley. With a curse,
Sebastian lunged into a run and gave chase.

The Saracen led him on a mad, zigzagging path, deep
into the lower part of the city. Sebastian felt like a bear chasing a gazelle, his chain mail like lead on his legs and shoulders, weighing him down. But his quarry seemed uneager to
lose him completely, the hunt reminiscent of another chase
through Ascalon's streets, a chase that had ended when
Zahirah walked out of a baker's shop and into his heart.

That chase had been a trap, and this one likely was, too,
but if it would lead him closer to her, he was going to follow
it to the end, and to hell with the consequences.

The Saracen skidded around the corner of a dilapidated
building and tore off down a sliver-wide alley. Sebastian
slipped between the crowding walls on either side and jogged
to the end, just in time to see the man dash into a hunk of
sandstone that might have at one time, perhaps a century before, been something passably inhabitable. With one hand on
the hilt of his sheathed sword, he moved aside a worm-eaten
board that seemed to serve as a door, and ducked inside. It
was dark within, but his vision adjusted enough that he could
that he was alone there; his quarry had vanished.

There was only one small window in the place as far as
Sebastian could tell, a hole burrowed into the wall of the
hovel. Draped over it was a moldy square of dark cloth; he
yanked it down, turning his head aside as the dust and dirt
stirred, then settled. Now, with the aid of some daylight, he
saw another door opposite where he stood, a door that
opened on oiled leather hinges into the floor. He lifted it and
stepped down onto a steep, dark stairwell carved out of the
earth.

At the bottom of what seemed a never-ending descent, was a wide rock-formed cave with a sand floor and the low rush of water flowing somewhere within. From out of the void of darkness came several pale fingers of light. Sunlight, he presumed, stepping through a slender beam that splintered in from the sidewall of the cavern.

"Well, well," purred a smoothly elegant voice, an Arabic voice, obviously well educated in the language of the Franks. "Captain Montborne, we meet again."

Sebastian did not have to see the gaunt, bearded face to know that he was being addressed by none other than Masyaf's elusive Old Man of the Mountain, Rashid al-Din Sinan. The same old man he had encountered in the city with Zahirah the other day. He had suspected it then, but it was not until Zahirah's attempt on the king that he put it all together.

"Where is she?" he demanded, turning toward the sound of Sinan's voice.

The King of the Assassins stepped out of the shadows, flanked by three armed men. One of them held Zahirah; her spine was stiff, her wrists bound together before her in a biting coil of rope. A dark bruise rode high on her cheek, and her lip had been split and swollen as from a severe blow.

"You son of a bitch," Sebastian growled, instantly furious and ready to tear the old man apart.

"Sebastian, no!" Zahirah cried. "He'll kill you!"

He took a step toward Sinan and the two bodyguards advanced to create a wall between him and their king, their hands gripped around the handles of their scimitars. The man holding Zahirah shifted and Sebastian caught the glint of a dagger blade held snug at her side.

"She's right, sirrah," Sinan warned. "Mind your temper. I promise you, I would be happy to rid myself of you both if you prove a tax on my patience."

"What is the meaning of this? Why did you send your man to lead me here?"

"I have a job for you," Sinan said. He slid a scathing look

on Zahirah. "Some unfinished business, if you will, with your king."

Sebastian laughed. "You're mad."

"Am I? Well, I wonder." Sinan smiled, seeming very amused with himself. "Am I mad to think you care for this woman? You cared enough to come here, when you had to know I would be waiting. I think you might care enough to do just about anything where she is concerned."

"You thought wrong," Sebastian replied, a bluff, but one he prayed would buy him some time to puzzle a way out of this spider's web. "I didn't come for her, Sinan. I came for you. If there is unfinished business, it's between you and me. As for the woman, she is—" He glanced to her, then back to the Old Man, and gave a shrug of his shoulder. "—she's inconsequential."

"Really." Sinan's smile widened, a slash of white in his beard. Still staring at Sebastian, gauging his reaction, the *fida'i* king issued an order to his man. "Cut her."

The guard flexed his beefy arm against her side and brought the blade of the dagger up where Sebastian could plainly see it. Holding it against Zahirah's cheek, he began to press the edge of the knife into her smooth skin. One slash and he would ruin her face forever.

Zahirah averted her gaze, but she would not turn away from the blade. She would not cry out. Faith, but she would stand there and let them mutilate her before she asked Sebastian to help her. The guard looked to his master for confirmation. Expressionless, Sinan gave an affirmative flick of his hand.

"Wait," Sebastian said. "Jesus Christ, you sick bastard. Wait."

At Sinan's nod, the dagger eased off. Sebastian blew out a curse. Zahirah was looking at him in anguish now, biting her lip and shaking her head. "Sebastian, don't let him use you. He wants Richard dead, but he will destroy you, too. He's going to kill me either way."

"She might be right, you know," Sinan mused. "Then again, would you be willing to test me?"

Zahirah's brows were knit together, her eyes swimming with tears. *No*, she mouthed. *No.*

Sinan knew he had him precisely where he wanted him; Sebastian could see the satisfaction blazing in those soulless eyes. "I'm listening," he growled.

"You have the benefit of certain access. Access that would take me months to establish again," said the Old Man. "So let us make a trade, you and I. Your king's death for your lady's life. Bring me the heart of the English Lion and I'll let you have the girl."

Sebastian smirked, scenting the stench on Sinan's so-called trade. "I'm not leaving here without her. Zahirah goes with me now, or we have no deal."

"Really, Captain." Sinan chuckled, but there was no humor in his expression. His eyes narrowed to glittering black slits. "Do you think I would surrender her to you and trust that you will uphold your end of the bargain?"

"Do you think I would leave her with you, and trust you to uphold yours?"

Sinan drew back at the challenge, his bearded chin rising to a superior angle. He grunted. "It seems we are at a stalemate, sirrah."

Sebastian drew his sword. "I don't think so. I'm taking her with me."

As his blade rasped out of its scabbard, Zahirah's eyes flew wide. "Sebastian, no!" The Old Man's two bodyguards raised their scimitars and held them in a battle stance, ready to pounce at their master's command. Zahirah's captor jerked her tighter against his dagger.

Standing behind his guards, Sinan did not so much as flinch. "Don't be a fool, Captain. You're moments away from watching her die. Her death won't be pretty, I assure you. Neither will yours, for that matter. My guards can have you disarmed and disemboweled in a heartbeat."

"Then bring them on," Sebastian taunted, knowing he needed to get them away from Sinan if he stood any chance of getting close enough to slay the Assassin King. "Do you forget, Old Man? I've seen your men in action, and I've sent a fair number of them to the devil where they belong. Nothing would please me more than to see you go next."

"Very well, you've made your choice." Sinan scowled at Sebastian from behind the wall of his guards. "Kill him."

The two *fida'i* stalked forward.

"No!" Zahirah screamed, bucking against the man who held her and, railing at Sinan. "Damn you! You bastard, damn you! I hate you!"

"Control her, will you?" Sinan barked, jerking his head toward the struggle going on beside him.

Sebastian saw the guard strike Zahirah, saw her stumble with the impact, her knees buckling beneath her. She pitched forward into the sand at her guard's feet. Sebastian let out a roar, but there was nothing he could do to help her at the moment. Sinan's two bodyguards rushed him, their weapons cold slashes of arced silver coming at him in a blur of flashing steel and murderous intent.

Sebastian met one with the edge of his sword, knocking the blow aside. The other man struck hard, his light blade slicing at the steel links that covered Sebastian's left arm. He whirled toward the attack, raising his weapon and bringing it down into the assassin's spine. Unprotected in just a leather jerkin and tunic, the man's back crunched like a beetle smashed under a boot heel. Sebastian jerked his blade out of the bleeding carcass and spun to meet the second man, who charged at him now in a fury.

In the corner of his eye, while he fought against this further assault, he saw Zahirah come up off the ground, jerked to her feet by her captor. Although her wrists were tied together, Sebastian was relieved to see that she was not entirely defenseless. She had managed to fill her hands with sand; now, with a yell, she threw it in the assassin guard's face. He roared, and in his momentary blindness, he dropped his dagger. Zahirah dove for the weapon, and, holding it between her bound hands, she lunged, and buried the blade in his chest. As he slumped, dead, Zahirah pivoted to find Sebastian in the fracas.

"Run!" he commanded her. "Save yourself. Get out of here!"

Sebastian's assailant landed a decent gash on his hand in the second Sebastian's attention was turned on Zahirah. Sebastian went down, but he was able to retaliate with an upward thrust of his blade. The two swords clanged against each other and held, force against force, rage to rage. Sebastian kicked him off, just in time to see Sinan inching toward a passageway in the cavern.

Rolling onto his feet, Sebastian bolted after the Old Man before he could slip away. He seized a fistful of Sinan's flowing robes and yanked him down to the ground. In the distance, above the crash of the surf outside the cavern, he heard voices shouting. English soldiers, no doubt, Fallonmour's men, poking around on the beach. He shook off the distraction, and put the tip of his sword at Sinan's throat. "Now you die," he growled and sucked in a breath of the briny air, ready to lean into his thrust.

"Not before she does, Captain," the Old Man sneered up at him, defiant, insanely confident.

Sebastian heard a muffled grunt nearby, heard the sifting of feet kicking in the sand. He swiveled his head over his shoulder and his heart sank. The last of the guards, the one he had knocked down but regretfully left living in his haste to catch Sinan, now had Zahirah. He held her before him, her bound hands trapped at her abdomen, pinned beneath the band of his beefy forearm. His scimitar gleamed from under her chin, forcing her to hold her head at a stiff angle to avoid severing her neck on its razor edge.

"You'd be wise to let me up," said Sinan. Sebastian eased off only slightly, allowing him a small space to regain his feet. He kept his sword leveled on Sinan's chest, balancing his gaze between his sly quarry and the brute who held Zahirah.

There was more commotion coming from outside the cavern along the shore, getting nearer now. Whoever it was, had evidently found a way into the cave. Sinan realized the threat as well. His gaze like twin fires, he stared at Sebastian. "Ahmed and I are going to take the girl, and we're going to leave now. And you are going to hold up your end of our bargain here today, aren't you, Captain?"

"Go to hell," he growled. "Tell your man to release her. Now. Unless you prefer to wait here like this until those knights arrive. I'm sure Lionheart would love to get his hands on you. Think back on Acre's massacre, if you have any doubt. Richard ordered twenty-seven hundred prisoners gutted that day; just imagine what amusements he'll devise for a cur like you."

Sinan's thin little smile faltered. His gaze slid to his man, and he gave a vague jab of his chin. "Let her go."

The assassin bodyguard seized a fistful of Zahirah's hair and savagely thrust her away from him. Without the aid of her hands to brace her, she went down hard, striking her head on a craggy rock nearby.

"Zahirah!" Sebastian shouted, and lunged toward her crumpled form. His attention focused elsewhere, the distraction gave Sinan the chance he needed to get away. The Old Man turned and fled down a dark artery of the cave, with his man, Ahmed, a few steps behind him. "Zahirah," Sebastian said, kneeling down beside her and gathering her into his arms. She roused, dazed, her forehead scraped and bloody.

"Go after him," she murmured, pulling herself up. "Don't let him get away."

Sebastian considered it for less than a moment. He shook his head. "I'm not leaving you. I'm not ever leaving you again."

"Down here!" came a Norman soldier's shout, echoing from somewhere along one of the passageways. "I think I heard something from down here, sir!" On the heels of that report, an untold number of knights seemed to be approaching at a run; their heavy armor jostled like chains in the cavern's arteries, the sound growing louder as they drew nearer to the assassin hideout.

Sebastian grabbed Zahirah's hands and cut her bonds loose with his dirk. "Can you stand?" he asked her as the ropes fell away. She nodded, marshaling herself to the task with the strength of will he so admired in her. "Then let's get out of here, my lady."

He took her hand and towed her with him, heading for the path that would take them back up the stairwell and out to escape through the city's underbelly. They rounded the wide jut of rock that separated the cave from the stairs—just as two armed English knights thundered down to head them off.

"This way!" Zahirah cried, spinning with Sebastian to attempt escape down another route.

They drew up short, met in force by Fallonmour and Blackheart and half a dozen more men. The soldiers came in from the direction of the beach, spilling into the wide cathedral of the cave to surround them like a pack of wolves.

Chapter Thirty

They were trapped. The tidal river surged below the ledge at their backs; on every other side of them were Frankish soldiers brandishing their broadswords. With nowhere left to go, nowhere to turn, Zahirah clung to Sebastian as he put himself in front of her like a shield, and faced off against his own countrymen.

At the front of the knights was a man with a lumpy, bandaged nose. Zahirah recognized him: he had been the one who accosted her at the feast tent in Darum. Fallonmour, Sebastian had named him as he charged to her rescue that night. How long ago that night seemed to her now. She might have forgotten the unpleasant part of the evening, if not for seeing her attacker before her now to remind her.

Fallonmour, evidently, was still holding a grudge for the punishment he suffered at Sebastian's hand. His gaze was scathing as it lit on her, but it burned all the worse when he turned it on Sebastian. "I might have known I'd find you here. *Traitor.*"

There was another knight present whom Zahirah feared, and that was the one known so infamously as Blackheart. He stood among the others like a mountain of leather and steel, all darkness and cool reserve. "Stand down, Fallonmour," he growled, turning a black scowl on his companion. "You forget yourself; you are addressing a fellow officer."

"Nay, not anymore," sneered the nobleman from beneath the bandaged pulp of his nose. "Haven't you heard? He lost his rank for letting this Arab whore twist his loyalties."

Zahirah's heart clenched at the knight's revelation. "Sebastian," she whispered, remorse heavy in her breast, "is it true?"

That he did not reply was answer enough. She was sick to think what her mistakes had cost him. What they might cost him, still, if the wicked glee in this leering soldier's eyes were any indication.

Fallonmour lowered his head like a bull incited to charge. "By the king's decree, Montborne is no longer captain here. He is a common sergeant, mine to command. And I command he kill this assassin bitch, or face a charge of treason."

"I'll kill you first," Sebastian replied with deadly calm. He reached around behind him with his left hand, as if making sure she was still there, as if to reassure her that he would bring her no harm, whatever the threats against him. "If you're looking for blood, Fallonmour, search out Rashid al-Din Sinan. He's here in this crag somewhere. You've got more men than him; you should be able to catch him."

Fallonmour seemed in no hurry to consider it. "My orders are to apprehend the woman. That's what I intend to do." He took a step forward, motioning to the other knights to follow his lead. They moved en masse, crowding them against the lip of the river ledge. "Now, are you going to assist me in this endeavor," Fallonmour asked, his voice echoing above the roar of the water below, "or will you defy me?"

The muscles in Sebastian's arms tensed beneath Zahirah's fingertips. She felt his right arm flex as he gripped his sword tighter, preparing himself to strike against one of his own.

Allah, help her, but she could not allow him to do it. She could not permit him to sacrifice any more than he already had in his association with her. She would not let him lose anything more when he had given her so much.

Wrapping her arms around him as far as she could reach, she embraced him with every ounce of devotion in her heart. She rose up on her toes to put her mouth near his ear.

"I love you," she whispered. "Sebastian, I will always love you, my lord."

She released him and took a small step back.

"Zahirah," he said, and pivoted his head over his shoulder as she shrank away from him. "Zahirah, be careful—"

She looked over that sheer drop of rock and at the surging black water below, and told herself it was the right choice. Her only choice, if she wanted Sebastian to have a chance at a happy future.

"I love you," she said, emotion choking her throat.

And then she turned and stepped off the ledge.

"Zahirah, no!" Sebastian reached out to pull her back, but she was gone.

Gone.

Nothing but empty space behind him, and the impossible idea that Zahirah had just willingly flung herself into that void. He was vaguely aware that the knights had moved in to crowd past him along the edge of the cavern shelf, staring over it, stupefied at what they had just seen. His heart was hammering in the hollow cavity of his chest, his mind screaming in torment, limbs numb with shock.

Slowly, as though in a dream, he heard Fallonmour call for someone to seize him, and he realized that he was standing at the very edge of the cliff now. He had tossed aside his sword. A hand clamped around his forearm as if to forcibly take him, and he shook it off with a roar. He looked down into the abyss of rushing surf below, trying to see if he could spy her somewhere in the water, yet praying he would not.

In his peripheral vision, he saw Blackheart break from the other knights and skirt down along a narrow decline in the side of the sheer wall of rock. Like a hound on the scent of fresh blood, he was going after her. Sebastian could not let him get to her first. He had to save her, if he could.

Tearing his surcoat to free himself from the grasping, gauntleted hands that tried to hold him, Sebastian pushed away from the side of the ledge and plummeted into the river below.

He fell fast, and hit the water like a stone. His chain mail pulled him down, below the racing current, which roared all around him like a raging, thrashing beast. He struggled with the added weight of his armor, commanding his limbs to move, to raise him up above the surface. He broke through, and, gulping in a mouthful of air, he began to search the water for some sign of Zahirah. Above him on the ledge, the soldiers had decided to look for her outside, someone guessing that the receding tide would eventually wash her out to the shore, dead or alive, as it had the man they found that morning.

Sebastian did not want to give up. He called her name, looking for her, feeling for her, diving down as deep and as long as he could, holding his breath until his lungs wanted to burst, and opening his eyes to the churning salt water that was too wild and too dark to provide any answers.

The current dragged him with it, no matter how hard he fought its pull. Relentlessly, it beat him against the rocks, thwarting his every move as it sucked him toward the mouth of the cave, toward daylight, and the immutable conclusion that he had just lost Zahirah for good.

Zahirah came out of the water, clinging to the side of a rock and gasping for air. The river had carried her swiftly, like driftwood caught in a tempest, ushering her nearly to the mouth of the cave. Her tunic had torn on the jagged walls of the tidal inlet, a shredded piece of it snagging on a toothlike rock and holding her while the water rushed all around her. The current rose up over her face, filling her nose and mouth, and while she worked to free herself from the tether, her groping fingers found a crevice in the stone.

Like the corner of a building, the sheer-rising wall bent around, creating an alcove where the water pooled peacefully, tucked away from the angry roil of the tide. She pulled herself into that alcove and followed its deep cleft, listening as the soldiers shouted in the cavern outside and the current raced past without her. She had not expected to live, but life swelled strongly within her, and so she pulled herself out of the water and lay on the flat surface of the stone she clung to, waiting while her burning lungs filled with air.

After a few moments, she could breathe without gasping. Her limbs could move again. Her head urged her to run. Dripping wet and shivering from the chill of the water, she got up onto her feet and stood . . . and then she saw him.

Blackheart.

He was not twenty paces from her in the alcove, a dark shadow in a place where everything was black. His sword was down at his side, unsheathed and menacing. Zahirah stared at him, this harbinger of death, and found she could not move. She would not ask him for mercy; she had no reason to believe he would grant it. And so she simply watched him, waiting for him to charge at her in a bloodthirsty rage, or save himself the trouble and call her out to Fallonmour and the other Franks.

He had his chance when someone yelled to him from outside the cave. "Sir Cabal! Are you there? Have you found any sign of the woman?"

"Aye," he answered back, his voice flat and emotionless. "I found her."

Zahirah swallowed hard, wishing the current had dragged her under as had been her plan. Only her death would satisfy the king, and only her death would give Sebastian a chance to gain back that which he had lost because of her. Her heart heavy with regret, she stared at the knight called Blackheart and waited for him to give the reply that would seal her fate and Sebastian's along with it.

To her astonishment, he did no such thing.

He stood there, looking at her much the way she was looking at him, and then he simply turned and walked away. His voice boomed over the pounding surf outside as he told his companions, "The assassin is dead."

Chapter Thirty-one

Ascalon, Three Months Later
September 1192

"They're loading the last ship, my friend. With any luck, we'll be moving out within a few hours."

Sitting in his favorite garden courtyard of the Ascalon palace for what had been the first time in more than three months—for what was certain to be the last time—Sebastian looked up and met Logan's gaze. "Have they started on the wall yet?"

"Aye. They're knocking it down as we speak." The Scot shook his head. "All that work building it up at Richard's command, only to tear it down on Saladin's."

"Just one part of the treaty signed between them," Sebastian said as he picked up his wine goblet and stared into the deep red bowl. "Ascalon has seen centuries of demolishment and repair. She'll rise to thrive again."

"You're going to miss this place."

It was not a question, and Sebastian was not inclined to answer. He was going to miss Ascalon, miss all of Outremer for that matter. It was a harsh, brutal land, nothing like his homeland, but it had its own beauty. And it would always have her.

Zahirah.

He said her name in his mind, as he had done a thousand times since the day she vanished into the blackness of his darkest day. He had thought of her constantly in the three months since, took her memory and his love for her with him into battle when Lionheart and his troops left Ascalon to march on Beit-Nuba, Acre, and Jaffa. He won back his rank and his king's trust during those final campaigns, but it seemed a hollow victory, knowing Zahirah was gone.

And he could not imagine leaving Outremer without her.

"I'm heading down to help the men with the wrecking," Logan said, pulling him out of his thoughts. "The sooner they pull down those walls, the sooner I can be back home with my sweet, bonny Mary. Why don't you ride down with me, my friend?"

"You go on ahead," Sebastian said, setting down his cup of wine. He was not yet ready to leave the tranquillity of the courtyard. He could almost feel her there, almost hear her voice again, smell the perfume of her skin and her glossy hair. He could stay there forever. Maybe he would.

"Go on," he said when Logan stood there, staring at him as if he knew the direction of his thoughts. "Go on. I'll be right there."

The Scot nodded, doubtless not believing him, then he turned and left.

He had been gone but a few moments when another knight came into the courtyard and interrupted. "Beg pardon, Captain, sir, but there's a group of English pilgrims arrived outside, requesting passage with us to England. Shall I send them in?"

Sebastian gave the knight a careless, affirmative wave of his hand. He had been entertaining requests such as this for days now, ever since the word had spread that King Richard and his army were moving out of the Holy Land. This most recent group, half a dozen men and women, had come all the way from Jerusalem, according to the knight as he showed them into the courtyard. Their long gowns were dusty from the road, their gnarled wooden staffs standing tall and brittle, like bones left to bleach in the desert sun. There were four men in this little group; they stood at the front of the party, their wide-brimmed pilgrim's hats tattered and sweat-stained.

Behind them were two women, one slender and petite in

her pale blue garb, the other a matron, with a round ruddy face that framed kind brown eyes and a serene smile. She seemed protective of her meek companion, who kept herself hidden behind the men, her covered head down, gaze averted. Sebastian guessed it was the other woman's daughter, but there was something peculiar there—something that made him come up from his seat on the bench, staring a bit harder than was seemly, willing her to look up so he could see the face she seemed determined to hide.

"You've all come from Jerusalem," he said, addressing the man who stood at the fore of the group, though his gaze kept straying to the woman behind him. "It is a long journey to make, and you've reached us just in time. Our last vessel leaves for England today."

"Aye," agreed the man. "'Twas a long trek, and a gamble, but we were hopeful, and we had God on our side. Actually, 'twas at the suggestion of our young sister that we came here at all, my lord. She said that Ascalon was a pearl in God's crown, and I must say she was correct. 'Tis a fine city, indeed . . ."

The man went on, but Sebastian was no longer listening. He took a step forward, watching the young woman shift nervously behind her companions. She fidgeted with a loose thread on her modest gown, and then, as if she could bear the weight of his gaze no longer, she lifted her head and looked at him.

Sebastian's heart soared to his throat. "My God. Zahir—"

She smiled, as if trying to bite back her joy and failing. She gave a small shake of her head. "No, my lord, I am not she. My name is Gillianne. It is a pleasure to meet you . . . to see you, Sebastian."

Ignoring the looks of astonishment and confusion from the others, Sebastian crossed the space of the courtyard. He went to her and embraced her, and her pilgrim companions disappeared without his notice, taking their leave as if they understood the meaning in this moment. "God . . . God," Sebastian said, kissing her, rejoicing in the feel of her, almost disbelieving that she could really be there, alive, in his arms once more. "I thought you dead. I searched for you in that river, and everywhere I've been since then. I thought you had drowned, or that Blackheart—"

"No," she said, pulling back to look at him. "He didn't tell you, then? No, I don't suppose he would have told anyone what he did that day." She gave a soft laugh. "He could have killed me, but he let me go. I don't know why; I've wondered all this time. Maybe he pitied me. Maybe he understood that the person I had been, the person Sinan had created all those years ago, was in fact dead and drowned in that river."

"I owe him everything for sparing you," Sebastian said, smoothing his hand over her face, realizing just then how faded her tan had become in the months since they had been apart. In a few more months, it would be gone completely, returned to the porcelain color she had been born with. "What happened to you?" he asked, still finding it hard to credit that she was there, standing before him, whole and hale. "Where have you been? Where did you go?"

"To Jerusalem," she said. "I went there to start over, to finish the pilgrimage my parents began when I was a babe . . . and to wait for you. I thought eventually the army would march there, and that maybe I would see you again."

Sebastian shook his head. "The king's health grew worse as we campaigned, and there has been trouble back home with his brother. We never made it to Jerusalem. Richard and Saladin agreed to a peace treaty before we were able to march on the city."

"I know," she answered. "And when I heard that some of the king's men had returned to Ascalon, I knew—well, I hoped—that you might be among them. Sebastian, forgive me, but I could not stay away. I have missed you so." She caressed his cheek, her fingertips like silk against his skin, her silver eyes tender and loving. "There is just so much to say . . ."

He took her hand and placed a kiss in her palm. "We'll have a lifetime to say it now," he said, his heart swelling with love for her. He knelt down before her, holding her hands in his. "My lady, my love . . . come back with me to England. Be my bride in truth."

She smiled down at him, laughing through her tears. "Oh, my lord. I thought you would never ask."

Epilogue

"I wish we hadn't come, my lord. What if he recognizes me? This may prove to be a terrible mistake."

Sebastian reached down and took his wife's hand in his as they entered the great reception hall of the royal castle in London. Usually unflappable and composed, Gillianne was trembling. "Don't be worried, my love. It's been nearly two years since that handful of days in Palestine, and much about you has changed. Save your stunning beauty, that is."

Gillianne smiled at his praise, her pale ivory cheeks flushing as pink as the brow of the sleeping babe she cradled in her arms. She had borne Sebastian a son just two months ago, and motherhood suited her well. Her husband was utterly besotted with the both of them, and he could think of nothing that gave him more contentment than the family he had with Gillianne.

While her tan had faded along with her accent since she had been living at Montborne, there were certain aspects of her life before that Gillianne had maintained. She was still every bit as fierce and stubborn as the tigress that had so captivated Sebastian, always ready to debate with him about philosophy and faith and the finer points of *shatranj*. She had fire and wit in equal measure to her beauty, and Sebastian never tired of the pleasure of her company. She charmed and fascinated him, and he was the proudest man in the room to have her on his arm.

"Relax, my love," he whispered beside her ear. "Now that Richard is returned to England, he will expect to meet the lovely lady I wed while he was indisposed."

Indisposed was something of an understatement. Richard had been waylaid by his enemies on his return from the Holy Land, abducted and held for ransom in Austria for these past two years. His ransom had been steep, paid in part by taxes and levies, and a rather sizable donation from the Earl of Montborne in exchange for license to marry a beautiful but dowerless orphan he had fallen quite in love with on his return from Crusade.

Sebastian's brother, Griffin, and his wife, Isabel, along with their growing brood, had accompanied Gillianne and him from Montborne to bestow their praises on the king and renew their pledges of support. Together the group of them took their places in queue to await their approach to the dais, where Richard and his venerable mother, Queen Eleanor, sat greeting their subjects.

The court was full to bursting with nobles and courtiers, but one gaze reached Sebastian's through the shoulder-to-shoulder crowds. It belonged to Sir Cabal, the knight Sebastian could no longer think of as Blackheart, his formidable *nom de guerre*. The two men exchanged glances, and Sebastian gave him a knowing nod.

The dark knight returned the gesture, but then his attention was snagged by a lovely blond lady who stood at his side, her belly big with child. She clung to his arm the way Gillianne clung to Sebastian's, her gaze as loving and warm as that which Sebastian enjoyed each time his wife looked upon him.

Curious, Sebastian leaned over to his brother. "Who is that woman there with Sir Cabal?"

Griff lifted his head and peered discreetly in that direction. "Ah, that is Emmalyn of Fallonmour."

"Fallonmour?" Sebastian asked, taken aback as he looked again at the love shared between them. "The earl's widow?"

Griffin's lady wife spoke up in answer. "Garrett's widow,"

Isabel confirmed, smiling, "but more recently, Sir Cabal's bride."

Before Sebastian could express his astonishment, he and Gillianne were escorted to stand before the king. He bowed low; beside him, Gillianne hugged their babe close and dipped into a graceful curtsy. "We thank God you are back, Sire. Your country has missed you."

"Rise, rise," said the king. "Let me have a look at you, and this lovely treasure which I understand you found en route from the Holy Land."

"My lord," said Sebastian, helping Gillianne up when she was slow to stand. "It is my honor and my great pleasure to introduce my bride, Lady Gillianne of Montborne, and our son."

The king's grunt of acknowledgment seemed more a leonine purr of appreciation. "Well met, my lady," he said, his blue eyes glittering with unsuspecting interest. To Sebastian he said, "Your wife pretties up this court like a gem, Montborne. I do hope you will bring her here often."

Sebastian cleared his throat and pulled her a little closer to him. "All due respect, my lord, but Gillianne is a treasure I intend to hoard selfishly for all my days."

He looked at her and she smiled, and the king and queen and the throng of hundreds in the room faded away to nothing, as was always the case whenever Sebastian was looking into his lady love's eyes.

Author's Note

"What would you think of a book set in the Holy Land during the Crusades, where the heroine is a Syrian assassin who's sent to kill the king of England, unless the hero can stop her?" I asked my editor, excited as I pitched my story idea to her over iced tea at an RWA National conference.

"I love it," she said. "It sounds like a fun book to write."

And it was . . . until the unimaginable happened on September 11, 2001.

I was putting the finishing touches on the manuscript when a friend called to tell me to turn on the TV. Like everyone else who sat in their living rooms or at work, transfixed in horror, I could not believe what I was seeing. Some days, I still can't believe the attacks actually happened. But they did, and while we will rise above our sorrow and fear, we will, as a nation and as individuals, be forever changed. It is my hope that we will emerge a stronger, more unified community, and that peace can still, one day, be ours.

I'm a hopeful romantic; I have to believe and trust whole-heartedly that love truly does have the power to conquer all. That message is at the core of all romantic fiction, and is a large part of what I find so appealing about it, as both a reader and a writer.

With regard to Sebastian of Montborne and his Assassin bride, I hope you enjoyed their love story in the spirit in which it was intended. I would like to share with you some of the interesting things I discovered in my research for this book, many of which found their way into the story.

The mysterious clan of the assassins did, in fact, exist. A

adical Ismaili sect, they first gained notoriety among the crusading Christians with the murder of King Richard's sometime ally, Conrad of Montferrat. Their leader at that time was Rashid al-Din Sinan, a reclusive man of great power, who commanded his agents from a mountain fortress called Masyaf. It was said that Sinan's grasp on his followers was so strong, men would willingly fling themselves to their deaths off the ramparts of the castle upon his command.

Some early scholars believed that the Old Man of the Mountain bewitched his agents with hallucinogenic drugs, such as hashish, from which the name "Assassin" is purportedly derived. This hypothesis has earned its share of doubt, skepticism I tend to share. The Ismaili doctrine is essentially one of authoritarianism; to the believer, there is no individual right of choice. He must follow the teachings of his leaders without argument or sway. It is not so hard to imagine—particularly today—that Sinan's followers, steeped in the fanaticism of his preaching, would be perfectly willing and able to carry out their covert, and often prolonged, missions without the aid (or the potential hindrance) of mind-altering drugs.

While the Assassins generally targeted non-Christians, they did occasionally reach beyond their established enemies, as evidenced by the alleged revenge-based murder of Conrad of Montferrat, then King of Jerusalem. Historical sources have never confirmed that Richard the Lionheart was ever in danger from Sinan's agents, but there were rumors of animosity, and I have taken the liberty in this novel of saying, "What if . . ."

I was very impressed, and quite often surprised, to find that the Arab nations of the twelfth century enjoyed many technological advances over their English counterparts—things like plumbing, irrigation, architectural advances, and an appreciation for cerebral pursuits. Perhaps you recognized the ancient Arabic game that Sebastian and Zahirah played in this book. The strategy game of *shatranj* is better known by its popular European incarnation, chess. It is believed that the checkered gameboard and miniature warrior pieces were first brought to England and France by the soldiers in the Third Crusade—as I am sure Sebastian and Gillianne would have done upon their return to Montborne. Chess became a popular form of entertainment in the Middle Ages, enjoyed by both men and women of the noble classes. The pieces underwent some changes from the original Arabic version, making it more Anglicized and giving certain pieces more freedom and power.

The most significant changes were the addition of the Queen and Bishop, replacing the Arabic *firz* (prime minister) and the *alil* (elephant), respectively. For the sake of simplicity and reader understanding, I used the more widely recognized European pieces in my story. I also changed the gameboard from its Arabic red-and-black squares to the black-and-white battlefield you see in chess today. One other interesting bit of trivia: *Shah mat*, the Arabic declaration of victory in *shatranj* eventually became the more English, if less relevant, "checkmate" we still use after the execution of the winning move today.

There is much more fascinating information available on these and further topics related to the Holy Land and the era of the Crusades. For additional reading, please visit your local library, or log on at my website at www.TinaStJohn.com for a list of articles and reference sources.

In the meantime, I hope you enjoyed this book, as I hope you will enjoy all the rest still to come.

LORD OF VENGEANCE

by Tina St. John

Set in majestic medieval England, this is the story of two valiant people who struggle with the sins of the past to forge a love as turbulent as the land they live in. Devilishly handsome Gunnar Rutledge has spent years plotting against the man who nearly destroyed his life. He seeks the ultimate vengeance on Raina d'Bussy—his enemy's daughter—a proud beauty who will be slave to no man. Gunnar sets out to break Raina's glorious spirit but instead finds himself bewitched by her goodness and strength.

*Where the desire was born…the destiny began…
and the whole story started!*

WHITE LION'S LADY

by Tina St. John

Abducted on the way to her wedding, heiress
Isabel de Lamere is unaware that the scoundrel
planning to use her for his own gain is the
cherished champion of her childhood, the
man who lingers in her dreams:
Griffin, the White Lion.

Then a twist of fate puts a price on both their
heads, embroiling them in a life-and-death chase
that will force Griffin to choose between his own
freedom and his fierce desire for the woman who
would redeem his noble spirit.

Published by Ivy Books.
Available wherever books are sold.

Subscribe to the new Pillow Talk e-newsletter—and receive all these fabulous online features directly in your e-mail inbox:

♥ Exclusive essays and other features by major romance writers like Linda Howard, Kristin Hannah, Julie Garwood, and Suzanne Brockmann

♥ Exciting behind-the-scenes news from our romance editors

♥ Special offers, including contests to win signed books and other prizes

♥ Author tour information, and monthly announcements about the newest books on sale

♥ A *Pillow Talk* readers forum, featuring feedback from romance fans...like you!

Go to **www.ballantinebooks.com/loveletters** to sign up.

Pillow Talk—
the romance e-newsletter brought to you by Ballantine Books